SHE KNEW HER FATHER WOULD NEVER GIVE HER UP TO A SUTHERLAND WITHOUT A FIGHT . . .

Still, her hand tightened in his, clutching at the fading dreams. Her love. Her starcatcher. She had looked for that star every night and prayed for him. As long as it hung bright in the night sky, she had known he was safe.

But that was no longer enough.

Patrick pulled her to a halt beneath an old, gnarled oak. His arms crushed her to him as if he needed her as much as she had needed him. No man had ever held her like this, so close that she could feel every inch of his lean, hard body pressed to hers. He was so tall and strong. For an instant, she was afraid.

But the green gaze that regarded her so intently was familiar—and filled with hunger. She had never hoped that he loved her. Yet as she melted into his tight embrace, she realized that she wanted everything. Everything, including love, that Patrick could give her.

When his head slowly lowered, her heart started to race. She felt his hand at the small of her back tremble, and it astonished her to see a trace of uncertainty flash in his eyes. Surely this confident man who held her so boldly couldn't be waiting for her permission.

Still, she gave it, whispering, "Patrick . . ."

Starcatcher

Patricia Potter

BANTAM BOOKS

NEW YORK TORONTO LONDON SYDNEY AUCKLAND

STARCATCHER

A Bantam Book / January 1998

ISBN 0-553-57507-4

Published simultaneously in the United States and Canada

Bantam Books are published by Bantam Books, a division of
Bantam Doubleday Dell Publishing Group, Inc. Its trademark,
consisting of the words "Bantam Books" and the portrayal of a
rooster, is Registered in U.S. Patent and Trademark Office and
in other countries. Marca Registrada. Bantam Books, 1540
Broadway, New York, New York 10036.

PRINTED IN THE UNITED STATES OF AMERICA

OPM   10   9   8   7   6   5   4   3   2   1

To my parents,
William and Adelaide Potter,
who are a living example of
what love is really about.

Starcatcher

Prologue

The Highlands of Scotland, 1648

She was eight years old and destined to be his bride.

Patrick Sutherland saw the small figure of Marsali Gunn huddled at the corner of one of the parapets as he walked the ramparts of Abernie for the last time. Tomorrow he would leave the Gunns, the family who'd fostered him all these years, and go to war in Ireland.

He would miss them all, especially Gavin, his best friend. Yet anticipation coursed through him. He was sixteen, at last considered a man ready to do a man's service. He intended to do it well and bring credit to a father he had tried—unsuccessfully—to please all his life.

Then, in ten years, he would return to claim his bride.

The betrothal agreement had been signed this day by Donald Gunn, Marsali's father, and Gregor Sutherland, his own parent. And this same day, Donald's sister, Margaret, was wed to Gregor, a widower for many years. The family would be doubly connected.

Patrick did not object to his match with the Lady Marsali. Since birth he'd been taught that the interests of his clan came before any personal consideration. Marriage was almost always a matter of convenience: for protection, money, or bloodline. But even at eight, Marsali had a winning way about her, and he found it endearing that she sometimes followed him around.

It was more than unusual to see her looking heartbroken. Studying her huddled form, Patrick wondered whether the formal betrothal ceremony, Gregor and Margaret's wedding, and the noisy, drunken celebrating had frightened her. He could still hear the revelry in the courtyard beneath them. He himself had only left because he'd wanted a few moments of quiet to say his goodbyes to a life he would never know again.

Patrick approached her slowly so as not to startle her. In the bright moonlight, he saw that she was hugging one of her two pet ferrets.

"Marsali," he said softly. "Should you not be abed?"

She whirled around, and he saw the tear tracks on her cheeks. The ferret she held scampered to perch on her shoulder, while the other sat at her feet, its nose peeking out from beneath the hem of her night rail. Both of the small animals eyed him distrustfully.

Gently, he asked, "Are you so unhappy, then, about today's ceremony?"

Her eyes widened. "Oh no, Lord Patrick."

"Then why the tears?" he asked, tucking a finger under her chin and forcing her to look up at him.

She bit her lip. Her long dark hair, unbound by a cap, fell over her cheek. "I will . . . miss you."

Real sorrow edged her words, and he felt humbled. He was sixteen, a man, and he'd paid little attention to the feelings of his best friend's sister, his future wife.

He took a long look at her face. Her eyes were a dark blue, and they glistened with tears and moonlight. Her face was delicately molded, and her wide mouth was made for smiling, which she did a good deal of the time. In truth, she showed signs of being a true beauty someday.

Seeing the way she stared at him, something tender moved within him. No one ever had looked at him as she did, with complete adoration. His mother had died at his birth, and his late stepmother had considered him a hindrance to his half brother's inheritance. His father was a rough and prideful man who knew nothing about affection and cared only that his son would be a great warrior and carry on tradition.

"I will be back before you have a chance to sprout," he said.

"Promise you will not get killed," she demanded with uncharacteristic force, her dark blue eyes boring into his.

"Aye," he said. "I swear it." And he could, in all honor, for he felt invincible. After all, had he not defeated much older, much heavier men in mock combat? He would vanquish his enemies and live forever.

She watched him steadily, too steadily for a child. It was as if she were willing his words to be true with the force of her desire.

The ferret moved down her arm and she caught it in her right hand, rubbing the animal's head with her left.

"Antony and Cleopatra will miss you, too," she said. "They will pray for you, as will I."

Stifling a smile, he said solemnly, "I now know I have nothing to fear."

Her eyes appeared to dance for a moment, but then they grew solemn again.

He bowed slightly. "You must hurry back to bed. But first, a favor to carry with me."

Her mouth widened briefly into a smile, then her look became dismayed. "I have nothing."

"What about this?" he said, lifting the end of the ribbon that graced the neck of her night rail.

He could see her pleasure at being treated like a true lady as she untied the ribbon, snaking it through the small holes of the cloth. Shyly, she handed it to him.

"I thank you, my lady," he said.

"Do I get one, too?" she asked.

He looked down at his clothing. He wore only a linen shirt and plaid of his clan. His dagger and sporran were in his room. Glancing toward the heavens for guidance, his gaze was caught by the night sky. It seemed extraordinarily bright. The moon was a huge, luminous globe. Stars crowded the sky, and he felt he could reach out and grab them. Suddenly, he was struck by a rare moment of whimsy.

"A star, Marsali?" he said. "Can I pluck one for you?"

"But then there will be an empty space where there should be brightness," she replied. "Tell me which one, and I will look at it every night and remember it is mine, and that you are my starcatcher."

He stared at her. She seemed much older than eight years. He would truly look forward to knowing her better.

Lifting his gaze, Patrick searched the skies for exactly the right star, one she could always find. He saw it at the heel of a formation of stars that never changed. His tutor had pointed it out to him long ago as a marker by which one could determine direction. He stooped down, balancing on the balls of his feet as he described to Marsali how she could always find the star he had chosen for her.

She listened intently. "I will look for it every night," she promised.

"And so will I," he said, knowing that he would not. But the lie was worth the joy he saw in her eyes.

His wife-to-be. It was difficult to imagine this child in that role. Nor, for that matter, could he envision himself as a husband. But that was years away.

"You had best be off to bed before Jeanie finds you gone," he warned.

She leaned over and swiftly kissed him on the cheek before turning away, small feet flying as she disappeared down a set of steep stairs.

He was left with the scent of roses, a piece of silk ribbon, the feel of silken hair against his cheek, and a lingering sense of the first sweetness he had ever known.

Chapter 1

The Highlands, 1660

I t was a splendid day for a wedding. Everyone said so. The sun sparkled, its rays dappling the rich green fields and nearby loch. The previous day's wind had eased into a gentle breeze.

A good omen for a future filled with happiness, Marsali's father had insisted. A fine day. A splendid alliance.

That he—and others—said it with apparent sincerity impressed the bride. The level of self-delusion among her clan had risen, she thought as she allowed Jeanie to brush her waist-length hair, then braid it with fresh flowers. "Edward Sinclair is a bonny man," Jeanie said hopefully.

"Aye," Marsali agreed. Jeanie was her maid, as well as her best friend. Indeed, she could not quarrel with Jeanie's assessment of the man her father intended her to wed. Still, she could not believe that no one else saw the coldness in the depths of Edward's eyes, the ruthlessness in his smile—a smile that, to her, seemed as stiff and unreal as a mask.

Four more hours. Four more hours of freedom. Four more hours to dream of a young man who, once, long ago, had offered to pluck a star from the sky for her.

She'd heard no news of Patrick for such a long time. Twelve years had passed since the evening he had taken his leave of her on the ramparts of Abernie, but she had never forgotten that night. Nor had she forgotten his next visit, when she was fourteen. She'd seen him note the changes the years had wrought in her, the look in his eyes transforming from mere kindness to something else altogether, something that made her tingle inside with delight and anticipation. She had treasured that look these past six years.

It seemed she had waited for Patrick all her life. She'd waited when he had gone to war to fight against Cromwell and been outlawed as a result. Their wedding had been postponed first one year, then another. In all that time, only two messages reached her, both stilted and formal and saying only that he was still alive. She would have waited forever.

But today she would become another man's bride.

Marsali's heart ached, but she knew that she had no choice. If she did not go through with the ceremony, her fourteen-year-old sister would be forced to take her place, and she could not abide the thought of sacrificing Cecilia to Edward Sinclair.

A splendid day for a wedding, they all continued to insist. Her brother. Her father. Even Jeanie.

Why, then, did she feel as if she were preparing for a funeral?

One of her ferrets climbed onto her lap. Tristan and Isolde had replaced Cleopatra and Antony, who she imagined were still together in ferret heaven. She wasn't sure why she kept naming her pets after legendary—and tragic—lovers. Perhaps another omen.

A tear trickled down her face and dropped onto the fur of the elongated animal.

"Ah now, lass," Jeanie said. "It is so bad for ye?"

Marsali pressed her lips together. There was nothing to be done anyway. Even if Patrick was alive, her father would never permit her to marry him. Not now. Not since he, as laird of the clan Gunn, had declared a blood feud against Patrick's family. The betrothal had been cried off by both her father and Gregor Sutherland, and though the two families already had many blood ties to one another, they were now more likely to kill each other than to feast together.

And it was all because of Marsali's aunt, Margaret, who had married Patrick's father on the same day that her betrothal to Patrick had been formalized. There had been much rejoicing that day by both clans, and for years afterward Margaret and Gregor had appeared to reside happily enough at Sutherland's Brinaire.

Then, two years ago, Patrick's father had accused Margaret of adultery and publicly branded her a whore. He had sought a divorce through Parliament, but the only two witnesses had disappeared. The divorce had been denied for lack of proof. A week later, Margaret vanished. Murdered, Donald Gunn claimed. Murdered by the man he had once called a friend: Patrick's father, Gregor Sutherland, the marquis of Brinaire.

Marsali didn't know the truth of it. No one did. She knew only that her aunt Margaret was her father's only sister, and that he was grief-stricken at losing her. Grief-stricken and enraged that her honor, and the honor of their clan, had been impugned.

Donald Gunn filed charges of murder against Brinaire, but again there was no proof. Marsali watched her father's hatred grow until he lost reason, until nothing was more important to him than revenge. She'd realized then that she would never have Patrick as a husband, even if he still lived.

She turned to Jeanie, wiping the tear from her cheek. "I do not like Edward Sinclair, nor do I trust him."

"And why, lass?"

Marsali could only shrug in response. How could she explain the cruelty in Edward's eyes? She'd tried to tell her father that she mistrusted Edward, but he had proclaimed it a woman's whim. Look at Margaret, he had argued. She married for love and was betrayed. No amount of talk had changed his mind.

But Marsali knew that what her father really wanted was the added strength an alliance with the Sinclairs would afford him. He could attack Brinaire and take his revenge. He had closed his mind to all else, including questions about Edward's character and rumors about the suspicious death of his second wife. As far as Donald Gunn was concerned, they were hearsay created by the lying Sutherlands. After all, had not Edward shed tears at the grave?

And Edward, too, had grudges against Patrick's family. He was a natural ally in her father's eyes. Although not of noble birth, Donald Gunn acknowledged, Edward was laird of a fine clan known for valor. Known better, Marsali thought, for brutality and trickery. But again her father would hear none of it. The marquis of Brinaire was the greater villain.

Marsali felt Jeanie's hand on her shoulder. Was it trembling slightly?

She turned and looked at her friend. Jeanie had lost her husband and her bairn at twenty, and had been engaged as wet nurse for herself. She'd been with Marsali ever since. Forty now, her auburn hair had only a few strands of gray. Marsali was shocked to see Jeanie's blue eyes glimmering with tears.

Marsali whispered, "Father believes Edward will make a fine husband."

"But my wee lassie doesna," Jeanie said. "Ye still dream of Patrick?"

Marsali sighed. "How can I do otherwise? I thought for years to one day call him husband."

"Ye have not seen him for a long time. Mayhap he has changed."

"Patrick?" Her voice softened. "Nay. The goodness in him will not have changed." Then, with a slow shake of her head, she added, "I see no goodness in Edward."

Jeanie was silent for a moment. "If it were not for your sister . . ."

"I would run away to Patrick," Marsali said without hesitation. "I know he still lives. I would know if it were otherwise."

"His father wouldna accept you," Jeanie reminded her.

"Then we could go somewhere else. South, toward the border," she said wistfully. She didn't even know whether Patrick would want her, much less give up everything for her.

"Truly?" Jeanie asked.

"Aye. But I canna sacrifice Cecilia for myself."

Marsali was silent a moment. Finally, she looked up at Jeanie's grim face. Reaching to place her hand over her friend's, she said, "I told Edward I want you to come with me."

"And did he agree?"

"He couldna do otherwise," Marsali said, remembering the argument. Edward had not wanted her to take her own servants. There were plenty at Haiford, he'd insisted. And although he'd eventually relented, Marsali feared that once married he would forgo his word.

She closed her eyes, praying for the strength to last the day. Thoughts of her wedding night made her clutch the fabric of her gown more tightly around her, and she trembled.

Jeanie's hand touched her cheek. "So cool," the older woman whispered.

With a heavy sigh, Jeanie laid down the brush and stepped away to eye her charge carefully. Her expression was tormented. Finally, she said, "Ye have been like me own bairn."

Marsali felt tears gather in her eyes, and she started to reply.

Jeanie cut her off, turning away as she spoke. "Take yer sister to the chapel," she commanded. "Pray for God's guidance."

Astonished, Marsali rose from the chair and took a step toward her. Jeanie was Catholic, one of those very few who refused to relinquish her ties to the Church despite the danger. She'd made little effort to conceal her contempt for those who'd shed their faith for self-interest and embraced Protestantism during the Cromwell years. She had refused to step one foot into the transformed chapel, instead slipping off at night to secret Catholic services. Why was she sending Marsali to pray to the Protestant God she disdained?

Jeanie moved away at her approach. "Get yer sister now. Prayers may well help ye." She gestured toward Tristan and Isolde, who had jumped to the floor when Marsali stood. "And take the wee beasties with ye."

Perhaps a few silent moments with God would lighten the enormous heaviness inside her soul. And perhaps Jeanie believed that, in such dire circumstances, it did not matter whether the building in which one prayed was designed by Catholics or Protestants. The chapel would be empty at this early hour; at least, Marsali thought, she would have a chance to say a private farewell to Cecilia.

Marsali found her younger sister in her room. Cecilia's eyes lit as she entered, but the brightness was quickly dimmed by dismay.

"Oh, Marsali, I'll miss you," Cecilia said. "You're the only one I can talk to."

"Gavin will look out for you," Marsali said.

"He's only interested in hunting and the estates," Cecilia said, adding with a hint of disgust, "and conspiring with Father to plan an advantageous marriage for me."

"You're still too young," Marsali said, knowing it was not altogether true. In her mind, Cecilia *was* too young, but age often meant little to men who used marriage as a tool to enrich themselves. She had once thought her father was different, that he would allow his daughters a choice, but the feud with the Sutherlands had disabused her of that notion.

"I wish . . ." Cecilia began hesitantly. "I wish . . ."

"What?" Marsali encouraged gently.

"I would have liked to have been a nun," her sister said quietly.

"You must never say that," Marsali whispered, alarmed. Such beliefs were so dangerous still.

"I know," Cecilia said. "But I do not believe I ever want to marry."

Marsali had no words of comfort. She had once believed in love and honor and happiness. Yet today she would marry a man she abhorred. And if she refused to speak the words, Cecilia would never have the strength to do likewise.

"Come with me to the chapel," she said. "I do not think God cares if it is a Protestant or Catholic house when we pray to Him."

"Truly?" Cecilia said. "Jeanie says—"

"Truly," Marsali said firmly. "There shouldn't be anyone about."

She took Cecilia's hand and led her down the stone staircase of the keep, staying in the shadows. The two ferrets scrambled after her. What would become of her pets when she went with Edward? He had made little secret of his distaste for them, and Tristan and Isolde were intelligent enough to keep their distance. . . .

Noise came from the great hall, where her father was entertaining guests. She and Cecilia reached the outer door and went into the courtyard, which was humming with activity. Visitors had been arriving for the past two days, and any number of clan plaids were visible. Marsali recognized many of them, but some were new to her. Everyone except Sutherlands had been invited to the wedding and made welcome. She guessed even her father didn't know all the guests.

Marsali took a deep breath. She felt like crying, but she did not want Cecilia to see her fear. Her loneliness. Her despair.

Her thoughts of Patrick.

She led the way across the crowded courtyard to the chapel. Opening the heavy door, she peeked inside. Empty and quiet. A relief.

Motioning for Cecilia to follow, she entered the dark, high-ceilinged building. Their slippers made little noise as they moved toward the altar. So plain now that the rich carvings and stained windows had been replaced by boards and shutters to conform with Cromwell's Puritan ways.

Of course, now that Cromwell was dead and King Charles was on the throne, the chapel undoubtedly would change again. Her father had been careful to shift with the political and religious winds.

She and Cecilia made their way to a pew at the front of the chapel. The ferrets scrambled onto the bench and began exploring. With a glance and a nod at her sister, Marsali knelt and bowed her head. Cecilia knelt beside her.

Marsali tried to concentrate on God, but all she could think about was Patrick. She knew the very day she had lost her heart to him. She had been only five, and one of her father's hunting hawks had swooped toward one of her ferrets. Patrick had heard her scream and caught the jesses of the hawk before it grabbed her pet. His hand had been badly mauled by the bird in the process. He had been her hero ever since, her knight. Her starcatcher.

Her husband-to-be.

She had relished that thought, in her eight-year-old way, when he had gone away that first time. When he'd returned from fighting on the continent, a wanted man, she'd been fourteen and he twenty-two. He'd been taller than she remembered, and his smile had come more slowly. He'd also carried a new scar on his face, but his eyes had been just as warm and his touch just as gentle as he'd brought her hand to his lips and exclaimed what a beauty she'd become. . . .

Marsali shook her head. She had to rid her mind of these thoughts.

Once more, she tried to pray. Then, suddenly, she felt a new presence. She started to turn.

Hands, strong and sure, seized her. At the same moment, she heard Cecilia gasp. She had no time to react. A piece of cloth was stuffed into her mouth, and her hands were quickly bound behind her.

A deep voice whispered in her ear. "My apologies, my lady." She registered a sharp pain at the back of her head, and in the next instant, everything went black.

Patrick Sutherland, earl of Treydan and son of the marquis of Brinaire, paced impatiently on the grassy knoll beside the waterfall.

Marsali had brought him to this spot during his last visit to Abernie. At fourteen, she'd been prettier than he'd ever imagined. He remembered vividly how she had appeared here, telling him shyly that no one else knew of her secret refuge. She had touched his heart as no one else ever had. During the last few years of horror, he'd thought frequently of that clear, bright morning, of Marsali's lovely face and giving nature. Instinctively, he believed she would bring him the peace he so desperately needed.

He was sick of war. Sick of slaughter perpetrated in the name of God and religion. Because he had been outlawed by Cromwell, he was unable to return home until the Restoration and the ascension of Charles II to the throne. In the meantime, he had survived as a mercenary on the continent, often under Charles's banner. After the last battle, though, he had sworn never again to raise his sword against a fellow Scotsman.

He'd left France when the young Prince Charles had been invited home; and along with Rufus and Hiram, he had ridden hard through England to get to Brinaire, only to find that his betrothal was no more, and that his intended was to marry Edward Sinclair, laird of the Sinclair clan.

Patrick had been chilled at the news. He knew the Sinclair. He had fought with him once, only to see the man's back at the height of battle.

Edward would not have his Marsali. Not the tender-hearted girl who could coax wild animals to eat from her hands, and whose faith had seen him through more death and destruction than he wanted to remember. No, it simply could not be.

Ignoring his father's warning to leave the matter alone, he had stormed away from the banquet planned in his honor. Another kind of honor demanded that he protect the woman who, for twelve long years, he had thought of as his bride.

He had taken with him Rufus Chisholm and Hiram Burnett. The three of them had saved each other's lives more times than Patrick could count. Together they had ridden to this waterfall, a hidden grotto on the border between Brinaire and Abernie.

He barely remembered the ride. His thoughts had been entirely of Marsali. Starcatcher, she had called him. She had made him feel as if he could do anything, even reach up and pluck stars from the sky. Did she still feel that way? Or did she want the marriage with Edward Sinclair? He had to know.

But Patrick knew he would never get inside the Abernie gates without being recognized, and he would only be recognized, according to his father, as an enemy. The last thing he wanted was to be faced with killing Marsali's kin.

So when he and his companions had arrived here and laid their plans, he had done something completely abhorrent to him: He had sent other men to do what he could not. Both Rufus and Hiram were unknown to Marsali's father, and Highland hospitality demanded their entrance to Abernie.

His comrades would seek out Jeanie MacDougal and ask the truth of Marsali's feelings. If she seemed content with the upcoming marriage, so be it; Rufus and Hiram were to return to him alone. If she was not, they were to bring her to him.

Still, Patrick acknowledged, patience had never been his strong suit. After two days of waiting, he had reached his limit.

He'd been staring at the narrow gap between the rocks, willing Hiram and Rufus to appear, and he tore his gaze away to face the waterfall. A lively tumble of water spilled in zigzag fashion through crevices and over boulders, falling some thirty feet. At its base, the water swirled gently in a quiet pool before continuing on its course.

Patrick remembered the last time he had been here.

"You must promise never to tell anyone of this place," Marsali begged. *"It will be ours alone."*

Following her through a narrow space between two enormous boulders, he was amused. She was part seductive woman, part enchanting child. She had planned the expedition carefully, even managing to escape Jeanie's watchful eye.

"Not even Jeanie knows of this place," she whispered, casting glances at him in search, he knew, of his reaction.

It was hard not to express his wonder. The cliffs rose on all sides to create a small wooded sanctuary that was bisected by the bright, noisy waterfall. The tiny oasis sat not far from the heavily traveled road leading from Sutherland land to Gunn land. Yet he had never suspected its presence among the fierce, barren mountains.

"I was riding one day," she explained, *"and saw a fawn dart between the rocks."*

He thought then that he'd never met anyone more gentle. He was certain that she would be a wonderful mother. Even at fourteen, she possessed the maturity of a woman even as she retained the eager hopefulness of the young. Through her eyes, he saw life as bright and beautiful and glorious.

"I promise," he told her. *"I will tell no one."*

But two days ago, he had broken his vow, bringing Hiram and Rufus to Marsali's hiding place. He hadn't known where else to go, where else to bring her that would be safe.

Patrick continued to pace. The waiting was driving him almost mad. He thought he'd learned to control his feelings long ago, but he was discovering that, where Marsali was concerned, the lessons had been for naught.

Chapter 2

Hiram caught the woman as she fell, her slender body collapsing into his arms. Rufus had accomplished the same with the girl.

"Patrick will kill us for using force," he grumbled.

"Aye, he might," Rufus replied amiably. "But then he might be glad we didna have to fight our way out of Abernie, which we would if that woman, Jeanie, is mistaken. If either one of the lasses cried out, blood would flow. He did say to avoid tha' above all."

Hiram cast Rufus a doubtful glance, watching as he balanced the lass in his arms. "He won't take kindly to ye undressing her, either."

Rufus grinned. " 'Tis not always easy being Patrick's friend. He canna do anything the simple way."

Hiram nodded his head. "If it ha' been up to me, we would ha' stormed our way in and taken her bold as daylight."

"And litter the ground wi' her kin?" Rufus said dryly. " 'Tis a foine way to start a marriage."

"Ye really think he plans to marry the lass? His fa' said he would disown him."

"Aye, I do think he will. When Patrick gets an idea in 'is head . . ."

"Now I see her, I ken his reason." Hiram leaned down to touch the rich dark hair, but as he reached out, a small animal suddenly threw itself on him, biting his hand.

"Bluidy devil," he spit, then remembered his pledge to the serving woman. He would treat the lass, and all that was hers, gently. He had promised to take her sister and what

Jeanie had called the "wee beasties" with him in return for her help.

Wee beasties, indeed.

He took the animal gently but firmly by the neck, then was suddenly attacked by a second. Out of the corner of his eye, he saw Rufus grin and knew he must be a sight. As big as he was, he'd often felt awkward, except in battle. It was all well and good to know that a swing of his arm would down an enemy, but what use was strength in the face of an unconscious woman and two small animals? Angry, hissing animals, trying to protect their mistress.

Feeling miserably inadequate, he growled, "Dammit, man, come help me."

"Ah, 'tis foine to hear ye need my help," Rufus said, approaching cautiously.

Grabbing the ferret perched on the woman's chest, he dropped it into Hiram's sizable sporran. Hiram sent the one he held to join its friend. The bag moved wildly against his belt—and lower—as Hiram tied it closed.

Hiram nodded his thanks. "Ah, as you said, Patrick's no' an easy friend. But he's been aching to get home to his bride. Even I could see tha'." He mused a moment, then said, "To imagine 'im in love is a wondrous thing. Didna think I would see the day."

"Ye may not see another if we donna get away from here."

"I gave the guards at the gate enough drugged wine to lay out a regiment, those that are no' sick from last night."

"Nothing like a wedding to make a mon thirsty," Rufus agreed. "Still, stealing the bride could make them a wee bit testy."

He took off the older lass's outer clothes and replaced them with a lad's trews over drawers and shift. "Ye best be looking out the door."

"The woman—Jeanie—said no one would come here wi'

all the celebratin'. She's fair bonny, tha' one. Wouldn't mind takin' her, too."

Rufus chuckled. "I didna think ye had romance in yer blood."

Hiram reddened but remained silent.

Rufus finished tucking the girl's hair under a man's bonnet that he cocked halfway down on her face. "This one's but a mite," he said. " 'Tis a sorry mon Abernie must be to sell either of them to a mon like Sinclair."

"Aye," Hiram agreed. "It would take a coldhearted villain to my thinking."

"Ah, and now ye be thinking. Wonders. Always wonders," Rufus said. "Now, watch over them while I go fetch the horses and a rug for the wee lass."

Hiram ignored the jibe, posting himself above the two unconscious lasses as he watched Rufus walk to the back of the church. At the door, Rufus glanced back at him briefly, then, opening the door a crack, he slipped outside.

Hiram heaved a deep sigh and prayed no one would come.

Minutes ticked by. When, after what seemed an eternity, the door slowly opened at the back of the church, his heart pounded in his chest and every muscle in his huge body tensed. An instant later, Rufus appeared, and he relaxed.

Rufus walked quickly to the front of the church. "You take Patrick's lass," he said. "I will wrap the wee one in the rug and carry her. As small as she is, she will look no more than a bundle of rags we are carrying off for the winter."

Hiram put his arm around the Lady Marsali and pulled her to a standing position, holding her up as her legs folded under her unconscious form.

He watched Rufus carefully roll the wee lass into the rug he'd brought, then just as carefully pick her up. Standing in the open doorway, Rufus whistled, and their horses moved to the steps of the church.

Hiram hesitated as they both looked out. Food and wine were being distributed to crofters in another part of the courtyard, so this area was virtually clear. No one seemed to be taking any note of them. With any luck, they looked like two wedding guests, one supporting a boy who was obviously drunk and the other carrying a bundle of castoffs.

They both deliberately swayed in their saddles as if drunk as they slowly walked their horses to the gate. Rufus mumbled something unintelligible to the now almost unconscious guards, who did nothing to stop them from passing. Hiram expected, at any second, to hear the cry of alarm behind them, but he curbed his impatience and kept his horse to a slow plod as they meandered down the road, toward the small village that served the castle.

Once out of sight of the gates, Hiram looked at Rufus and grinned. Then they both dug their heels into the sides of the horses and took off.

They'd absconded with the bride.

Patrick heard the horses and strode quickly to the opening in the rocks. At last.

But was Marsali with them?

One horse, a huge animal Patrick recognized as Hiram's, emerged from between the rocks. His heart stopped for a moment as he saw a lad slumped over in the saddle in front of his friend.

Rufus followed, holding a girl slumped against him. But the girl had red hair, and Marsali's was black, like fine silk.

Hiram came to a halt and swung out of the saddle, carrying the still figure with him.

He laid the figure down and bowed to Patrick. "Your Marsali, milord," he said with rare formality.

"What in the bloody hell did you do to her?" Dropping to the ground, Patrick gathered her into his arms and tugged the bonnet from her head. Black hair, still laced with flowers, tumbled out. Her dark lashes lay gently against creamy white skin.

He knelt, holding her, his own heart thumping as it had

not for years. He laid a hand over hers. When he felt the steady beat of her pulse, relief flooded him.

"A wee tap only," Hiram said apologetically. "We had no time, Patrick. The woman you sent us to, Jeanie, wasn't any too sure what to do, not until this morn. She told us to wait in the chapel, and she would send the lassies if she believed it the right thing to do. We had no time to talk to the lassies, not if we were to escape before the wedding."

Patrick felt his heart miss a beat. "You mean she did not agree?"

"Jeanie said she would not send her to us unless she was certain of the girl's heart," Hiram insisted. "When they appeared, we assumed . . ."

Patrick's stomach turned. He'd wanted Marsali's consent. But he was not angry at Hiram. He should have gone to her himself. He should have somehow found a way.

His gaze fixed on Marsali's face, he swore softly. Then, glancing at the younger lass Rufus had laid upon the ground a few yards away, he asked, "And who is that?"

"Yer lady's sister," Rufus replied.

Patrick's eyes widened in surprise, and he studied the unconscious form more closely. Cecilia had been so much younger the last time he had seen her, he truly hadn't recognized her.

"Jeanie said the lass would not go wi'out her sister," Hiram explained. "She said the earl had threatened to marry the wee one to Sinclair if yer lady wouldna'. That is why yer lady agreed to the wedding."

Patrick cursed under his breath. He could scarcely believe it of his foster father, whom he had both admired and respected.

But what in God's name would he do with Cecilia now?

Rufus was trying to offer water from a pouch to Cecilia in an effort to waken her. He nodded to Patrick that the girl was unharmed.

Marsali moved in his arms, moaning quietly, and her

thick lashes fluttered. Then her eyes flew open, and he saw the deep blue depths that had haunted him. Confusion clouded her gaze as she tried to focus.

"Marsali," he said gently.

They widened then, those eyes, shock replacing confusion. What did he look like to her? He was used to the scar that left his lips turned permanently upward on the left side, to the lines that stretched outward from his eyes. But he knew he looked ten years older than his age and that his face was no maiden's dream.

"Patrick?" The sound of his name was soft and full of wonder.

"Aye," he said, his hand going to her cheek.

For a moment, something glorious replaced the bewilderment in her face, and she smiled, a marvelous smile that made his heart lurch crazily in his chest. In the years since he'd last seen her, she'd become, if possible, even lovelier.

"I was so afraid for you," she said. "No one has heard from you for so long."

The words were a balm to all the pain of past years, to the sickness of heart at the killing.

"And I for you," he said softly, "when I heard about Sinclair."

When he spoke that name, her eyes lost the soft luster of wonder they'd had as she looked at him. She struggled to sit upright. A frown marred her brow now, and her eyes seemed to shimmer with moisture. "I canna stay with you," she said brokenly.

"We have your sister," Patrick said. "I will pledge her safety."

Her frown deepened, and her gaze found Cecilia's still form. She looked back at him briefly, then turned toward Hiram and Rufus. "How? Why . . . ?"

"These men are Hiram Burnett and Rufus Chisholm," he said. "They are my friends. And they were not supposed to hurt you, but . . ." His voice trailed off as she rose and went to kneel by her sister.

"Cecilia," she whispered, holding her sister's hand.

Patrick watched her, unable to do anything but drink in the sight of her. She was uncommonly graceful. The lad's clothing did nothing to detract from her loveliness, but rather emphasized the willowy slenderness of her body.

Her hands touched Cecilia with a tenderness he wanted for his own, and he heard her call softly to the still-unconscious girl. He looked up to see Rufus watching both lasses intently, his lean, saturnine features, usually inscrutable, twisted into something Patrick could only identify as regret.

Rufus? Regret? Doubtful. Still . . .

Patrick frowned and moved to Marsali's side. He remembered Cecilia as a child, quiet and obedient with little of her sister's curiosity or precociousness. She was now the age that Marsali had been when last they met, but she looked younger, impossibly innocent.

Finally, at Marsali's coaxing, Cecilia began to wake.

"We didna harm her," Rufus said awkwardly in a voice that Patrick didn't recognize. His tone was apologetic, without a trace of his usual sardonic humor.

Marsali looked up at Rufus accusingly.

When Rufus gave him a helpless glance, Patrick thought he might have laughed under other circumstances.

"They said your sister might be forced to marry," Patrick said. "Jeanie told Hiram and Rufus that you would not come without her."

"Jeanie?" Marsali repeated, staring at him. "She told me to take Cecilia to the chapel. She knew?"

Kneeling on one knee beside her, Patrick nodded. "Aye, I would not have interfered with your wedding had I thought you . . . wanted it. Rufus and Hiram were instructed—" He broke off at the sight of tears forming in Marsali's eyes.

But just then, Cecilia let out a weak groan, bringing both of their gazes down to her.

"Cecilia." Marsali gave her sister's shoulder a gentle shake.

The girl's eyes flew open. They were blue, but not the same deep blue as Marsali's. Marsali's eyes reminded him of the evening sky; Cecilia's were more like the sky at noon. Her hair was lighter, too, a rich, dark auburn.

"Marsali?"

Patrick cursed himself silently. He'd never purposely harmed a woman in his life.

"Do not be afraid, Cecilia," Marsali said softly. "Patrick is here. He wants to help us." She looked up at him sharply. "Or did you come to make us your hostages?"

The question made him wince. That she would even consider such a possibility was a dagger in his heart.

"No," he said. "You may leave if you wish. I wanted only to save you from a marriage you may not have wanted."

"My father will come after me," she said quietly, "and I canna believe your father will accept me. Where do you propose my sister and I go?"

Cecilia was sitting now. Quiet. Watchful.

"I still consider our betrothal valid," Patrick said.

Marsali stared up at him. "And what about me? Do I have a choice? Or are you like my father? Using me for your ends?"

He heard the pain in her voice, sensed the betrayal she had felt at being thrust between their families.

Patrick looked toward his two companions, then, bringing his gaze back to Marsali, he asked, "Will you walk with me?"

She hesitated, and he said, "Your sister will be safe. Hiram and Rufus have been with me these past ten years, and there are no men more trustworthy."

"Aside from kidnapping maidens?" she asked, and though her tone was dry, he thought he heard a trace of humor in her voice.

"Aye," he said with the briefest of smiles, "except for that."

She looked at Cecilia, and, casting Rufus a quick glance, Cecilia nodded her assent.

Hiram cleared his throat, and Patrick followed the man's look. The big man's sporran was jumping frantically below his belt, as if his manhood had gone berserk.

Patrick nearly burst out laughing but managed to stifle the sound in a cough. His large companion, a warrior through and through, looked chagrined as he opened his sporran. Two creatures jumped out, hissing and chittering. Even Hiram jumped back.

"Tristan! Isolde!" At the sound of Marsali's voice, the two ferrets abandoned their attack on Hiram and ran to her, tumbling over each other in their eagerness. She petted them, her touch bringing them calm.

"Mistress Jeanie said ye would be wantin' them," Hiram said.

She gave him a slow, delighted smile, and Patrick's heart melted. He'd waited years to see that smile again.

He rose and held out his hand to her, and after a moment's hesitation, she took it and allowed him to help her to her feet. He felt her fingers tighten around his as their gazes met. Wanting desperately to be alone with her, and wondering how in God's name he would restrain himself once he was, he led her away from the others.

With her hand held securely in Patrick's, Marsali allowed him to lead the way toward the other side of the secret grotto, where a high pile of rocks and a thicket of hawthorn provided some privacy.

She couldn't believe this was happening. Hours ago, she had been dreading a ceremony that would bind her to a man she distrusted. Sick with dismay, she'd hopelessly prayed that Patrick would come to her. And here he was. The man she'd loved all her life.

He had changed. Her handsome prince was a man now, one whose face bore physical scars, and his soul, she sensed, scars of another kind. Yet his glittering green eyes, as vivid as emeralds, softened each time they looked at her—only to turn cautious and wary again when he looked away.

He held her hand as if he were afraid she might escape and, for a moment, Marsali was seized by uncertainty. More than twelve years separated the boy and the man. There was a hardness to him now, an aura of danger that she did not remember.

She wanted to put her arms around him, and feel *his* arms around her. She wanted the touch of his mouth, the comfort of his closeness. But their clans were at war. And while she told herself he was still Patrick, her Patrick, her recent, bitter experience told her to be cautious. Her father had been willing to trade her to achieve his own ends. Her brother Gavin had supported him. So would not Patrick want to use her, too? Did not all men think of women as weapons to be used to wage their bloody wars?

She would be a fine trophy to flash before Gregor Sutherland. It would please the marquis greatly if his heir were to bring home a Gunn hostage. And she knew her father would never give her up to a Sutherland without a fight.

Still, her hand tightened in his, clutching at the fading dreams. Her love. Her starcatcher. She had looked for that star every night and prayed for his safety. As long as it hung bright in the night sky, she had known he was safe.

But that was no longer enough.

Patrick pulled her to a halt beneath an old, gnarled oak. His arms crushed her to him as if he needed her as much as she had needed him. No man had ever held her like this, so close that she could feel every inch of his lean, hard body pressed to hers. He was so tall and strong. For an instant, she was afraid.

But the green gaze that regarded her so intently was familiar—and filled with hunger. She had never hoped that he loved her. It had always been sufficient that she loved him, and that he'd consented to their betrothal. Yet as she melted into his tight embrace, she realized that she wanted everything. Everything, including love, that Patrick could give her.

When his head slowly lowered, her heart started to race. She felt his hand at the small of her back tremble, and it astonished her to see a trace of uncertainty flash in his eyes. Surely this confident man who held her so boldly couldn't be waiting for her permission.

Still, she gave it, whispering, "Patrick . . ."

An instant later, his lips seized hers.

It wasn't the first time he'd kissed her. Six years ago, in saying goodbye, he'd held her hands and touched his lips to hers in a sweet parting. A gentle kiss. A passionless kiss. A kiss that was nothing at all like this.

And before she knew what was happening, fire was raging between them. The joining of their lips seemed to contain an energy so intense she thought she would be consumed by it. So much longing. And desperation—aye, that, too.

All doubts sank to the recesses of her mind as the heat between them intensified, and a need she'd never known before exploded into raw hunger. This was Patrick. And he was here, at last. Until that moment, she'd never realized how much she'd feared for him, how much she'd needed him, how deeply her spirit had yearned for him.

She knew it was madness to stay here with Patrick, when the result could be his death. Yet she couldn't forgo the shelter of his arms. Nor could she force herself to end the heated flow of desire between them.

A deep growl rumbled in his chest. "Sweetness," he whispered into her hair. "I dreamed of this."

He had dreamed of her. It was so much more than she'd ever expected. Her legs trembled as his tongue touched her lips, then slipped inside her mouth. A wave of new sensations rushed through her. Yet she did nothing to discourage the intimate way he explored her. Instead, she found herself responding to his every touch.

Somehow, with what was left of her wits, she realized she was clinging to him, as if her life were forfeit. She heard the small, throaty sounds she was making. She felt his entire body shaking, and she felt the hard, vital evidence of his manhood pressed against her. She had heard servants talk; she knew where this was leading. And she wanted it, wanted to move even closer to him, to join her body intimately with his.

But she could not build her own happiness on the blood of others, especially not the blood of her kin and the kin of the man she loved.

She had to return to Abernie. She had to go through with the wedding. . . .

Tearing herself from Patrick's embrace, Marsali uttered a pained, hopeless cry. Surprised, Patrick let her go, his arms dropping to his sides. His breathing was ragged as his eyes questioned her.

"I canna," she said brokenly.

"We were pledged," he replied, his voice hoarse. "You are mine, Marsali."

The note of possessiveness in his voice, even given the feelings he aroused in her, stunned her. The flat, almost emotionless tone was so authoritative, so . . . certain. He'd become a stranger again, one who made decisions without consulting her.

"Our betrothal was broken," she said quietly, "cried off by both families."

"Not by me," he said.

She studied him obliquely. "My father and Edward . . . they will go after your family," she said.

"They will *try*." Coldness underlined his voice. She had never feared him before, but now she wondered whether she knew him at all.

"Your father killed my aunt," she said desperately.

"Nay, my father is as puzzled by her disappearance as any man, and, despite his faults, I do not think he would lie."

"Not even with death as a consequence?"

"Not even then."

Lifting her chin a notch, Marsali continued. "He accused my aunt of adultery."

"He says there was proof," Patrick replied.

"Nay," she denied.

His eyes glittered with the hardness of stone, and she glimpsed what his enemies must have seen of Patrick Sutherland. The thought of him at war with her father and brother made her shiver.

Dear Mother in heaven. The wedding should have started by now. Everyone would be looking for the bride. When would they begin to suspect the Sutherlands?

"I have to return to Abernie," she whispered.

"Jeanie said she would not help us if she wasn't sure you didna want the wedding," Patrick said flatly. "Was she wrong, lass? Do you want to wed Sinclair?"

"Aye," Marsali said defiantly, even though she was certain the lie must be plain on her face.

"Because of your sister?" Patrick guessed.

"Because you and I can never be."

He studied her for a moment, then, slowly, the tension left his face. He lifted his hand to trail a finger along her cheek. "You have become a beautiful woman," he said quietly. "But then, I always knew you would."

Her resolve melted under the words, under the intensity of his gaze, under the force of his demand for the truth. She leaned into his touch, craving it.

His hands were strong, she thought, from years of wielding a sword. But she could well destroy him, as well as both of their families, if she did not return.

"I *agreed* to the marriage with Edward," she said as firmly as she could. "I gave him my troth."

His hand trailed downward over her shoulder, her arm,

until he took her hand in his. He squeezed her fingers, saying, "You had already given it to me with your words and, a minute ago, you gave it to me with your body. Your heart is mine, Marsali."

"And *your* heart?" she asked.

A muscle flexed in his throat, but he said nothing, and she wondered for a moment whether he had come for her out of affection—or simply because she was a belonging he wasn't ready to forfeit.

She pulled away and turned to gaze at the rocks, the hills, anything but the face made even more attractive to her by the character the years had given it. "Where would we go?"

"To Brinaire," he said flatly.

"And Cecilia?"

"She will come with us. You will both be safe there."

"Your father? He agrees?"

He hesitated long enough that she knew the answer.

"He will have to," he said. "Or we will go to France. I have friends there."

She turned and looked at him again. "And then our clans will fight one another. You know that. Many will die or starve because of us. Can you live with that?"

His mouth twisted. "They seem determined to fight now in any event."

"But there has been naught but a few minor raids," she said. "If I were to go with you, my father would not be satisfied with anything but blood. His pride—"

"Damn his pride!" Patrick burst out. "I canna stand aside and see you marry Sinclair. The man is a coward. And his wife's death was more than a little odd."

When she only stared at him, saying nothing, he sighed heavily and shoved his fingers through his thick, black hair. Her gaze followed the gesture, falling on the scar on his wrist that he'd gotten saving her ferret's life so many years ago. Reaching out, she took Patrick's hand in hers, her fingers touching the rough, white mark from the hawk's talons.

Its jagged length ran from the first knuckle of his fourth finger up his forearm to four inches past his wrist.

"Will you make an oath to me, Patrick Sutherland?" she asked, lifting her gaze to meet his.

"Aye," he said, nodding slowly. "Anything but return you to Sinclair."

"Send my sister away. Send her someplace safe. I know only my father's friends."

His gaze bore into hers. "I do know someone. Rufus's family. I was wounded, and they cared for me. There are five sisters, as well as Rufus and an older brother and his wife. It is as fine a family as I've ever known—and as generous a one. They live in an old keep in the Lowlands and socialize very little, though they bear a fine name. Their clan is very loyal to them."

"Will you see her safely there? Do you swear? No matter what happens between you and me?" She heard the desperation in her voice and saw, by the fierce glitter in his eyes, that he'd heard it, too.

"I swear it, lass," he said.

"Thank you." Marsali closed her eyes briefly.

She didn't resist when he took her in his arms again, pulling her gently toward him. She leaned against him, listening to the beating of his heart, the fine strong rhythm of it, and savoring the warmth of his body.

For a long minute, she huddled within his embrace, trying not to think of Abernie Castle, trying not to imagine the worry everyone—everyone but Jeanie—must be feeling by now. Shortly, when a search of the castle didn't turn up either her or Cecilia, panic would seize them. The two daughters of the keep gone without a trace.

She had to return. Still, she would not be returning the same person as she was when she left. Fear had turned into hope, if not happiness. Patrick had given her the means to refuse the marriage to Edward Sinclair. As long as she knew Cecilia was safe, no one would be able to force the words from her mouth. And by refusing marriage with Sinclair, she would break the alliance that would have crushed Patrick's family. Her father could not attack the Sutherlands on his own. Perhaps a war could be prevented, after all.

She would make her father believe that no Sutherland was involved in her sister's disappearance. Only herself. He would be furious. But he could do little.

Her heart would never be whole again. She could already feel it breaking, shattering into tiny shards of pain. But she would have the comfort of knowing she had prevented bloodshed.

She only wished that, one day, her father—and brother— might understand what she had given up.

Chapter 3

Patrick wondered whether he had promised too quickly. He knew how determined Marsali could be. Her independent spirit had always intrigued him. But what was she bent on doing that put such a fierce light in her lovely eyes?

"No matter what happens between you and me." Her words echoed in his mind. What had she meant? Surely, she did not intend still to marry Sinclair.

"Marsali?"

She did not look at him but at the hawthorn brake that shielded their view of the others, on the opposite side of the grotto. "Cecilia will be frightened," she said.

"Rufus will entertain her."

"I doubt it not," she said. "He must have a way with ladies if he convinced Jeanie that he would be a safe escort."

"Look at me," he demanded.

With obvious reluctance, she turned toward him, and just as reluctantly raised her gaze to meet his.

"I know," he said, "that I have changed. The scars . . ."

She uttered a small cry of denial, cutting off his words. "Nay," she said, placing her hand upon his face, her fingers running the length of the white mark where the tip of a sword had laid open his cheek. "I have always thought you very handsome, and never more so than now."

Hearing the sincerity in her voice, he realized how much he had feared her reaction. Her rejection.

Her eyes filled with tears, and she turned away again. "I am sorry," she whispered. "I canna bear to think of your pain. You've been wounded, and you could have been . . . killed . . ."

"Is that why you agreed to the marriage to Sinclair? You thought me dead?"

She shook her head. "I agreed only because of Cecilia. My father would do anything to gain Edward's troops so he could ride against Brinaire."

"The rest of your clan? How do they feel?"

"A fourth of them have Sutherland blood," she said, "and nearly all have Sutherland friends. But they are sworn to my father, and they will follow him."

"And Gavin?" he asked, not truly wanting to hear the answer. Not wanting to learn that his closest friend now wanted to slay him and his family.

"He has missed you," Marsali replied carefully. "He talked of you much until . . ."

Patrick wanted to swear. "A woman," he muttered instead. "All because of one woman."

"And I would make it worse," she said. "If I go with you. It would only deepen the hatred."

Patrick couldn't deny her words, yet he wasn't ready to give up the argument.

"You said you would let me return if I wished," she said.

"Aye," he replied, regretting his first words to her. "But you have said you do not want the marriage."

She gave her head a quick shake. "I will not be responsible for more hatred. I canna."

"I want you for my wife," Patrick said, trying to bury the sudden desperation he heard in his voice.

"The marriage was meant to unite the families, not destroy them," Marsali said gently. "I canna marry you, but you have given me the means to refuse Edward. Without Cecilia at Abernie, my father canna force me to marry Edward."

"Are you sure of that?"

"Aye. He will be very angry, but I will tell him that it was I who smuggled my sister from his gates. He wouldna doubt me. Nor will he hurt me. He believes striking a woman is cowardly."

Patrick wished he could believe her, but Abernie had clearly changed a great deal, enough to force his daughter into an unwanted marriage.

"Nay," he said. "I willna allow it."

"You gave me your oath," she accused him.

"I willna allow you to take the blame for something I did."

She searched his face. "I will be ruined if it becomes known that you kidnapped me."

"We would have to wed," he said. "There would be no disgrace."

"Nor would there be peace," she argued, her voice trembling.

"There canna be peace, anyway," Patrick said bitterly. "Our fathers have made that clear." Then, sighing heavily, he murmured, "If only we knew what happened to your aunt."

"She would not take her own life," Marsali insisted. "She still believed—"

When she stopped abruptly, he prompted her. "Believed what?"

She hesitated.

"Believed what?" he asked again.

"That it is a mortal sin," she said finally, her gaze locked with his.

Patrick felt a shiver of apprehension race up his spine. He understood immediately what Marsali was telling him. But if Margaret was a Catholic, was Marsali one, too? He cared not at all what form Marsali's prayers took, but these days, to be Catholic in Scotland was to risk death.

Answering his unspoken questions, Marsali shook her head. "I was not taught Catholicism. My aunt never mentioned her beliefs, but Jeanie let something slip once about attending a mass with Aunt Margaret. I am certain my father didna know."

"I doubt mine did, either," Patrick replied, his head whirling with the implications. If it was true, Margaret would never have considered suicide. But then, divorce was also a mortal sin to Catholics, and his father, convinced he'd been cuckolded, had sworn to divorce Margaret. Which would she have considered the greater sin: suicide or divorce?

In his mind, Patrick could still picture Margaret. She had been a beautiful woman, reserved and sweet natured. Her marriage to his father had been a political alliance, and, where his father was concerned, that might have been as much as it ever meant. Gregor Sutherland would never admit to an emotion as sentimental as love. But Margaret? Had she loved his father?

Perhaps, Patrick thought. He couldn't be certain. She had not seemed the type of woman to betray a husband, even one she did not love. Yet he had believed his father's version of the story because, as brittle and uncaring as he could be, the marquis of Brinaire did not lie. Truly, why would he invent a story of his wife's adultery? Nay, it made no sense. Nor would he see the need to lie about Margaret's death—not to his own son.

Marsali's revelation only added to the mystery.

She was watching him closely, misery still clouding her eyes, and all he wanted was to wrap her in his arms and be her starcatcher again, a hero who, by his very will, could solve all of her troubles.

"Patrick." She made his name sound like a whispered prayer.

Looking down at her, he drew a ragged breath. He knew he was not going to like what she was about to say. Delaying her words, he dug into his sporran and extracted an item, dangling it in front of her.

She stared at the tiny piece of shredded fabric, stained

with dirt and sweat and blood. Then her eyes grew wide with astonishment. "My ribbon," she breathed.

He nodded. "I told you I would have nothing to fear if you gave me a token. It has been my talisman."

"Such a small thing," she said. "But you had my prayers, too, and they were very big."

He smiled slowly, capturing her hand in his. "I have been waiting for you to grow up, Marsali."

She bowed her head, but not before he saw surprise and, yes, pleasure sparkle in her eyes. Using a finger to tip her chin upward, he forced her to look at him again.

"You are even prettier than I dreamed you would be," he said. "And I *did* dream. I think those dreams were all that kept me alive."

"Then I am content," she said, but the words were marred by anguish. "And I will remember that always. But you *must* let me return to Abernie."

"How can I?" he countered. "How can you even ask—"

"What about your family?" she interrupted. "What about your clan? Your brother? Your sister? You know you canna subject them to war any more than I can mine."

Patrick stared at her in silence, jaw clenched. Finally, he muttered, "Our fathers are bent upon war. It will happen no matter what we do. And I have waited too long for you as it is."

She shook her head. "No. If I go with you, Father and Edward will join together, and nothing will satisfy Father's pride but to destroy your clan. But if I return to Abernie and refuse Edward, he will never join my father against the Sutherlands." She squeezed his hand hard. "Patrick, we can stop this. We *have* to stop it."

"Are you that brave?" he said gently.

"Nay," she said. "I am no' so brave at all. I am only a coward who canna bear the thought of you or Gavin or my father dying, especially at each other's hands."

Patrick had seen bravery on the field, courage so great

he'd been both awed and humbled by it. But never, he thought, had he seen bravery as pure as hers. She was prepared to sacrifice her own needs for the sake of those she loved.

For a moment, he was filled with pride, but it soon gave way to defeat. During all the years he'd been in Europe, fighting other people's battles for them, enduring cold and hunger as well as wounds in return for money, he had clung to two dreams that he expected, one day, to fulfill: Marsali and peace. But he was finding that he could have one or the other, but never both. It seemed to him that the devil had finally decided to demand his due, for, surely, this was hell.

She had spoken truly; he could not bring disaster upon his family. Yet looking at Marsali, he did not know how he would bear the loss of her.

Patrick bent his head. He felt something odd, something he hadn't experienced in years—a tightness behind his eyes, a mist blurring his vision. Then he felt her hand, soft and sweet, on his face.

His hand flew to cover hers and press it to him. "I will find a way," he swore. "Wait for me, Marsali. I swear, I will find a way for us to be together. And until then, if you need anything . . ."

She gave a soft sob. Biting her lower lip, she nodded.

"If your father tries to marry you to Sinclair, I will come after you again, and—"

She placed a finger to his lips. "Donna say it. Donna make promises you canna keep."

A knot in his throat kept him from replying. Sick with frustration, Patrick pulled her into his embrace, holding her tightly, trying somehow to capture some part of her to hold when she was gone.

"Jeanie's sister is married to a Sutherland," Marsali said brokenly. "Mayhap I can get a message to you—"

His lips crushed hers, stopping the words. Bittersweet longing ripped through him as he tasted that for which he'd hungered so long. God, he wanted her more than he'd ever imagined wanting any woman. Desperation guided his mouth to take hers, and she responded with the same kind of fierce recklessness. He savored the possessiveness with which she returned his kiss. She *was* his. She would always be his.

Her arms entwined around his neck, demanding more, and his tongue thrust into her mouth in intimate possession, exploring, tasting, seducing. Desire, raw and demanding, coursed through him. In another minute, he would have her on the ground and be inside her, filling her with his seed.

Only the thought of the consequences of that act forced him to curb his passion. By force of will, he gentled the kiss, then, finally, ended it—while he still could.

Drawing a ragged breath, he looked down at her, framing her face with his hands, memorizing it so that he might remember her exactly as she was at this moment: beguiling, soft, her eyes glowing with passion.

"I *will* have you," he said, and the depth of his determination stunned even him. "I'll find a way."

They were both trembling, and the smile she managed was a bit shaky. "I never knew . . . I never dreamed it could be so . . . so . . ."

He returned her smile. "Neither did I, my lady."

"I will wait," she whispered brokenly.

He brushed her cheek with the back of his hand. "Are you sure you will be all right?"

She nodded.

He did not want to let her go. He particularly did not want to let her go back to her wedding day. Damn the Fates, it should have been *their* wedding day.

He forced himself to take a step back, away from her, and his words sounded more impersonal than he intended as he spoke. "I will send Rufus and Hiram ahead with your sister.

The faster they're away from here, the better. Your father's men are probably combing the castle for you both."

She nodded, but her gaze reflected uncertainty. "You *know* she will be safe?"

"I swear it," he said. "Hiram and Rufus are completely trustworthy, but I will have them stop at a farm on the edge of our land. A widow lives there who will go with them. Cecilia will be well chaperoned." He hesitated. "It might be better if you two exchanged clothes."

She looked down at the lad's clothing she wore, and an impish smile brightened her face. "I like them."

"Aye, and you look enchanting in them," he said, eyeing her slender form. "But your sister will need them more."

She nodded.

"Will she be willing to leave?"

"I think so. She no more wants to marry Edward than I do."

He leaned down and kissed her cheek, drawing away before his desire could overrule his good sense again. "Go talk to her."

Her eyes expressed her reluctance to leave him. "Thank you," she said softly. "Thank you for saving me from Edward."

"I will kill him if he lays one finger on you," he promised. And he would, though it would be breaking his vow not to kill another Scotsman. But then Sinclair was unworthy to be called a Scot. Patrick could only hope that God was as discriminating.

She held his gaze a moment longer, then turned and left him.

He let her go, afraid to touch her again.

As she disappeared behind the brake of hawthorn, he cursed the Fates that had led him home to the one thing he'd ever wanted—only to find that he could not have her. As God was his witness, he would find a way for Marsali and him to be together, without bloodshed—or he would die trying.

Marsali tried desperately to hold on to her courage. Clasping her hands together in her lap, she prayed that her father could not see how badly they were shaking.

She had never seen him so angry. He had been a good father. He had never struck her. She could see, though, that he wanted to do so now. His hand was clenching and unclenching at his side, and his face was mottled red.

Her voice was none too steady as she spoke. "I will not marry him. You canna make me. I will take my own life first."

Her father paled, staring at her. Then, swearing, he began stomping around the room. "You dare defy me? Shame me?"

She darted a glance at her brother, Gavin, who had stood behind her father throughout the ordeal. He'd always shown her a rough affection—when he'd had time—and had often taken her side in small battles. This time, though, he remained silent, his dark eyes shadowed, a frown marring his handsome face.

Marsali's gaze went to him, beseeching him to intercede. "We will be bloody lucky if Sinclair doesna declare war on us," he said stiffly. "The insult was great."

She could not argue with that. Returning to Abernie the morn after the wedding was supposed to have taken place, she had found things exactly as she expected. The entire castle was in a state of panic. Crofters had been searching the keep for her and Cecilia and riders sent to scour the Gunn lands. Her arrival had been greeted, at first, with joy and relief. But as she had stood, wearing her sister's soiled gown, and announced that she herself had spirited her sister away, happiness had turned to confusion. When she'd added that she would not marry Edward Sinclair, confusion had become anger.

She would never forget the look on Edward's face. Fury

had transformed his handsome features, and he had looked as if he truly wanted to kill her. He had stood by, raging silently, as her father had tried to reason with her. But no one could force her to speak the words, and the vicar, though obviously disapproving of her conduct, had refused to perform the ceremony without her spoken consent.

Finally, the crofters had been sent home. Some guests, clearly afraid that battle might break out, had quickly disappeared. Others had stayed out of curiosity, and Highland hospitality forbade sending them away. Marsali suspected that most, even now, remained oblivious to anything but the casks of wine still being provided.

At some point amid the chaos, Edward had stormed away with his men, warning her father that either he set the matter to right or face another enemy.

Her father certainly had tried. She had been threatened with everything from the tiny dungeon below the castle to a beating to bread and water forever, but all seemed preferable to Edward Sinclair.

"Well, girl, what do you say?" he demanded.

Her fingers clenched together until they hurt. "I told you I could not marry him," she said. "And three years ago you never would have agreed to it."

"I did not need him three years ago," Donald Gunn boomed. "You have a duty to me and to your clan."

"No one but you wants to fight the Sutherlands," she said recklessly. "A full quarter of our clan are related to them."

"They killed your aunt!" he raged. "Your own blood! They shamed our name, and now you have shamed it worse."

She hung her head. Her father had doted on his sister, his only living sibling. He had rejoiced when Margaret had married Patrick's father; it had strengthened the bonds between two clans that had been allies for a hundred years. But Margaret was gone, leaving hatred behind her.

"Marsali." Gavin's voice was low, reasoned, when he finally addressed her. "Where is Cecilia?"

"Safe," she said.

"How do you know?"

She pressed her lips together. She knew a large part of their anger was rooted in worry for her sister.

"Marsali?"

She could bear Gavin's anger, but it was much harder to remain silent in the face of his anxiety.

"Cecilia is only a child," she said desperately. "I couldna let you marry her to someone like Edward. And I will not, either. I do not understand how either of you could even consider—"

"Edward is a laird with rich lands," her father reminded her.

"With an army, you mean," she replied bitterly. "He's also had two wives who died when they were young."

"One in childbirth," her father said.

"And the other?" she said. "There are whispers—"

"Sutherland lies. He lied about Margaret."

"You have condemned the marquis of Brinaire on less."

Blood rose in his face, turning it an angry shade of red. "You willna mention that name again," he said.

Gavin spoke from his position by the door. "You could not have gone far. We will find her. Men are out combing the countryside now."

She was silent. Cecilia should be far out of reach by now. She had seemed a little nervous but had not argued with the plan for her to travel south with Hiram and Rufus. Indeed, to Marsali's surprise, her sister had donned the boy's clothing almost eagerly. Charmed by Patrick's companions, despite the rough introduction she'd been given to them, she'd expressed no hesitation about riding off to who-knows-where with them. Seeing this, Marsali had realized, to her surprise, that her quiet, studious sister possessed a certain desire for adventure.

Halting a few feet from Marsali's chair, her father spun to face her. "You will stay in your room with only bread and water until you are willing to marry Sinclair," he said, "and you tell us where your sister is. Gavin, see to it."

Gavin's frown deepened, but he did not attempt to contradict the order. His gaze rested on her for a moment, and she saw sympathy in his eyes. But she also saw steely resolve.

Rising from her chair, she turned blindly toward the door. Any further argument was futile. Still, she felt a stirring of triumph. She had escaped marriage to Edward Sinclair.

"Father," she acknowledged, bowing her head slightly as she swept from the room.

Gavin waited for her by the door, and she followed him up the stairs. Now that the worst was past, she wanted some time to herself to remember the moments she and Patrick had shared. She wanted to remember the hunger she'd seen in his eyes. She wanted to remember his kiss. She wanted to believe that he would find a way for them to be together. He had not changed very much, after all, she told herself. He was still the boy who had saved her ferret. He was still the young man who had reached out to pluck the stars from the heavens for her.

She stopped at her door and, hesitating a moment, turned to Gavin. "Cecilia is safe," she said.

"And what about Patrick?" he asked quietly.

Chapter 4

Marsali stared at Gavin, her heart in her throat.
Of course, he would have heard about Patrick's
return. There were few secrets in the Highlands.

"Marsali?" Gavin's tone was rough. "What about Patrick?"

"I donna know what you mean," she said.

"I think you do. Have you seen him?"

She hesitated, feeling very much alone. Her family had always been close. Perhaps because they had known so many losses. Three of Marsali's siblings died in infancy, and her mother had succumbed to fever shortly after giving birth to a stillborn babe. When her stepmother had died just weeks after giving birth to Cecilia, a strong bond had formed between herself and her new baby sister.

Her father and her aunt had shared a similar relationship; but Marsali just couldn't accept his version of her aunt's disappearance, nor could she condone his desire to shed Sutherland blood. Even if it meant pushing her only brother away.

She was silent under Gavin's intense scrutiny, his question hanging between them. "Patrick *is* back, then!" he exploded.

She turned toward the stairs leading to her bedchamber, but her brother's hand on her arm stopped her progress.

"It is no good, Marsali," he said. "Father will never allow another marriage between our families."

He, nearly as much as Jeanie, knew how she felt about Patrick. Over the years, she had plagued Gavin with questions about the man who'd been raised alongside him, and he, in turn, had teased her countless times about her abiding interest in her husband-to-be.

"He was your friend," she accused him. "You've said he was your brother."

"Aye," Gavin replied. "But I canna go against Father on this. Patrick's blood spilled ours."

"You do not know that."

"I know Aunt Margaret would never leave without saying a word."

"And I don't think Patrick's father would lie," she retorted. "The marquis of Brinaire might not be known for his kindness, but I have never heard anyone call him a liar."

Letting out a long breath, Gavin demanded, "Where is Patrick? And where is our sister?"

"I donna know," she said, and she didn't. Not exactly. She did know that wherever Cecilia was, she was safer than she would be here, in the middle of a clan war or, worse, married to Edward Sinclair.

"I will have to find her," Gavin said. "And God help anyone who hurts her."

Marsali placed a hand on his arm. "She will be safe," she said. "I swear."

Gavin frowned. "Fa is convinced that the Sutherlands are responsible," he said. "He wants me to raid their southern borders. He also wants me to take Patrick's brother hostage—or Patrick himself, if indeed he is back—in exchange for Cecilia."

Marsali's heart pounded. "Patrick had nothing to do with this. I planned it myself so that Fa could not force me to marry Edward by threatening to marry Cecilia to him in my place. Surely, Gavin"—her voice broke—"surely you canna trust the Sinclairs."

Gavin looked away. "It would have been a good alliance."

"You may give yourself up for dubious alliances," she said, tears forming behind her eyes. "I will not."

"You will, if Fa commands it."

"He canna command my heart."

Gavin sighed. "Marsali, you have no' seen Patrick since you were a child. You know nothing of him now."

She drew herself up to her full height, which, maddeningly, was still a good foot shorter than her brother's. "I was fourteen."

Something flickered in his eyes, and she knew that he'd been trying to trick her into admitting she had seen Patrick recently.

"You've changed, Gavin."

"So have you, little sister. You have always been so . . ."

"Malleable?"

He had the grace to look embarrassed. "That is not what I meant. You—"

"Always wanted to please?"

"Aye," he said, allowing himself a small smile.

She looked into blue eyes very much like her own. "You have always known how I felt about Patrick," she said. "You encouraged it with your tales of his honor and courage and reports of his deeds in battle. I am not as inconstant as you with my friendships or my loyalties."

His lips thinned at the rebuke. "Our loyalty belongs to our father."

"When he is right."

"No! He is our father, regardless." Gavin's fist hit the stone wall beside them. "And he *is* right! Margaret must be avenged."

"No one knows the truth of the matter," she charged. "I think it is the disgrace of the charges against Aunt Margaret that you and Fa canna bear, not the loss of her." The moment the words left her lips, she wished she could reclaim them. She did not want to wound him. She simply wanted him to understand.

"I willna explain myself to you," he said coldly. "I loved Margaret, and I know she would never leave without a word. She is dead, and the Sutherlands are responsible." A muscle in his throat flexed. "God's blood, do you not know how much I cared for Patrick? How much I wanted you wed to him so we truly would be brothers? But duty and honor are more important than my personal wants. You would do well to remember that."

"Your sense of honor and mine are different," she said, her voice shaking. Her life, Cecilia's life—and Patrick's, too—might all depend upon her strength of will. She would give nothing away. Nothing.

Yet the bleak look in Gavin's eyes wounded her heart. She turned and entered her room. This time, he did not stop her.

Gregor Sutherland, marquis of Brinaire, glared at his son. "Where in the devil have you been?"

Patrick returned his father's glare. "I went exploring. 'Tis a long time since I have seen these hills."

"You missed the homecoming I intended." The bushy brows, silver now where once they'd been black, knitted together. "I wanted to present my brawny, braw son to my friends. They have heard of your great deeds." He spoke with the pride that Patrick had always hoped for. But now it meant little.

"I had the homecoming I wanted."

"And what was that?"

Startled, Patrick studied his father more closely. The marquis of Brinaire had never asked him what he wanted before. Years ago, he had been a handsome man, but now he appeared far older than his years. His once strong body was gaunt, his face drawn and haggard, and a tic pulled at his right cheek, below his eye. Where was the powerful, uncompromising man who had been his father? Patrick wondered.

Gone. Just as the home he had known was gone.

The great hall of Brinaire was in shambles. Dirty rushes half covered an even dirtier floor, the table was still uncleared from the morning meal, and years of accumulated soot and grime had turned the once-beautiful wall hangings a dingy gray. Only one fire was being kept, and given the stench and smoke emanating from it, he had to wonder when the fireplace had last been cleaned.

He wanted his old home back, the Brinaire he had left twelve years ago. He wanted to see the rushes changed daily and the floor swept clean. He wanted to hear the clomp of his clansmen's feet and the sound of their laughter as they strode through the door, into the great hall, by the dozens. He wanted to see Margaret's warm smile that had brightened the place beyond measure.

But Margaret was gone, too.

His father, he'd been told, had fired all of the servants, accusing them of aiding his wife in her adultery. Only a few new clansmen had been hired, all inexperienced. His sister Elizabeth found herself the chatelaine, attempting to manage the household with neither experience nor her father's support.

Gentle Elizabeth, who crept around the keep like a mouse. His sister had been but three years old when Patrick had left home. Since his return, Patrick had seen a girl who was painfully shy and afraid of their father's temper. His brother Alex, now seventeen, was similarly restrained, seeking refuge from his father's wrath wherever he could.

In all truth, it seemed to Patrick that the entire keep and all of its occupants were in sad and immediate need of attention.

His father's voice broke into his dismayed thoughts. "I asked where you went."

"I told you. I wanted to see the hills," Patrick said. "I wanted to smell the heather and breathe air that didn't smell of death. I am through with fighting."

The tic in his father's cheek twitched. "Nay, I willna be hearing that talk. You will do what needs be done. The Gunns have been raiding our cattle, and they have threatened to burn out some of our clansmen. If they join with Sinclair, there will be killing, you can be sure of that. And it is your duty to protect your clansmen." His lips thinned, and he swore. "Gunns!"

"I fostered with the Gunns," Patrick said. "I was betrothed to one. God's truth, but a fourth of our clan is related to them. I canna fight them."

"You will do what I tell you, lad." The marquis turned away.

"Nay," Patrick said. There would be no misunderstandings between them. "I willna be killing for you."

His father turned back to him, his dark gray gaze turning ebony. As a child, Patrick had melted under that look; even now, he felt the old urge to give in.

"That girl is marrying a Sinclair," his father said. "You know what that means. The Sinclairs have been our blood enemies for centuries."

"Nay," Patrick said. "Marsali willna be marrying Edward Sinclair."

His father squinted at him. "How would you be knowing that?"

"I have ears."

"You have no' seen her?"

Patrick hesitated. He might oppose his father, but lying to him would be dishonorable. "I have," he replied simply.

Rage mottled Gregor Sutherland's face. "You went on Gunn land?"

"To the edge of our own."

"That Gunn wench was on Sutherland land, then."

"We were betrothed. Neither of us consented to breaking it."

Without warning, Gregor Sutherland raised a hand and struck his son's face as hard as he was able. Patrick stepped backward with the force of the blow, but he remained silent.

"You willna wed a Gunn whore," his father said. "I'll not be having another one in my home."

Patrick stared at his father, from whom he had received not a single loving gesture and bloody little approval. Even

the welcome at his homecoming had been distant. No wonder his sister had grown into a frightened wisp and his
younger brother kept his nose buried in books and wanted,
he'd said in a whisper three days ago, to go into the church.
His father had become a demon.

"If you want to go to war with the Gunns, it will be without my help," Patrick said. "I canna exchange years of
friendship because—"

"Then you can leave my house," Gregor raged. "I will
disown you. Alex—"

"Alex told me that he wants to go to Edinburgh. He
wants to study there."

"Alex will do what I tell him."

And he would, Patrick thought, feeling as if a noose were
tightening around his neck. Alex would try to fight their father's battle. And Alex would die. What would become of
Elizabeth, alone with a bitter, fanatical old man? No, he
could not leave them to fend for themselves at Brinaire
again. Yet if he left his father's house, Patrick knew he
would leave without a penny. And he had only one occupa-
tion: the one he'd forsworn.

He was trapped. As trapped as Marsali had been when
she'd known that Cecilia would be forced to take her place
if she didn't marry Sinclair.

"Well?" his father said, a gleam of triumph in his eyes.

Patrick thought of Marsali's willingness to sacrifice herself. What would he have to do to save his sister and
brother? Betray his sworn oath? He wondered about Gavin,
and whether he, too, was facing impossible choices. They
had vowed to be friends forever. Dear God, how had things
come to this pass?

Margaret. Lovely, wise Margaret, who had been missing
for nearly two years and was presumed dead.

"Patrick?"

His father was still waiting—waiting for his capitulation.
He needed time. "The men must be trained," he said.

"They could take Gunns any day," his father sneered.

"I willna fight alongside anyone, nor ask them to fight with me, until we know each other's skills. I've been gone too many years. I canna ask them to trust me."

"You will be the Sutherland," Gregor said. "They owe you their loyalty."

"I will *earn* their loyalty," Patrick replied.

His father made another attempt to stare him down, but the effort was halfhearted. Finally, he shrugged.

That, Patrick thought, was more revealing than anything his father had actually said. He could not remember Gregor Sutherland backing down, not once, not ever. The past two years had indeed taken their toll on both him and his spirit.

"A few days more or less won't make a difference," his father grumbled.

"We will start tomorrow," Patrick replied, turning to leave.

His father's voice stopped him. "Alex will train with you. I should have fostered him. He would have gotten over his idea of going to the University of Edinburgh. Margaret told him . . ." His voice died away.

Patrick knew better than to pursue the subject, but he decided to inquire elsewhere. Had Margaret encouraged Alex's love of books? There was still so much he didn't know, so many currents running through his family. A family he no longer knew.

"Where are those two men who came with you?" The question came unexpectedly.

Patrick stopped at the door to the hall. "They had some business of their own."

"Will they be back?"

"Aye."

"They look like braw men."

"They are. And they have saved my life many times over."

"And you theirs, I am thinking," his father said, a calculating gleam in his eyes. "They owe you, then."

"No man owes me anything," Patrick said. "Indeed, I owe them."

"They will ride with you?"

Patrick smiled. Perhaps Hiram and Rufus could be used as another delaying tactic. It might be weeks before they returned. Especially if a messenger advised them to take their time.

He nodded. "Yes, they will ride with me, and you willna find two more valuable warriors."

Gregor Sutherland pressed his lips together in a bloodless smile. Patrick could almost guess his thoughts. Gavin would lead the Gunns—Gavin who, although trained in battle, had never been tested. The times were peaceful in their part of the Highlands. But for the occasional cattle raid, no opportunities existed for a warrior to ply his skills.

"You will remember many of our clansmen," Gregor said. "They ha' heard of your deeds, and are eager to follow you."

Into battle against men they knew? Patrick doubted it, but none would defy their laird in such a matter.

He had come home to this. To more killing. The killing not only of Scotsmen but of neighbors.

Still, he had bought a little time. Now, if only he knew what had happened to Margaret Gunn Sutherland.

Chapter 5

M arsali looked down from her perch on the window seat in her bedchamber. Horsemen were riding into the courtyard: Gavin and their kinsmen, returning from their latest search for Cecilia. It had been days, but they hadn't found her. At least, Marsali thought, that made her captivity a little more bearable.

Sighing, she turned to survey the room. It had been a fortnight since she'd seen anything but these four walls and the view from the window, but her father showed no sign of relenting. In the past, he'd usually softened after a day or two. But not this time. It was only good fortune that he had not remembered the ferrets. Otherwise, he probably would have taken those, too.

She petted Tristan and Isolde, both curled on her lap, asleep. She wished her father had forgotten Jeanie, as well. But he had issued orders that Jeanie was not to enter her chamber, and she hadn't seen her friend in two weeks. Nevertheless, with the help of Flora, the kitchen maid who had been waiting on her, Jeanie had sneaked in tidbits of food to supplement the bread and water her father had decreed.

Marsali appreciated the gesture, but she could only pick at the food. She ate because she knew she must. It would not do to become weak in body, for weakness of will was sure to follow. Still, she had only to peer into her small mirror to see that her face looked thin and that her body was becoming almost gaunt.

How much longer could she go on?

As long as it took, her heart answered. She clung to

Patrick's promise and the memory of their brief moments together. They were all she had.

A knock came at her door, and the sound of a key grating in the lock followed. She would never grow used to that sound, not as long as it signified she'd been imprisoned by her own father.

Expecting Flora, Marsali was shocked to see Jeanie open the door. With a glad cry, she dumped Tristan and Isolde unceremoniously onto the window seat and flew across the room to hug her onetime nursemaid.

"Here, now," Jeanie said. "Let me at least put down the tray before ye be spillin' yer food all over the floor."

"I donna care about the food! Oh, it is so good to see you."

Casting her gaze over Jeanie's face, Marsali saw that her friend's pale blue eyes were red rimmed, their sparkle gone.

"You have been crying," she said.

"Well, what did ye think I would be doin' with ye locked in here and me not bein' allowed in?"

"Oh, Jeanie, I am sorry." A sudden thought deepened Marsali's frown. "Why are you here? You didna sneak in without Father knowing, did you, because I would not want—"

"Nay, he knows I'm here." Jeanie gave her a conspiratorial grin. "Flora has a toothache, ye see. She be moanin' up a storm in the kitchen. Yer fa said I could bring yer tray." As she spoke, Jeanie held her by the shoulders and looked her up and down. "Ah, love, I canna bear to see ye this way."

"I am fine," Marsali said. "I have Tristan and Isolde to keep me company, and my chamber, after all, is not a dungeon."

"Hmph." Jeanie clearly was not convinced. "Come, sit and eat, then."

Marsali glanced at the tray of food—the pitcher of water and the half loaf of bread—without interest. Still, she returned to the window seat and watched as Jeanie bustled about, picking up clothing and straightening.

"Gavin is back," Jeanie said.

"I know. I saw him."

"He says there is no sign of Cecilia."

Marsali remained silent.

"Canna ye tell him enough to—"

"No," Marsali said, noting Jeanie's subsequent sigh.

"There is talk that Patrick Sutherland is training his clansmen," Jeanie continued, "that he will attack a Gunn village within a few—"

Marsali shook her head. "He wouldna do that."

"Are ye so sure, love?"

"Aye," she said, taking the smaller ferret, Isolde, into her hands and petting her. In some far corner of her mind, one tiny doubt nagged at her. After two weeks, it was not possible to keep all the demons at bay.

How well did she really know Patrick? So many years had gone by, years that he had spent soldiering, warring. Killing. Despite his tenderness toward her, he must have become a hard man. He would not have survived had he not, and doubtless he bore scars other than those that were visible. Besides, would not his loyalty belong to his father, as Gavin's belonged to his?

Marsali tried to banish these thoughts, not wanting Jeanie to guess her doubts. Tristan, sitting on the floor at her feet, aided her cause by erupting in chatter, expressing his displeasure at being ignored. With a weak smile, Marsali held out her hand to him, and Tristan darted onto her lap beside Isolde, flopping onto his back to bare his stomach for fondling.

"I brought ye some meat pie," Jeanie said.

"You must not do that," Marsali scolded. "If you get caught, Fa will be furious. He might make you leave Abernie, and then I would have no one."

Jeanie dismissed her concern with a wave of her hand. "Do ye suppose that big one might still be wi' yer young earl?"

"Who—" Marsali frowned, confused. She gave Jeanie a surprised glance. "Hiram?"

"Is that his name?" Jeanie said. "It fits a braw man like him."

Marsali stared at the older woman. For as long as she had known Jeanie, her friend had never shown interest in a man. She had spoken little about the husband she had lost so young, though Marsali suspected she still grieved for him, and never so much as mentioned any other. As she straightened Marsali's bed, Jeanie said, "He seemed like an honorable man, or I wouldna have let him take ye."

"He is that," Marsali said. "He and his friend, Rufus. They were very kind, and very troubled at hitting us."

"*Hitting* ye?" Jeanie whirled to face her.

"They knocked us out," Marsali said with a smile. "They were afraid to risk some kind of outcry. But, truly, Jeanie, they did it as gently as possible, and they did apologize most profusely."

Jeanie's frown wavered. Finally, she let the matter go and, in a hushed voice, asked, "And ye talked with the young earl?"

"Aye," Marsali replied wistfully.

"He is as bonny as before?"

"Bonny is not the word," Marsali said. "He is a man in all ways. But yes, he is very handsome. He bears a scar on his face now, but for some reason that I canna explain, it only makes him more appealing."

Marsali didn't miss the knowing look Jeanie gave her.

"And he allowed you to come back?" the older woman said.

"He did not want to. He wants to marry me. But it would mean war. Edward would most certainly join with Fa." She could not stop the tears from spilling down her cheeks.

"Ah, love . . ." Jeanie crossed the room to gather Marsali to her, her hand gently patting her charge's dark hair.

"Patrick's father will never countenance the marriage," she said brokenly. "Not after . . . after Margaret . . ."

Jeanie murmured soothing sounds.

"But, truly"—Marsali pulled away to look up at Jeanie—"Patrick willna take up arms against our family. I know it."

Jeanie nodded. Taking a kerchief from her pocket and wiping Marsali's face, she said, "There now, 'tis no good ye takin' on so. Dry yer eyes, love, and eat this meat pie I made for ye." Producing another kerchief from her other pocket, she unwrapped the morsel and set it on the plate. "Eat that, love. Ye must keep up your strength. For everyone's sake."

Sniffling a little, Marsali nodded.

"Now I must go," Jeanie said. "I suspect Gavin will be here soon to badger ye some more for an answer to where ye have hidden yer sister. So ye best eat quickly."

Marsali watched her leave, knowing she was right: Gavin would try again and again to extract the information from her. Wondering what threats he would use this time, she felt the sadness within her deepen.

Patrick greeted Hiram in the courtyard at Brinaire, where training exercises were taking place. It had been two weeks since he'd sent his two companions-in-war off with Cecilia Gunn.

"The young lass is safe," Hiram said, dismounting from his tired horse.

Sheathing his sword, Patrick cocked one eyebrow. "And where is Rufus?"

Hiram handed his horse's reins to the stable lad, then shrugged his massive shoulders. "He thought to linger a few days, make sure the lass is comfortable."

Patrick eyed his friend cynically. Rufus's attraction to—and for—women was legendary.

Hiram grinned. "She's well guarded by Rufus's sister, as she was by me and your cousin Anna. That Anna Sutherland took to the wee lass like a mother cat to a kitten, and she's staying there wi' her." Hiram's grin deepened. "Rufus ha' been on his best behavior."

"And I imagine that is paining him," Patrick murmured, his gaze turning back to the men training in the courtyard.

"Aye, but he is handlin' it well enough," Hiram said. "He said he would be back by the middle of next week."

"Are you ready for more travel?"

It was Hiram's turn to cock an eyebrow. "To Abernie?"

"Aye," Patrick said. "If you think it is safe for you to be seen there again."

"It is," Hiram said. "The only Gunns who saw us leave were too drunk to recognize their own wives."

"Then go and tell Marsali that her sister is safe," Patrick said. "And find out whether she is well."

Hiram inclined his head in agreement. "I will that." Following Patrick's gaze to the men engaged in swordplay on the opposite side of the yard, he asked, "Are you planning something?"

"Delay," Patrick replied flatly. "Until I can make some sense of all this."

Hiram said quietly, "Ye willna hold him in check long."

"I know." Patrick was not surprised that Hiram had assessed the marquis of Brinaire so quickly. Or so accurately. He was silent for a moment, watching his clansmen's mock battles. They were improving, which should have given him satisfaction. He shook his head. "While you are in Abernie, learn what you can about Margaret."

"It might take several days."

Patrick saw the gleam in his friend's eyes. "That does not seem to displease you."

Hiram shrugged. "There is a lass . . ."

"Hiram!" Patrick couldn't hide his shock. "Not you?"

Hiram looked abashed, and Patrick chuckled. Hiram's shyness with women was as legendary as Rufus's charm. "Who is she?" Patrick asked, almost afraid of the answer. One slip inside Gunn territory and Hiram might well forfeit his life.

"Mistress Jeanie," Hiram grumbled.

"In truth?"

Hiram turned several shades of red but stood his ground. "She is a foine woman."

"She is that," Patrick said. "But be careful. I donna want to lose you, nor would I have Marsali lose Jeanie. They have always been close."

Hiram shifted from one foot to the other. "I wouldna leave ye with only Rufus to guard yer back."

Patrick had to smile at the well-meaning taunt. Rufus and Hiram had always been competitors as well as friends.

"Stay with us tonight and have supper. My father has been asking about you. I told him that you and Rufus went to visit friends in the south."

"Aye, and so we did," Hiram said. "And yer sister and brother, how do they fare?"

Patrick sighed. In the past two weeks, he had tried to befriend Alex and support his sister's attempts to put Brinaire into its previous well-groomed state. But Alex avoided him, and Elizabeth faced an impossible situation, since their father refused to take back former servants and cared nothing about disciplining the present ones.

"Alex still hides in his books and Elizabeth is thoroughly frustrated," he told Hiram. "I think she would do well given some authority, but my father refuses to give it to her. He criticizes everything she does and belittles her constantly. I fear she is afraid of doing anything, lest it displease him."

"How do the other Sutherlands feel about this feud with the Gunns?"

"They will do what my father tells them—until I earn their loyalty. Then perhaps I can persuade them to do my bidding."

Hiram looked once more toward the men training. "And how do ye earn their respect without attacking yer father's enemies?"

Patrick gave him a clap on the shoulder. "That, my friend, is the puzzle. Still, I have a few ideas."

Hiram's dark brows knitted together. "Be careful not to outwit yerself."

"I have you and Rufus to keep me in check," Patrick said with a grin.

But Hiram didn't share his humor. " 'Tis a dangerous game ye play, Patrick. A miscalculation could destroy both ye and the lass."

"I know," Patrick agreed softly. "I know."

Weeks after the humiliating scene at Abernie, Edward Sinclair could scarcely contain his fury. Stalking back and forth across the weapons chamber of his keep, he brooded over the defeats he had suffered. He had been mortified in front of representatives of nearly every northern Highland family. Years of sowing distrust between the Gunn and Sutherland families had come to naught.

He wanted Marsali, and he wanted an alliance against the Sutherlands, who were hereditary enemies of his clan. Together, the Sinclairs and Gunns would surround the Sutherland lands, choke off any assistance from other clans, and eventually claim Brinaire's rich grazing land as their own.

Most of all, though, he wanted the girl. She was a true beauty, and her indifference toward him—only increased his desire. He would break her as he broke his wildest horses. She would pay for insulting him.

He also wanted sons, and neither of his wives had been able to serve even this simple purpose. One had died of fever, along with a sickly daughter, and the other had been barren. It had taken years to find a woman who could take his second wife's place. He'd found what he wanted in Marsali Gunn.

The time had come, Edward thought, to force Donald Gunn's hand. Edward had little doubt that the old man could compel his daughter to marry the man he chose if given the proper motivation; if nothing else, he could find a clergyman who would not be too particular about the woman's responses.

Edward had already been successfully manipulating the earl of Abernie. He'd guessed correctly that the old man had a soft spot for his sister, and he'd exploited that situation. Now he knew where he could strike next. The earl's concern for the safety of his crofters was well known.

"Gordie," Edward barked. "Come in here."

Two men entered the study. Giving the first only a nod of acknowledgment, Edward turned to Gordie, a mercenary who, although disliked by his own men, was loyal to him and absolutely ruthless. Gordie waited, his soulless gaze earning Edward's approval.

"Take a troop to Abernie," Edward ordered. "They are to wear Sutherland plaids. Burn out tenants, take as many of the cattle as possible. But mind you, be careful. I do not want any of your men taken prisoner. This must be seen as a Sutherland raid."

"I understand," Gordie said.

Edward nodded with satisfaction. It would not be the first time Gordie and his men had donned Sutherland plaids. Indeed, he had two women working continuously on the dyes.

"And send someone over to Brinaire," Edward continued. "Someone the Sutherlands do not know. I want to find Cecilia Gunn, and I suspect the Sutherlands may know something about her disappearance." Finding Cecilia, he knew, would be the quickest way to change Marsali's mind about marrying him. "One way or the other, I want that alliance."

"I know the man," Gordie said. "He just joined us from the Lowlands, where he fought with Cromwell."

"He can be trusted?"

"If he is paid well enough."

"See to it, then. Tell him a greater reward awaits him if he succeeds in obtaining the information we need."

Gordie nodded. "It will be done."

"You ride tonight. And make it costly."

"Women?"

Edward hesitated. "No. I want you in and out of there, and I do not want anyone to remember your faces. Paint them."

Disappointment flashed in Gordie's eyes. Edward ignored it, though he knew that Gordie, like many soldiers, believed rape to be a side benefit of war.

"You will have other opportunities," Edward said, then, with a sly smirk, added, "The Sutherland's daughter is a pretty piece. If everything goes as planned, we will be occupying Brinaire before long, and . . . enjoying all its riches."

The man who had stood silently next to Gordie throughout the conversation took a step forward. "Patrick Sutherland is mine," he said, his voice a tortured rasp. A scar stretched across his throat from his left ear to the point of his right collarbone.

"Aye," Edward agreed. "He is yours. I swore it."

The man nodded, his amber eyes like two cold stones. "As long as it is understood. I will kill any man who gets in my way."

"You are welcome to him," Edward said. "Now let us plan tonight's attack."

Chapter 6

Marsali dreamed she heard male voices shouting. Then came the clank of armor and weapons. The rush of booted feet on stone floors brought her fully awake from her afternoon doze. She sprang from her bed, knocking to the floor the precious illustrated book Jeanie had smuggled to her, and ran to the window.

The courtyard was filled with clansmen, and even from so high above them, she could hear the urgency, as well as the anger, in their voices. Dread filled her as she watched Gavin, heavily armed, mount his horse and thunder out of the gates. He was followed by a troop of thirty men.

Even after their departure, the courtyard teemed with people, and Marsali ached to be among them. She watched the stream of women and children entering through the gates. She was too far away to recognize faces, but her stomach contracted sickeningly when she saw several men, clearly wounded, staggering over the rough ground.

Dear God, the war has begun, she thought. Aloud, she prayed, "Please, *please* don't let it be the Sutherlands who have started it."

Hurrying to the door of her chamber, she pounded on the thick oak portal until her fists hurt, but no one answered.

With a screech of frustration, Marsali ran back to the window, scanning the growing crowd for her cousin Duncan, who acted as Gavin's lieutenant and carried a set of keys to all the doors in the keep. In the courtyard, crofters were sinking to the ground, either with weariness or wounds—

she couldn't tell which. She heard children crying and their mothers trying to soothe them. She saw no sign of Duncan.

Marsali's hands clenched where they rested on the windowsill. It was her place to be with her clansmen, nursing them if necessary and providing what reassurance she could. It was her duty. No punishment her father had levied against her should take precedence over it.

Marsali began pounding on the door again, and finally a key grated in the lock.

Breathless with relief, she stood back as it opened. She was shocked to find herself facing her father.

"The Sutherlands attacked the crofters near the Sutherland border," he said grimly. "Four were killed, twelve other men and women wounded. And a child."

"Are you sure they were Sutherlands?" she asked, regretting the question when she saw the rage that contorted his face.

"Aye, our people are sure." His big hands shook, as if he wanted to strike something. "The raiders were wearing Sutherland plaids, and a woman heard one man call another Patrick. Spawn of the devil! To think I harbored that bastard and even considered—" He broke off, his jaw working. "You should have taken Sinclair," he said. "This wouldna ha' happened with the alliance. The Sutherlands wouldna ha' dared."

Marsali trembled under his violent glare. Finally, she forced herself to ask, "Where did Gavin go?"

"After the bastards," her father said, his voice quaking with rage. "After the animals that killed our people."

I don't believe it. Marsali wanted to speak the words aloud, but she knew her father was convinced of the Sutherlands' guilt, and nothing short of absolute proof would change his mind.

But doubt plagued her. She would not, could not, believe it of Patrick. But his father? She was not as certain.

"You are needed," her father said stiffly.

She nodded. "I will fetch the herbs from the kitchen. Are the children . . . ?"

"One is hurt, and several are missing. Quick Harry's son was hit by a hoof," her father said. " 'Tis only by God's will he was not killed. I pray he willna lose the use of his leg." He turned without saying another word and started for the steps.

Marsali had to work hard to bank her own anger. The boy was only seven, the son of a man who had been given his name when he was a lad. The older Harry had won every footrace he had ever joined, and he had become the clan's messenger. Everyone thought his son would be just as fast and would follow in his father's footsteps.

"Father." Marsali called after him.

He stopped at the top of the stairs but did not turn.

"What about Quick Harry?" she asked. "Is he all right?"

"He is missing," her father said, casting an accusing glance over his shoulder. Then he turned away from her again.

The burden of guilt her father had levied upon her was almost more than she could bear. Patrick had not been involved, she told herself again and again, repeating the litany as she ran for the kitchen.

The wounded were crowded into the guardroom, where they were sheltered from the cold wind that swept the Highlands. A fire jumped high in the fireplace that stretched across the back wall of the room.

As Marsali moved among the injured, it was eerily quiet. Highlanders—even their women and children—prided themselves on endurance and courage. But pale faces looked at her in bewilderment, their gazes clouded with pain, and the fresh rushes on the floor were splattered with blood.

Marsali took in the scene, clutching her basket of herbs and fresh linens and giving Jeanie a grateful look when she appeared at her side carrying buckets of clean water. A quick survey of the wounded told her that the raiders had been on horseback, the defenders on foot, for most of the injuries were sword strokes to the arms and shoulders.

"See to Wee Harry first," one of the wounded men said.

Marsali looked down at the man, hesitating. Unable to help herself, she asked the question that was pounding in her head. "You are sure it was Sutherlands? Did you know any of them?"

The man grimaced, supporting his injured arm with his good one as he straightened to sit against the wall. "They came too fast, lass," he said. "I couldna recognize faces, but I knew the plaid."

"Do you know Patrick Sutherland?"

"Aye," a woman sitting next to the man replied. "I remember him well. I didna see him, though someone said his name was called." She looked up at Marsali. "*Why?* Why would they do this? The cattle, mayhap. But burning us out? My cousin is married to a Sutherland."

Marsali wanted to cry out that Patrick would not have done this, nor would he ever condone it. But did she know?

Heartsick, she made her way through the packed room to Wee Harry, stopping next to him.

"Ah, braw boy," Marsali said gently as she examined the lad's bloody left leg. A hoof had opened a long, jagged tear in his calf, but someone had tied it off and stopped the bleeding. The bone, however, was broken. Examining it carefully, she saw the boy wince and felt the pain as if it were her own. What kind of man could ride down a child like this?

The boy bit his lower lip until it bled but made no sound as she washed the wound, then sewed it closed. With his head cradled in his mother's lap, he valiantly blinked back tears as Marsali bound a long piece of wood to his leg to hold it stiff and straight.

Marsali raised her gaze to meet his mother's concern.

"Will he be able to walk again?" the woman asked.

"Aye," Marsali said. "I think he will be as good as new. What of your other son?"

"My sister is caring for him. Her husband went lookin' for Quick Harry."

Marsali finished tying the splint, then took the other woman's hands in hers. "Tell me what happened."

Dazed, the woman shook her head. "They came from nowhere. At least twenty riders. They took the cattle, burned our cottages. Harry was in the fields an' came runnin', but they were gone. He took off after them on foot an' didna come back."

"Fa said they were Sutherlands."

"Och, they were Sutherlands right enough," the woman said bitterly. "I saw their plaids, but I didna recognize faces. They were painted. Mayhap when Quick Harry returns . . ." But her voice trailed off, her eyes misting with tears.

They both knew that chances of Harry's returning were slim.

The despair assailing Marsali grew more intense. Her heart wept for the child who might have lost a father, for the woman who might have lost a husband, for Quick Harry, who had a ready smile as well as swift feet. She wanted to flail out at whoever had done this thing. At that moment, she understood her father's rage at those who would hurt innocents. *His* people, who depended upon him for protection.

Had she been wrong to refuse Edward? Had it been a mistake—a terrible mistake—to trust Patrick?

As she went from one injured crofter to the next, her thoughts were in turmoil. Despite her efforts, a blood feud had begun. The bitter murmurings swirling around her were like the first rumbles of thunder before a storm. And there was nothing she could do to stop it.

What in holy hell had happened? Hiram rode into Abernie Keep, one of many entering the gates at this hour. Something was gravely wrong. In contrast to his arrival weeks ago, he saw no smiles and heard no laughter, nor did he receive any drunken greetings. Instead, he found a scene only too familiar. He recognized the words of vengeance. He recognized the hate.

Pulling his horse to a halt in front of the stable, he dismounted. He expected to be recognized. He wore the plaid of his own clan, one that bore no resemblance to the Sutherlands', but he knew his very size made him memorable. Still, he did not think anyone would connect him with the disappearance of the earl's younger daughter, especially as Marsali had taken the blame onto herself.

The stable lads were trying to handle too many horses coming in at once, so Hiram stabled his own horse. He cooled the animal, then fed him oats, listening to the snippets of conversation around him.

The things he heard sent his estimation of Patrick's lady spiraling upward. Imprisoned in her chamber for nigh onto a month. Unbroken in her vow not to marry Edward Sinclair; nor would she reveal her sister's whereabouts. Released to care for her wounded kinsmen, and doing a fine job of it at this very moment. A rare lass.

But he heard other things, too. Things that made his blood boil. The Sutherlands had raided cattle, burned homes. Killed several and wounded many, including a child named Wee Harry. Horses were being readied to chase "the craven scum."

Giving his horse an absentminded pat, Hiram went to find Jeanie, hoping that she was not infected with the anger pervading the stables and courtyard. Moving cautiously now, he stopped a boy taking water inside and asked about Jeanie MacDougal.

"She is wi' the wounded," the boy said. "Along wi' the lord's daughter."

"Will ye be telling her that there is someone to see her?"

"And who might tha' be?"

"A mon who admires her," Hiram said.

The boy snorted. "Then ye are in fer sorrow. Jeanie cares naught for romance."

Hiram shrugged his shoulders. "Mayhap. Will ye be giving her the message?"

"Aye, but she will be busy awhile. Those cursed Sutherlands . . ."

"I see horses are being readied."

"Aye. Lord Gavin left hours ago, and more go to join him."

"If I had not been on a horse these past four days, I would go wi' him myself," Hiram replied.

"If I were older . . ." the boy started, then bit his lip and, remembering his errand, hurried inside the castle.

Hiram waited an hour, leaning against the wall beside the door the boy had entered. Fires dotted the yard inside the keep, and the walls above had double the usual number of guards. He watched the activity, wondering what Patrick would do when he heard the news, until, finally, Jeanie appeared in the doorway.

She stood, hands on her hips, her gaze searching the courtyard. When she spotted him, she hurried over to him, and he swept off his bonnet in an elaborate gesture. Marsali was his public excuse for returning to Abernie, but, in truth, he would have returned in any case. He wanted to see Jeanie again.

But neither the look she gave him nor the words she spoke were welcoming. "Go away," she said. "Ye will only cause more trouble."

"They are saying the Sutherlands burned out yer people. 'Tis not true," he replied.

"They wore the plaid," she said stubbornly. "They spoke the young lord's name."

" 'Twas not Patrick. I swear it. He's been doing everything he can to stay his father's hand, which is not easy while yer laird spreads calumny about him."

Jeanie eyed him warily until, finally, she grumbled, "The Gunn has been calling Gregor Sutherland a murderer to all that listen. That's true enough."

Hiram shifted on his feet. "Patrick sent me to see how his lady fares."

"Hmph." Jeanie frowned. "She is no' eating well. Worryin' herself to death, she is. I think now there will be even more pressure on her to marry the Sinclair. The Gunns canna fight the Sutherlands alone."

"There is no way for her to escape?"

"She willna do that," Jeanie said, "even if she could. She feels it might cause war."

He shook his head. "I ken there is little to stop it now."

"I will talk to her," Jeanie said. "I will tell her ye came, but ye canna stay. It is much too dangerous."

"Ye say she is locked in?"

"Aye."

"Who has the key?"

"Duncan Gunn. He is a chieftain and second only to Gavin."

"Can you get it from him?"

She looked askance at him. "Be ye daft? No, I canna. He keeps the keys on his person. Whoever takes her tray has to ask permission to be let into her room."

Hiram did not push further. He had discovered what he needed to know—what Patrick needed to know.

"Ye must go now," she said. " 'Tis dangerous for Marsali. And for ye. Leave before the gates close for the night."

Pleased that her worry was not for Marsali alone, he replied without thinking. "Aye, love."

Her eyes widened, but she could not have been any more surprised than he that he had spoken so boldly. He had never been a lady's man, nor quick with words, but it seemed as if he had known this lady forever.

Confusion clouded Jeanie's eyes for a moment, then she backed away.

"Patrick wanted ye to tell his lass that her sister is safe in the Lowlands," Hiram said as she retreated from him. "Well and happy, as I saw for myself."

"I will tell her. Now go."

She turned and nearly ran back into the keep. He watched her disappear inside the heavy door, her skirt swishing on well-formed hips.

Retrieving his horse from the stable, Hiram rode through the gates unhurriedly. Once out of sight of the guards manning the walls, he spurred his horse. Patrick was waiting, probably most impatiently, for his news. Och, but he hated being the one who had to deliver it.

Two days after the raid, Gunn clansmen were still streaming into Abernie.

Patrick pulled his bonnet far down on his forehead. Hoping his disguise was adequate, he walked through the gates amidst a crowd of men, women, and children seeking sanctuary. A new beard all but covered his face, and what it did not cover was caked with dirt. He had rubbed dye into his hair, turning it gray, and he walked as if with difficulty, using a cane. The plaid he wore bore the MacDougal colors. And he doubted that anyone would really want to take a long, close look at him anyway. He smelled none too sweet.

Taking in the scene in quick glances, he confirmed Hiram's report. Controlled chaos overlaid by anger. Witnessing it, he could barely contain his anxiety. Hiram had wanted to come with him, but Patrick feared his friend's presence would only increase the risk to all of them. Besides, he knew Abernie as well—perhaps better—than he knew his own home. He knew every nook and cranny, every hiding place, every escape, and he possessed a speed that Hiram did not. Grudgingly, Hiram had agreed to wait, with the three horses they had brought, in a wood a mile or so from the keep.

Shifting his bag from one shoulder to the other, Patrick limped through the courtyard. His back was bent, and he moved as if every step were an effort, though his bag was not heavy: It contained only two flagons of wine, a length of rope, and a plaid. Nothing out of the ordinary, at least not in appearance. No one could see that one of the flagons of wine was drugged.

He had to get Marsali out of here. Hiram had said she was being held prisoner on a diet of bread and water, and he feared it was only a matter of time before she would be forced into marriage with Edward Sinclair. At Brinaire, he could protect her, and her presence there would also protect his clan from a retaliatory Gunn attack. Her father would not deliberately endanger his daughter. Patrick did not believe his two aims were contradictory. He hoped Marsali would feel the same way and accept the logic of his reasoning.

He wondered if she believed the stories that he had participated in the raid. Surely, she could not. She had bared her heart to him. He knew what was in her soul, and he knew his dreams of her had not been based on illusion. The moment he had seen her again, he had understood that his life was entwined with hers.

Which was why he could no more have allowed her to remain imprisoned than he could have stopped breathing. And so he would take her from Abernie, willing or not.

He would much prefer to have her willing.

Patrick knew that his greatest problem was Marsali's concern for her people. She might not be able to leave them in their time of need. Nor would she want to leave her father and brother, he was certain, when they needed her. He respected her loyalty. But he simply could not allow it to override what he believed to be common sense.

He would worry about making his apologies later, when she was safe.

Similarly shoved aside were worries about his father's reaction to his bringing home a Gunn bride. At least, he thought, his father could not actually throw him out. Beset with gout and unable to sit a horse for more than a few hours at a time, the Sutherland needed his eldest son.

Patrick made his way to a corner of the keep and slipped

into the shadows, pulling the bonnet lower over his eyes. Gavin was the one person who would probably recognize him despite any disguise: They had lived together, played together, and trained together for nearly eight years. His best friend, who now considered him an enemy.

As darkness fell, the gates were closed. He was trapped now, unless he could obtain the keys: the one to Marsali's room and the one to the cistern that ran underneath the castle floors. He would have to find Duncan Gunn.

Patrick remembered Marsali's cousin. Built like a tree trunk, Abernie's second-in-command was about two decades older than he was, but Patrick was certain Duncan would still be able to swing a sword with the best of them. Though he was a kind man, Duncan was also battle-wise, cautious, and fast. His room, Patrick recalled, was located near the armory. All he had to do, Patrick thought wryly, was get inside, outwit the guards, break in to Duncan's room, and find the keys—all without being detected. And then kidnap Marsali.

The sound of horsemen brought his gaze flashing upward. From under his bonnet, he saw Gavin and several other men riding in through the postern. Settling back farther into the shadows, he watched and listened as the riders wearily dismounted and left their horses to the stablehands.

The arrivals reported no sign of the raiders, nor of Quick Harry, who apparently was missing. Patrick cursed silently, hearing that Gavin and his party had picked up some Sutherland cattle in exchange for the ones that had been stolen. The theft would prompt his father to act. Where in the devil would it all end?

The last of the riders dismounted and headed toward the great hall for food and drink. Patrick prayed they would sleep well tonight. He kept his head down as several servants came out and distributed food to those in the courtyard. One man nudged him with a foot, and he fought not to react. Another voice interceded.

"Let 'im sleep. I saw 'im come in. 'E could barely walk."

Patrick heard the sound of retreating boots on solidly packed earth.

Hours passed. The night deepened. Voices finally quieted, replaced by snoring. He glanced at the sky. The moon was only half full but very bright. He judged the time to be well past midnight. Fires had flickered out; only a few embers glowed against the gloom of the courtyard.

Patrick stumbled to his feet, leaning on his cane. Two men in Gunn plaid stood by the door that led to the interior of the castle. Patrick grunted as he reached them, removing the flagon of undrugged wine from his bag and taking a deep swallow.

The two guards looked at him thirstily.

"And what do ye be wanting inside?" one asked.

Patrick handed him the flagon, keeping his eyes on the door. "A bit of food," he said hopefully. "I heard I would find some 'ere."

"They were giving out food earlier," one of the guards said, taking a hefty draught from the flagon and passing it to his partner.

Patrick ran a hand over his forehead. "I must ha' been asleep. I came a great distance and was told I would be welcome here for a night."

"Aye," one man said, "Abernie has always been known for hospitality. But there be trouble now."

The other man regarded Patrick dubiously, then looked at the flagon. " 'Tis good wine."

"Ye can have it," Patrick said. "I ha' only hunger in my belly."

"Let him go in," the first guard said. "Ye know Jeanie's generous heart, and he looks to be a MacDougal."

"Are ye?" asked the other guard.

"Aye." Patrick handed him the wine.

"Do ye know Jeanie MacDougal?"

"Nay," he said. "But I ha' heard of her."

The guards looked at each other, then one said, "There should be some bread in the kitchen. Go through the hall, down the corridor tae the back. The kitchen is tae the left. There should be someone there."

Patrick bowed slightly. "Och, but my stomach thanks ye." He shuffled forward, tapping his cane on the uneven stone floor.

The corridor was quiet, the double doors to the great hall closed. The place rang with memories. He had been happy here. Happier than he had been anywhere else in his life.

But this was no time for reminiscing. Patrick started for the stairs, careful to keep to the shadows. When he reached the second floor, he heard footsteps and voices from above. He moved swiftly along the dark corridor and pressed himself against the wall, wishing he could melt into the stone.

"Surely, Father, you canna continue to keep her locked up." It was Gavin. "She worked all afternoon and evening on the wounded. They need her."

"Jeanie and the other women can assume her duties." The laird's voice was harsh and unforgiving. "We need that marriage now more than ever. She must get over these romantic notions of hers and see reason."

"She doesna trust Edward Sinclair, and I canna say that I do, either," Gavin said. "The Sinclairs have never been our friends. Never been anyone's friends but their own."

"She made no complaints about the first marriage I planned for her," the laird said plaintively.

"She thought Patrick was a good man," Gavin said. "She never liked Sinclair and made no secret of it. And you know Marsali can be very stubborn."

"God's blood, but she will destroy me. D'ye think, lad, she dreams still about that devil's spawn? Ach! By God, she will do what I wish if I have to take everything away from her, including those cursed ferrets."

In the brief silence that followed, Patrick heard the

sound of a candle sputtering very close by. He pressed his body harder against the wall.

Finally, the laird spoke again, from the landing only a few feet away. "I thought you approved of the alliance with Sinclair."

"I did not realize how strongly she felt," Gavin said. "I didna know you had told her you would marry Cecilia to Sinclair if she didna marry him." Anger deepened his voice. "Cecilia is still a child!"

"Many lasses are married at her age," his father retorted. "And Marsali openly defied me in spiriting her sister away. Ach! Even now, I canna believe she did such a thing!"

"Aye, she did it," Gavin said, "but she thought she had reason."

The older man grunted. "You want her to marry the Sutherland whelp? A man who would attack peaceful farmers?"

Patrick missed Gavin's response as father and son continued descending the stairs and their voices faded. How much time did he have before they returned to their chambers? He could only hope Duncan had already retired.

Moving silently down the corridor, he found the door he sought, standing outside it for a moment to listen for any movement within. Hearing none, he gently pushed the door open and slid inside, closing it swiftly and silently behind him so that no light from the corridor would enter and give him away. As his eyes adjusted to the darkness, he took the dirk from his belt. He would do what he needed to do to find Marsali.

His gaze came to rest on the large form lying on the bed. Duncan. With luck, he had drunk his fill of wine tonight— and Patrick could get in and out of the room without rousing him. Wishing there were more than a sliver of moonlight coming through the window, he scanned the room until he made out the outline of a table with an irregular object on its surface. He moved to it quickly and in seconds his fingers had closed around a ring of keys. He wrapped his hand around them tightly to keep them from jingling, and stepped carefully toward the door.

A soft snort came from the bed. Patrick held perfectly still, not even breathing, until the sleeping man settled once more into deep slumber. Thanking God, hoping that He was receptive to this bit of thievery, Patrick opened the door a crack and checked the corridor. No one in sight. Stepping out of the room, Patrick closed the door as gently as he had opened it and stood in the hallway.

He hung on to the thought that, in another hour, two at most, he and Marsali would be gone from here—together. If only she would hear him out.

After listening for several moments, he steadied himself and moved stealthily up to the third floor. Reaching the top of the stairs, he hesitated, then turned down the corridor toward Marsali's room—and let it be, he prayed, that she still occupied the same chamber as when she was a child.

Candles flickered from several sconces set high on the walls. He looked down at the keys. There were five, two especially heavy. These would most likely open the armory door and the other the huge iron door leading to the interior of the keep. The key to interior rooms would be one of the other three. He tried one, wincing at the loud grating noise it made, cursing under his breath when it did not turn. The second key, however, slid easily into the lock and turned.

She was standing at the window, her slim form outlined by moonlight. It did not seem that she had heard him, but she turned then, and he knew the instant she saw him. She came to a sudden stop, and her sharp intake of breath was audible from across the room. Before she could utter another sound, he had crossed to her and placed a finger on her lips.

"Shhhh," he whispered. Then, bending her head, he silenced her with a kiss.

Chapter 7

arsali knew instantly whose lips covered hers. She could never mistake the taste of him, the feel of his mouth against hers. Even the unfamiliar beard, an oddly pleasant sensation brushing against her skin, could not make her doubt what her heart knew was true.

Her first impulse was to melt in his arms, to forget the day, forget the dead and wounded and Wee Harry's tears—but the impulse was short-lived.

"Patrick." Her lips slid away from his and she whispered against his neck. "Oh, Patrick, what are you doing here? How did you get inside?"

With her hands on his biceps, she pushed away to look up at him. Her eyes, accustomed to the dark, took in his appearance. God above, it was well he had kissed her, for if she had but seen him, she would not have recognized him.

Cautioning her with a finger to his lips, he held up an object for her to see. A key.

Her eyes widened.

"I took it from Duncan Gunn's room," he whispered.

She stiffened. "Duncan?"

"He was sleeping. He is *still* sleeping."

"You didna hurt him?"

"Nay, lass. I didna touch him," he said, his fingers skimming her face reverently.

"And if you had been discovered?"

"Even then, I would not have hurt him," he assured her. "Do you not know that I would never hurt anyone who is dear to you?"

She wanted, to the depths of her soul, to believe him. But

the Gunn crofters had been so absolutely certain, and she had spent the evening bandaging wounds that had come from somewhere. And he looked so unlike himself, this man standing boldly in her room—in his enemy's keep.

She did not truly know him, the voice of doubt reminded her. The man before her was a warrior, tested time and again on the battlefield. For the past twelve years, he had lived and breathed violence. Could it be that violence had become such a part of him that he could not forsake it? And would she know if he was lying to her? Or, because she had loved him and waited so long for him, would she be gulled into believing what her heart wanted to hear?

Reading her hesitation, he said, "I heard about the raid. You must know I had no part in it."

"Your father?"

"No," he said. "He could not have ordered it without my knowing. I am certain of it."

She caught her lower lip between her teeth, backing away from his arms, arms she wanted so badly to hold her. "You have to go," she said. "This is dangerous."

He moved toward her, and she took another step backward.

"Hiram told me you were being kept a prisoner," he said. "Jeanie told him that you were not eating."

"Jeanie never believes I eat enough," Marsali replied. "And now that you see I am perfectly well, you must go."

He ignored her request. "Did she tell you that your sister is safe? And content?"

"Aye," she said. "And I thank you for that. But now . . ."

Her words trailed off when he came to a halt mere inches away from her. With the back of her knees against the window seat, she could not move. She felt his gaze boring into her. Its heat stopped her words, stopped her very breathing. His hand went to her face, his fingers following the planes of her cheek with featherlike strokes.

"Marsali," he finally murmured. "You must have heard that my name was mentioned during that raid."

She nodded, unable to speak.

His finger tucked a wayward curl behind her ear. The touch was like the caress of the wind.

"Marsali . . ." he whispered.

That was all he said, but the *way* he said it, the way he spoke her name, his deep voice filling the single word with hope and longing, found its way straight to her heart. She could not help herself, could not prevent her hand from going to his face or her fingers from touching him as he had touched her.

"Ah, God," he breathed.

Then she was in his arms and his lips were on hers again. This time she did not push away. Rather, she let herself be swallowed in a moment so wondrous that she did not care whether it was real or magic. She only wanted it to go on and on.

A new sensation settled deep in her belly, a sweet craving that made her tremble inside. His kiss deepened, and when he opened his mouth over hers, inviting her, leading her, she followed. His tongue entered her mouth, stirring her need into a tempest.

Of its own accord, her body pressed closer to his, relishing his lean strength and his heat, fitting so naturally against him that she could no longer deny the truth. She belonged here, in his arms. This was real. This was Patrick, and she loved him. She'd always loved him. As their mouths blended and their bodies strained toward each other, the woman she had become realized that the reality of this love was a far greater, far more compelling thing than she had ever dreamed. It made her heart sing and her senses reel. It made her lose all caution, all fear. . . . It made her want more. . . .

His arms encircled her, and she clung to his neck. Her legs were suddenly weak and her heart pounded. She wanted to touch every part of him. She wanted to believe there was no one and nothing but the two of them.

She gasped for breath when he dragged his mouth away from hers, dragged it across her cheek to bury his face in her hair.

"Tell me that you believe I had nothing to do with the raid," he said, his voice ragged with both desire and anguish. "I need to hear you say it, lass."

"Nay," she breathed. "I know you did not."

She could feel some of the tension go out of him, heard it leave in his heavy sigh. He kept his face buried in her hair for a moment, then lifted his head to look down at her.

"I know you were not among the raiders," she told him. "But most think you were."

"Gavin?"

"Aye," she said.

In the moonlight, she saw his lips thin. "Marsali, I swear to you, I didna even know about it, nor do I believe that any Sutherlands did."

She was silent a moment. "They were wearing your plaids."

He nodded. "It is clear that whoever did it wanted your father to think it was Sutherlands. If the plaids were ours, then someone went to considerable lengths to put on the ruse. The dyes are not so easy to make."

"I know," she said. "But it wouldna be impossible. Sutherland women make them, after all." Then she paused before continuing thoughtfully, "The Sinclairs?"

"Hmm. 'Tis a reasonable assumption," he replied.

"My father is not reasonable about your family."

His strong hands came up to grip her shoulders. "That is why I am here. Marsali, I want you to leave with me."

She stared at him in astonishment. "Leave with you?" She uttered a brief, shocked laugh. "I am still wondering how you got in."

He drew back a little, and his voice was colored by mock

indignation. "Have you not noticed my appearance? Canna you see that I am a master of disguise?"

"I can barely see you at all," she chided gently.

"Ah, but you can smell. 'Tis sorry I am about that."

"It doesna matter. Oh, Patrick"—her voice broke a little—"I have missed you so."

"Marsali . . ."

His head lowered, his lips grazing her cheek, her eyelids, his voice whispering in her ear words that turned her insides into liquid fire. When his mouth slanted across hers, his tongue swept inside in intimate possession. The embers still smoldering between them flared instantly to a full blaze.

They clung together in desperate need, and Marsali found it odd but right that, in his arms, she felt both helpless and steady. Somehow, he made her believe, for the briefest moment, that all would be right.

"Marsali," he groaned, his voice full of a desire that she knew burned as deeply in him as it did in her.

Caution fled. Their heartbeats quickened, pounding against one another's. She felt his muscles flexing in response to each of her soft caresses. Oh, how much she wanted him, how much she wanted to live with him and be his wife, to wake up with him and go to bed with him, to sing with him and even cry with him. She wanted to give him everything.

She greedily tasted the aching sweetness of his mouth. Nothing had prepared her for this—the sweet explosions, the overwhelming hunger, the excruciating tingling that reached to her toes.

By the time he drew away from her, the kiss had rendered her all but senseless. She was trembling all over, and her breathing sounded like whimpering panting to her ears.

"This is madness," he said hoarsely. "Will anyone be coming back here to check on you?"

She shook her head. "I—I donna think so. They were here . . . earlier."

"They still want you to marry Sinclair?"

"My father does, but I willna. Not now that Cecilia is safe—" She broke off. The thought of her sister was like a strong wind, blowing all other thoughts from her mind. She gripped his hand. "Patrick, tell me truly, you are *sure* she is safe?"

"Aye," he said gently, reaching into his sporran and extracting something that he held out to her. "She sent you this. She said you would know what it meant."

A white rose. Marsali took it in her hands. Cecilia loved white roses, and before she had left with Rufus she had whispered that she would send one to signal that she was safe. A red rose would have meant she was in danger.

Smiling, Marsali felt the worry that had plagued her drain away. "Thank you," she said.

Patrick returned her smile. "Hiram said your sister became a member of the family immediately. Rufus, I fear, is besotted. He decided to stay several additional days to make sure she was 'comfortable.' "

"She is so young," Marsali said.

"Aye, she is. And Rufus will not take advantage, nor would his family allow it. I would not send her there otherwise."

"I will never be able to tell you how grateful I am."

"Ah, lass, it was little enough." He brushed her forehead with his lips. "I wish I could slay you a dragon, but instead I can only carry you off."

"No," she replied softly. "I canna go. It would only make things worse."

"It canna get worse," he said. "But if I take you as hostage, your father willna ride against us. It will give me time to find the real raiders—and the man behind them."

"Hostage?" Marsali felt the warmth draining from her. She was hardly aware of moving stiffly out of his embrace.

He caught her arm. "Marsali, I would not use you against

your father. But I canna see you imprisoned by him, either. I will not leave you here."

"And if I will not go?" she said, a note of defiance coloring her tone. As much as she loved him, she would not be controlled by him, or by any other man. Not again. Not ever.

"Marsali—" he began.

"Tell me, Patrick, what do you plan if I will not go?" She was unaware that the sudden change in her tone had stirred the ferrets, who had been dozing on the window seat behind her. With only a single low growl, one leaped onto Patrick's leg and chomped on it.

Startled, he cried out more loudly than caution dictated. "Ach!" He gingerly plucked the animal from his bare leg, where its teeth had drawn blood. "Devil take it!"

"Isolde!" Marsali scolded, taking the animal from him at the same time she tried to soothe the other chittering ferret, perched for attack on the bench behind her.

"The female?" Patrick asked wryly as he examined the blood trickling down his leg.

Marsali nodded, cuddling the small animal against her cheek and making soothing noises. How could she scold the animal for trying to protect her?

"I should have known," Patrick said.

She was pleased to hear the dry humor in his voice, but she could not let him get away with the implied insult. "And why should you have known?"

"I, uh, hear things," he said, still smiling.

Reason told her that in all the years he had been away, it was improbable to think that he had remained chaste. Still . . .

"I had best put them in their basket," she said stiffly.

He remained wisely silent as she placed the adventurous ferrets safely in the round basket that served as their home when she left the room.

When she had finished, Patrick pulled her back into his embrace. "Where were we?" he murmured.

"You were about to tell me how you knew about women who bite."

He chuckled. "That was not what I had in mind. And I really know very little about women who . . . bite."

"Why is that not comforting?" she asked.

His chuckle died, and his hand moved to her face again. The gesture was meant to soothe, just, she thought, as she had tried to soothe her ferrets. She did not like the comparison at all. But as she tried to move away, his hand caught hers.

"Ah, Marsali . . . my bonny lass," he whispered, "you have grown into a lovely woman. And a gallant one to risk yourself for your family's sake." His lips touched her hair, and he spoke in a raw, oddly vulnerable tone. "Why will you not come with me? Do you not trust me?"

"It has nothing to do with trusting you," she said, resisting the seductive pull of his gentle voice. "To begin with, we would never escape the keep."

"I know a way."

He would, she thought, for he had been allowed to play with Gavin in the cellars and dungeons. Her bitter complaints about the injustice of their freedom and her lack of it had fallen on deaf ears.

"Marsali?"

"Oh, Patrick, do you not know what it would do to my father and brother if I went with you?"

"Aye," he replied. "That is why they must believe it is a kidnapping—for a time, at least. They willna be hurt or angered if they believe you were taken by force. Aye, it will increase their anger at my clan, but they willna take vengeance as long as they think your safety is at stake. And, meanwhile, it will buy us some time—time to look for a more lasting solution."

A lasting solution. It seemed impossible. But his words

sounded frighteningly like sense to her. *Everything* sounded like sense when he held her so closely.

"And *your* father?" she asked, hearing the quaver in her voice.

Patrick's face went hard, harder than she'd ever seen it. The soft moonlight, filtering through the window, settled around him like a halo, but any resemblance to an angel ended there. His green eyes glittered like polished emeralds, cold and distant. She shivered. At that moment, he looked more than capable of killing, more than capable of ordering a battle . . . or a raid.

"My father needs me," he said tonelessly. "He will accept my decisions."

Perhaps, Marsali thought, but as she remembered the cold man who had married her aunt, who had later announced to her father that he would divorce Margaret, she could not imagine his acceptance of anyone else's commands.

Patrick's arms tightened around her. "Marsali, trust me. Come with me now, before it is too late. It must look to the world as if you are my hostage, but we can be wed. Come live with me, lass, and be my wife in truth, as you are in my heart."

His wife. Oh, how sweet the words did sound. And, oh, how she longed to say yes. But at what cost?

Needing desperately to gather her wits, she extracted herself from Patrick's arms and turned toward the window. From lifelong habit, her gaze went unerringly to her star. The star he had given her.

How much harm would she cause in leaving? She simply did not agree with Patrick. Her father would be furious, and he would feel honor-bound to strike. And if Patrick brought her home as his bride, Gregor Sutherland would disown his heir. Could he still love her if she caused him to lose his birthright?

And Gavin. If he came after her, would Patrick be able to honor his vow not to harm anyone dear to her? Or would he be forced, in self-defense, to fight her brother—his friend. . . . Her breath caught in her throat on a sob.

"Marsali . . ." he pleaded, coming to stand behind her.

Turning to look up at him, Marsali searched his features. The coldness was gone from his eyes, replaced by warmth and compassion.

He truly was two different men, she thought. One familiar, one not. One she trusted. One she did not.

"I can surrender myself," he said mildly. "Perhaps then your father will have the weapons he needs and free you."

"Nay!" she cried, horrified. "Fa will kill you."

"I canna believe he would."

"You donna realize how much he has changed. He feels your father has betrayed him. He even feels responsible for Aunt Margaret's . . . disappearance, since the marriage was his idea. He is not the same man he was when you knew him."

Patrick looked down at her for a long moment.

Finally, he let out a heavy sigh. "So I canna stay, and you are reluctant to go."

She might as well die, she thought, for her heart, like her dreams and hopes, was broken, and she did not think it would ever mend. "Patrick," she said, "I donna think we can ever be together. Not as long as it would mean we would be trailed by blood."

"I willna let that happen."

"You canna stop it. It *is* happening." Drawing a steadying breath, she whispered, "You must go. Alone."

He stared at her, his gaze inscrutable in the moonlight.

"At least," he said finally, "share a cup of wine with me before I go."

She blinked, surprised at his surrender, despite his forceful words. "Aye," she said, "I would share one with you, but there is none in the room."

"Ah, but there is," he said, giving her a small, crooked

smile. He retrieved the bag he had been carrying when he entered and withdrew a flagon from its depths.

She sighed. She did so want to prolong these last few minutes they would have together.

"Let me light a candle," she said.

"Nay, it is not needed."

Clouds had smothered the moonlight, throwing the room into almost total darkness, but she sensed his movements as he found her cup on the table beside her bed and poured a measure of wine into it. Returning to her side, he handed her the cup. She took it gratefully, needing the courage and warmth of the wine. Taking a sip, she handed it to him and turned to look out the window at the cold night. He lifted the cup to his lips, briefly, then handed it back to her.

It was a surprisingly fine wine, she thought, but then, perhaps it only seemed so because of the manner in which they were sharing it. There was something intoxicatingly intimate about the ritual.

When she tried to pass the cup to him once more, he refused it. "I have a long way to go tonight, lass," he said.

"But you need sleep."

The thought of his leaving, of the danger he had put himself in by coming here, made her shudder. She wanted to postpone such thoughts. As long as he was here, he was safe. And so was she. He made it so.

She was also tired. Very, very tired.

She put a hand to her forehead, her head suddenly beginning to swim. She gave him a bewildered look. "Patrick?" she said.

But that was all she could manage. She felt herself falling, felt his arms catch her. And in her last moment of foggy awareness, she thought she heard him say, "Ah, lass, I am sorry."

Chapter 8

Patrick laid Marsali gently on her bed, praying that he was not destroying any chance of love between them. "Patrick?" Her voice was slurred.

" 'Tis all right, love." He sat next to her, holding her hand. "I am here with you."

"I . . . feel . . ." She sighed. "Patrick . . ."

He leaned down and kissed her cheek. "Forgive me," he pleaded. But she did not hear him. She was asleep.

He watched her for a moment, listening to the soft whisper of her breathing. Then he went to the window. The clouds completely covered the moon. Good. He needed a few more hours like this. And rain. Or a fine Scottish mist.

A scratching in the ferrets' basket brought his attention back to his next task. Pouring a tiny portion of wine over a chunk of bread, he placed the morsel inside the basket, avoiding two pairs of sharp teeth. He held his breath, watching, exhaling as he saw the wee beasts start to nibble the wine-spiced bread. He could not have risked taking them if they were awake—and noisy—but he did not want to leave them behind when he was already taking Marsali away from everything else she loved.

She will never forgive you for this. His conscience berated him as he waited to be sure both Marsali and the ferrets were soundly asleep. Yet, as the minutes passed and he thought, for the hundredth time, about the possible alternatives, he could see no other choice.

When he was certain the drug had been given a chance to work, he lifted the top of the ferrets' basket and peeked inside. Isolde and Tristan were curled up against each other, breathing quietly, and he tucked them into his sporran. Then he turned back to the bed. Although it was dark, he saw her form. She looked small and defenseless. Yet her father had used her as a weapon—a tool to accomplish his own ends. Sinclair wanted to do so as well. And he himself was doing so at that very moment.

For a moment, Patrick wavered. He could still leave without her. She would awaken in the morning wondering what had happened but with no harm done to her.

But as he leaned down to touch her face, a question rose in his mind: What if, tomorrow, her father brought her before Edward Sinclair and an unscrupulous vicar who was willing to marry her to Edward without her consent? The thought of Sinclair touching something so fragile, so precious, sent streaks of rage knifing through him.

Devil take it. This was the only way. He could agonize over his guilty conscience some other time. Now he needed to get moving.

Quickly plaiting her hair into a loose braid, he looked at her nightdress. He could not take her out in the cold air wearing so little. Cursing under his breath, he found a plaid overskirt and pulled it on her.

His hands brushed her breasts—firm and high and altogether lovely—and he ached to caress them. But his sense of honor would not allow him to take such liberties.

Leaving Marsali on the bed, Patrick went to the door and listened. When he heard nothing, he returned to lift Marsali into his arms and gently place her over his shoulder. Making sure he had the stolen keys still tucked into his belt, he walked cautiously down the corridor to the stairs and began a careful descent. Once he reached the floor beneath the kitchen, he hesitated. He had descended into pitch blackness, and he had to pause to allow his eyes time to adjust. No candle still burned in a wall sconce. No window provided even a cloud-covered hint of moonlight.

Relying on instinct and memory, he mentally constructed

the path he planned to take, one that led to the back of the keep and the stairs that went down into the cellars. There, one corridor led to another set of stairs and the dungeon below, while another led to the wine cellar. A third went under the kitchen, where a large drain carried water to a cistern that ran under the keep to emerge on the other side of the walls, above the moat. It was the third corridor he wanted. The one that would lead him out of Abernie.

Making his way slowly in the blackness, he remained mindful of the treasure he carried; if he hugged the wall too closely, he would bang Marsali's head against it. He reached the kitchen, where a loose stone caused him to stumble. He froze at the clatter it made. When no other sound followed, he continued downward, more warily now, to the cellars.

Beneath the kitchen, he stopped. There, a circular well filled part of the room. A pulley system could raise a series of buckets up to each of the higher levels of the keep. To the left lay the drain that emptied into the cistern, which collected runoff from several other grated openings in the courtyard. That sewer was none too clean, since rainwater often mixed with animal droppings. Yet it was a far preferable route to freedom than the privy shute.

Studying the drain, Patrick sighed. It would be a devil of a long crawl, especially with an unconscious woman and two similarly sedated ferrets, whom he would have to be careful not to squash.

He shifted Marsali to the floor, then yanked on the grate over the drain, trying to work it loose. It did not move. Indeed, it probably had not been removed since he and Gavin had been through it some twelve or thirteen years ago. Never assume anything, he reminded himself—too late. It had not even occurred to him that he would be foiled by something as simple as a stuck drain cover.

Anchoring his feet against the wall, Patrick pulled at the iron grating in earnest. After several attempts, he felt the grate begin to loosen. Another tug, and it came off. Relieved, he laid the heavy piece of iron aside and lowered himself into the drain opening, pulling Marsali in after him. Settling her over his shoulder again, he climbed down a ladder some five feet, then had to shift her to his arms in order to enter the cistern.

It seemed to him, as he had to bend nearly double to fit through the sewer arch, that the cistern had shrunk. He had been able to move through it swiftly as a boy, but went only a few feet this time before realizing he would never make it in this fashion. Dropping to his knees, he swung Marsali's limp body onto his back and began to crawl.

Within seconds, his clothing was soaked, as was the sporran in which the ferrets slept. He tried to keep Marsali from getting wet as well, but it was impossible. He cursed his size and the cold and anything else he could think of as he slogged along through two feet of slimy water and mold. How could he ever have considered such a journey an adventure? Even as a boy?

Trying to ignore the occasional squeal of a disturbed rat, he followed the rounded wall. After endless movement in darkness, he finally felt cool, fresh air and knew he was near one of the overhead grates. He slowed his pace and moved more cautiously, lest any sound he made disturb those in the courtyard above. Past another grate. He must be close to the outer wall now. What hour was it? Near dawn? Each passing minute gnawed away at the time he needed.

Finally, a lightening of the gloom signaled the end of the dark journey. Balancing Marsali's dead weight on his back, he made his way as quickly as possible to the outer-wall grate, praying it would not be as rusted as the one in the floor of the cellar. Squinting to see through the darkness, his groping hand reached out until it touched iron.

Carefully, he rolled Marsali off his back, catching her in his arms. Clutching her slender body against him with one hand, he dug for the key with the other. He searched for the lock, cursing. It was simply too dark to see. He had no choice but to lay Marsali against the wall in the fetid water as he blindly sought the lock. It had been too bloody long since he and Gavin had come here to play Robert the Bruce, and he had no memory at all of where to look for it.

And he found it only by pure luck, for it was covered with dirt and moss. Cursing steadily now, Patrick cleared the lock's mechanism as best he could, then tried the first of the larger keys. It would not go into the keyhole even a half inch. The second one did, albeit with a rasp of protest. Reluctantly, it turned, and the harsh click it made as it opened was the sweetest sound he had heard in a long while. Patrick thanked God as he pulled on the bars of the large grate, but when it did not budge, he wondered if his gratitude had been offered too soon.

Light bouncing against the shallow water of the moat below told him that the clouds had passed, at least for the moment. He kept listening for an alarm, for the sound of loud voices, but there was only the noise he himself was making: the rattle of the grate and his own labored, desperate breathing.

He checked on Marsali. She seemed all right, though she was soaked and he felt the tiny raised bumps on her chilled arms. He was sweating from his labors, but as he sat still for a moment, he realized how very cold it was. He had to get her out, and get her warmed. If he could not open the grate, he would have to return her to her room and summon help. He would *not* allow her to become ill through his efforts to rescue her. The irony would be too awful to bear.

Taking a deep breath, Patrick wrapped his hands around the grate and heaved until sweat poured down his face and beneath his beard, and every muscle in his body was quivering. Then, as he was about to give up, the thing came loose without warning. The sudden lack of resistance sent him backward, cursing, into the slimy water with the grate on top of him. Quickly, he put the damnable hunk of iron aside and scrambled to his knees at the exit, listening hard, expecting to hear shouts from the guards on the wall above.

He heard only the wind, and he blessed it, guessing it had carried any sounds he had made away from the guards' ears.

Easing his head outside the opening, he scanned his surroundings. Clouds still swirled in the sky, but they hid the moon only partially. Moisture was heavy in the air, and, with luck, there would be mist by morn. Just as he was ruing the fact that he could not wait for it, a thick bank of clouds overran the moon, as if by request. He wasted no more time. Lifting Marsali in his arms, he stepped out onto the narrow ledge four feet above the moat.

The earl of Abernie had allowed the moat to disintegrate over the past twenty years, feeling that the keep's thick walls and its position high on a hill were sufficient protection against attack. Water had accumulated in the deepest part of the moat, but in the back side, where he stood, the moat was shallow, water having worn away slices of earth to create runoffs.

Holding Marsali tightly to him, Patrick sat on the ledge, then jumped into the water. He could not avoid the splash that inevitably accompanied the action, and once in the water, he held still for a full minute, again expecting to hear that the alarm had been sounded.

When he was certain that his worst fears had not been realized, he started across the moat. The water was knee high, no more, and he moved with assurance. Though there was little light, it seemed almost bright after the deep darkness of the cistern. He found a ditch, cut into the side of the moat by runoff, and stepped into it, his feet sinking into several inches of mud. A fine rain started to fall, and with it came the blessed mist. Though it made the steps more difficult, the cover it provided could save them both.

Making steady progress, he came to the end of the ditch, where the banks leveled out and the trickle of water was absorbed into the rich dirt of a meadow. Patrick shifted

Marsali onto his shoulder and, taking a few deep breaths, started running.

A mile to go to the forest. And, God help him, he had to make it before dawn.

Gregor Sutherland, marquis of Brinaire, laird of the clan Sutherland, glared at his younger son. "Where in the devil is that brother of yours?"

He watched Alex flinch and did not try to hide his contempt. Why was he so plagued? An unfaithful wife. And of two sons, one was disobedient and the other a coward. And his daughter! Och! She crept about like a ghost that had lost its way to the beyond.

"Well, where is he?" he demanded.

Alex shifted. "He did not tell me where he was going."

Gregor struggled from his chair. His joints were swollen, and every movement caused him unfathomable pain. Any change in the weather made it worse. It took several men to help him mount a horse, which caused him enough humiliation to prevent him from doing it.

Gregor knew he had never been a temperate man, and the events of the past two years had only quickened his anger. The fear he saw in his son's face both shamed and enraged him.

He had never known how to reach out to anyone. Not to his first wife, whom he had loved. Not to his second wife who was a shrew. Nor to his third, Margaret, whom he had tried not to love. And not to his children, whom he might have loved if he had but known how. His own father had viewed love as a weakness, forgiveness a sin. Hate your enemies, suspect your friends. Do unto others before they do unto you, his father had been fond of saying.

But he had not listened at first. He had called Donald Gunn, the earl of Abernie, his friend. They had hunted together and fought together, and Gregor had seen Donald's easy affection with his family and envied him. It had given him great satisfaction to send his oldest son to foster with Donald's family.

Somehow, he had allowed himself to become entranced by Margaret Gunn. After losing his first wife in childbirth, he had sworn never to care too much for anyone again. It had been altogether too painful to lose her. Love, he had decided, *was* painful, as well as foolish and sentimental. Duty and loyalty to clan: Those were the only two things that really mattered.

He had married Margaret to solidify an important alliance—for his clan. But she had chipped away at the shell surrounding his heart. She had made him care for her. But he had only come to know how much he cared when she had betrayed him.

And now his children were betraying him, too. Even Patrick, who had more than surpassed his highest hopes; Patrick's reputation as a warrior had filled him with pride. But he had disappeared, leaving guests who had come in his honor behind. He had admitted to seeing the Gunn wench. And now he was gone again. This was the third time this month. No word. No explanation. And Gregor was certain Alex was covering for him.

Yet, the marquis knew he had no real basis for complaint. Since Patrick had begun training his clansmen, their battle skills had improved dramatically. Moreover, it was evident that Patrick had already gained their respect. He radiated a natural leadership that Gregor silently had to admire. Indeed, these changes should have pleased him, but they did not. He saw his authority, his control, slipping away, just as everything else had slipped away.

The cursed Gunns! His cattle had been raided; lies were being spread. The Gunns were accusing him—*him*—of killing and stealing, even as they stole his best cattle. And where was his son? Wandering about the countryside.

He threw a goblet into the fireplace. "I want Patrick here, and I want him now," he told Alex. "Tell David to find him. I donna care how many men it takes. I want those cattle."

Alex started to back out of the chamber.

"And you will start training again," Gregor ordered. "You will fight beside your brother."

A muscle moved in his son's cheek. Och, but he had sired a tender lad, good for nothing except keeping accounts. He could employ someone to do that.

"Aye, Father," Alex said, turning hurriedly to the door.

"I want to know as soon as Patrick arrives," Gregor shouted after him. "I want one worthy son near me."

He saw Alex falter as the arrow hit its mark, and he wanted to take back the words. But his pride would not allow it. He watched in silence as Alex slipped out of the room, closing the door quietly behind him.

Gregor stared at the closed door. He took a step toward it, then slumped against the table. Lowering himself into a chair, he snatched up a large vessel of wine and took a long drink without bothering to pour it into a glass. The alcohol would aggravate his gout, but he did not care. It would also dull his senses and bring him momentary respite from the loneliness in his soul.

And what choice did he have left: Only drunkenness and rage.

Dawn's first rays had dispersed a blessedly dense mist when Patrick reached the place where he was to meet Hiram.

The horses were tethered to a tree off the path, deep in the forest. Hiram was not in sight, but Patrick knew where to find him. For all his size, Hiram was agile, and could climb a tree like a cat. Finding a branch that would hold him was another matter.

That was, in fact, how they had first met. Hiram had fallen on him, nearly breaking both their necks in the process. After they concluded that neither had sustained life-threatening injuries, and Hiram learned that Patrick was to be his new commander, Hiram had stuttered apologies.

Patrick had grinned. "How did anyone as big as you get up there?"

"Och," Hiram replied. "Not as quickly as I came down."

From that moment on, Hiram had made it his particular role to protect Patrick's back.

Casting a quick glance at the leafy branches above him, Patrick put Marsali down and knelt beside her. Her eyes were still closed and her breathing normal. But she was very cold. Even unconscious, she was shivering.

"Hiram!" Patrick called. A thud announced his friend's arrival a few yards away.

"Ye didna see me?"

"Nay," Patrick said. "Like a bird, you were."

Hiram chuckled. "Ye lie."

"A large bird, then."

"More like a bear," Hiram said, squatting beside Patrick to study Marsali. "The lass is unconscious?"

"She was afraid it would only brew more trouble if she came with me."

"She will be angry."

"Doubtless." Patrick sighed. "But right now I have to get her warm."

Hiram handed him an extra plaid they had brought along and turned away as Patrick wrapped Marsali in it, holding her tight until some of her shivering quieted. Then Patrick lifted her into Hiram's arms while he mounted his horse. Checking the two ferrets inside his sporran, he assured himself that they were still sleeping. Marsali truly would never forgive him if he harmed her pets, any more than she would forgive him if his actions brought harm to her family.

Acutely aware of the fine line he was walking, Patrick gestured to Hiram to give Marsali to him. He settled her onto the saddle, her legs straddling the horse and her back leaning against his chest. She felt as if she belonged there.

All he had to do was convince her of that. He would not leave their future in the hands of two stubborn old men.

Waiting for Hiram to mount, Patrick watched with regret as his friend gathered the reins of the third horse, which was to have been Marsali's. They would have to lead the animal. But he had no room for more regrets. What was done was done.

He spurred his horse forward, and Hiram followed. Though dawn had broken, the night was not yet over. They were still on Gunn land with a half day's ride ahead of them.

Chapter 9

S he will be treated as an honored guest." Patrick
spoke through clenched teeth.

"I am still lord here," his father replied. "I will
say where she stays, and a tower room is sufficient. She is
naught but a prisoner."

"She is a lady. I was betrothed to her. She will be treated
with the courtesy of her position."

"You dare dictate to me?"

"No, I am merely stating what *I* will do."

"I make the decisions. The clan will obey me."

Patrick spoke softly. "Will they, Father? They donna like
this feud with the Gunns any more than I do. Do you really
want to put it to a test?" He kept his features impassive and
his gaze steady under his father's angry glare.

The old man sitting in the stuffed chair was a stranger to
him. Of course, his father had always been a stranger, but
now even his appearance was radically changed. The spare
body, the gray hair, the perpetual frown, and the trembling
hands were unfamiliar to Patrick's eyes, as were the gri-
maces of pain and the almost continuous drinking. Yet it
was his father's hesitation, his apparent retreat from their
battle of wills, that told Patrick the changes went far deeper
than a few gray hairs.

"Father?"

The marquis waved his hand as if the matter were beneath his interest—or as if it required too much effort to
speak. Patrick could not be sure which was true. "As long as
she is well guarded," he finally said.

Hiding his shock at having won so easily, Patrick continued. "She will take her meals with us, and she will be treated cordially by *all* of us."

"You give *me* instruction?" His father struggled up from the chair, his face mottling with outrage.

"Aye," Patrick replied calmly. "I brought her here to stop this madness, not to compound it. You know the Gunns will petition the king and seek to have us outlawed. I can justify the kidnapping by saying I only took my betrothed bride. We canna justify taking her as a hostage. Those days are gone."

His father's hands clenched. "They stole our cattle."

"They think we stole their cattle—and worse."

"You know that is a lie. They invented the tale to put us in the wrong."

"No, Father."

"Whose side are you on?"

"The side of reason," Patrick said. "I would wager everything I have that someone else is involved. The Gunns *were* attacked. I saw their wounded."

"How did you get in, lad?" His father cocked his head to the side, an unholy light dancing in his eyes. "Can you take others back in there?"

Patrick's lips thinned. As usual, his father was only hearing what he wanted to hear. "I am sure, by now, Gavin has discovered my route," he said. "He will have blocked it."

His father looked momentarily disgusted. But then another thought put the light back in his eyes. "Och, I would like to see Gunn's face when he learns you were inside his keep."

"I take no pleasure in deceiving him," Patrick replied. "He was kind to me when I was a lad."

"He thrust that she-witch on me," his father roared. "Then he questioned my honor in front of all of Scotland."

Patrick let a few seconds of silence pass. Finally, he spoke quietly. "What happened, Father? I canna imagine Margaret betraying you."

His father looked away. "There was ample proof."

"But not enough for Parliament?"

"The two accusers disappeared, but I spoke to them myself. I know Margaret went out riding, alone, every day. Two men saw her meet a man at the abandoned hut in the north woods."

"Did they give you a description?"

"Only one that would fit dozens of men."

"It could not have been Edward Sinclair?"

His father's gaze snapped to his face. "Nay, it wasna him. Sinclair is the only one around with light-colored hair, and the men said the man was dark."

"Why did you trust the two men? Did Margaret admit it?"

"Nay," the old man grumbled. Then, more forcefully, he said, "But she didna deny it, either."

Patrick spread his hands. There was even less proof than he had guessed. "When she disappeared, she didna leave a note?" he asked.

His father shook his head.

" 'Tis strange indeed she didna return to Abernie, do you not think? She and her brother were very close."

"She drowned herself," his father said. " 'Tis as simple as that. She was disgraced, despite Parliament's ruling. No man would have had her."

But she would not have killed herself, Patrick thought. No good Catholic would commit a mortal sin against God only to avoid social disgrace.

"And these two men?" he continued. "Were they our people?"

"Mercenaries," his father said uncomfortably. "Sinclair was making threats, and I hired them."

"Sinclair has spent his life trying to make trouble between the Gunns and Sutherlands," Patrick said. "Can you think of a better way to accomplish it than to make you believe that Margaret—your wife and Donald Gunn's sister— had betrayed you?"

"She didna deny it," his father said stubbornly.

More likely, his father had not given her a chance to deny it.

Patrick sighed. He would not convince his father, but the word of two men who killed for money and who had conveniently disappeared was not enough for Patrick. Although he himself had been a mercenary, pledged by his father in return for alliances that would secure more land, he had met few other than Rufus and Hiram who had gained his respect; most would sell each other out for a pence.

If Margaret was innocent, then there was only one likely explanation for her disappearance: murder. Patrick felt chilled. Uncovering a murder that had been planned and executed two years ago was an overwhelming task—and not one suited to a trained warrior. But if he did not solve the puzzle, no one would. And his dreams of a life with Marsali would be doomed.

Marsali. He needed to get back to her. She had still been asleep when he had carried her to the guest bedchamber and laid her upon the feather bed, but she should be waking soon. He wanted to be there when she did.

"I want your word, Father," he said, breaking the tense silence. "I want your word that you will be civil to Marsali. Or I *will* leave Brinaire and take her with me. No one here will stop me."

He watched the anger flash in his father's eyes, but it was anger laced with cunning. "I am always civil to guests at Brinaire," his father said.

Patrick recognized that the reply was not a surrender. Rather it was a temporary cease-fire. The old man was undoubtedly plotting a strategy of his own. The Sutherland would not risk a test of his leadership for fear it would be denied—he was not certain that his clansmen's loyalty was still his to command.

Neither was Patrick certain that he himself could claim

that loyalty—not yet. Not when he was working to gain fealty that his father had held inviolate for thirty years.

He nodded to his father, then, in respect, backed out of the room.

His sister, Elizabeth, was waiting outside, and Patrick wondered whether she had been listening.

"Did Father agree?" Elizabeth asked.

"She will stay as our guest," Patrick said. "I hope you will lend her some clothing."

"Aye," Elizabeth said shyly. "I have always liked Marsali. I had hoped she would be my sister."

"Then make her welcome, little one. She will need friends."

"Do you . . ." She glanced at him from under her thick lashes. "Do you wish to marry her?"

Patrick considered his sister carefully. Then he said, "I *will* marry her." When Elizabeth's surprised gaze flashed upward to meet his, he touched the tip of his index finger to her chin, smiling. "But that is between you and me at the moment. I donna think our father is ready to accept it as truth."

A hint of pink crept into Elizabeth's cheeks, and Patrick knew she was pleased that he had trusted her.

"And Marsali?" she asked.

He sighed. "She will be none too happy with me when she wakes."

She gazed up at him with adoration. "Then she is daft, and I will tell her so."

His eyebrow lifted in surprise at her uncommon display of spirit. Perhaps there was more to Elizabeth than met the eye. "Then you donna share this ill will toward the Gunns?" he asked.

"Oh no. Margaret was ever so good to me. I do not believe any of what they say about her," she said. Standing on tiptoe, she leaned toward him to whisper in his ear. "She even said she loved Father and that she really believed Father loved her, even if he could not say so. Imagine that!"

She said the words with such amazement that Patrick felt sick. Had she been so unloved these past years that she could not even imagine their father having the capacity for affection?

He smiled down at his sister. Elizabeth was no beauty, but she had lovely, golden-flecked green eyes that made her rather pretty when she smiled, which was much too rarely. Her normal expression was pinched, as if she was trying very hard to please but did not expect to succeed.

"And you, little one?" he asked. "Has someone caught your eye?"

"Oh, I am much too plain," she said, pushing a listless piece of hair back behind her ear.

Anger flared inside him at her easy repetition of this untruth. "Did Margaret tell you that?"

"Oh no," Elizabeth replied. "She always said I had the kind of face that was nice to live with. It was Father who told me that meant plain."

Patrick had to forcibly tamp down his temper. "Margaret was right," he said gently. "You have very fine eyes and a smile that could break hearts. You are not plain at all."

"Really?" she said hopefully.

"Really," he replied. "And now I am going up to see Marsali. Does she have food and fresh water?"

"Aye, I have already sent them up, along with one of Margaret's gowns. They are prettier than mine."

"You are a treasure, Elizabeth," he said.

Her hesitant smile widened. "I am so glad you are home. So is Alex." Then she turned and ran from the hall.

Patrick knew at that moment that he could not leave again. Elizabeth and Alex needed him, or his father would destroy them both. He could not flee to France with Marsali if things did not go as he hoped. Come what may, it would be here that they would make their stand. And they would have to make it together, if they were to win the war.

But drugging his comrade-in-arms, mayhap, had not been the best way to begin.

Sighing, Patrick went up the stairs to Marsali's chamber. She was still asleep, lost in the folds of the huge feather bed. Crossing quietly to the bedside, he noted her freshly scrubbed face and clean nightdress. Elizabeth had been efficient.

As he watched her sleep, the ferrets, which he had also placed on the bed, began to stir, their movements as unsteady as those of a drunkard after a long night of revelry. They poked slowly around their mistress, thrusting their faces against her, trying to wake her. Little noises of distress came from their small throats as they found no response. When one noticed Patrick, it started for him but tripped over its shaky feet. He would have to work hard to repair his image in those dark eyes and valiant little hearts. He could not blame them.

Drawing a chair close to the bed, Patrick sat down to wait.

Marsali's head pounded as though it were full of Scottish drums as she struggled toward awareness. Patrick was kneeling with her at the betrothal ceremony. No, he was with her at the waterfall, and he was kissing her. His face was scarred. But how could she see that when he wore a beard? No, that was not right. Patrick had no beard. It must be some other man kissing her, his beard dark and scratchy and his hair thick with white dust. But why would she let another man kiss her . . . ?

It was the wet nose poking her chin that brought reality back. Or mostly so: Everything, her limbs as well as her mind, felt sluggish. A furry body tumbled over her face. She raised a hand to catch it—but missed. Isolde. She recognized the chittering voice, a fraction higher than Tristan's.

Marsali opened her eyes slowly, blinking several times before she could focus. Tristan joined Isolde in sitting on her chest and making anxious noises, and she patted them limply as she took in her surroundings.

The room was not familiar, but she recognized the man sitting close by in the chair to her right. It was Patrick, and he *did* have a beard of sorts, and his uncombed hair *was* white—or gray, at least. And he was watching her intently. Memory came back in a sudden rush: They had been standing at the window in her room, moonlight cloaking them as they kissed and talked and shared a cup of wine.

"Come with me," he had said to her.

Her eyes widened as realization and horror filled her. She looked again at the unfamiliar room, much plainer than her room at Abernie.

"Patrick?" The sound was a mere croak, but she knew he had heard her. In his hesitation, she had the answer to her unspoken question.

"I could not leave you," he said softly. "I brought you to Brinaire."

Anguish, deep and painful, sliced through her. He had not listened to her at all. He had assumed he was right, and he had done as he saw fit. Worse, he had not considered her honor as important as his own. He was no different, no better, than her father or brother. Like them, he thought a woman was to be bartered and stolen and claimed like livestock. Why had she ever expected anything else? And she had. She had *believed* in him.

"Marsali?"

Her answer was bitter, flat. "So I am your prisoner."

"No," he said. "Never."

"Then what?"

"A guest. A very honored guest."

She uttered a sound of disbelief. She would not let herself cry. *She would not.* "I may leave?"

She saw him shift in his chair. Good. He should be uncomfortable. Still fighting the tears that stung her eyes, she turned her face away from him. This was the cruelest betrayal of all.

"It was the only way," she heard him say, his voice bleak.

She did not hear him approach the bed, but she sensed his presence and, as always, it overwhelmed her. She did not want him near her, did not trust herself to resist whatever spell it was he cast over her.

"I couldna leave you there," he said again. "I couldna risk your father forcing the marriage with Sinclair."

"I told you I wouldna marry him.'" She forced the words past the lump in her throat. "You didna trust me."

"I trust you. I didna trust your father."

"And you trust yours?"

"No, God, help me, I do not," he said.

"Then why bring me here? He has been accused of murder."

"You know as well as I he didna kill Margaret," Patrick said. "He is surely guilty of other sins, but not of murdering his wife. There is no danger here for you."

"I must go home."

"Will you listen to me, lass?" he pleaded.

She rolled her head back toward him. "I did listen to you. I thought you listened to me. But you didna. As my fa and brother didna. I am nothing to you, am I? Nothing but a trophy to be claimed by one side or the other."

His eyes darkened and his lips thinned. He looked like a brigand, unkempt and unwashed and thoroughly ruthless. Indeed, he had a reputation for being so. Had she believed he had left that behind, on the battlefield? Perhaps not, but she had surely never believed he would use it against her.

She had believed what she wanted to believe, seen what she wanted to see, and she had only herself to blame.

When he moved toward her and she stiffened, the ferrets stopped nuzzling her and came to attention, ready to attack.

Patrick stopped short, eyeing the creatures, and she wanted to smile. It gave her satisfaction to think that a man who would drug and kidnap the woman he claimed he wanted to wed was afraid of a tiny animal.

She did notice that he had gone to the trouble of bringing her pets—and appreciated that small tenderness. It could not have been easy. In fact, she could not imagine how he had left Abernie without hue and cry. However he had done it, it appeared that he had gotten soaked and filthy in the process. And he looked as if he had not slept in days.

But she was too angry to care. And too hurt.

"I must go home," she said again. "Immediately. This will kill my father. First Cecilia disappears, then he awakens to find me gone, too. If he believes I came willingly—"

"I will send word," Patrick interrupted her. "I will tell him that I took you, that you are being held here, that it is my right as the man to whom you were legally betrothed."

"He will appeal to the king."

"Aye, I expect he will, but Charles will not interfere. He has enough to worry about with his quarreling lords and so many seeking back estates confiscated by Cromwell. I only took my promised bride."

She heard the hardness in his voice, the finality. *He* had decided, and he would not change his mind.

"Then I am your prisoner," she concluded, "no matter what you choose to call it." Struggling to sit up, she pressed a hand to her forehead in an effort to ease the pounding. "I had a dream, a wonderful dream. I felt safe and protected and loved." She looked up at him. "I will never feel safe with you again. I will never trust you again."

She saw a muscle twitch in his cheek before she turned her head away from him. "Am I allowed privacy? Or are you taking that away, too?" she asked, her voice low.

"Marsali . . ."

"Please leave," she said with all the dignity she had left.

She stared sightlessly at the window, her hopes—her dreams—shattering, and each shard piercing her heart. She prayed he would go soon, for she did not know how much longer she could maintain her strength.

A long silence passed, then he spoke again. "I hope you will join us for supper," he said.

"Is that a command, my lord?' she asked bitterly.

"Nay, only a hope," he replied.

"I donna feel well. Someone gave me something disagreeable," she said. After a long silence, she heard his footsteps crossing the room and the sound of the door closing. Only then did she collapse on the bed and allow the tears to come.

"I will never trust you again." Marsali's words echoed in Patrick's mind as he walked toward the stairs. He had expected her to be angry. He had not anticipated how deeply hurt she would be by his actions.

She was right. He had asked her to trust him, but he had not trusted her. His concern had been for her safety; but he should have been concerned for her honor.

He remembered the way she had looked at him last night, after he had kissed her—her face bathed in moonlight, her eyes filled with passion and pure adoration. She had given him everything, her trust, her heart, her life. The idea that he may have lost that precious gift forever frightened him to the marrow.

He had to win her back. Neither an apology nor any excuses about her well-being would suffice. But what would? What did he know of these things?

He had been making decisions on his own for so long. He had led men into battle where the ability to make instant decisions meant the difference between life and death. He knew no other way to survive.

Mayhap he would have to learn. And soon, if he had any hopes of repairing the damage he had done.

With renewed determination, Patrick ran down the last flight of stairs. First, he had to clear a path for himself and

Marsali to walk together. He had to put a stop to the war with the Gunns.

At the bottom of the stairs, he came to a sudden halt, his eyes widening at the sight of his father dressed in battle gear, sword and pistol strapped to his side. He deserved to be wet and cold, and worse. Fully armed clansmen stood on either side of him.

"Since you seem to have no desire to take back what is ours," his father said to him, "I am going after the cattle."

Nothing Patrick could think of would make matters worse. By now, Gunns would be scouring the countryside for their lady. Furious Gunns. Any encounter with them would mean bloodshed—an end to any hope of peace between them.

"I will go," he said. "I will bring back the bloody cattle." The gleam that appeared in his father's eyes told Patrick that the old man's intention had only been to force his hand.

"I want your pledge," Patrick continued, "that you will treat Marsali as a member of the family." Then, as he had second thoughts about that quality of care, he corrected himself. "As an honored guest."

His father nodded his assent, a triumphant smile on his lips.

Patrick allowed him that. He had schemes of his own, one every bit as devious as anything his father could concoct.

Chapter 10

Patrick rode out of Brinaire at eventide. He took ten men with him: Hiram and nine others carefully selected from the clansmen he had been training. They were the smartest of the lot, the ones who had understood defensive as well as offensive fighting. The ones he thought would obey without question.

Taking little with them, he and his men rode through the night, expecting to reach Abernie long before dawn. The Sutherland cattle would be held close to the castle gates, and Patrick planned to bring them home to his father. His main goal, however, was something entirely different.

He did not share his scheme with anyone but Hiram, who stared at him as if he were daft. But then, it was not the first time, and doubtless would not be the last, that he had been on the receiving end of that look.

Patrick was grateful for the wind that whipped his face as he rode. The cold air, combined with the anticipation of conflict, sharpened his senses, despite the mere two hours of sleep he had managed to snatch.

He tried to keep thoughts of the problem he had left behind from distracting him. It was crucial to stay focused on what lay ahead if his plan was to be successful. He was going to talk to Gavin. Surely, something was left of their friendship. There had to be.

Patrick kept his raiders to a hard pace until they came to the pass that bridged the domains of the two clans. There, they were forced to go more cautiously. The soft mist that shrouded the mountains made the pass treacherous, despite the torches carried by the two men at the front of the line.

The clatter of hooves against rock and the metallic sound of swords scraping against the sheer stone walls rang ominously in the thick night air.

They traversed the pass without incident, and Patrick picked up the pace once more, tossing a quick order to the torchbearers to quench their flames. Two more hours and they would reach the pastureland around Abernie. With the exception of Hiram, all of the men had grown up in these mountains, had been back and forth between Abernie and Brinaire for weddings, births, and deaths. They knew Abernie land as well as their own.

Patrick could feel their tension growing. Although they had all been eager at the prospect of a raid, time and the cold mist had blunted their excitement. They were proud of their new skills and wanted to test them, but none of them had been in battle. And most had friends at Abernie.

They had been surprised when he explained that he wanted no bloodshed. He had laid out his plan in every detail: the raid, the trap. Still, many things could go wrong. A hothead. A blade struck with too much force. Was he truly daft, as Hiram thought, to think he could succeed?

An hour later, they left the well-worn path that drifted past a cluster of cottages, and made their way through the forest. Taking the lead, Patrick rode ahead, listening for signs that guards had been posted, although he did not expect to find any. Most likely they would be stationed along the roads, not the more difficult terrain through the gorse. Still, several times, his tightly strung senses caused him to lead his small troop in another direction.

Finally, they neared the pasture where, the previous night, he had seen the Sutherland herd. He heard the soft lowing of the cattle before he saw them, and he stopped his men. Gesturing for them to dismount, he silently assigned one man to stay with the horses, then led the others onward by foot. Each man had already been told exactly what to do. One by one, they moved stealthily toward the beasts.

Patrick saw one of the herders leaning on a huge staff, alone at the edge of the cattle, and crept up softly behind him. With one hand, he covered the man's mouth, and with the other struck the back of his head with his fist. The man slumped in his arms, unconscious. After dragging him out of danger from the cattle's hooves, he looked toward the castle. Nearly eclipsed by the mist, it rose against the sky like a great black behemoth. Several barely visible lights flickered in the distance. But he was certain that no one, no matter how fine their eyes, would be able to see what was happening in the pasture outside the gates.

Three additional herders were taken, knocked out, and dragged to the edge of the pasture, where Hiram quickly bound and gagged them. Then, as quietly as possible, the raiders started to herd the cattle toward Sutherland land.

Patrick and Hiram gave them a good lead. Then Patrick shook one of the unconscious men until he stirred.

He had chosen one he recognized: Johnny Gunn. Patrick remembered the red hair, the teasing Johnny always took with such good nature. Johnny's eyes flew open, squinting as he tried to focus on his attacker through the black night.

Patrick took the gag from his mouth, replacing it with the palm of his hand. "Donna make a sound except to answer me," he said. "Your life and your friends' lives depend upon it."

He read the anger—and fear—in Johnny's eyes, and kept his voice hard, even cruel.

"I have two messages," he said. "The first one is for the earl. Tell him that Sutherlands had naught to do with the raid that wounded and murdered your crofters and burned their homes. Tonight, I am taking back what is ours—and what is mine. Do you understand?"

Johnny stared at him for a moment, then gave his head a quick nod.

Patrick continued. "The second message is for Gavin and no one else. Give it to another person, and I will know it. And God help you if I discover you betrayed me. Do you ken what I say?" He lifted his hand enough from Johnny's mouth to allow the man to speak.

"Aye," Johnny said. "I give my word."

"Good. Tell Gavin he knows where to find me." Without further discussion, Patrick replaced Johnny's gag, then stood.

"Go on ahead," he told Hiram. "I will follow later."

Hiram hesitated, as if he wanted to protest. But he could not misinterpret the hard set of Patrick's jaw, and he shrugged, disappearing into the darkness. He reappeared a few minutes later with two horses, Patrick's black stallion and his own. Handing the black's reins to Patrick, he mounted and rode off into the darkness, leaving Patrick alone with the captured Gunns.

Patrick picked a spot near a tangle of gorse and crouched down to wait. He needed to ensure that the herders did not free themselves and sound the alarm before his men had completed their tasks. The cattle were being driven in two small herds, in two separate directions; Hiram would take two men and several extra horses in yet a third direction, then circle around to meet the two herds. The result would be a confusion of crossing trails, and they needed a full two hours to accomplish it.

Guessing that the herders would be relieved at dawn, Patrick looked at the sky. It was going to be close.

Marsali dressed for the evening meal, determined not to give in to the impulse to stay in her room for a second night. She examined her face closely in the small mirror: She did not want anyone to know she had been crying. Deciding the blotches had faded sufficiently, she made a vow to herself that, no matter what happened at dinner, she would not be brought to tears in public.

Having brought her a simple linen tunic and jeweled

belt, Elizabeth stood by, watching. "I thought the blue would be pretty with your eyes," the girl said shyly.

Marsali could not help but smile at her. She was so clearly eager to be of service.

"Will Patrick be at supper?" she asked.

Elizabeth's eyes darted to the window, and her obvious discomfort gave Marsali her answer.

"Where is he?" she asked.

Elizabeth's face reddened, and she looked away. Marsali's skin prickled with fear. Where had Patrick gone? With her own experience fresh in her mind, Marsali was willing to consider him capable of nearly anything. The possibilities frightened her considerably.

Feeling more than ever that she was in an enemy camp, she felt her determination to appear at dinner waver. But to stay in the room would be cowardly, and she would not give them that satisfaction. Nor would she take out her anger on Elizabeth, who was trying so hard to befriend her.

God help me, Marsali thought, but I need a friend.

Tristan, who had been curled contentedly on the bed, roused himself to approach the unfamiliar girl. Elizabeth smiled with delight and knelt on the floor to hold out her hand.

"He bites," Marsali warned.

But Elizabeth's hand remained steady while Tristan sniffed it, then nuzzled it. In a moment, Isolde joined him, and they tumbled over each other in their eagerness to be fondled. Elizabeth seemed glad to comply.

"Isolde bit Patrick," Marsali said.

"He would not dare," Elizabeth replied in horror.

"She," Marsali corrected. "And she did. Tristan would have also, given the chance."

"But animals like Patrick," Elizabeth protested.

Marsali knew it was true, remembering not only the day Patrick had saved Antony from the hawk but the way he had handled the pet rabbit she had once owned and the firm but gentle manner he had with the horses at Abernie. The head stable lad had admired him greatly. She did not understand why Tristan and Isolde had not taken to him. Perhaps they sensed, where she had not, that he was untrustworthy.

Watching her pets make friends with Elizabeth, she mumbled grudgingly, "I suppose I should be grateful that he brought them when he took me."

"Patrick would do anything for you," Elizabeth said.

Marsali gave the girl a look of disbelief.

"He has been arguing with Fa. No one argues with him," Elizabeth stated gravely, as if she could ask for no more solid proof. Then, when Tristan rolled onto his back and squirmed to have his stomach rubbed—his favorite form of entertainment—Elizabeth forgot about any more serious matter and laughed aloud.

Marsali was stunned at how completely laughter changed the girl's face. The small worried furrows around her eyes and mouth disappeared, and her green eyes sparkled. Heartened by the change, Marsali yearned to take Elizabeth under her wing, to brush the dark brown hair until it shone, to instill in her the confidence she needed to straighten her back and lift her chin and challenge the world.

Not that she herself was doing very well in challenging the world at the moment.

The ferrets were darting in and out between chairs and bed, gowns and table, teasing Elizabeth to catch them. She plopped down on the floor, disregarding her gown, which was little more than a linen tunic, as totally absorbed in the little animals as they were in her.

For a few moments, Marsali forgot where she was and why she was there. She had missed her sister, and Elizabeth reminded her of Cecilia—although Cecilia's serious look came to her naturally, and Marsali suspected that Elizabeth's came from another source: fear. What had made the girl so afraid that she would thoroughly disguise her natural, outgoing nature? Suddenly Elizabeth sat up, her smile disappearing.

"We will be late," she said. "Father will be displeased."

And there was the answer: her father. Marsali was afraid of him, too, she acknowledged to herself. But she would never let him know it. The only reason she cared if he was displeased at their lateness was for Elizabeth's sake.

Deciding she had done all with her appearance that she could, she held out a hand to Elizabeth and helped her to her feet. The girl's present concern had not entirely erased the signs of recent pleasure from her face.

"You really are very pretty, you know," Marsali said to her.

Elizabeth blushed and murmured a polite, if somewhat disbelieving, "Thank you." Then, with her eyes glowing, she blurted out, "Oh, Marsali, I am so pleased you are here."

Marsali gave her a smile filled with genuine fondness.

She was ready to go down to dinner. She was a Gunn. She would not be daunted by the Sutherland men.

Giving Elizabeth a determined smile, she said, "I am ready. Let us both go beard the lion in his den."

Gregor Sutherland could not help but admire the Gunn wench. She hid her discomfort well as she approached where he sat in his chair in the great hall. She curtsied before him, and her blue eyes met his without flinching. Indeed, she was all grace and charm and composure. She had everything he wanted in a daughter-in-law. Everything except the right name.

He motioned her to a seat far down the table, not next to him or his family, as was customary. She did not acknowledge the slight but merely squeezed in between two large clansmen, ignoring, too, their awkwardness over her presence. Instead, she smiled at both and turned her attention to the food being placed in front of her.

Gregor felt uncomfortably bested. So he decided to attack.

Turning to Alex, he spoke in a booming voice. "Your

brother should be returning with our cattle soon. Bloody Gunn thieves."

He saw his daughter's face turn red and heard Alex gasp. The Gunn lass's face went ghost pale, and an unaccustomed shame filled him as she turned her steady gaze toward him.

All sounds of goblets clanging on wooden tables and amiable chatter ceased. Everyone turned to look at the Lady Marsali.

She slowly pushed back her chair and stood. Slender as she was, it occurred to Gregor that she could still dominate a room with her quiet dignity. She reminded him, in that way, of Margaret, which only made him even angrier.

"I was informed that I was a guest," she said, her voice trembling at first, then growing stronger. " 'An *honored* guest' were the words I believe your son used when he invited me to join you for your evening meal. Now that I know the value of Sutherland manners, I believe I would prefer to keep my own company."

Silence followed the soft sound of her slippers as she left the table and disappeared through the great doors.

"She has spirit. I can say that for her," Gregor grumbled. "Too bad she is a Gunn."

He bent over his meal once more. He owed the Gunns nothing. Not even simple courtesy. They were treacherous, all of them. And this one—she was like her aunt, all perfidy wrapped in pretty trappings. If Patrick could not see that, then it was up to him, his father, to show him. He would not want his son to suffer the same pain that he suffered every waking hour of his life.

When the gray mist lightened, heralding the coming dawn, Patrick mounted his stallion. His captives were all awake and all, he knew, fighting their bonds each time he glanced away from them. He had left himself little time to gain a lead over the Gunn riders who would surely follow him, but, by now, his raiders should have been able to scatter the stolen and reclaimed herd in the hills.

He spurred his horse, hearing a shout behind him. One of the men must have loosened his gag. Gavin, he guessed, would be less than an hour behind him. Would Johnny honor his word and give Gavin the message? Patrick believed he would. He was less sure that Gavin would heed his call.

As Marsali had her secret place, so did Gavin. Perhaps coincidentally, perhaps not, Gavin's hideaway was also a waterfall; in gentler times, he had often mused that brother and sister were, in some ways, much alike. Both were attracted to small, closed-in places where a person felt as if he had entered another world. He himself preferred an open meadow or a mountaintop.

Patrick remembered the pool of water beneath a waterfall, where he and Gavin had splashed as boys. It had been icy cold, but the frigid water had been part of the boyish challenge between them. On three sides of the pool, the cliffs rose high, making the spot inaccessible to riders from all but one direction. Yet the cliffs also provided dozens of hiding places, all easy to abandon. If Gavin brought riders with him, Patrick would know before they were sure he even was there.

Gavin, of course, knew that.

Patrick rode hard for an hour, then slowed, giving his black some rest. The mist had cleared, and a golden glow stretched over the mountains. He had missed that sight. He had missed these mountains.

He had missed Gavin.

Patrick reached the path leading up to the cliffs. He was a half day's ride from the border of his land, a full day's walk. But his horse could not climb, and he did not wish to leave him tied to a tree where, if everything went wrong, he might starve. Dismounting, he gave the animal a slap to its withers.

"Go home," he said. "Your job is done."

The horse needed no further urging. He headed for Brinaire, where he knew he would find feed in his trough.

Patrick climbed up among the rocks. And waited.

Gavin rode slowly to the pool, feeling the weight of disloyalty like an iron collar around his neck. He had not been to the pool in two years, not since the trouble started with the Sutherlands. The spot was close to the border, a small niche in the rugged terrain separating the two clans. But it was memories, not fear, that had kept him away.

He had never had a better friend than Patrick. He had loved Patrick as a brother, had missed him like the devil all the years he had been gone. He had also been secretly envious. Patrick had gone off to have adventures while he, as the only heir, had been required to stay home. He had heard tales of Patrick's exploits, his bravery, and had wished a thousand times to be at his side. He had lived vicariously through the troubadours who had sung his foster brother's praises, and he had hungered for deeds of his own.

Six years had passed since Gavin had last seen his friend, twelve since they had lived together at Abernie. Their world had changed in that time, and the changes were not, Gavin thought, for the better.

What did Patrick want? Why had he asked to see him alone? Was it a trap? Gavin had wrestled with his doubts after hearing the herder's message. Should he tell his father? Should he take others and try to capture Patrick, to exchange him for Marsali?

Gavin knew that, in his present state of mind, his father was capable of killing Patrick without hearing him out. In all his life, he had never seen rage like his father's when he had discovered Marsali gone. Donald Gunn claimed Patrick's explanation that he was claiming his betrothed bride was but a ploy to prevent the Sutherlands from being charged with kidnapping. Gavin thought it was bloody clever.

But if Patrick truly wanted Marsali—and peace—why had he taken the cattle? Surely, they were little enough payment for the Gunns' murdered clansmen, wounded children, and burned homes.

The greatest question, though, was why was he on his way to meet a man who was his family's enemy?

Unable to provide his conscience with a satisfactory response, Gavin gave up trying. In truth, he wanted to see his old friend. How much had Patrick changed? he wondered. Six years ago, he had been different—far different—than when he had first gone off to war. He had borne scars, and the lighthearted mischievousness was gone from his eyes. He had been harder, his laughter forced, his gaze cautious. Gavin recalled badgering Patrick to tell him about the battles he had fought, but Patrick would not; nor would he talk about the men he had killed.

Instead, he had looked at him and said, "I pray that you will never know how it feels to kill a man. It eats at your soul, Gavin. There is no glory in it."

At the time, he had thought there was no glory, either, in nursing cattle and sheep and helping his father preside over petty arguments.

No glory. Gavin touched the pistol he wore tucked into his belt, then the hilt of the dirk he carried.

When he reached the bottom of the path leading to the pool, his eyes began searching the cliffs around him. He must be daft, coming here alone, trusting a man he no longer knew, a man who had stolen his sister from her bedchamber. It would serve him right if there were a dozen Sutherlands concealed among the crags and rocks—and there very well could be.

But he heard no sound other than the music of the waterfall, saw nothing other than the rise of a hawk above the rocks and the ripples of the pool beneath the fall.

He pulled his horse to a halt, dismounted, and walked to the pool. He knew he was a perfect target for an arrow or a pistol shot. His fingers clenched into fists, but he would not take a weapon in his hand. He would not show fear.

Gavin forced himself to stare downward, at his reflection in the pool. Several minutes passed, and he continued to hear nothing. Suddenly, he knew he was no longer alone. A distorted face appeared beside his in the water's mirrored surface, and he turned.

Patrick stood beside him, his hands empty of weapons, his face expressionless, his eyes wary.

"Thank you for coming," he said.

"I am not certain why I did," Gavin said, feeling the stirrings of old friendship. He reminded himself that Patrick Sutherland was his family's enemy. Moreover, he was a man who could charm a wolf out of his supper.

"You came," Patrick began, "because you want this insanity to end as much as I do."

"Do you?" Gavin asked. "Then why did you take Marsali?"

"I feared your father would force her into a marriage with Sinclair," Patrick said. "I acted only after I was certain she didna want the marriage. Gavin, you know I have always cared for her. I still intend to make her my wife, and I swear to you she is well protected."

Searching Patrick's features, Gavin believed him, although he did not believe the explanation sufficient to justify kidnapping. A sudden thought occurred to him. "And Cecilia? Was her disappearance your doing, as well?"

"Aye," Patrick said, surprising him.

He had only been thrusting in the dark. He had believed Marsali's claim that she had done it all on her own. It did not help his mood to realize that she had lied to them, that she and Patrick must have met and concocted the plan together.

Gavin's hand went to the hilt of his dirk as he recalled the nights and days he had spent looking for his younger sister. "Is Cecilia at Brinaire?"

"No," Patrick said. "She is safe with a family in the south."

"She was *safe* with her own family," Gavin replied curtly.

"Was she?" Patrick asked. "Would you have approved of her marrying Sinclair if Marsali had refused? Christ help us, but she is only a child."

"Father never meant . . ." Gavin's voice trailed off. "I donna believe he would have gone through with it."

"But he would have sacrificed Marsali?"

"Sinclair is a suitable match," Gavin protested weakly.

"I thought you cared for her," Patrick said with contempt that stung Gavin to the core.

"*Your* father bears responsibility for that engagement," Gavin shot back. "Do you think Father could have gone through with your marriage to Marsali after *your* father disgraced Margaret, perhaps even murdered her?"

Patrick did not reply for a moment, then he said, "I want you to know that I had naught to do with that raid on your lands. Neither did my father."

Gavin's eyes narrowed. "Then who?"

"I donna believe you have to look farther than your chosen prospective brother-in-law," Patrick replied.

"Do you have proof?"

"No more than common sense."

"They were wearing your plaids."

"So I heard," Patrick said. "And one mentioned my name. But I wasna there, and if one could steal my name, they could certainly steal our plaids."

"Why?"

"Edward Sinclair wants an alliance with your clan. With it, he can wipe out the Sutherlands, which has been his most fervent desire all his life."

That much, Gavin could not deny. "Sinclair had nothing to do with Margaret," he pointed out.

Patrick cocked an eyebrow. "Did he not?"

Gavin stared at him. "Are you accusing Margaret . . ."

"Nay," Patrick said. "I was fond of her, and she was kind to my sister and brother. I donna believe she betrayed my father any more than you do."

The reply stunned Gavin. So did the direction of the conversation. He had expected denials, assurances of innocence. He had expected charges against Margaret and justifications for the marquis's inexcusable behavior.

Gavin walked away from the pool and leaned against the granite wall. "What do you want, Patrick?"

"First," Patrick said, "I want to know if you trust me."

Gavin uttered a harsh laugh.

"You trusted me enough to come alone."

"Aye," Gavin said, "but I called myself a fool the whole way."

"But you came."

Gavin hesitated. Finally, he spoke. "Aye, I came because I trusted the boy I grew up with and trained with. And I trusted the man who came home as an outlaw to see his loved ones. But six years has passed since then, and six years can do much to a man. I donna know if I trust who you are today, and so far your actions have not given me cause to think I can."

He saw Patrick's shoulders heave in a sigh. "You have reason to be skeptical, and you are right, six years can change a man. But no amount of time will change his nature." Pausing for a moment, he looked hard at his old friend. "Gavin, have I ever lied to you? Have you ever seen me hurt someone weaker than myself? Have I ever blamed anything I did on another?"

Gavin stared at the man who was both familiar and not, searching for any sign of guile. But he knew he could search forever and find none. Patrick Sutherland was neither a liar nor a bully, and he would never, as a matter of honor, allow someone else to shoulder the blame for something he had done.

"Nay," Gavin replied. "But your father—"

"My father is no saint, and no one knows that better than I. But he didna kill Margaret." When Gavin tried to interrupt him, he waved him off. "He truly felt betrayed, and he would have believed killing her to be within his rights. If he had done it, he wouldna have denied it."

"She didna kill herself," Gavin said. "She was still Catholic in her soul."

"Then she left of her own volition," Patrick said. "Or someone took her."

Gavin frowned. "If you are right, then someone is playing us all for fools."

"And who but one has reason?" Patrick replied softly. "King Charles is trying to bring order to the Highlands. If we fight each other, he could outlaw both of our clans. Who would be free to take our cattle and our land?"

"Sinclair," Gavin said, his mind spinning with the implications of what Patrick was proposing. If it was all true, the scheme was diabolical. "But if Sinclair is behind this and joined my father," he said, "he could be outlawed, as well."

Patrick shook his head. "Nay, not if he is clever enough. And so far he has been. In two years, no one has found even a trace of Margaret. And he has kept our fathers at each other's throats by making sure they blame each other."

"What do you propose?" Gavin asked warily.

"Can you talk to your father?"

"About your father?" Gavin gave a harsh laugh. "He will not even allow the name Gregor Sutherland to be spoken."

"And your clansmen?"

Gavin shook his head. "They would not go against him. Neither will I. It would destroy the clan if I were to try to usurp him."

Patrick sighed grimly. "And so we must find a way to keep two stubborn old men from bringing destruction to their clans for the sake of their own pride. I need to know, before we begin, if you still trust me. My plan willna work if you do not."

Gavin straightened. He looked into Patrick's clear green eyes and searched his own soul. He had watched his family slowly being destroyed over the past two years. His father was no longer a happy, genial man. Margaret, whom he had loved like a mother, had disappeared. His two sisters were gone. His clansmen had lost both lives and the cattle they needed to survive the coming winter.

But still and despite everything, he trusted Patrick Sutherland. God protect him, but he did.

Gavin nodded. "Aye, Patrick. I trust you. I donna think I would have come here today if I did not."

The reward for his honesty was seeing Patrick's face crease into a smile.

"I have a plan," Patrick said. "But first I have this to say, Gavin: By God, it *is* good to see you."

He held out his right hand, and Gavin stepped forward to take it, clasping each other's forearms with their other hands as they held each other's gaze. Still, a hint of awkwardness— or perhaps it was caution—kept Gavin from letting the handshake become the rough, bearlike embrace that had been their standard greeting, a test of strength as well as a show of masculine friendship. He would wait and see.

"Tell me of this plan of yours," he said, smiling at the eager look that lit Patrick's eyes and animated his features. It was so familiar. He had been afraid that, in learning how to hide his feelings, his friend had forgotten how to show them.

"Do you have people you can trust?" Patrick asked. "Men who donna have wives and children but who, perhaps, do have ties to Sutherlands?"

Gavin nodded his head. "Aye." God knows, their clans had been intermarrying for years. It was harder to find Gunn men *without* ties of some kind to Patrick's clan.

The scar on Patrick's face seemed to deepen as he grinned. It was an expression Gavin recognized, one that had inevitably gotten the two of them into trouble.

"All right," Patrick said. "Here is what I am proposing that we do."

By the time Gavin had heard the whole of Patrick's plan, he had decided that the past twelve years had rendered the Sutherland heir daft—although Patrick's eyes were quite clear, and he had given voice to his wild notions with complete confidence. His plan was insane. Utterly impossible. Gavin wished he had thought of it himself.

"We could both be disinherited," he said.

"Aye, we could be," Patrick agreed. "If we are caught."

Despite himself, Gavin felt a grin creeping across his face. Patrick was as audacious as ever.

"All right," he said. "I will do my part. You have my word on it." As he spoke, he felt some of the heaviness that had enveloped his soul fall away.

"I have missed you, friend," Patrick said softly. "You and Abernie."

"You will be back," Gavin said, amazed to see a glistening sheen appear briefly in Patrick's eyes.

It was the sun, he told himself. Why else would his own eyes be burning, too?

Chapter 11

Patrick returned to Brinaire to find Hiram and Rufus talking in the courtyard. The former was in a state of extreme agitation; the latter appeared unaffected.

"I thought to find ye dead," Hiram scolded as Patrick dismounted and handed his reins to the stable lad.

Patrick gave Rufus a nod of greeting and turned to Hiram. "The cattle are safe?"

"Scattered, like ye said," Hiram replied.

"Guards?"

"The ones ye chose. Patrick, do ye not know I always do as ye say?"

Patrick laughed. Hiram seldom did as he said but rather as he saw fit. Nevertheless, Patrick knew that, in the end, his interests were well served.

Turning to Rufus, he said, "And what do you have to say for yourself?"

Rufus bowed with a flourish. "Ye summoned me?"

"Aye, I missed your impertinent tongue."

"And my charm, no doubt."

Patrick nodded, waiting for an explanation.

Reading his silence correctly, Rufus spoke in casual tones—too casual, Patrick thought. "I wanted to be sure the young lass was comfortable."

"And is she?"

Rufus's saturnine face became inscrutable. "She appears content. I brought a message for the Lady Marsali, but I have no' had time to gi' it to her."

"I will take it," Patrick said.

"And why were ye so anxious for my return?"

"I know of a new employer for your unique talents."

"And who might that be?"

"Edward Sinclair."

Rufus flashed him an unholy grin. "Ye require my more devious skills, then."

"Mmm. I hear Sinclair is in need of mercenaries."

"And I, being the finest of them all, have a duty to accommodate him."

"I will miss your modesty."

"And my fine right arm."

Hiram coughed. Loudly.

"When do ye want me to leave?"

"Now," Patrick said. "While you were gone, there was an attack on the Gunns."

"Aye, Hiram told me."

"I want you to find out if, as I suspect, Sinclair was responsible. Also listen for word of a man called Quick Harry. He tried to follow the raiders and no one has seen him since."

"And when I uncover an evil plot?" Rufus asked with false humility.

Patrick smiled. "There is a wood near the Sinclair border. Hiram will show you the way. Pick a place. Either he or I will be there every Monday and Thursday at noon. If you learn anything, anything at all, meet us or leave a message."

Rufus nodded and turned to go.

"Rufus?"

He glanced back to raise a dark eyebrow.

"Stay alive."

Rufus nodded. "Aye, I will. I have reason now to want to live a long, long time."

Rufus's words echoed in Patrick's mind as he mounted the stairs toward the guest chamber. He, too, had reason to want to stay alive. If she would still speak to him.

As he approached Marsali's room, he noticed the door

ajar and heard voices and soft laughter. Weary as he was, his heart rebounded. Complete disaster had not occurred. He knocked on the partially open door and, without waiting for a reply, opened it to stand in the doorway.

Marsali and his sister, their faces flushed, were sitting on the bed, playing with the ferrets. His gaze made a thorough scan of Marsali, looking for any sign that the drug had caused her harm. But she looked well and, as always, lovely, wearing a dark blue tunic that matched her eyes. His sister's appearance, on the other hand, surprised him. Although Elizabeth's laughter seemed to have choked in her throat at the sight of him, her eyes were sparkling and her cheeks were a rosy pink; her otherwise ordinary features were transformed into a quite pretty face.

At that moment, one of the ferrets noticed him and bared its teeth. Chagrined, he watched as the small animals allowed his sister to fondle them while they bristled at him. Turning to Marsali, he found her gaze steadily upon him, searching, her eyes wide and appealing and so very, very blue.

Several moments of tense silence ensued until, finally, his sister murmured, "I must go." She handed the ferret she had been holding to Marsali, then hopped off the bed and scurried past him.

The ferret squirmed in Marsali's hands, ready to defend her with its small life.

"Can you convince him . . . or her . . . that I mean no harm?" Patrick asked.

She quirked an eyebrow. "Afraid?"

"Aye."

A smile flickered across her lips, then abruptly died. "Your father said you were going to Abernie to steal cattle," she said.

"It is not stealing to take back what is yours," he corrected.

"Was anyone . . ."

"Nay," he said gently. "No one was hurt."

She relaxed visibly.

He took a few steps into the room. "And you, Marsali, how did you fare?"

She said nothing, but something flashed in her eyes that told him all had not gone well.

"Father? What did he do?"

"No more than I expected from a Sutherland," she replied.

"That bad?" he teased, trying to coax a smile.

"Why does it matter to you?" she asked. "I am naught but your prisoner."

"Marsali . . ." He moved slowly toward the bed. When the ferrets bared their teeth again, chittering angrily, he came to a halt, muttering an oath.

She gave a brief laugh. "They sound like your father."

"He would not appreciate the comparison," Patrick replied, pleased to see that her spirit was intact.

Marsali took the two squirming ferrets from her lap, whispered something to them, and placed them in a basket Patrick imagined his sister must have provided. Then she stood, looking at him, her dark blue eyes as warm as a loch covered with frost.

"What do you want?" she asked.

He reached inside his belt and took out the piece of parchment Rufus had given him. "From your sister."

Without a word, she took it from him and held it, her fingers clenching it as if she expected him to take it away.

"Marsali?" He wanted so desperately to touch her.

She backed up a step, and he stopped.

He spoke in solemn tones. "I have not seen my sister laugh since I returned home. Thank you."

Amazed, he watched a tear appear at the corner of her eye. And as it did, the frost melted. Suddenly, her eyes were filled with pain and longing.

"Ah, lass . . ." Reaching across the space that separated them, he snagged her wrist and pulled her stiff body into his embrace, one of his hands gently wiping away the tear that had started rolling down her cheek. "Donna cry," he whispered. " 'Twill be all right." He would make it so if it took his last breath.

She started to speak, then closed her mouth, and he saw the veil come down over her eyes once again, shutting herself in, shutting him out. He could not ask her to trust him again, but, sweet God in heaven, he wanted to. He wanted her faith, her love. But he understood why he did not have them.

His hand fell to his side, and she immediately stepped away from him.

"I should leave you to read your letter in privacy," he said, but her voice stopped him from leaving.

"You look tired," she said.

So she still cared. At least a little.

"It has been a long night," he replied.

"For Gavin, too?"

Stunned, Patrick stared at her. It was as if she had read both his mind and his heart. When he did not reply immediately, she spoke again.

"You saw him, did you not?"

"Aye," he replied, unwilling to lie to her, yet cautious. The path upon which he and Gavin had embarked was fraught with danger, not the least of which was discovery. The fewer who knew about it, the better off—the safer—they would all be.

"Did you have words?" she asked.

He noticed her gaze skimming quickly over him, and he realized she was looking to see if he had come to harm.

"Aye," he said.

"You did not fight?"

"Nay."

"He was alone?"

"Aye."

"Then you *did* talk with him?"

"Aye."

"Can you say naught but nay and aye?"

"Only that you look very bonny this morning."

She stamped her foot in frustration, and the ferrets, shut inside their basket, started chittering again.

They both looked at the basket, then back at each other. For one long minute, their gazes held. The distance between them, although only a few feet, seemed like an ocean. He wanted to hold her, to soothe away the disillusionment he saw in her eyes. He wanted to be her hero, her star-catcher, once again. And, God help him, most of all, he wanted to kiss her and feel even a small spark of the wondrous fire that he knew lay there, waiting, for them.

But the time was not right. With every step she took away from him, she was telling him that she was not ready to yield.

"Patrick," she whispered, her tone anguished.

"I never wished to hurt you," he said hoarsely. "Marsali, I swear, I did not. God help me, I am trying to put a stop to all this."

Her lips trembled. "I want to believe you. But I donna see how taking me from my bedchamber, unconscious, or stealing cattle from outside Abernie's walls can be helping matters. It seems more like pouring oil on a fire already out of control."

He let out a heavy sigh. "I can but tell you that I believe I am doing the only thing that can be done to put an end to a war that no one wants."

"You are very good with words," she said. "You always could make magic with them, talk Gavin or me or even Fa into believing whatever you wanted us to believe. *I* came to believe you could do anything"—she uttered a bitter laugh—"even pluck stars from the sky. I thought you were different from other men, that you cared for more than battle and revenge."

"I do, lass," he said. "I care for a great deal more. Please—" He broke off, closing his eyes briefly. "Please, have faith. Just a while longer."

When he met her gaze once more, her look was wounded, accusing. "You want me to have faith, but you explain nothing. You expect me to be a mindless pawn in a game you—and Gavin, too, I suspect—are playing between our clans." Her frown deepened. "All those years, I was so proud of you every time I heard another tale of your bravery and the victories you had won. But now"—she shook her head—"now I have seen the price you and other men are willing to pay for such reputations. I know now that there is nothing noble about creating widows and orphans. There is no honor in wounding innocents. And there is certainly no valor in death and destruction." She closed her eyes. "I want no part of your game."

"I want no part of you." Patrick heard only the words she did not speak. They could not have been clearer if she had said them aloud.

He turned away from her to face the window, his back rigid with the effort it took not to cry out his anguish, for no wound he had received on the battlefield had ever cut more deeply. For a long time, he stared sightlessly at the mountains that stretched across the horizon. When he thought he could speak without breaking, he turned back to her, though he did not meet her gaze.

"I apologize for the inconvenience I have caused you," he said. "I will return you as soon as possible to Abernie. I know you do not believe me—and of course there is no reason you should—but there are things I must do first." He heard the iciness in his voice, but he could not alter it. "If you require anything, please ask Elizabeth. She will see to it."

Before she could say anything more, he crossed the room and closed the door softly behind him.

Hurt and angry and utterly bewildered, Marsali stared after him. She did not regret her words, though they had caused her deep pain. If there could be no truth between them, then they had nothing worth saving. They could not build a life on mutual desire alone, not even a desire so strong that it crackled in the air like lightning every time their eyes met.

She did not know this man who talked of ending the conflict between their families at the same time he held her hostage and raided her clan's cattle. She did not understand him, the enigmatic man who, one moment, could be so tender and, the next, so ruthless. No, she neither knew nor understood him.

If only, God help her, she did not love him.

Chapter 12

The mountains called to him, the mist-shrouded peaks that had always given him a measure of peace. He rode toward them, Marsali's eyes haunting him over every mile he traveled. Over and over, he saw her pain, her confusion. Her horror as she looked at him and saw truly, for the first time, who he had become.

Had she seen death on his face? Could she tell that every line was a hatch mark for a soul he had destroyed? Did she know his fear, the terror that had dogged every minute he had spent on the battlefield? Whatever she had seen, whatever she understood, she did not like it. Of that much, he was certain.

Spurring his large bay into a gallop, Patrick crossed a grassy meadow between two rocky peaks. The bay felt sluggish beneath him, and he curbed the impulse to take out his feelings on the animal. He preferred a fine gray that he had found in his father's stable, but one of the first lessons he had learned as a warrior was never to choose a distinctive horse when he knew he might encounter enemies.

The hut that was his destination was not much farther. Legend had it that his Sutherland kinsmen had used the place when being hunted by the English during Edward the Hammer's reign. It was old but sturdy, with walls of stone, and it was well hidden by the forest. Except for an occasional hunter, the ancient structure was seldom occupied; it was simply too far away from Brinaire, and the land surrounding it was too rocky for farming or grazing.

If his stepmother had wanted a truly secret place for trysting, the hut would have been a good choice.

Patrick's horse climbed over rocky paths and through narrow passages, past a waterfall that went tumbling over jagged, iron-gray rock. He looked up at the peaks that disappeared into the sky. He was wet from the moisture in the air, a fine mist that coated everything, yet he felt no discomfort.

His father had brought him to this place once, before he had gone to foster with the Gunns.

"Remember the Sutherlands that have gone on before you," his father had said as they stood together surveying the northern reaches of their land. His father had told him the legend of the hut, how their ancestors had fought with William Wallace against Edward, then with Robert the Bruce. They had been hunted and outlawed, and they had survived because they were united.

"Never forget your clan, lad. 'Tis the most important thing in life. More important than God, or even family. More important than life itself."

Patrick had looked up in astonishment at the tall, distant man, at the unusual passion that transformed his face.

"Promise me, lad," his father had said. "Swear on your life, your honor, that your clan will always come first."

Patrick had promised. At six years old, he had not known exactly what his vow meant, but he would have done anything to win approval from his father. And if he had not known then what he had promised, he had since learned. It had been hammered into his head, over and over again by the same man who had extracted the oath from him. That sworn oath had been used to send him to fight with Montrose, and later others.

Knowing how his father felt about clan loyalty, Patrick realized it must nearly have destroyed the old man to believe his wife had cuckolded him in a place that held so much meaning for the Sutherlands. Standing there now, he wondered who else would know of its importance to the marquis of Brinaire. Perhaps Donald Gunn; yes, his father might have told his longtime friend during one of their hunting trips.

For a moment, Patrick entertained the wish that Marsali were here, with him, and that he could tell her his thoughts and listen to hers. That together they could work out what might have happened two years ago to her aunt.

But in truth, he had held his own counsel for so long that he would not have known how to do otherwise, as much as he wanted to share himself with the woman he loved. Even Hiram and Rufus seldom knew what he was planning until it was absolutely necessary to tell them. In this way, he had to acknowledge, he was his father's son.

The underbrush was heavy near the hut, the path almost overgrown. Patrick wondered whether anyone had been there in the last two years. His father would have searched the place for evidence, would have taken anything he thought was helpful, and yet Patrick felt he had to look.

He pulled his horse to a halt in front of the hut, dismounted, and tied the animal to a low branch. He started toward the old structure, only to be stopped in his tracks by the sight of a dark blotch on the earth in front of him. He found another a few paces ahead, then another near the door. He had seen enough of those dark blotches to know their origin.

Opening the door to the hut with one hand, he kept his other hand on the dirk tucked into his belt. Light entered the tiny room with him, and his gaze went immediately to a figure lying on a filthy pile of straw in the corner. He quickly scanned the rest of the interior, found nothing of concern, then strode over to stoop at the prone man's side.

Patrick recognized him immediately. Anyone who had ever spent a night at Abernie knew Quick Harry. His gaze took in the rust-colored stains on Quick Harry's plaid at the same time he put his fingers to the injured man's neck. His breath rushed out when he found a pulse, though it was weak and thready. Quick Harry's skin was hot and his breathing labored.

Unwrapping the blood-soaked plaid, Patrick saw the sword stroke across Harry's chest. The slash was wicked looking, and infected, but not deep. Fever had downed him, fever and loss of blood. Patrick was amazed Harry had reached the hut, given that the raid had taken place many miles to the north.

Helplessly, Patrick stared at the wound and damned himself for not bringing anyone or anything with him. No wine. No water. No food. No help.

But Quick Harry could not afford the time he was wasting on self-chastisement. The first thing the injured man needed was water.

It did not take long to search the hut or to find that all of the crockery had been smashed; shards littered the floor. Violence had also been done to the chairs and table; what was left of them were mere sticks. For a brief moment, Patrick saw the scene in his mind, saw his father systematically destroying everything.

Clenching his jaw, he looked closer and finally found a chunk of broken crockery that seemed solid enough to hold water. He ran to the stream that meandered nearby, where he collected as much water as the pitiful excuse for a cup would hold. Then he set about waking the injured man.

He tried gently at first. When that did not work, he tried shaking the man. Patrick did not want Quick Harry to slide easily into oblivion, and he admitted to himself that his motives were not entirely unselfish. Harry had to know something, had to have seen something. And he did not want another man's soul on his conscience.

A soft, agonized moan told him that Harry had not entirely given up.

"Harry," he said. Then louder, "Harry!"

Eyes flickered open, shut, then open again. They were a milky blue. Unseeing. But slowly they seemed to focus and come to rest on the plaid Patrick wore. Harry started to push him weakly away, but Patrick held him down.

"Nay," he said softly. "Ye are in safe hands. I willna hurt ye." He let his speech lapse into the dialect he had spoken as a child, before the tutors, a language he knew Harry would more easily understand and find soothing.

"Water."

"I ha' some for ye," Patrick said. He put his hand behind the man's back, helping him up enough to swallow water. Then he guided the broken crockery to Harry's mouth and watched as he drank greedily.

When he had taken the last drop, Quick Harry looked at him. "Ye . . . be Patrick Sutherland."

"Aye," Patrick said, meeting Quick Harry's eyes. "And I ha' naught to do wi' the raid. I suspect ye ken tha'."

"I followed," the man said. "I followed on foot. I heard yer name spoke, but I remembered ye as a lad. I knew ye were no' among them." Quick Harry tried to rise, then groaned with the effort.

"Where did they go?" Patrick asked.

"South. Toward yer land." The effort to speak was draining him. Still, he asked, "My wife? My son?"

"Safe at Abernie," Patrick said. He could not bring himself to tell the man that his son had been gravely injured.

Quick Harry sighed. "Demmed villains. I wa' following, and one saw me. He came back. Thought he ha' killed me, but I only played dead."

"How did you get here?"

"Came on it as a boy," Harry said.

"Did you see any faces, mon?"

"Only one. The rest were painted. I ha' ne'r seen this one b'fore and I willna forget. He be the one who came back fer me. As ugly a face as I ha' ever seen, and he spoke wi' a rasp. He laughed as he swung the sword. I ha' ne'r heard sech a terrible sound."

"A rasp?" Patrick's heartbeat quickened. "The man spoke?"

"Aye, he said . . ." Quick Harry moaned again.

"He said . . . ?" Patrick prompted.

Harry's eyes fluttered. "He said . . . . 'Ye ran all tha' way for naught, old mon.' "

"Not for naught," Patrick said softly. "I will fetch you some more water, and then go for help."

"The . . . raid?"

"It wasna Sutherlands," Patrick said. "I swear it. I would take ye to Brinaire, but I fear ye might not make the journey. Ye've already lost much blood, and I canna take a chance ye might reopen that wound. I will bring help back to ye. Food, medicine, bandages."

Quick Harry looked at him with red, watery eyes. "I didna think it could be ye, Lord Patrick."

Patrick savored the rough sincerity of the man's words. He would need the trust of both clans before this was over. If he had to gain it one by one, then so be it.

He did what he could to make Harry comfortable, then he started a fire in the hearth with the broken pieces of furniture, piling it high. It would be late—and much colder—before he returned. Then, reassuring Harry that he would be back, he ran for his horse.

As Patrick rode for Brinaire, a single memory overwhelmed him. A raspy voice. An ugly face. A description that could fit many men. But one man haunted Patrick. The man was dead; he had to be.

But he could not dismiss it. Nor could he dismiss the dread that filled him.

Marsali stood in the middle of Brinaire's courtyard, hugging herself against the cold wind that was blowing in over the mountains. Had she been wrong to speak her mind as she had? She had not meant to drive Patrick away. Not entirely.

Surely, he would not leave her here, alone, among her enemies.

But morning went by, then midday, and she did not see him. Elizabeth and Alex both claimed ignorance of his whereabouts. Finally, when she could not stand pacing the floor of her chamber any longer, she had tried the door and been surprised to discover it was not locked. Gathering her courage, she had gone in search of Hiram.

No one had stopped her from walking out of the castle. As she ventured cautiously across the courtyard, some curious glances had followed her, but few hostile ones. She had thought about simply trying to walk out the gates, but then she had noticed the two men behind her. To give them credit, they were being discreet, but as she stood wondering where to go next, she could not help but be aware of their presence.

At about the time she decided she might as well go back inside, Hiram appeared from the stable. He hurried to her side as soon as he spotted her.

"Lady Marsali," he said, his tone worried. "Be there something ye wanted?"

He was standing so close—hovering, really—that she had to tip her head almost all the way back to look at him. Dear heaven, he was huge. "I was looking for Patrick," she said.

Hiram shifted uncomfortably, which had the fortunate effect of putting a bit more distance between them and allowing her neck to assume a more reasonable angle.

His expression was sheepish as he replied, "I am sorry, but I donna know where he went."

She was not sure she believed him, but then, it was hard to know what to believe anymore.

"Is Rufus here, then?" she asked. "I received the letter he brought from my sister, but I would like to hear from him how she is faring." Actually, Cecilia's letter had been so dotted with references to Rufus that she had decided she should assess the man more thoroughly for herself. "Would you tell me where to find him?"

Hiram shifted again on his feet. "He has gone, milady."

"Already? Where?"

"I canna say."

Her lips thinned. "Canna or willna?"

His face turned red, and Marsali immediately felt guilty. She was directing her anger at someone who was not responsible for her situation. Hiram was following orders—orders issued by Patrick.

She turned away, toward the stables. Perhaps she would look at the horses. Deep in her mind were thoughts of escape.

Behind her, Hiram spoke in a low rumble meant only for her ears. "He loves ye, milady."

She stopped, her back to Hiram, her breath caught in her throat.

"And ye are not as alone as I ken ye feel," he said.

She swung around to face him again, the sturdy Scots Highland face framed by red hair. His eyes were light blue, his nose crooked as if it had been broken, his lips full with a bit of a twist at one end. It was a solid face, a comforting face. A face her intuition once would have told her she could trust. But she was in an enemy camp, and she had been brought here by the last man her intuition had told her to trust.

"How long have you been with him?" she asked, and watched the skin around Hiram's eyes crinkle as he smiled.

"Och, eight years or better," he said. "I would follow him to hell and back."

"Why?"

He shrugged. "Why does any mon follow another? He sees a better mon, mayhap, a mon he wants to be."

"Do *you* want to be like Patrick?"

Hiram chuckled. It came from deep within his barrel chest. "At one time, mayhap. He is a foine leader and braw fighter. But I donna have his conscience, lass. Neither would I like to have it. A conscience is a liability in a warrior."

"Then why do you stay with him?"

"Because I admire him more than any mon I ha' ever known. I know he would never desert me, never abandon me, never betray me. 'Tis not many men I would trust wi' my life."

She was silent a moment, then spoke softly, mostly to herself. "I wish that I believed as strongly as you do."

Hiram heaved a sigh. "Sometimes, he can be a hard man to ken. He keeps his thoughts to hisself. Rufus makes up for him. Blethers on about everything. Patrick, now, he's a mon who thinks things through first, then speaks." He smiled down at her. "But his eyes light up every time he looks at ye, milady. He even gets a little befuddled. 'Tis a joy to see him act like a mortal man. Truly, it is."

Marsali could not prevent a small smile from curling the corners of her lips at the thought of a befuddled Patrick. She had seen him tender and passionate, playful and serious, hurt and angry. She had never seen the slightest sign of befuddlement. She thought she would like to see that, very much.

In fact, despite her confusion about him, Marsali felt as though she was seeing new sides of Patrick every day. She understood now, in a way she had not before, what it must have been like for him, living here at Brinaire as a small boy. He was already living at Abernie when she was born, and she had grown up knowing a boy whose smile could beguile anyone. But now that she had met Elizabeth and Alex, now that she had spent even a single day in the same house with Gregor Sutherland, she wondered whether Patrick, as a wee child, had been more like his brother and sister. Whether smiles had been infrequent and happiness a rare commodity. It was not hard at all, thinking in those terms, to imagine him confused, insecure. Lost.

But Patrick was no longer that little boy. He was a grown

man who had been to war. He exuded confidence. He never seemed even slightly bewildered, no matter what Hiram said. And he certainly seemed to know where he was going—even if he did not care to share that knowledge with her.

And, her conscience reminded her, he had come home to find his home and his family in shambles, his twelve-year betrothal broken, and his clan on the verge of a bitter and bloody feud.

If only he would come back . . .

Seeking refuge from the anxiety that was threatening to turn into panic, Marsali glanced at Hiram. "Do you have a family?" she asked.

"Nay," he shook his head. "Most were killed by the English. The rest were proscribed and scattered to the winds. They were stubbornly Catholic, and independent." He looked toward the mountains, remembering. "I was fostering with another family when it happened. I returned to find an Englishman lording over our land. Never did like them joyless bas—"

He stopped in midsentence and Marsali saw a tightness to his mouth and a coldness in his eyes that chilled her. This was not the good-natured man who blushed easily and appeared so awkward. This was a different man altogether.

Just as Patrick was sometimes so different. Was it always so with men? Were there always two of them inside the same body?

A strong gust of wind swirled through the courtyard, flattening her gown against her. She shivered, but it was not only from the cold. The lessons she was learning about men and their way of life were not pretty ones.

Hiram looked at the clouds overhead. "Ye best go back inside, my lady. 'Tis going to be growing colder."

"I would like a ride, Hiram. Can you arrange it?"

"No, my lady, I canna," he said. "But I will ask Patrick's sister to find ye a warm shawl."

"I donna want a warm shawl. I donna want to wait here

for Patrick's convenience." Suddenly, without warning, a tear hovered in the corner of her eye, but she resisted the impulse to brush it away.

Hiram shuffled his feet. "I will try to find him," he finally said.

She glared at him, unwilling to give him quarter. "And you might as well tell him I will starve before I eat at his father's table again."

"Aye, my lady," he replied, troubled.

She wanted to say more, but she knew it was no use. He would not go against Patrick's wishes, no matter how much she pleaded. Nor would she humble herself any further.

Turning into the freezing wind, she walked back toward the castle.

Fighting exhaustion, Patrick galloped into the small village east of Brinaire, to the cottage of Bridie Fitzpatrick. Her father had been a Sutherland, but it was said her mother had been a gypsy. It was also said that Bridie had the Sight, as well as a talent for the healing arts. When her husband died, she had returned to live with her aunt, who was a midwife, and together they had served the Sutherlands. Now her aunt was gone, too, and Bridie survived by collecting herbs and making potions. Love potions, healing potions, potions to scare away spirits.

Patrick did not know Bridie. She had not come to live with her Sutherland kinsmen until after he had left Brinaire to foster with the Gunns, but he had heard enough stories about her during his visit home six years earlier that he remembered her reputation.

He did not know exactly what to expect as he strode up to her cottage door and raised his hand to knock. But he did not knock even once before the door opened.

The woman who stood in the doorway was gaunt, her hair black as a gypsy's and her eyes just as dark. He saw instantly that she had been a handsome woman once; vestiges of a kind of ageless beauty remained. Her eyes were piercing, knowing, and her face unwrinkled, though he guessed her to be over sixty.

"Milord," she said.

Her unsurprised tone made him raise an eyebrow. "You were expecting me?"

She appeared amused. "Everyone comes to me."

"Everyone?"

"Aye. At some time or another. And what would your need be? A love potion, mayhap. I hear of an angry young lass."

The cynic in him said it would require no special talent to guess that Marsali was furious. Most people would assume it. By now, everyone knew he had written to her father saying he had kidnapped her.

Nonetheless, he was fascinated by the woman's confidence. "Do you hear of everything?" he asked.

" 'Tis not difficult if you keep your ears open," she said.

He smiled. "I think I would like to talk to you more, but at the moment, I need healing herbs. Poultices—for a festering wound."

She stared at him for a moment as if taking his measure. He felt uncomfortable under her dark eyes, but then she nodded. "I will get what ye need. Come in."

He took a few steps inside. Flames played in the fireplace, and herbs of all kinds hung from the thatched roof. A variety of smells mingled with the familiar odor of peat, turning it sweet and soothing. Patrick watched as Bridie gathered an assortment of minced herbs from containers and carefully sorted them into two piles, putting one batch into a leather pouch and the other into a bottle.

"The contents of the pouch are for the wound," she instructed as she worked. "It contains meal as well as herbs. Mix it with water and spread on cloth. The other is to be taken by mouth. It should help lower a fever." She added several pieces of clean linen, wrapped them all up in a larger piece of cloth, and tied it together with a piece of hemp.

Patrick took several gold coins from his pocket and handed them to her. "My thanks."

Her dark eyes seemed to bore into him. "Come again, milord."

Again, he had the odd impression that she knew something that concerned him. He nodded. "I will do that." As he turned to leave, she spoke again.

"And milord," she said, "take care. There be danger out there for ye."

He stopped in the doorway to look back at her, his eyes searching her face. "Is there something I should know?"

"Nay, milord. Just a feeling. I sense death."

"I have known enough of it, Mistress Fitzpatrick. I fear it clings to me."

"Bridie," she insisted. "Everyone calls me Bridie."

"Bridie, then," he said, then gave her a nod in parting.

He would need a fresh horse, water, food, and blankets, he thought as he mounted and spurred his horse onto the road toward Brinaire. If he hurried, he might get back to the hut before the wee hours of the morning, before true darkness came. He blessed the long gloaming hours of this time of year, the long dusk that stretched late into the night.

He hoped he would have company for that ride. Willing company.

Marsali took supper in her room. She had debated the matter carefully, hating to give the old marquis the pleasure of her absence, yet determined not to give him another opportunity to publicly humiliate her. Finally, the former seemed the less hateful choice.

She picked at the fish and partridge that had been brought on her tray, finding it ill cooked. But then all of Brinaire seemed bedraggled and mismanaged. She had seen few servants. Indeed, it had been Elizabeth who had brought everything to her, and the great hall had been in shambles each time she had seen it. Brinaire was no longer grand and stately, as she remembered it.

She took another bite of fish, trying to apply her thoughts to plans for escape. She felt it her duty to try. But it was hard to concentrate on such weighty matters when the problem under her nose kept distracting her attention. Lord above, but the food was inedible.

Still, she was hungry. And the tunics Elizabeth had selected for her fell gracelessly from a body that was no longer merely slender but far too thin. Taking a deep breath, she forced herself to take another bite of the partridge.

She wished Elizabeth were with her, but the girl had been summoned to supper. As clear as it had been that she wanted to stay, she would not disobey her father.

Marsali handed a piece of fish to one of her ferrets, then became dismayed when even greedy Tristan sniffed disdainfully and refused it. Isolde chittered away, as if scolding her for providing such inferior food. It was a mean state of affairs when one of the oldest and most noble houses in the Highlands provided food for guests that even a ferret would not eat.

Finally, Marsali rose, put the ferrets in the basket, and headed for the chamber door. She would try a trip to the kitchen, both for her stomach's sake and to see how much freedom she had. She opened the door, expecting to see her huge Sutherland guard outside of it. Instead, she found Patrick.

Stunned, she simply stood there, staring at him. He had shaved off the growth of beard that had shielded his scar, but he had a day's worth of new bristle.

She wanted to be angry at him. But any furious words she might have hurled at him died when she looked at his eyes. They were very green—and incredibly tired. And his face was lined with both weariness and worry.

"Marsali," he said. "I need help."

And with those few simple words from him, she was lost.

Chapter 13

Marsali relished the feel of the cold wind against her face and the smooth gait of the horse beneath her. Both spelled freedom. After more than a month of captivity, her exuberant spirit savored every sensation.

Patrick rode at her right, Hiram to her left. But they were not guards. They had become companions—fellow conspirators in a mysterious adventure. After Patrick had come to her and asked for help, they had slipped silently down the stone steps and out the great door to where Hiram waited, mounted on one huge horse and holding the reins of three others.

Patrick had helped her into the sidesaddle of a small bay gelding, then bounded into the saddle of a sleek black stallion. The fourth horse was laden with full sacks; what the sacks contained, she did not know. With a grin in her direction, Patrick had spurred his horse forward. The three of them galloped out of Brinaire, leaving the guards at the gate staring dumbfounded.

She had no idea what Patrick intended. No idea where they were going. And she did not care. They were sharing an adventure and he needed her help. She could not have refused the plea in his eyes if her life had depended upon it. And she liked the dashing, reckless way he was behaving. It spoke to her own need to take control of a situation in which she felt she had none.

When Hiram winked at her, any lingering apprehensions she may have felt were dispelled. Hiram had no guile about him.

They rode hard, their horses' hooves pounding over the

rocky terrain as they traveled north. A wild, pulsing delight filled her as the wind tangled her hair and buffeted her body, and the smell of heather scented the air. The night itself seemed magical, the time of the gloaming—the long hours where twilight hovered and streaks of gold painted the sky above the rugged Highland mountains.

They were going deeper into Sutherland land, into the wilderness where little survived other than hardy flowers and gnarled trees and wild animals. No fields. No sheep or cattle. The territory was new to her, and she drank it in as they wound around steep paths, finally emerging on the floor of a valley. There, the rocky ground forced them to slow, the horses picking their way across the valley to a wood, where a hut, sitting protected by trees, soon came into sight.

Patrick swung out of the saddle, then helped her dismount. He kept his hands on her waist, and she looked up to meet his gaze. The devil-may-care light in his eyes was more subdued, and his tone was serious as he spoke.

"Someone inside needs your healing skills," he said.

She sucked in a quick breath. "Who?"

Maddeningly, he did not answer but, instead, went back to his horse, untying the bags from his saddle and slinging them over his shoulder. Then, with Hiram at his heels, he headed for the door, opening it wide to allow in the light.

The man was infuriating, she thought, never uttering a single word that did not absolutely have to be spoken. With a sound of frustration, Marsali followed Patrick and Hiram into the cottage.

It was cold inside, the only source of heat the dying embers in the fireplace. Her gaze went to the form of a man lying on a bed of straw. An instant later, she was on her knees beside him.

"Quick Harry," she said softly, placing a hand on his face. The injured man did not stir at her touch, but she knew he was alive; indeed, he was burning up with fever. Raising her gaze, she found Patrick looking at her over his shoulder as he built a fire in the hearth.

"I found him here," he said. "Earlier today."

She would have answers to her myriad questions later. Now she had work to do.

"Harry," she said again, trying to stir him. She took his hand and squeezed it tightly.

His eyes opened, blinked, then he tried a weak smile. "Lady Marsali," he whispered. "How . . ."

"Patrick Sutherland brought me," she said.

"He said he would bring help. My wife . . . my son? Have ye seen them?"

"Both at Abernie," she said.

He released a sigh of relief. "The Sutherland said as much, but . . ."

Marsali glanced at Patrick, who was nudging the fire to life. If he had heard the doubt in Quick Harry's voice, he gave no indication that he was offended by it.

"Here. Ye might be needing this." Hiram squatted beside her to offer Quick Harry a flagon of wine.

She saw that the big Scot had emptied one of the sacks, piling the articles on a blanket in a corner of the hut: several loaves of bread, potatoes, a roasted chicken. Marsali sincerely hoped the chicken was better than the one she had eaten at Brinaire, lest it finish Quick Harry before the wound had its chance. Seeing the food, she had to wonder how long Patrick intended to keep Quick Harry here. Given the number of sacks, there must be enough food for several weeks.

"Who be ye?" Quick Harry asked Hiram, his voice weak but suspicious.

"A mon bearing gifts," Hiram said, "and a friend to Patrick Sutherland and, I hope, to the young lass."

Quick Harry looked to Marsali for confirmation.

She wished she felt certain in giving it. She liked Hiram, but he was clearly Patrick's man.

She felt as if she were navigating rough seas with no compass. Grabbing hold of the most expedient course for getting Harry help, she simply nodded, and Quick Harry took the flagon, his shaking hand guided by Hiram's strong, steady one. He took a long draught, then smiled faintly, his hand dropping. Hiram caught the wine before it fell.

Quick Harry was weak, too weak. He needed more than wine, and his wounds needed stitching. Marsali wished that Patrick had told her the purpose of their mission before they had left Brinaire; she could have brought what she required.

No sooner had she completed that thought than Patrick dropped down beside her and spread another blanket on the earthen floor. He began emptying one of the other sacks onto the blanket. She watched as he laid out each item. A needle. A spool of rough thread. Pieces of cloth. Powders.

He caught her startled look and gave her a brief smile. "A healer gave me herbs for poultices and other things you might be needing."

Patrick Sutherland, she was learning, was not a man who left anything to chance.

As she examined Quick Harry's injuries, she noted that someone—undoubtedly Patrick—had already cut away the cloth around his wound and cleaned it as well as possible. The skin was red around the wicked slice, and the wound was seeping yellowish blood. It had already been much too long. Four days.

"Give him some more wine," she told Hiram. "I have to sew up that wound, and it will be painful."

Hiram helped lift Quick Harry's head and put the flagon back to his lips. Marsali watched as he sipped slowly, his lashes slipping over his eyes even as he tried to stay conscious.

Marsali smelled the powders that Patrick had set out on

the blanket. She recognized them all, and they were exactly what she would have selected. Taking one bottle—a mixture comprised mostly of powdered Saint-John's-wort—she sprinkled its contents in the wound, then readied the needle and thread. Meeting Patrick's gaze as he crouched on the other side of the blanket, she asked, "Will you heat some water?"

"Aye." He rose to see to the task.

Marsali still did not understand why Patrick would want to save the life of a Gunn clansman, but she was grateful that he did. She was also grateful that he trusted her skills as a healer. His faith in bringing her here said more than simple words could.

Trying to be as gentle as possible, Marsali cut away the damaged skin, washed the wound as best she could, and started a row of stitches in the gaping flesh, bringing the edges together to stop the bleeding. Although Quick Harry grimaced with the pain she caused him, he made no sound.

The process was slow. As she worked, she wondered why Patrick had not simply taken Quick Harry to Brinaire—or sent him with Hiram to Abernie. And what was Quick Harry doing here on Sutherland land, so far from home, in the first place?

She looked at the blood soaked into Quick Harry's clothes, remembering his wounded son and the awful night of the raid. Had they suffered injury because of her? Because she had refused to marry Edward Sinclair? Because Patrick had returned and given her a reason and a means to resist? Indeed, had Patrick's return been the catalyst for simmering violence?

When she had finished sewing, she sat back on her heels and drew a deep breath. She only hoped she had not locked the poison inside the wound. " 'Tis all, Quick Harry," she said. "The worst is finished. You can relax now."

Quick Harry offered her a weak smile, then closed his eyes once more.

Marsali rose and went to the fire. Wordlessly, Patrick took a bowl of water from the flames and set it down next to the herbs. She put what she needed into the bowl, added meal to the solution, and mixed it together. Then she spread the paste across a piece of cloth and placed the cloth over Quick Harry's wound, watching his mouth tighten at the sudden heat against his injured flesh.

" 'Twill draw out the poison," she said. "In the meantime, you must eat and drink. I am going to make a broth with some chicken, and I will want you to drink as much of it as possible."

He nodded, and she left Hiram kneeling next to him, urging what water and wine he could drink on him.

Patrick covered the wounded man with several blankets, then stood to lean against the wall beside the hearth. His stance seemed casual, even lazy, but she knew the appearance was deceptive; she sensed the tension in his hard, lean body, and she felt his gaze on her, watching every move she made, as she cut the chicken into a pot, added water, and set it in the fire to simmer. When it was ready, she would add the herbs from the bottle Patrick had brought.

While she was preparing the broth, Hiram left Harry's side and murmured that he was going to tend the horses. When Marsali straightened from her task, she met Patrick's gaze, wondering if he could read the questions in her eyes.

He nodded toward Harry. "Will he live?"

"With God's help," she said. "Thank you for bringing me to him. He is a dear friend."

"I want no more deaths on my conscience," Patrick said without emotion.

"Do you have so many, then?"

"Enough."

His tone did not invite further inquiry, and Marsali let it go.

Almost afraid to hear the answer, she asked, "What are you going to do with Quick Harry?"

Patrick heaved a sigh. "Hopefully see him hale again."

Marsali chewed on her lip for a moment. "Do you hope to use him as another hostage?"

When he did not answer immediately, she thought that it must be true. His motives had not been altruistic at all. She wondered if there was anything she, or anyone else, could say to change his mind.

"Quick Harry saw the face of one of the raiders."

Patrick's quiet words made the breath catch in her throat. Her gaze flew to his, and for a moment, she was afraid to speak. "A . . . Sutherland?" she finally managed.

Patrick shook his head. "He didna recognize the man, but he described him. I think I might know who he is. And he is no Sutherland."

"Then who?"

"A man I once knew," Patrick said. Then, hesitating, he pushed off from the wall and paced to the opposite side of the tiny cottage. Turning to face her, he said, "Marsali, no one must know that Quick Harry is alive, or that he could recognize this man."

"He would be safe at Abernie," she said, taking a step toward him.

"I canna be sure of that."

"But his wife!" she exclaimed. "You canna let her think he is dead."

"I believe he is safer that way," Patrick said implacably.

"*You* believe," she mocked, angry at the implication that someone at Abernie was a traitor.

"I *know*," he answered quietly. "Marsali, I have been gone too long, and I have learned to trust very few men. I have also learned that treachery comes easy to far too many Scots. I saw it with Montrose, with men who turned against him." He shook his dark head. "I put faith in no man, other than Hiram and Rufus."

Marsali understood at least a bit of how he felt. She, too, had lost faith in those she trusted. Still, in her heart, she chose to think the best of most people. To go through life believing in only two men? She could not imagine it.

"And Gavin?" she asked.

Patrick's eyes shuttered, a muscle jerking in his scarred cheek.

Marsali sighed. She was weary of men's pride, heartsick over their stubborn and unreasonable sense of honor, which sent other men—and women—to their deaths. She did not want to believe that Patrick was as prideful and unreasonable as all the others, but at the moment she could not be sure.

She looked up at him through narrowed eyes, measuring him. "So, you will keep Quick Harry prisoner?"

"I will keep him safe," Patrick replied.

"Because you need him."

"Because he is hurt and he was once a friend. Because I would do it for any man." Briefly, a wry smile pulled the scarred side of his mouth upward. "Well, almost any man," he corrected.

"There are those you wouldna help?" she asked.

"A few. Or, at least, I would do so with . . . difficulty." When she only stared at him, he shrugged. "A soldier makes enemies, lass. Alliances shift." He uttered a humorless laugh. "Our families have proven that to you, surely. I never would ha' believed the Gunns would join with the Sinclairs."

She bristled, but she could not deny it. Neither of them would ever have imagined the truce between two clans who were traditionally enemies, nor war with the clan that was traditionally a friend.

Glancing at Quick Harry, she asked, "How long do you plan to keep him here?"

"A few days," he said. "I hoped you would stay with him."

"Alone?" she exclaimed.

"Nay, either Hiram or I will be here with you."

"I am still your prisoner, then?"

"Nay, a much treasured guest," he replied. "And one I want protected."

Which meant guarded.

"What of my ferrets?" she asked.

"My sister will look after them, or I can bring them here," Patrick said.

"They donna like you."

For a moment, he looked nonplussed, and she relished the expression. It made him seem more . . . well, as Hiram had said, 'like a normal mon.'

Finally, he spoke a trifle stiffly. "We will have to adjust."

She resisted the urge to giggle at the thought of her ferrets "adjusting" to his command. More likely, they would try to take a rather large chunk of him.

His eyes narrowed at her suspiciously, as if he thought she might will them to disobey across the miles, and the impulse to laugh became harder to control. Finally, she could not contain her amusement, and had to allow her lips to curve into a smile.

He scowled at her a moment longer, then, slowly, the scowl disappeared and he smiled in return.

And suddenly, for that instant, everything between them seemed right again. For a long while, they stood without moving, without speaking, just drinking in the sight of each other. As the seconds ticked by, Marsali felt the coldness drain away and, in its place, a hot, sweet warmth began to grow.

And they were alone. Almost. Quick Harry's eyes were closed, and Hiram had not returned. She saw, in Patrick's eyes, that he realized it, too. His gaze, locked with hers, radiated green fire, a fire that reached out and scorched her. She watched, her heart pounding, as he slowly closed the distance between them. She held her breath as his hand lifted and his fingers touched her face, tracing her cheekbone in a slow movement both erotic and tender.

Tremors of sensation ran down her spine, and the air seemed to sizzle between them. When his head began to lower toward hers, she knew she should move away. But she could not make her body obey. Instead, she moved closer to him, raising herself on tiptoe, her head tilting back, her lips parting slightly in invitation.

"Marsali," he groaned as his lips came down on hers.

Shudders ran through her at the contact, glorious shudders of desire and anticipation. Suddenly, she felt as if she were filled with shooting stars, her body teeming with small, exquisite explosions of pleasure. He kissed her tenderly, yet with a possessiveness that thrilled her. She was brimming with the smell and taste and feel of him, of that wonderful, warm intimacy that made her feel both safe and imperiled. The contradiction was intoxicating.

He was dangerous. The way he made her feel was especially dangerous. She was bewitched by it—her body thrummed with it, sang with it.

You canna trust him. Her brain said the words, but her heart and body refused to listen, not when his fingers were feathering the back of her neck, not when his lips caressed hers, not when his breath became as uneven as her own.

She sensed he was holding himself back, forcing a patience he did not feel. But she did not want his patience, or even his tenderness. She wanted the fierce exulting wildness she had felt in his arms only a few nights before. She wanted to forget her fear and mistrust. She wanted to be wrapped in the enchantment that made them the only two people in the world. . . .

Patrick felt Marsali's breath quicken, felt her trembling in his arms, felt her body speak to his of her desires. Exultation filled him as her lips responded hungrily to the movement of his upon them. Dear God, he had feared he'd lost her forever, yet she was responding as if the past few days of distrust and anger had never had happened.

Her body curled against his, and he shuddered, the

stroking of her fingers in the hair at the back of his neck making him groan. He reveled in the sweet awakening of her passion, the innocent way her body clung to his seeking something he knew she did not truly understand. Sweet God in heaven, he wanted her, needed her, the pulsing demand in his body becoming more insistent with every touch of her hands on his face, his back, his hair.

His body was burning, his mind fogging with need for her, his breathing growing more and more ragged. Hunger racked him, hunger for the woman whom he had dreamed of for so long. Hunger for the taste of her body, the feel of it, naked against his.

Then, in an awful flash, cold reason struck. This was madness. He would lose her, surely, if it continued. He had drugged her once with wine. If he drugged her with passion, seducing her into doing things she assuredly would regret, he would never have her completely of her own free will. And what was he thinking, kissing her like this with Hiram outside and Quick Harry lying on the floor only a few yards away?

Groaning, Patrick dragged his mouth away from Marsali's, forced himself to hold her away from him. Her eyes opened to look at him, passion-glazed, bewildered. Dear God, she was lovely, with her hair tousled from the wind and his hands, her lips rosy from being kissed. In all his life, he had never felt like this, never wanted a woman as badly as he wanted *this* woman.

But she deserved more than his lust. She deserved to be honored. Honored and respected.

Knowing he would not keep his hands off her if he continued looking at her, Patrick made himself turn away. He had to leave. He could not stay here, for if he did, he knew he would bring disgrace upon them both.

Moreover, he reminded himself, he had to see to other matters. He had to be available to Rufus, and he had to be at Brinaire to blunt his father's anger when he learned of the latest raid on their cattle. He felt like a court jester, juggling balls in the air. If one fell, they would all fall.

"Patrick?"

At Marsali's soft query, he drew a steadying breath. Then, cautiously, testing his capacity for restraint, he turned to face her once more.

"I have to leave," he said, trying to ignore the beseeching look in her eyes. "You will be safe here with Hiram. He'll see to the fire, and he is a good huntsman."

"But where—" She broke off, hesitating.

"I want you to promise not to try to leave," he said, holding her gaze.

"You would believe my promise?"

"Aye. If I did not, all this would be for naught."

A small frown marred her brow. "All what?"

He hesitated. "I have a plan, lass. If all goes well, perhaps we can solve the mystery of your aunt and learn who is responsible for the raid on your land."

"Tell me," she pleaded.

He wanted to. He knew she needed reassurance. Most of all, he knew she needed to know that her trust had not been misplaced. But years of trusting no one made him cautious to the point of obsession.

"The fewer who know, the better," he said gently, his hand tucking an errant curl behind her ear.

He noted the flash of disgust that passed over her features. He couldn't have missed it.

"Is Quick Harry a part of your plan?" she persisted.

He frowned. "I am not sure. Mayhap."

"Patrick, please," she said. "His wife and children are frantic with worry about him. *Please*, donna make them suffer any longer."

He looked at her. If she were missing and believed dead, he knew he would go insane. Despite his instinct to the contrary, he relented. "I will try to get word to his wife that he is alive."

Her eyes closed briefly on a murmured "Thank you." But she was quiet only a moment. "Please, tell me about your plan," she said. "Is Gavin involved? Have you learned something about Margaret? Please, Patrick, I have a right to know."

She did indeed, he thought. Still he could not bring himself to shed twelve long years of habit borne of the struggle for survival.

"I asked you to trust me before," he said finally. "I know you believe that I betrayed your trust. Mayhap I did, no matter how well intended my actions were, no matter that I still believe I did the only thing I *could* do to protect you. But I have not lied to you, lass. Not once. And though I know you have no reason to trust me again, I am asking if you will try."

Holding his breath, he watched her face.

Finally, she said, "I donna know."

It was an honest answer. At least she had not rejected the notion outright.

"Will you stay here, without trying to leave?" he asked.

Her gaze fell from his, and she hesitated a long time before offering a reply. "I will stay at least until Quick Harry is better."

It was not enough. He could not risk her return to Abernie, not now. If she were safely home, her father might launch an all-out attack on the Sutherlands. And he might persuade Edward Sinclair to join him.

"I canna risk it," he told her. "Too many lives are at stake. Yours, Gavin's, our fathers', our clansmen's. *All* of our lives are at stake, Marsali. I must have your word that you will stay until I return." He paused, tasting bile at the words he felt compelled to speak. "If you donna give it, I will have to tell Hiram to keep you confined to the hut."

Her back straightened, her chin lifting in instant, righteous anger. "I forgot that you are my jailer," she said bitterly. "But I swear, I willna make that mistake again."

Her barb hit home, but he did not flinch. "Promise me, Marsali," he said. "Please, do not force me to do something that will only cause both of us anguish."

He saw the doubt in her eyes. Did she not understand? Did she believe he *wanted* to keep her a prisoner? Did she think he could treat her so and not be affected? The notion astonished him.

She looked for a long time at Quick Harry, lying on his bed of straw, wan in the firelight. At last, with a sigh, she met his gaze once more. "You have my word," she said, her voice flat, defeated.

The warmth had left her eyes, and not a trace of a smile remained on her lips. Looking at her, Patrick was deeply afraid that, though he had won the battle, he might well have lost the war. The only war he had ever truly wanted to win.

Chapter 14

Gavin looked over the woolly figures of the Highland cattle. They were exactly where Patrick had said they would be. Still, this seemed too easy.

Was it a trap? He had asked himself the question so many times it had become a litany. The consequences would be grave—disaster, really—if Patrick betrayed him. But in his heart, he did not believe that Patrick Sutherland would ever betray anyone he called a friend.

Gavin looked at the three men with him. Boyhood friends all, which meant they had also been friends of Patrick's. He had selected them carefully; they had no wives or children, but all had some tie, either through family or friendship, to the Sutherlands.

Ian Gunn, a cousin of Patrick's, moved his horse next to Gavin's.

Ian grinned, his teeth gleaming in the darkness. " 'Tis a long time since I have gone reiving," he said. "Ye are sure there are no Sutherlands about?"

"Aye," Gavin said. "They apparently think the cattle well hidden here. I happened on them earlier while looking for Quick Harry." God, he hated lying. Damn Patrick, he thought, this madness had best work.

"Yer fa will be pleased."

"Aye," Gavin said, feeling even worse about deceiving his father. In this case, though, the end justified the means. If it brought an end to the Gunn and Sutherland feud, a little deception would be well worth it.

Gavin looked at the sky, noting the sliver of moon that had risen. In a few hours, the mist would rise to obscure what light the moon provided. His gaze scanned the mountains, then the trees to the east, looking for movement. He saw none. The night was quiet. It was time.

With a nod, he gave the order to start driving the cattle. Poor beasts. If they had known Patrick's scheme for them, they surely would not have liked it. And if this feud continued for long, the cattle were going to be bloody thin.

Edward Sinclair glared at the messenger. "The bastard has Marsali?" he demanded.

"Aye. He has 'er at Brinaire. Even sent a message to 'er father, he did, telling 'im so. Claimed it were his right to take 'er, that his betrothal to 'er is legal."

Edward swore. He took no notice, when he began pacing, of Gordie moving quietly out of his way. "And the earl," he said. "What is he doing about this?"

"Naught," the messenger said.

"Naught! He is simply going to accept that his daughter is being held hostage?"

The man shrugged. "There is little he ca' do. Abernie is furious. He wanted tae go after 'er, but 'is son warned 'im off."

"Why?"

"He said the new king favors Sutherland. And he said Charles wouldna act to stop a marriage tha' could end a feud between the Gunns an' Sutherlands. Charles wants peace, 'tis true enough."

"Abernie listened to this argument?" Edward raged.

"It took convincing, but, aye, he did. He 'as not the strength to attack Brinaire alone. So, instead, he 'as lodged a protest with the Scottish Parliament and the king. Tha' was the young lord's idea."

Edward could barely contain himself. He was already snickered at for having been left at the altar. To have his humiliation trotted before all of Parliament! By God, it was . . . unthinkable.

"Charles will side with Sutherland," he muttered.

Edward's gaze snapped to the man standing at the back of the room, in the shadows. Foster. The half-Scot, half-English mercenary who had appeared at his gate two years ago. An ugly man, with a voice like gravel and a bright, nearly maniacal light in his odd amber eyes. Yet there was a magnetism about him that oddly seemed to appeal to women.

Foster hated Patrick Sutherland, and Edward neither knew nor cared why. He only knew that the man's hatred matched his own. Together, they had hatched a scheme to divide the Gunns and the Sutherlands, and for two years, the plan had worked perfectly. Then Patrick Sutherland had arrived from Europe, and, since then, nothing had gone as it should.

Foster sauntered slowly toward the front of the room, ignoring Gordie as he passed him. "Gavin Gunn is right. The king will favor Sutherland. The Sutherlands fought for Charles's father, and Charles remembers such things. You will have to take matters into your own hands."

"How?" Sinclair snapped. He disliked admitting his own helplessness, and Foster was the kind of man who would use any weakness against him.

"Another raid or two," Foster said, "and Abernie will be forced to do something or lose the respect of his clan. And we must discover the whereabouts of the younger sister. From what you say, Marsali will do anything to protect her."

Edward whirled to look at the messenger. "You must have heard something," he said. "Have they found Cecilia?"

The man shook his head. "Nay, no' a trace. 'Er brother 'as looked hisself, but there is no sign."

Edward cursed. If the girl was held at Brinaire, he had no chance of taking her. The keep was well fortified, impregnable without artillery.

"Gavin," Foster said. "Was he not Sutherland's friend

once? Could it not be that he stays his father's hand now because he is *still* Sutherland's friend?"

Edward stopped pacing.

"And could it not be," Foster continued, "that he does not find his younger sister because he does not *want* to find her?"

Edward's mind whirled. Given his experience with Gavin Gunn, it seemed ludicrous to think that the younger man would betray his father. And yet . . .

"It *would* have been far easier," he said, "for Sutherland to get inside Abernie and kidnap Marsali if he had had a willing accomplice."

"Aye," Foster said.

Edward swung around to face the messenger again. "Get back to Abernie and watch Gavin Gunn. If he leaves the keep, you are to follow him."

"Aye," the man agreed.

"You may go."

The man dipped his head in deference, then left the room. Sinclair turned to Gordie, who had remained silent throughout the interrogation. "This new man, you have just employed," Edward began, turning his attention to another matter. "Do you know anything about him?"

"Only that he is good with a sword. He says he fought against Montrose, and I have questioned him. He knows the officers and units. I believe him, and I know his ilk. All he cares about is money."

"Then he canna be associated with the Sutherlands."

"Nay, I doubt it," Gordie replied. "I questioned all of our men. He is unfamiliar to them. One said he saw him at Abernie, but Rufus had already told me that he had gone there seeking employment. He was told Abernie did not employ mercenaries."

"We can trust him, then?"

Gordie shrugged. "As long as we pay him well."

Edward gave him a tight smile. "That's true of all of you."

"Except Foster," Gordie said, "who has a bone to pick." He looked at the other man with distrust.

Edward's gaze went from Gordie to Foster and back again. They did not like each other; that much was clear. Foster regarded Gordie with contempt; Gordie eyed Foster with suspicion.

"We will pay the Gunns another wee visit," he said finally. "Take the new man with you. I want to see how he fights. We might need him."

When Foster and Gordie had gone, Edward sank into a chair and downed a cup of wine. All his carefully laid plans could not—simply could *not*—fail now. His clan had fought the Sutherlands for a hundred years; the enmity was of long standing. But his hatred of Patrick Sutherland went far beyond any clan feud.

For Patrick Sutherland had seen him run from a battle, and Edward still remembered the contempt in the other man's eyes. Even now, years later, he saw himself through that all-knowing, green gaze. Until those eyes had been permanently closed, he would have no peace. He wanted Sutherland's death every bit as much as he wanted Marsali in his bed. And he would have both.

Marsali grumbled to herself as she changed Quick Harry's bandages. She missed her sister. She missed Jeanie. She missed her father and brother. She missed her ferrets. Most of all, heaven help her, she missed Patrick.

He had said he would return, had he not? He had said he would bring Tristan and Isolde, too. Or had they left it that Elizabeth would care for them? She did not remember. In any case, she was *sure* he had said he would return. But it had been three full *days*.

Quick Harry took a deep breath, and she realized she was attacking the bandage. Her hands immediately gentled.

"I am sorry, Quick Harry. My thoughts were wandering."

"Aye, lass. I couldna help but notice."

She felt herself turning red. She could not avoid Quick Harry's questioning eyes, nor the worried set of his mouth. The poultices were working well; the pain was fading as was the heat in his body. He had even tried to stand a short time ago. Though he had quickly slumped back to the ground, he had gained his feet for a moment. She knew he was becoming restless. She also knew he was as worried as she about Patrick's plan for him.

She wished that she could ease his concern, but she could not even ease her own. Inwardly, she railed against the promise that kept her from leaving. It was galling that Patrick had made her an accomplice to her own imprisonment.

Hiram did little to help matters. He slept outside like an overgrown watchdog, entering the hut only to bring in wood for the fire, water, or meat that he had hunted. She did not know whether to consider him a guardian angel or a jailer.

The latter, she thought, with growing resentment. She was tired of Patrick's asking her to trust him when he trusted her not at all. And tired of not knowing what she wanted from him. One minute, nothing would satisfy her except to melt into his arms and love him. The next, she wanted only to fight him, to force him to consider her as a human being, not a thing to be used. And she had no idea which she would do first when next she saw him: kiss him or pummel him. Mayhap both.

Needing some fresh air as well as fresh water, Marsali finished tending Quick Harry, picked up the empty water bucket, and left the hut. Despite her promise, Hiram had secreted the horses away; she was certain Patrick had told him to take no chances. She guessed that she was supposed to be grateful for being allowed the run of the clearing.

She headed for the stream, which meandered past the

hut about a hundred feet into the wood. Halfway there, she met Hiram, on his way back from a hunting foray.

She eyed the rabbits and their bearer balefully. "When will Patrick return?"

Falling into step beside her, Hiram cast his gaze upward, which she supposed meant he was praying that she stop plaguing him with the same question.

"Never mind," she sighed. "I know the answer." A few steps later, she asked, "Can we go riding?"

He gave her a sideways glance, hesitating.

"Please," she said. "I swore to Patrick I wouldna try to escape."

Hiram frowned. "What about Quick Harry?"

"He will be fine," she assured him. "I changed his bandages and gave him his meal. He willna need me again for several hours."

Hiram studied her for another moment, then smiled. "Aye, if ye would like."

"Alone?" she said hopefully.

"Nay, my lady," he said, adding hurriedly, " 'Tis not that I do not trust ye. But Patrick would roast me alive if aught happened to ye. 'Tis wild country about here."

She wanted to argue that she was very competent on a horse, but the set of his jaw told her that he would not relent.

"Then that is as it must be," she conceded. "I would certainly not like to see you roasted."

He gave her a rare smile and, surprise of surprises, a dimple appeared. Hiram? A dimple? It defied all logic on the large, rough face, with its wide nose that looked as if it had been broken a score of times. She suppressed a giggle.

"Tha' relieves me, lass," he said, lapsing into the familiarity so natural to Highlanders. "Ye ha' been glaring at me."

"I have been glaring at Patrick," she said, "Unfortunately, he has not been here, and you have been."

"Then I will try to be gone when he does appear," Hiram chuckled.

"A worthy notion, indeed," she said.

"Aye," he said. "But Patrick always has good reason for what he does."

She was tired of hearing that. Bloody tired. "He simply never cares to explain."

Hiram's smile turned back into a frown. " 'Tis Patrick's way."

"I donna care for his way."

Hiram sighed. "He is a difficult mon, but a loyal one. And loyalty is a rare commodity. So is mercy, though sometimes mercy be not so verra wise."

They had reached the stream, and Marsali dipped the bucket into it. When it was filled, Hiram took the bucket from her, though she could have carried it herself.

As they started back toward the hut, she asked, "What do you mean, mercy is not always wise?"

Hiram glanced at her, hesitating. Finally, he replied. "Patrick permitted no looting of villages, and no rape, though it was customary. And he always gave quarter when it was asked."

Such things did not sound particularly noble to her. They sounded like acts of any honorable man. She did not say so, however, for she did not want to end Hiram's uncustomary volubility.

"War changes men," Hiram said, "but it didna change Patrick."

"Nay?" she asked. "He was always so stubborn? So arrogant? Odd that I donna remember him that way. Nor do I recall him taking women as hostages and holding them against their will."

Hiram looked wounded. He stared at his feet, reluctant to respond. She, guiltily, felt a momentary satisfaction.

"He is no' accustomed to explaining his actions," Hiram mumbled.

"Obviously," she said bitingly.

"But he means well."

Hiram was about as forthcoming as Patrick, she thought, especially when she attacked the man he obviously thought sat next to God. The next time she would try honey; it might produce more information.

They left the water bucket and the rabbits at the hut, then Hiram led her through the underbrush some distance away to a small, dry cave. Inside, the horses occupied a makeshift stable. She was surprised that he had led her there, and evidently it showed.

Hiram gave her a knowing smile. "I wasna hiding them from ye, lass," he said. "Patrick said ye gave him yer word."

"Then why hide the horses at all?" she wondered.

He raised an eyebrow. "Quick Harry found this place. Mayhap others might wander onto it. I didna want them to find our horses. That is also why I didna want a fire during the day."

Chastened, Marsali felt her spirits lighten. Patrick *had* accepted her word. He *did* trust her. A little, anyway. Why had Hiram not said anything earlier? Probably, like his lord, Hiram believed that the less said, the better.

She watched as Hiram saddled the horses, then allowed him to help her mount. Mounting his own horse, he followed her out of the cave. When she realized he was trailing behind her deliberately, she appreciated the small measure of freedom. Or was it simply that he did not want to answer any more questions?

Holding her horse back, Marsali waited until he was by her side. "Patrick told me you saved his life," she said.

" 'Tis more like he saved mine," Hiram replied in a tight voice.

"Where did you fight together?"

"Scotland, Ireland, France, Prussia."

"How did Patrick get the scar on his face?"

"A whoreson Englishman gave it to him. But Patrick

gave as much," Hiram said with satisfaction, mumbling something that sounded like "should ha' killed . . . bastard."

"What was that?" she asked.

" 'Twas nothing." he said. "Would ye like to race, my lady?" It was one of the few times he had called her "my lady," and she knew he meant to end the conversation.

She flashed him a grin. "Aye, I would."

Marsali nudged her mount with her heels, and the eager animal responded immediately. Marsali felt the horse's gathering speed, its muscles bunching powerfully, and she heard her own laughter as the gelding wove in and out between the trees. Hiram was to her left, keeping pace, but obviously holding back to keep her from becoming reckless.

But she *felt* reckless. She felt wonderful, and she knew it was because Patrick had accepted her word, because everything Hiram had said led her to believe that Patrick was still the most honorable of men—even if he was not facile with words, nor given to sharing confidences. Mayhap he would change once he felt he could trust her completely, and once the weight of so many lives had been lifted from his shoulders.

She put her heels to the gelding again, feeling its burst of speed as it broke from the trees and ran across the broad valley, toward the mountains. Behind her, she heard Hiram shout, and she looked over her shoulder to see him pointing. Her gaze followed the direction of his gesture, and she saw two men riding down the path from the mountain pass.

At that moment, something startled her horse. The gelding reared and twisted. Caught unaware, her attention on the riders, Marsali lost her balance and tumbled out of the sidesaddle.

She felt herself falling and tried to regain her balance, but it was to no avail. She hit the ground, and, instantly, everything went black.

Chapter 15

Marsali woke to the sound of a roaring argument. At first, she thought it must be a dream. The male voices were immediately familiar, and they were carrying on their fight directly over her. She wished they would be quiet. Her head hurt like blazes, and she felt very foolish; she had not fallen from a horse in years.

"You said she was safe!"

"You were not so concerned about her safety two months ago!"

"*I* never gave her an untamed horse!"

"*You* were ready to hand her over to a traitor and coward as his bride!"

"I doubt he would have dragged her through a bloody cistern!"

"Och, she is waking," a third voice chimed in, "and yer prattle is doin' her no good."

"Puir lass," said a fourth voice.

She heard a low curse, then complete silence. She knew they were all staring at her. Deciding she might as well face the inevitable, she moved slightly, testing her bones. Pain rushed through her head as she half opened her eyes and blinked.

Four worried faces stared at her. They were inside the hut, and she was lying on a blanket against the wall next to the hearth. And she had not been dreaming, nor had her ears deceived her; it was true: Patrick and Gavin were there, kneeling next to her.

Was Gavin a prisoner, too? He certainly did not act like one.

"Gavin?"

"Aye. This blackguard said you were safe, but I wanted to see for myself. Safe? Humphhhh!"

He was grumbling, but Marsali could see that his anger had subsided since she had awakened.

I wanted to see for myself. He was no prisoner. He was here of his own volition. Dawn suddenly broke in her mind. "You are *together*."

Gavin chuckled. "You have not lost your ability to reason," he teased. "Obviously we are together."

"But how . . . when . . . ?" Her voice trailed off.

"You always were one for questions," Gavin replied fondly. "Always wanting to know why the moon rose at night and the sun at day."

"May the devil fetch you," Marsali said irritably. Her head hurt and she did not want riddles. She looked at Patrick. "Patrick?"

"Ah, love, " Patrick said, looking helpless. The mere word was like a balm to her hurts, and she took the sound and feel of it, locking it tight in her heart.

Hiram thrust a cup of something at her, and she took a sip of wine as she tried several different parts of her body—arms, legs, fingers. All seemed to work. All except her mind. She was still trying to determine what Gavin and Patrick were doing here together.

She moved her head again, wincing, and a pair of small, wet noses nuzzled her. Two elongated bodies wriggled into the crook of her arm.

"How do you feel?" Patrick said, his mouth twisted in a frown.

"How do you think she feels?" her brother said, obviously ready to start the argument about her safety again.

"You must not blame Patrick," she said. "For *that*," she added.

"Nay, 'twas my fault," Hiram put in. "I shouldna ha'

shouted at her, much less allowed her to ride, but . . ." He hung his head.

"You are not to blame, either," Marsali told him. "I was distracted."

She tried to sit up, but her head felt as if it were exploding. Falling back onto the blanket, she frowned, her gaze shifting from Patrick to Gavin and back again.

"What are you doing here?" she asked Gavin, trying to ignore the pounding in her head. "You are not a . . . hostage, are you?"

It was Patrick who replied. "I brought him here to see Quick Harry," he said. "And to see you. To ease the worry I saw on both of your faces."

"But . . ." she started to say, then another wave of pain crashed through her head, forcing her to close her eyes.

He made a movement toward her, and the instant he did so, the ferrets left their nest in the crook of her arm and Isolde immediately scurried across her chest, chittering madly.

Gavin laughed and picked up Isolde, only to have the animal turn and bite him. Startled, he dropped it on Marsali. "She has never done that before," he said, disgruntled.

"I believe," Marsali said, "that they are both irritated with all men at the moment, and I donna blame them."

All four of the men frowned at her with varying degrees of confusion and chagrin.

"You and your secrets," Marsali said, her voice gathering strength as her temper finally reached the boiling point. "You and your wars and battles. You donna think we women have a brain in our head, or understand the ways of men. We understand far better than you, for we are the ones who deal with the wounds and the waiting and the losses. 'Tis far more painful to sit in ignorance than to go out and fight battles. Aye, and it takes more courage, too."

Again, she tried to sit up, and Patrick immediately took her hand in an effort to help her.

She jerked it away and glared at him, glared at the four of them. Then, gritting her teeth, she pushed herself up to sit propped against the stone wall. The two ferrets bared their teeth.

"Good God, Marsali, I didna know you had such a temper," Gavin said in awed tones.

"You never tried to know," she accused. "All you wanted was a well-run keep, and I tried to give that to you, and I loved you, and all I wanted . . ." Her voice faltered.

"All you wanted?" Gavin prompted softly.

"To be . . . treated as a person. To be . . . loved."

"You *are* loved," Gavin said, frowning.

"Then why did you try to sell me to Edward Sinclair?"

He looked away. "Father thought it would be a good marriage for you."

"He did *not* think it would be a good marriage for *me*. He thought it would be a good marriage for *him*. I *might* understand his reasoning as being blinded by grief and rage. But you? My brother? You didna agree with Fa from the start about Edward, but you said naught. Did you?"

"Nay," he agreed forlornly. "I should have fought for you, but I knew he would never allow you to wed Patrick. At least, I thought, with Edward, you would be nearby."

He looked so miserable that she could not continue to glare at him. Besides, glaring made her head hurt worse. But neither would she relent.

"And you," she said, her gaze flashing to Patrick. "You allowed me to sit here for three whole days, worrying that you and Gavin were out there somewhere killing each other."

"Marsali," Patrick began, "Gavin and I just met the day before I brought you here. I told you then . . ."

"You did *not* tell me you were friends again. You wouldna tell me what you talked about or how the conversation had gone—or anything else. For all I knew, you could have decided your only choice, given your fathers' positions, was to become blood enemies and to kill each other on sight the next time you met."

She watched as his gaze flickered to Gavin. Gavin shrugged helplessly. Hiram had backed away and was trying futilely to feign disinterest. Quick Harry was making no such attempt; he was listening avidly.

Staunchly, Patrick tried to defend his actions. "It was best that no one knew what Gavin and I discussed," he said.

"But Hiram knew, did he not?" she said. "And probably Rufus." Patrick's guilty look told Marsali that she was right.

"Who else knows?" she asked.

"No one," Patrick said. "I swear. I had to bring Gavin here to see Quick Harry. I didna think Harry would stay otherwise, and I didna want to keep him here by force."

"But you donna mind keeping *me* by force?" she said angrily, her increasing temper creating an equal increase of pain in her head.

"Nay, lass, I do mind," Patrick said, his voice tender. "I mind a great deal. 'Tis another reason that I brought Gavin. I wanted you to know that we are together in a plan." He hesitated, and she saw the uncertainty in his eyes as he continued. "After all that has happened, I didna know if you would believe me without your brother here to back up my word."

She started to say something, but he placed a finger on her lips. "Let me finish, lass. Please. I am not accustomed to saying these things. I have learned to keep my own counsel, but I realize now that I have been asking you for something that I wasna willing to give. I wanted your trust, but didna know how to give you mine."

He was asking her to understand. He was telling her that he was sorry. More than that, he was admitting that he had been wrong.

With their gazes locked, his finger, still lying on her lips, began to trace their outline. The simple caress warmed her to her toes, and her anger melted under the onslaught of his intoxicating apology.

Gavin coughed.

Suddenly, Marsali remembered the others. For a fleeting moment, she had been alone with Patrick. The left side of his lips turned upward in a rueful grin, silently acknowledging that he, too, had forgotten where they were.

Looking around, she saw that Quick Harry had retreated to his corner of the tiny room, and Hiram was lurking near the door. Gavin, on the other hand, still hovered close by. And Tristan and Isolde were poised, ready to attack if Patrick made the slightest move of which they did not approve.

It was all too much. Suddenly her headache overwhelmed her, and she grimaced.

"Hiram," Patrick called. "Bring her a cool, damp cloth for her head. Here, lass, let me help you lie down again."

He lowered her to the blanket, and she closed her eyes, feeling Patrick's fingers skim over the tender spot, just above her right temple, where she had hit her head. She winced, raising a hand to touch the spot herself. She had a rather large bump, but she felt no cut.

"Ah, lass," Patrick said. "I was afraid for you when I saw you fall."

"I never fall."

"Nay, not ever."

"I was distracted."

"Aye. So you said."

"You and Gavin seemed to come from nowhere." She was already feeling better, although when she moved too quickly, she would have sworn a blacksmith had been loosed inside her head and was using it for an anvil.

"Aye, that is the advantage of this place," Patrick said. "Few know of it, and the only way in from the south is treacherous. Still, if Quick Harry agrees, we will move him up to the cave where we've kept the horses. It would be even safer."

At that moment, Hiram appeared at her side with the wet cloth. Patrick laid it across her forehead. Then, pivoting on the balls of his feet to look at Quick Harry, he asked, "Can you walk outside?"

"Aye, with some help," Quick Harry replied.

Hiram moved to accommodate him, taking the injured man's hand and pulling him to his feet. Then, with an arm around Quick Harry's waist, Hiram helped him out of the hut. Gavin followed them. Patrick waited until all three were outside before turning back to her.

Marsali looked at him with disappointment. "Are they waiting for you to join them—so you can talk about your plans?"

"Nay," he said. "No more secrets, love. Hiram will be taking care of the horses. Gavin wanted to talk to Quick Harry alone. And I wanted *you* alone." His gaze skimmed over her, flickering to her injured head several times. "I wish I could take the pain away," he said.

" 'Tis nothing." And the ache in her head *was* nothing compared with the lovely warm feeling spreading over her.

"I feel that it is my fault. I feel that *all* you have suffered these past weeks has been my fault. Weeks in your bedchamber, being drugged and taken from your home, subjected to my father's ill humor, then dragged up here and made to stay—"

"Hush." This time, it was her finger placed on his lips that stopped the flow of words.

He snagged her hand in his and brought the backs of her fingers to his lips. His face was tormented. "My heart stopped when I saw you fall," he said softly.

"I never fall," she protested again.

"I know," he said. "I would not have told Hiram to allow you to ride if I thought otherwise."

Allow. The word rankled. He created so many opposing

emotions in her. He had called her his love, but she wanted to be loved as an equal, not as an inferior being. He placed his fingers on her temples and gently began massaging her head, and her irritation subsided along with some of the pain. His hands were very gentle.

"Elizabeth misses you," he said. "So do I."

The words swirled in her heart. But still, the questions plagued her. "What are you and Gavin planning?"

Patrick sighed, and shifted to sit beside her. When he moved, placing a hand on the floor as a brace, one of the ferrets took the opportunity and lunged. It planted small sharp teeth in his wrist, then scurried back to its mate to curl comfortably, satisfied now that it had made its feelings known.

"Isolde!" Marsali scolded, but the small animal merely lifted its head, gave her a ferret grin, and ducked back into the safety of Tristan's fur, believing herself invisible.

With a sound of distress, Marsali looked at the blood dripping from Patrick's hand. She wiggled herself into a half-sitting position and reached down to tear off a piece of her shift, binding the strip of cloth around the small puncture wounds.

Holding still for her attentions, he gave her a wry smile. "I am pleased you do not have leopards as pets."

She returned his smile with a small, embarrassed one of her own. When she had finished her ministrations, she started to lie back down, but he pulled her to him, wrapping an arm around her shoulders. Happily, she leaned against him, resting her head on his chest.

"How did you ever bring Tristan and Isolde here?"

"They seem to like a small nip of wine," he said, his smile spreading. "I have discovered that ferrets in their cups are more amiable. Right now, though, I think they are feeling the results of intemperance and are blaming it on me."

She giggled.

His tone became serious. "I brought them because I

didna know how Quick Harry would be, and whether you would need to stay longer. But he looks well enough, and I would like you to return with me."

"To Brinaire?"

"Aye."

Her face fell. She liked Elizabeth, but she had felt like a prisoner there. Here, at least, she had some freedom and felt as if she were doing something worthwhile. "I would prefer to stay here," she said.

He was silent a moment. "I am not sure it is safe," he said.

"You said no one knew of it."

"Someone does." He raised one eyebrow. "The person who informed my father that Margaret was meeting a lover here."

With a gasp, Marsali glanced around the tiny, ancient dwelling. "This was the place?"

"Aye."

"Are you planning to leave Quick Harry here?"

"Aye," he said, "but in the cave where Hiram kept the horses. Most likely, the hut is safe enough, but I willna take any chances, either with you or with him."

"I could stay in the cave, too," she said.

When he did not reply, she glanced up to meet his gaze and found him frowning unhappily. "Is Brinaire so bad?"

"Your father doesna want me there—I can feel his hatred—and you are always gone," she replied honestly.

Patrick let out a sigh. "You canna stay alone with Quick Harry, and I need Hiram."

He was right, of course. If someone did know of this place, she could not defend herself and a wounded man from harm. The last thing she wanted was to be someone else's prisoner.

Putting the problem aside, she returned to what she considered the most important issue. "What are you and Gavin planning?"

He studied her hard, then gave a short nod. "I suppose you must know."

She listened in growing amazement as he explained the scheme, and a more brilliant scheme she had never heard. By the time he had finished, she was grinning, and her headache was nearly gone.

"And Gavin agreed to this?" she asked.

"Aye. Some was even his idea."

"Who else knows?"

"Rufus, who has gone to the Sinclairs to see what he can discover. Hiram. Now you." Patrick grimaced a little, acknowledging, "I suppose it is inevitable that others will guess as time passes. But we have chosen our raiders carefully—men who have connections with both clans and who, for that reason, will be reluctant to use force." His voice became urgent as he continued. "What we need is time. I fear that Sinclair will grow impatient and do something precipitate."

"Something like what?" she asked quietly.

His tone was grave. "Another raid. He must be raging now that none of his plans have worked. He willna wait long."

As their gazes held, she placed her hand on top of his injured one. "Tell me what you have learned about Aunt Margaret," she said. "If we can solve that mystery—"

"Aye," he said, "Margaret is the key. That is why I need time. I have men chasing down the two who came to my father with the tale of her adultery. Two men who seem to have disappeared."

"Then you do not believe she committed adultery?"

"Nay. Elizabeth told me that Margaret truly loved my father and that she even believed he loved her. Someone worked very hard to make my father believe he had been cuckolded, and I think it was Sinclair."

It made perfect sense. Slowly, she asked, "Do you think she is still alive?"

His jaw tensed. "I doubt it, lass. But I swear to you, I will find out."

Her fingers tightened around his. "What about my disappearance from Brinaire? How did you explain that?"

"The truth," he said. "At least part of it. You are known as a healer, and I told my father you are assisting a man and his wife who are ill and that Hiram is staying with you as guard."

"He believed you?"

Patrick uttered a brief laugh. "He had no choice without calling his son and heir a liar, and he needs me too much now to take that risk. The clan is loyal only to the laird, not the title of marquis, and if they want, they can elect a new laird. He canna afford to see the clan divided. Gavin also canna risk dividing your clan and leaving it weakened—easy prey for Sinclair."

The pounding in Marsali's head returned as she realized the depth of the problem. Older members of both clans were sworn to their leaders—Donald Gunn and Gregor Sutherland. They had fought at their lairds' sides for years, and depended on them for protection. The younger clansmen might choose Gavin and Patrick, but such choices would tear the clans apart, pit family members against one another.

"Gavin wouldna do anything that might divide our clan," Marsali murmured. "I am amazed that you persuaded him to join your scheme, for if Fa finds out, he will surely disown my brother."

"Aye," Patrick agreed. "We will both be disowned if our fathers learn what we are doing. But Gavin and I are in agreement that the most important thing is to end the feud. We will do whatever it takes."

The thought that Patrick and Gavin were working together warmed her. They could do anything. She had always thought so.

Lifting his hand, she brought it to her cheek, nuzzling it.

She smiled, hearing the small, rumbling sound her action evoked from him. She liked that rumble. Just as she liked the strong, sure beat of his heart.

Nudging the now sleeping ferrets from her lap, Marsali shifted, turning so that her face was only inches away from Patrick's. Her heart raced as she examined his face with its rough, dark bristle. When her gaze met the emerald green fire of his, a shiver ran along her spine.

They were alone. For a few blessed moments they were alone.

Patrick's head lowered, and his lips brushed her cheek, then nibbled her earlobe before moving down her neck. At the place where her neck and shoulder met, his mouth lingered, igniting flames that streaked throughout her body.

"Marsali," he murmured, raising his head to look at her as his fingers smoothed her riotous hair from her face. Then he kissed her, a sweet, lingering kiss that was both gentle and, in some indefinable way, proprietary. She could feel the longing in his lips, a need that matched her own deep yearning.

Her hand moved in his, and she wondered at the hard, callused strength that disguised so much gentleness. His face was deceptive, too: the hardness so adept at hiding his thoughts—and his emotions.

But now she *felt* them. She felt his heart that had won such deep affection from men like Hiram, that held the courage to go against his father to save others from harm. He was a man who would always reach for the stars when others satisfied themselves with the ordinary.

Her hand moved to his face, to the scar, and her fingertips sought to ease the pain engraved there. She felt the movement of his muscles in response to every soft caress.

"Marsali." His arms tightened around her, careful at first, as if afraid to hurt her.

She answered the plea, her arms twining around his neck, her mouth joining his in a luscious, deep connection.

His lips pressed hard against hers, and she felt waves of emotion passing between them. Everything in her dissolved under the exquisite agony of his every touch. Tremors racked her body, and she gloried in the growing tension she felt in his body as he strained against her.

She wasn't sure how they got there, half lying, front-to-front, entwined in intimate embrace. Yet she wanted to be closer. As close as a man and a woman could be. She had never known wanting like this, wanting so fierce she thought she might shatter.

It seemed as though something inside of her did shatter when his hand slid up her side to cup her breast. Through the cloth of her gown, she felt her breast swell and grow hard. She gasped, a small, whimpering sound of shocked pleasure. He let his mouth trail down her throat, lips feathering her neck, at the same time his fingers untied the laces of her gown. With only her thin chemise covering her breasts, she felt his mouth slide downward to envelop one hardened peak.

"Oh!" she gasped as heat suffused her. She had a few brief moments of the most exquisite pleasure she had ever known, then, suddenly, he brought it to an abrupt halt.

With a muttered oath and a groan, he pushed himself away from her. "Sweet Jesu, what am I thinking?" Running a shaking hand through his hair, he heaved a ragged breath. "This is madness. The others could come back at any time."

Trembling, her breath as ragged as his, she reluctantly had to agree. But, dear heaven, she ached all over, and none of it was from the fall. She ached with passion and a hunger unlike any she had ever know. She wanted him so much. She wanted to be part of him. She wanted to see where these new, thrilling feelings would lead.

"Tonight?" she whispered, blushing at the boldness of the suggestion.

His dark brows knitted together. "At Brinaire?"

"Aye," she said, her body still trembling.

His smile was filled with warmth, and it was unlike any smile he had ever given her. It erased years from his face and gave her a glimpse of a man whom she longed to know completely. Her fingers traced the sensuous curve of his lips.

He caught her finger in his mouth and sucked on it with deliciously agonizing deliberation, holding her gaze. His eyes seemed deeper and greener than ever before. She could not breathe as she waited for his answer.

When he released her finger, his look became so solemn that, for a moment, she actually thought he might refuse.

"We should wed first," he said.

She stared at him.

He chuckled. "Do not look so stricken, love. Believe me, I donna want to wait any longer than you do." His brow lifted in query. "We could declare our handfast in front of Gavin and Hiram and Quick Harry."

Her eyes widened. "And your father?"

He shook his head. " 'Tis better to keep him in ignorance for a while. But a handfast would protect you if there is a bairn."

She had been so caught up in passion, *that* thought had not occurred to her. At his reminder, she felt heat creeping into her cheeks, yet the notion was quite a lovely one. A bairn with Patrick's green eyes.

Marsali nodded, a smile curving her lips. "Aye. I am willing. But do you think Gavin will stand as witness?"

"I donna know," he said. "But he must see that it would protect you from Sinclair. And a handfast wouldna compromise you if anything happens to me."

"Nothing will happen to you," she said fiercely.

His finger touched her chin. "Nay, love. You would no' allow it, would you?"

She felt him stiffen suddenly, his gaze flashing to the door. Seconds later, she heard voices approaching. His ears were far better than hers, she thought as her hands flew to help him lace her outer dress. They finished just as the door opened.

Gavin's large form loomed in the doorway, and she saw his eyes narrow as he took in their position. They were no longer mostly prone, but Patrick's arms were still around her and she was leaning against his chest.

Gavin scowled. "I think it is time to take our leave," he said sharply.

Patrick gently eased her out of his arms and stood as Quick Harry came in, his body partly supported by Hiram.

Patrick spoke to Gavin. "I would like to talk to you. Outside."

Marsali saw Gavin's gaze flicker back and forth between Patrick and her, his look inscrutable. Then he nodded and turned in the doorway. Patrick gave her a reassuring look before following him.

She tried to swallow her apprehensions.

Handfasting. It was not the wedding she had dreamt of. But it would do. It would do very well. Handfasted couples announced their intent before witnesses and lived together for a year and a day, then decided whether or not to officially wed. If not, no one's reputation was besmirched.

But they needed Gavin's cooperation. His presence as a witness from her family would be vital if the legality of the handfast was ever questioned. She bit her lower lip, unaware of her hands wringing each other at her waist. Her brother had not been pleased to find her in Patrick's arms. What if the two of them fought, after all, because of her? A shiver of fear ran through her.

She waited, every moment a lifetime, as the two men she loved most in the world decided her future.

Chapter 16

Patrick questioned his own sanity.

He was inviting disaster for them all, and yet . . .

Yet, he knew he could not remain around Marsali without loving her, and without making love to her. Having tasted only a small measure of what awaited them, he knew it was only a matter of time. He had nearly dishonored her twice already, and the thought of a bastard child was abhorrent to him. He *had* to protect Marsali.

But handfasting? He was genuinely nervous about Gavin's reaction. 'Twas a common enough practice in the Lowlands, but it was seldom used by Scot nobles. Would his friend think it good enough for his sister?

Gavin said nothing as they walked toward the stream, though Patrick felt tension radiating from his friend. Undoubtedly, he felt Patrick had taken advantage of his sister; God knew they must have looked guilty as hell when Gavin walked in.

When they reached the bank of the stream, Patrick turned to him. "Marsali and I want to handfast."

Gavin drew back, his gaze narrowing.

"I would like your approval," Patrick added.

Gavin studied him for a moment, then glanced down at the water rushing by between the narrow banks. For a long while, his gaze remained fixed on the tumbling water. A muscle twitched in his jaw.

Patrick waited. He knew he should not be asking this of Gavin. His friend had already committed acts his father might never forgive. But for Marsali's sake, Patrick would not handfast with her without her brother's approval. To do so would be to leave her with no family at all.

Finally, Gavin heaved a deep sigh. "She has always loved you," he said slowly. "I wanted to believe otherwise, but I knew it when I saw her face just now."

Patrick said nothing. He did not want to force Gavin's decision.

"It would protect her from Sinclair," Gavin said. Shaking his head, he murmured, " 'Tis true, I should never have agreed to support Sinclair's offer when I knew it was wrong for her." He cast Patrick a sideways glance. "Of course, she could still come home with me."

Patrick willed himself to answer calmly. "Can you be sure your father willna try again to marry her off to Sinclair?"

Gavin considered it for a moment. "Nay, I canna," he said. After another long pause, he said, "I want Marsali to be happy, but how can she be happy in a place she is hated?"

"Elizabeth adores her," Patrick said. "So does Alex. It will not be long before she wins more hearts."

"Bloody hell," Gavin muttered. "How did we ever come to this?"

"Two stubborn, prideful old men," Patrick said. "They willna listen to reason. They are destroying their own lives. I donna want them to ruin others."

Another silence ensued, then Gavin spoke again.

"The king will approve your alliance to Marsali?"

"Aye," Patrick said. "I served him in France. He knew of the betrothal and approved. He would approve anything that brings peace to the Highlands."

"I wish I thought a marriage would do it," Gavin said. "I canna help but wonder whether it might mean the spilling of more blood. Good God, if Fa learned that you and Marsali had handfasted . . . well, I canna imagine his rage. He canna learn of it. Not now."

"Aye, I agree," Patrick said, sensing victory. Though Gavin's words sounded pessimistic, if he were going to say no, Patrick thought, he would have done so immediately. "I will wager," Patrick said, "that Sinclair has been stirring the pot of trouble for years. He has finally found a way to divide us. First with Margaret, now with Marsali. But we will stop him, between us."

Gavin knotted his fists. "If it can be proved, by God, I will kill him myself."

"I have someone with the Sinclairs now," Patrick said, wanting to give Gavin back some of the trust his friend had given him. "If they plan another raid, we will know of it."

Gavin nodded. "I thank you for caring for Quick Harry."

"Tell his family," Patrick said, "but order them to tell no others. His life may be forfeit. Sinclair would want no witnesses to his perfidy. His head would be at stake."

"Aye," Gavin said. "His wife will do as you say, and be happy to do so."

"Be careful, Gavin. I wouldna be surprised if Sinclair has spies in both our clans."

Gavin turned to face him, studying him long and hard. The question that had begun the discussion still hung between them, unanswered.

Holding his friend's gaze, Patrick said, "I will take good care of her, Gavin. I swear it."

Gavin looked at him for a moment, then nodded. "Aye, Patrick, I know you will. So handfast, then. I will support you and uphold the match."

Patrick held out his hand, and Gavin clasped it. "I will be your brother in truth."

"Aye," Gavin said. "God help us all."

Handfasting required little formality. All that was needed was for the couple to say they both agreed.

Marsali stood beside Patrick, her hand in his. He turned and looked at her, his deep green eyes glittering with something she could not identify. "I will always protect and honor you," he said simply.

Marsali wanted more. She wanted an avowal of love, but with Gavin and Quick Harry and Hiram at their sides, she could not, would not, beg for it. One day, he would say the words.

"And I will honor you," she said, wanting desperately to say more—to say she loved him. But he had not said it, and without that neither could she. It was enough, now, to know he wanted her.

"It is your wish to handfast?" Gavin asked.

"Aye," Patrick said readily.

"Aye," Marsali agreed.

"It is done, then." Gavin seemed not to notice the absence of such words as love or obey. Instead, he merely kissed her cheek and wished her well.

She smiled and whispered, "Thank you."

"Come to me," he said, "if you ever need anything."

"I will."

He smiled at her. "Our little sister will be furious when she learns you did this without telling her first."

Marsali knew he was teasing, but a hint of underlying concern in his voice prompted her to answer seriously. "Cecilia truly is safe, Gavin. Ask Patrick. I am sure he will tell you where she is."

Gavin shook his head. "I trust you both. I am sure she is in good hands." Then he added, sadly, " 'Tis better she is gone for now."

He seemed different, Marsali thought. Though things hardly could have been worse for their family, he seemed more confident—almost as if in the few days since she had left Abernie, he had found himself.

Because of Patrick, she thought. He brought out the best in people. She had watched him with Hiram, watched the pride in the big man's face as he saw to Patrick's interests. Even Quick Harry, who had been suspicious at first, now grinned easily at the man who had saved his life.

She stood between her brother and Patrick as they

talked, making plans. She listened contentedly to their voices while she watched Hiram saddle the horses. After she and Patrick and Hiram left, Gavin would stay behind to help Quick Harry remove any traces of recent habitation from the hut. Then Harry would retire to the cave, and Gavin would return to Abernie.

As Patrick helped her into the saddle, his hand lingered on hers. "Tonight," he whispered.

Tonight.

Anticipation surged through her. She looked down at Patrick and his eyes were warm enough to heat all of Brinaire. His mouth twisted into a wry grin as he handed the ferrets, safely in their basket, up to her.

"I might not ha' brought them had I known we were returning so quickly," he said. "I didna know that you were so fine a healer or that Quick Harry would mend so well. But Elizabeth said they were brokenhearted and would not eat."

He may not have said he loved her, she thought, but the gesture showed her what he had not said. Her heart swelled as she looked down at him, at the hard body that contained a large and compassionate heart.

Her husband.

She watched as he moved away from her and mounted his own horse. She watched his every move, her eyes drinking in his lean grace, his fluid strength.

Tonight. Her body throbbed at the thought.

He settled into the saddle, then looked at her and smiled. A glorious smile. Warm and intimate. Promising.

Tonight. The word echoed in her head all the way to Brinaire.

Patrick listened to the litany of complaints from his father, allowing them to drift in one ear and out the other.

He had taken supper in the great hall with his clansmen. His father had demanded his presence. Marsali had decided to eat in her room, and Elizabeth had joined her.

His father had not bothered to ask about Marsali, apparently satisfied to learn she was again a hostage inside his walls. He was far more interested in the fact that the Sutherlands had lost a herd of cattle.

"Bloody Gunns," he grumbled.

"I will get them back," Patrick assured him.

"I want you to take Alex with you. 'Tis time he learned to be a man." Gregor directed his glare at his younger son, who sat several seats down from him.

Alex flushed.

"You will go tonight," his father ignored Alex's discomfort and spoke directly to Patrick.

"Nay," Patrick said. "I have been riding all day, and I am tired. We will go tomorrow night."

"Then Alex will take the men out tonight."

The clatter of dishes stopped. Sutherlands up and down the table looked down at their food, pretending to ignore the unexpected test of wills. One threw a bone on the floor amidst four of the dogs, who immediately began fighting over it. Several additional bones went bounding over the table.

"No," Patrick said. "I will go myself tomorrow. I will do this my way, or I will leave Brinaire for good."

The sudden silence in the hall was deafening. His father's face went red, then white. But Patrick knew he had to stand firm if he was ever to expect the clan's loyalty. He waited for an explosion. When it came, it was not at all what he had expected.

Abruptly, his father sat back in his chair and roared with laughter. "You are my son, at that," he said. "You take no sass from any man. Tomorrow night, then. Bring me back my cattle and the hides of those thieving Gunns."

Patrick raised an eyebrow at the bloodthirsty command. His father's demands were increasing.

He finished his meal quickly and without further talk. Marsali was waiting. The very thought of her warmed his blood, and he wondered whether anyone noticed how many times he glanced at the stairs.

A few more hours.

Rivers of gold poured across the gentian sky, cresting along the tips of the hazy gray-green hills that lay beyond Brinaire.

Marsali stood at the window of her bedchamber, her face bathed in the light of the gloaming. Usually, she loved this time of day, the long hours where day and night converged. This night, though, she wished the hours away. She wanted nightfall.

She wanted Patrick. Her husband.

She hoped Elizabeth had not thought her rude. She knew the girl had wanted to linger after their meal together, to talk and play with the ferrets. But Marsali had pleaded exhaustion and the need to bathe as excuses to end what she feared would be a long visit. Elizabeth had not seemed put out; rather she had scurried off to fetch hot water and fresh linens. In her typically shy way, she had asked if Marsali wanted her help bathing, but Marsali had thanked her and said she could manage alone.

It would have been heavenly under any circumstances to wash away the dirt of three days spent in the hut. But as she bathed, Marsali thought about the coming night, about Patrick touching her and about bare skin on bare skin, and . . . well, bathing had never seemed so erotic.

She had dried off by the time she heard a light knock at the door. She ran lightly across the room, her heart suddenly racing, and opened the door.

Patrick stood there. He had shaved and was dressed in a fresh linen shirt and plaid. He looked intolerably handsome with his serious expression and fire flashing in his vivid green eyes.

He stepped in and closed the door behind him, his gaze raking over her. She had not dressed after she bathed but wore only a shift; the fabric was thin, and she blushed under his bold, possessive look. When he held out his arms in open invitation, she stepped into his embrace.

His arms closed around her, and for a moment, they did not move, simply allowing warmth to flow between them. She rested her head on his chest, listening to his heart's steady beat, feeling his breath ruffle the hair at her temple. She sighed, filled with blissful contentment at being here with him. Alone.

Soon, though, it was no longer enough merely to hold one another. Marsali felt the tension begin to grow between them, felt the embers, still glowing from the morning's tryst, come to life. His arms tightened around her, and her body began to hum with anticipation.

"Marsali," he said her name softly, his hand stroking the hair that hung down her back to her waist.

She raised her gaze to meet his, and he smiled down at her.

"You are so very bonny," he whispered, his fingertips stroking her cheek.

As he leaned down to kiss her, a shiver ran down her spine, and, inside, a pressure started building. He feathered her face with kisses, then his lips found her mouth and lingered there. Tasting, nibbling, tracing the seam of her lips with his tongue. The pressure became fire, the fire an inferno when she opened her mouth and his tongue swept inside.

His mouth slanted across hers in a kiss filled with tenderness as well as desire. His hands stroked her back, her sides, her hips. She felt him shudder, heard the deep, rumbling sounds he made, and was thrilled by her body's familiarity with his. Alive with sensation, she clutched at his shoulders, fearing that soon she would be unable to stand.

Her knees weakened further when his arms enveloped her, pulling her to him, and she felt the growing hardness of him pressing against her.

"Sweeting," he whispered, his lips nuzzling her ear.

"Patrick . . . Oh, please . . ."

As incoherent as her plea was, he seemed to understand it. He picked her up and took her to the bed, placing her on the great feather mattress. Then, standing over her, he let his gaze make another long, slow trip downward, across her breasts, her stomach, her hips, down her legs, and back up again. When his gaze returned to hers, she felt as if he had actually touched every inch of her. But then he sat next to her, his hands cupping her breasts, and she learned that actually being touched was something much more than she had ever imagined.

He leaned over to kiss her neck; at the same time his hands stroked and teased her breasts. Swimming in desire, Marsali felt her nipples harden and her back arch. Her hands went behind his neck, and she pulled him closer until her body strained against his.

With a low groan, he straightened to tug her shift over her head. For a second, she felt completely exposed—and totally vulnerable. But then she saw herself reflected in his eyes, saw the tenderness in them, and the momentary uncomfortable feeling faded away.

Patrick forced himself to be deliberate, gentle, even though he was burning like all the fires in hell. She looked so innocent, even puzzled by feelings he realized were new to her. Yet, despite brief moments of uncertainty, her passion was clear in her eyes.

He allowed himself the pleasure of looking at her, the slim body with high, firm breasts and rounded hips, the face with the lovely cobalt blue eyes and fine cheekbones and stubborn chin. Sweet Jesu, but he wanted her. For twelve long years, he had felt she belonged to him, with him. Finally—despite wars and wounds that might have killed him, despite her father who had tried to give her to another man and his father who would disown him sooner than hear him call her *wife*, despite everything that had happened to keep them apart—finally, she was his. She was a part of him. Now and for all time.

He stroked her possessively, his hands caressing her shoulders, her back, and, finally, her breasts. Her look became languorous, passion laden. Yet a hint of surprise, a sort of awe at the sheer novelty of the things she was experiencing, lingered in her eyes, and that innocent look both charmed him and seduced him completely.

"Marsali," he said in a harsh whisper. "Marsali."

Her answer, little more than a moan, stoked the fire inside him. He leaned down and kissed one of her nipples, then the other, and he felt her fingers on his cheek, threading through his hair, curling at the nape of his neck. Her touch was sensitive, wondrous. No one had *ever* touched him with such tenderness. Such love. He knew he had been waiting for this all his life.

He reached up and undid the pin that held his great plaid at his shoulder. It fell, and he stood, unbuckling the belt that held the cloth at his waist. The plaid fell to the floor, and a second later, the linen shirt followed it. He caught a glimpse of her looking at his naked body as he dropped next to her on the bed, and when her hand tentatively touched his shoulder, he felt uncertainty in her again. Gritting his teeth and willing himself to be patient, he started to move away.

"No. Do not," she whispered, her hands clutching his shoulders and pulling him back to her.

The breath left his body in a great rush as he pulled her against him and felt, for the first time, the glorious heat of their naked flesh meeting. He tried to reassure her with every touch. Her eyes glowed with desire, and yet it was clear she was not quite sure what to do. She did not have a mother to instruct her, and he vowed to be slow and tender.

His mouth covered one of her breasts, his tongue flicking and circling the nipple. Her body straightened, tensed, and a small cry escaped her lips. His hands moved farther down, to the triangle of hair, and then below. Her body strained, trembling, as his fingers invaded the most private part of her. He heard her whisper his name, and he felt the moisture he sought.

When her body was writhing and he knew she was ready—and knew that he could wait no longer—he moved, positioning his body above hers. He held himself in check, allowing his manhood to caress and probe until she arched to meet him, asking for more. He heard her cry his name again, and slowly, deliberately, he lowered himself into her. . . .

Marsali thought she could bear the exquisite pain no longer. Patrick had built this need inside her, until it seemed her body would explode. Then she felt him probing. He was so large, and for a moment she was stunned by the feel of him. Then pain flared inside her, and she could not hold back a small scream.

He stopped moving, and his mouth covered hers briefly, kissing her. Then, tenderly, he whispered, " 'Twill pass in a moment, lass. I should ha' warned you." He started to withdraw.

But already the pain was fading, and she shook her head. "No," she whispered. "Donna go away."

He waited a moment, then moved again, and she felt ripples of pleasure, replaced by that aching need again as he moved deeper and deeper into her, filling her, becoming one with her. He moved slowly, allowing her to become accustomed to the feel of him, in what seemed like a deliberate, sensuous dance.

Billows of delicious sensation surged through her. Her arms wrapped tighter around him. She knew, somehow, that as fine as this was, there was more.

And there was.

His thrusting became rhythmic strokes, building the tension inside her. Her body quivered in response to his every movement, clasping him tightly and reaching for something she could not even understand. And then in one brilliant explosion she did.

Pleasure washed over her in waves, and her body trembled with the exquisite release flooding through her. At the same time, she heard him growl, felt his body straining, thrusting deep inside of her. And for the space of several heartbeats, she felt them enter another world, a place of pure sensation, a place of light and joy, a place where they were truly one: one heartbeat, one mind, one soul.

Chapter 17

The cattle were getting thinner.

Patrick sat on his horse and studied them. Blasted animals had been driven back and forth between Abernie and Brinaire so many times it was a bloody miracle they had any flesh left to hang on their bones.

"They look a wee bit disgruntled," Hiram noted judiciously.

Patrick felt disgruntled himself. He would have much preferred to be in bed with Marsali. But his father had insisted on seeing the bloody cattle with his own two eyes. Thus, he had to collect the hairy beasts from Abernie land and drive them to the keep's gates for inspection. Tomorrow, he would drive them to pasture, where Gavin could find them and take them to Abernie. The whole thing was a blasted nuisance, and why he had ever thought it a decent plan escaped him when he thought of Marsali, waiting for him at Brinaire. In bed. Alone.

Alex rode up next to him, his face creased in worry. "I see no guards."

Of course not. Gavin had seen to that. A few flagons of wine on a cold, blustery night and the herders, all on foot, were sound asleep. Gavin would wake them in the morning, berate them for dereliction of duty, and suggest they tell no one, especially not the earl. He would get the cattle back, he would say. Pitiably grateful for his mercy, the herders would thank him.

He himself had found a different method of assuring that the cattle were unguarded when they were in his possession. He simply sent his herders away, saying others would replace them. Pleased to return to the great hall's fire and hot food, they asked no questions, nor did they care who took their place. They did not want to be noticed and sent out again.

The earl of Abernie thought his herd was growing, compliments of the marquis of Brinaire, and he was well pleased with his son's craftiness. The marquis of Brinaire believed himself a richer man by stealing from his enemy; he would have liked to see some bloodletting, but all in all, Patrick thought, his father seemed satisfied with his son's reiving skills.

'Twas only the cattle who were dissatisfied.

Alex was still muttering about the absence of guards. "Perhaps it is a trap," he ventured.

Patrick looked across to Hiram, who shrugged. They had already discussed including Alex in the scheme, and Hiram had expressed reservations. But Patrick felt instinctively he could trust Alex. He had made a mistake in not trusting Marsali, and it had almost cost him her love. Mayhap it was time he started to trust more often. And there was a more pragmatic reason: Alex might express his puzzlement about the unguarded cattle to his father.

"Nay, lad," he said. "I think there are no guards for a reason."

Now Alex looked positively bewildered. They had waited until dark, which made it the wee hours of the morning, and the only light came from a thin slice of moon. But Patrick's eyes had become well accustomed to the dim light, and he could see his brother's confused expression. He also saw his fear; Alex would never feel the excitement that came from danger, the exhilaration before a battle that he himself had felt once, as a young man. And he prayed that his brother would never know the cost of those few illusory moments of thrill.

With a nod, Patrick told his brother to follow him, then guided his horse a short distance away from the five other

Sutherland clansmen who were with them. Once out of earshot, he halted his horse and waited until Alex had ridden up beside him.

"There are no guards," he said, "because Gavin and I planned that there would be none."

Comprehension came quickly. Patrick watched it dawn on his brother's face, his eyes widening and a slow grin spreading across his mouth. The lad was bright.

"You and Gavin Gunn have arranged this raid?"

"Aye."

"And the one on our cattle last week? Was that arranged, too?"

"Aye."

"And neither of you minds giving up the cattle to the other, because . . ."

"Because we know we will soon be getting them back."

Alex studied the herd briefly, his eyes narrowing. "You mean we are stealing the same animals over and over again?"

"Reiving, brother," Patrick said indignantly. "A traditional Highland practice. And, aye, they are the same cattle."

Alex gave a soft laugh. "Father thinks we have taken the entire Gunn herd."

"I am sure Abernie believes he has the entire Sutherland herd," Patrick chuckled.

"The poor beasts." Alex enjoyed another moment of amusement, then he frowned. "But why are you doing this?"

Patrick sighed. "To gain time. I am sure Sinclair was behind the raid on Gunn land, but there is no proof. I think if he becomes impatient enough, he might try it again. Hopefully, we can catch Sinclairs in Sutherland plaids."

"And thus put an end to Abernie's grudge against Father," Alex concluded. "But there is still Lady Margaret."

"Aye," Patrick agreed. "And I canna help but believe the

Sinclair had something to do with that, too. If we can catch him in the one mischief, we might find proof of the other."

After a moment, Alex said, "And the men with us know nothing about the cattle?"

"Nay, and I hope that they merely feel fortunate that the herders are neglecting their duties and they willna have to fight their neighbors."

Patrick watched his brother's back straighten, saw his chin come up; suddenly, there was pride, not fear or worry, on his brother's face. All for having been shown a wee bit of faith.

Patrick thought it would not hurt to emphasize the point. "Alex, the only ones who know of the plan are Hiram, Rufus, two of Gavin's men, Marsali—and now, you. I am certain others will know before much longer, but we must be careful."

Alex's back became even straighter, and Patrick knew he had been right in telling him, despite Hiram's doubts. He had seen how their father had systematically stripped his brother's self-respect because Alex had not been born in Gregor Sutherland's image. It was time to give Alex back some of what had been taken from him.

"Thank you," Alex said gratefully. "I will do anything I can to help."

"I am counting on it," Patrick said gently. "I will need your help. And so will Marsali."

"You need not ask me," Alex said. "I would do anything for the lady."

Not surprised that Marsali had won Alex's allegiance, Patrick smiled. His bride, after all, was no ordinary woman, and he suspected he was in for a lifetime of watching her unwittingly win other men's hearts.

Patrick held out his hand, and Alex grasped it.

"I am glad you are back, brother," Alex said. "Brinaire has been a sad place."

"We will try to change that," Patrick said. "You and I together. And now we best get the cattle to Brinaire before a Gunn wanders by."

Alex grinned. "And when will they be taken again?"

"Two nights, I would say," Patrick replied. "By then I hope to hear something from Sinclair. This reiving is hard on a mon."

"Especially when that mon would prefer to be with a certain lady," Alex retorted.

Patrick's brow shot upward. "You just wait, little brother, until love strikes *you*."

Alex snorted. "I doubt any lady will want me. I am neither brave nor gallant nor handsome." With a grimace, he muttered, "Father says I am a weakling and a coward."

"Father is wrong," Patrick said. "Bravery has naught to do with the use of arms. 'Tis often the opposite. Only a fool doesna care about life, Alex. Real courage is being true to yourself and what you believe is right—right for *you*, not for someone who finds glory in the death of others."

"But you . . ." Alex began.

"Aye, I went to war," Patrick said, hearing the bitterness in his own voice. "And at first I was eager for it. I killed men for no other reason than that other men told me to do so. But I soon became sick of killing. And I was given no option but to continue." Quietly, he added, "Many of those faces still haunt me, and probably always will. 'Tis not something I would wish for you, Alex."

Without waiting for a reply, Patrick urged his horse toward the waiting men and gave the signal to start the cattle moving toward Sutherland pastures.

During the course of the drive, Patrick kept his eye on Alex. He was surprised to note his brother's skill in steering the herd south. Alex was, he realized, a bloody fine horseman.

When Hiram rode up beside him, Patrick said, "It seems

my brother has learned something besides what he has read in his books."

"Aye," Hiram agreed. "He can ride. And he is a good lad. But I wonder whether it was wise to tell him your plans."

"If I canna trust him, then I might as well take Marsali, ride out, and never return."

"Still, he is only a lad."

"He is seventeen," Patrick said sharply. "I went to war at sixteen. And if anything happens to me, he is heir to Brinaire. He must learn responsibility."

Hiram nodded. " 'Tis plain he grew a foot or two tonight."

"You saw it, too."

"Aye. He will never be a warrior, but he has a brain if he will but learn tae trust it."

Patrick shot his friend a grin. "Mayhap you can teach him that lesson. I seem to recall that it took you some time to learn that your head could be as effective a weapon as your fists."

"Hmph," Hiram grunted. "I think I best give 'em a hand so ye can return to yer lassie."

"Now you are *really* using your head," Patrick said, spurring his horse into a gallop.

Marsali entered the kitchen with Elizabeth beside her. She would have much preferred to be in her chamber, dreaming about making love with Patrick.

Her body felt different after his loving invasion: full and warm and alive, as if her senses, like harp strings, had been tuned to a new, heightened pitch. When she thought about the night they had spent together, which was nearly all she *could* think about, her insides seemed to melt and tremble. Her disappointment had been acute when he had said he could not come to her the previous night, that he had to go reiving. At least she could be certain that Gavin had prepared the way, and, thus, she did not have to be concerned for her husband's safety. She had reminded herself of that often as she lay awake, aching for him.

That morning, she had risen determined not to spend another useless hour. And it seemed to her that the first thing she must do was make a place for herself in Patrick's family.

She had joined the family at their meal the prior evening, sitting with Elizabeth. While the clansmen had minded their manners, the marquis had ignored her; indeed, he had been in an unusually ebullient mood, which she attributed to his belief that he would be acquiring more Gunn cattle that night. His good moods usually meant ill for someone else.

But she resolutely ignored him and resolved at that meal to do something about the food. She might earn the undying gratitude of the clan if she made any progress toward improving the kitchen offerings.

First, she had enlisted Elizabeth's help. Since Marsali could not leave the castle, she gave Elizabeth a list of herbs she needed. Salt was at the top of the list.

Elizabeth, at fifteen, was eager to learn. She had been thirteen when Margaret disappeared, the age when girls begin learning to manage a household. But the household servants had all been discharged then, accused of aiding Margaret in her unfaithfulness.

The new servants had little supervision, and Elizabeth, constantly belittled by her father, was afraid to take charge. And no one had taught her how in any case.

After Elizabeth returned with the herbs, Marsali convinced her to join her assault on the kitchen. Elizabeth agreed shyly, darting looks about her as if she were a fugitive rather than lady of the manor.

Now, taking a steadying breath, Marsali looked at the kitchen servants. She had already prepared what she would say, knowing from experience the first step was to make friends with the cook. From the woman's frown, she deduced it might not be easy.

"I wanted to thank you for such lovely food," she said, directing her words to the woman who appeared to be in charge. She hoped God would forgive her lie.

The woman, who was thin as a reed—probably due to her own cooking—regarded her suspiciously. Probably no one had ever thanked her before.

"I thought," Marsali continued brightly, "that we might share some secrets. Someday I could take yours back to Abernie, and you can try mine here, at Brinaire."

Some of the suspicion faded from the woman's face. She lifted her chin, looking at the other servants as if to make sure they had all heard. *Her* recipes going to Abernie.

"Mayhap, milady," she said cautiously, as if suspecting a trick, "but milord has no complaint wi' what I gi' him now."

"Of course he does not," Marsali said. "But it never hurts to have some new tricks up one's sleeve, does it? And I am sure you must have many that I donna know."

The idea of teaching a lady obviously appealed to the cook. Her dull eyes began to brighten, and her expression cleared. Marsali hoped she might relax, having been assured that she was not about to lose her position.

"I am Colly MacAlister," she said. She named the others, and Marsali gave them each a smile as they bobbed a curtsy. "And this layabout is Angus Sutherland," Colly added, nodding her head toward a boy slinking in the corner, "and as useless a kitchen helper as ever was."

The boy flushed as he doffed his cap.

His face was dirty, his wiry body much too thin, and his clothes ragged. Marsali had a sudden urge to throw him in a tub of hot water, then feed him mounds of pastries. But she had to go slowly. She did not want Colly to complain to the marquis about her interference.

Tugging Elizabeth out from behind her, she said to Colly, "Lady Elizabeth would also like to learn from you."

Colly MacAlister preened before the others. "You are welcome, Lady Elizabeth," she said, though, according to Elizabeth's reports, the girl's previous appearances in the kitchen had been met with hostility.

Marsali caught the conspiratorial twinkle in Elizabeth's eyes and elbowed her lightly in the ribs to be careful.

"Now, how long do you cook the pheasant?" she asked. "It has such an unusual taste."

That night, Marsali lay in bed, worrying about Patrick. She could not help it. He had been gone all day, and he had not appeared at the evening meal. Nor had Alex, who she knew had gone with him. Where were they? Surely, Patrick had those poor cattle in hand by now. Surely, he should be home.

She had retired to her bedchamber directly after supper, grateful when Elizabeth said she had other chores and would have to forgo their planned romp with the ferrets. After undressing and brushing her hair, she had stood by the window for a very long while, watching the hills. It was a bleak, cold night. Rain was falling, and occasional streaks of lightning pierced the billowing clouds that rushed across the dark blue heavens.

Finally, Marsali had given up her vigil, quenched the candle, and gone to bed. She had been lying there for hours, unable to sleep, when a light knock at the door brought her bolt upright.

She sprang from the bed as Patrick entered, candle in hand.

"I feared you would be asleep," he said quietly, catching her in one arm as she flung herself upon him.

"Asleep!" she exclaimed, planting a kiss on his cheek. "How can I sleep when my husband is out reiving in the pouring rain?"

His deep chuckle was lost as their lips met in a brief but sweet greeting. Though his eyes looked weary, he had taken the time to wash, she noticed, for he smelled of soap and leather. And he had brought some wine with him. As he poured each of them a cup, he told her about the raid and, in particular, how pleased he was with the way Alex had carried himself. Sitting cross-legged on the feather bed, she listened happily.

When he came to sit beside her, handing her a cup of wine, the ferrets roused from their sleep and chittered fretfully. Patrick eyed them askance as they stirred from their makeshift nest in the center of the bed. But they did not attack him. A measure of progress, she thought. She watched cautiously as he offered them a piece of pastry he had brought. They sniffed it with disdain and refused to take it.

"They willna be bribed," she said, plucking the animals off the bed and taking them to their basket.

"Nay, I see," he said, his gaze following her as she closed the lid. When she returned to the bed, he lifted his wine cup in salute. "But at least they didna take another part of me."

"Mayhap they are thinking you are tastier than the pastry."

His look of offended dignity was spoiled by the mischievous glint in his eyes. Quirking an eyebrow at her, he said, "Colly told me that she was teaching you to cook today."

"Aye," Marsali agreed, lowering her head in mock deference. "I thought my lord would like a wife who can satisfy his stomach, as well as his . . . other needs."

His chuckle was warm and knowing. "Aye, a mon's stomach is a weighty matter."

"Aye, my lord."

"It must be cared for properly."

"Aye, I know, my lord."

He eyed the pastry in his fingers. "And do I not detect a wee bit of difference in this pastry? It seems not to have the same, uh, crunch as the last batch."

" 'Tis the eggs, my lord, that make the difference."

He looked at her blankly, and Marsali hurried to explain.

"You see, I said I had heard that eggs would lighten a heavy dough—though, of course, I had no idea where I had heard it. I thought to confirm the rumor with Colly, and when I asked if she knew of such things, she said of course she had. It was common practice. Well, I could hardly argue with her experience, could I? So as I helped her make the dough, I put eggs into it. She was most distressed. Apparently, she hadna planned to add them *this* time. But, well"—she gave a helpless shrug—"it was too late, you see. The damage had been done."

Patrick threw back his head and laughed, the sound filling the room. Marsali thought she had never heard so fine a sound.

Still chuckling, he said, "I wonder whether my wife is not every bit as sly as . . ."

"As you, my lord?" she suggested.

He laughed again, pulling her to him in a bear hug. She spilled across his lap, laughing with him. As their laughter died, she picked up his hand, lying atop hers, and toyed with his fingers. She loved all their calluses and tiny scars. Realizing she held his left hand, she examined it more closely, studying the lines engraved on the palm, tracing one in particular with her finger. The life line, the gypsies who came each year to Abernie called it. She had asked a gypsy woman once to explain how she told fortunes, and the woman had shown her the lines and what they meant. Patrick's lines seemed very long.

She gave a sigh of satisfaction.

"And what was that for?" he asked, his voice husky from laughter—and something else she was coming to recognize as arousal.

"Your life line," she said. "You will live a very long time."

"That is good to know," he said solemnly.

" 'Tis true," she protested.

"Mayhap."

"You will see." Her hand crept upward to the opening of

his linen shirt, untying the thong to open it wider as she spoke. "You will live a long life and have many children and grandchildren."

"As you say," he murmured, his body tensing as she began drawing small patterns in the silky black hair on his chest.

She leaned back in his arms and watched his face as she touched him, watched the weariness fade, replaced by something far more powerful. A muscle jumped in his throat, and the glow in his eyes grew brighter.

"You must be tired," she said, her fingers claiming more territory.

"I was," he murmured. "But now . . ." His arms tightened, drawing her against him.

His kiss was fierce and seeking. His tongue licked at her lips, and she opened them, welcoming him. Their tongues entwined, exploring and seducing—though no seduction was needed.

Tenderly he cupped her breast, and she sighed, expecting now the sweet ache that accompanied his caress. The small but exquisite transformations that took place in her body when he loved her were no longer new, but that made them no less extraordinary.

Her body moved instinctively against his, and she felt him growing hard against her. Such lovely sorcery, that bodies fit so well together.

His mouth left her lips and moved down her neck, licking and nuzzling until she arched wildly against him.

"I missed you," he whispered.

Beautiful words. Magnificent words.

Drawing her down to lie on the bed, he placed a hand on her stomach, his touch burning through the thin linen shift that served as her nightdress. A sound came from deep within her, a languorous, welcoming sound that seemed to arouse him more than any word. His mouth pressed against hers with a ravenous yearning that made her ache inside.

His hands moved over her body with poignant slowness, as if he were memorizing every curve. She tingled with anticipation, the need inside her growing as his hands continued their loving exploration. Just as she thought she would melt with delicious heat, he drew up her shift and his lips moved to trace patterns in her stomach, moving lower and lower.

Her fingers entwined in his hair, her grasp grew progressively tighter as he ignited a string of fires that ran through her body like lightning. When his mouth touched the opening to her womanhood, she gasped, her body arching convulsively. It was luscious, magical, and surely wicked what he was doing, and she could no more have prevented her body from responding, encouraging him with every move and sound she made, than she could have prevented the sun from rising.

When she thought she would simply go up in flames if he continued, he pulled away, groaning her name. An instant later, he was on top of her, his plaid hiked up haphazardly, his mouth claiming hers in a kiss that sent her soaring into the heavens. He plunged into her deeply, again and again, as if seeking the very core of her soul. There was no pain this time. Her body welcomed him and moved with him, their bodies, together, engaged in a stormy dance of unbridled passion.

The world became a sunburst of color and shooting stars. Exquisite spasms racked her body, growing stronger with each pulsing stroke, until, as one, they climaxed in a great and wondrous explosion.

He fell onto her, the muscles in his arms trembling, no longer able to support him. Sinking into the feather mattress, she relished the feel of his weight. His breathing was heavy in her ear, and she could almost hear his heart pound—or was it her own?

Her lips nuzzled his dark hair and her hands played with the back of his neck as their bodies quivered with aftershocks of pleasure. She felt as if she must truly be glowing, as if a thousand candles had been lit inside her.

He lifted his head and smiled lazily at her, and she thought that no one could be happier than she was at this very moment. Perhaps this night they had started a bairn. A boy with Patrick's green eyes and confidence and kindness.

"I must be as heavy as a horse," he said softly, rolling over and carrying her with him until she was on top of him.

It felt strange—and wonderful—to look down at him and watch the smile curl on his lips. She bent down and kissed his throat, feeling his pulse race against her lips. She wanted to stay like this forever. Holding and being held. When his hand swept slowly down her back, she thought of his long life line and smiled.

Outside the window, a clap of thunder startled her, and she jumped.

" 'Tis only the storm," Patrick soothed her.

"Aye," she said. But a chill had invaded her body. She shivered, wondering why the room had turned so cold so quickly.

Lightning flashed, and a few seconds later, thunder roared again.

"You are cold," Patrick said, his hands skimming up her arms, which were covered with gooseflesh. He pulled her down beside him and tugged the heavy feather cover over the two of them. Then, pulling her close, he wrapped her in his arms.

But the chills did not go away. She trembled when the next roar of thunder came, and she did not understand why. She had never been afraid of storms; indeed, she had always liked them, often taking the stairs to the parapet at Abernie to watch. And she was in Patrick's arms. Safe. Loved. Wanted. She had no reason to be afraid.

Yet, fear trickled through her.

Marsali believed in the Sight. She believed that some

people could foretell doom. But she had never been aware of having such a gift.

It was nonsense, she thought. She had brought it on herself, talking about gypsies and life lines. She was happier than she had ever been in her life. Indeed, she was so happy that, mayhap, she feared it could not last. And if that was so, then the obvious thing to do was stop worrying.

Relishing the kisses Patrick showered upon her, she snuggled deeper into his arms. He would warm her.

Yet the chill did not go away. It continued on, through the night, as she watched Patrick sleep. And it was still with her when dawn broke over the misty Scottish hills.

Chapter 18

Just before dawn, Patrick rose to leave Marsali's room. He was aware that something had disturbed her the previous night, and he did not want her to awaken alone. Standing beside the bed, he leaned over and brushed her lips with his own.

Though the kiss was light, her eyes flew open instantly. She blinked several times, then, focusing on his face, she raised a slender hand to take his. He felt a now familiar tugging in his groin, looking at her. She was naked, as beautifully naked as any statue, her body warm with sleep.

"I must go," he said, wishing he did not have to. But this was not the time to make his father doubt his loyalty, as finding him in bed with his enemy's daughter would surely do.

When he turned to reach for his plaid, lying in a heap on the floor, she held on to his hand. "Can you tell me where you are going?" she asked drowsily.

"I will check on Quick Harry, for one thing," he said.

"And other things?"

"I have to meet with Rufus."

"Where is he?"

He hesitated for a moment—but only a moment. Marsali was his wife, and this concerned her as much as it did him.

"My wily friend is ingratiating himself with the Sinclairs," he said.

Her eyes widened in shock. "You are not going to the Sinclairs, are you?"

"Nay," he replied. "I am to meet him, if he can break free."

"Can I go with you?"

He shook his head. "The meeting place is close to the Sinclair border. I will not endanger you."

"But you will endanger yourself?"

He smiled. "I survived twelve years of war, love. The Sinclairs donna frighten me."

Her brows knitted together. "They frighten *me*."

He gave a soft laugh. "I donna think anything frightens you."

She did not share his humor. "You won't go alone?"

The tips of his fingers brushed her cheek. "Do not worry, my lady."

"I do," she said, and there was no teasing in her voice.

He leaned down and kissed her again. "I should see you at supper." Again, he tried to take his hand back from her, but she held on, unwilling to let him go.

"Please, Patrick," she demanded. "Please take someone with you."

"I will try, Marsali," he said. And though he knew it was not what she wanted to hear, it was all he was able to offer.

Retrieving his plaid, he wrapped and pinned it quickly, tossing her a kiss from the doorway as he left the room. The vision of her eyes, dark with anxiety, followed him.

Gavin entered his father's bedchamber, took one look at his sire's face, and thought, *Here is trouble.*

His father had returned earlier that day from another unsuccessful foray seeking assistance in his feud with the Sutherlands. None of the other clans bore a grudge against the Sutherlands, and they were all tired of war. Aside from that, everyone was reluctant to anger Charles, the new king, who was said to hold Patrick Sutherland in high regard.

Gavin knew his father was disheartened and felt betrayed by friends and allies. As he came to stand before his father, he prepared himself for the worst: The earl had bloodlust in his eyes.

"Duncan tells me you have been successful in your cattle raids."

"Aye," Gavin said. "We have increased our stock."

"And the Sutherlands? What are they doing about it?"

"A small raid now and then, but we have been able to keep the cattle."

"And your sister?"

"Still at Brinaire. My spy there tells me that she is well. She has the run of the castle and is well treated."

"Hmph." The earl scowled. "And Cecilia?"

Gavin shook his head. "We havena found a trace of her." And he had not. Of course, he was no longer looking very hard.

"I want Elizabeth," his father said suddenly. "They took my daughter. I want Brinaire's daughter. Then we can trade."

Gavin cursed himself silently. He should have seen this coming. He could excuse Patrick for taking Marsali, because his friend truly loved his sister and had acted to save her from Sinclair. But he himself wanted no part in kidnapping Elizabeth Sutherland.

"But the king—" he started to protest.

"The king be damned," his father growled through clenched teeth. "Brinaire took my sister, and now my daughter. I willna have it. Have your spy smuggle the lass out. Do it soon."

Gavin thought it highly unlikely that Patrick would trade his new bride, but if it came down to it, he was not certain that Patrick would be given a choice. If Elizabeth were held hostage at Abernie, he knew Marsali herself would never stand for it. In the same way her strong feminine instincts guided her to protect Cecilia, she would feel compelled to protect Elizabeth. It had been more than two years since last he glimpsed the lass, but he knew her to be about Cecilia's age. Aye, Marsali would agree to come home rather than allow Elizabeth to suffer.

"I do not think my man could take Elizabeth Sutherland from Brinaire," he told his father. "He but works in the stable. He has sharp ears, but he lacks cunning."

His father snorted. "Enough gold might sharpen his skills."

"I will ask him."

"You will tell him."

"Aye," Gavin said.

"And I will go out on the next raid. I would not be minding shedding some Sutherland blood."

Gavin's heart began to pound. He had to work at keeping his tone mild as he spoke. "Some of that Sutherland blood is mixed with Gunn."

"Then they should come back to us," the earl retorted. "Anyone who stays there is a Sutherland and will receive no mercy from me."

Gavin thought of Marsali. If their father knew she had given herself willingly to Patrick, he might well consider her a traitor and disown her.

Time was running out. It was becoming imperative that Patrick—or someone—find proof of Sinclair's involvement in this feud. Quick Harry had given him a description of the one man he had seen. Perhaps it was time that he made his own visit to Edward Sinclair.

Stall him. Gavin told his father what he knew the earl wanted to hear. "I will get word to my man at Brinaire," he said. "And I think I will visit Sinclair, see if I canna convince him to join us despite Marsali's actions." He started to back out of the room.

"Gavin, lad," his father said, stopping his departure, "I want you to know I am proud of you. Duncan told me about all the cattle you ha' brought in. You've outsmarted that young Sutherland. I always knew you were the better mon."

Gavin had to force a nod of acknowledgment. He was a fraud, clear and plain. Everything had been Patrick's plan.

But mayhap now he would take things into his own hands.

Marsali dressed quickly, foreboding hovering over her like a bird of prey. She had tried to calm her fears after Patrick left her, but she could not. He should not be going alone to his meeting with Rufus, and she feared he would do exactly that.

Hoping to catch him before he left, she finished dressing and hurried toward the door. When she flung open the portal, she found Elizabeth standing there, her hand raised, ready to knock.

"Oh!" Elizabeth smiled in greeting. "I was coming to ask if you would like to break fast together, then mayhap make another visit to the kitchen for instruction." Mischief danced in her eyes, and her cheeks bloomed with color.

"I am sorry, Elizabeth," Marsali said, hurrying from the room. She continued talking over her shoulder as Elizabeth scurried after her. "I must find Patrick."

"But he rode out an hour ago," Elizabeth said.

Marsali whirled to face her, her heart thumping. She would never be able to catch him, even if she were free to leave. Still, he might linger with Hiram and Quick Harry.

"Alone?" she asked.

"Aye," Elizabeth replied, her eyes clouding with confusion.

"Do you ride?" she asked Elizabeth.

The girl nodded. "Aye, a little. Margaret taught me, but Father has not allowed me to ride alone since she left, and there is no one to accompany me."

"What about Alex?"

"He is always buried in his books."

"A good reason, then, for him to get out in the fresh air. I imagine he would enjoy it, too."

Elizabeth's look was skeptical. "Do you really think so?"

"Of course," Marsali said. "Mayhap we can all go today. This morning. Indeed, right now."

Elizabeth stared at her. "But . . ."

"I am a hostage," Marsali finished for her. "But I have given my parole, and with both you and Alex . . ."

Elizabeth's face brightened. "I will go talk to Alex."

Marsali waited in her room, pacing, for Elizabeth's return. Regardless of what Alex said, she was determined to find a way to get outside of Brinaire's walls. Somehow, she had to reach Patrick and warn him not to go near Sinclair land.

And what reason would she give him for her insistence? That she had an odd feeling? Mayhap the feeling was only that: a feeling. Mayhap she was overreacting to being a new wife.

But she did not believe it. Her insides were quaking with fear for him; it was unlike anything she had ever experienced, and she could not ignore it. Especially not when she knew quite well that danger lay all around them. No, regardless of what he might think, even if he laughed at her for being worried over nothing, she simply had to warn him.

Her plan was risky. Men from both clans were all over these hills, trying to steal cattle and whatever else was not too heavy to carry or drive off. And Sinclair—if he was sowing the seeds of war, he and his men would also be about.

She chewed her nails as she paced. Patrick would never forgive her if she led his sister and brother into danger. They would have to stay well within the Sutherland borders, which meant going no farther than the hut. She could only pray that Patrick would still be there.

Unable to bear the waiting any longer, she tried to put her nervous energy to use by plaiting her hair in preparation for riding. A glance out the window showed her that little activity was taking place in the courtyard. A good sign.

The sound of voices nearing her door sent her flying to open it. Alex stood beside his sister, a lopsided grin on his face. "Elizabeth said you would like to ride this morning. I would be honored to escort you."

"Your father?" Marsali asked breathlessly.

"His gout is worse. He has not left his room and probably will not," Alex said.

"I donna want to get you in trouble," she replied, paying cursory heed to a conscience that scolded her for putting both Alex and Elizabeth in line for their father's wrath.

Alex waved off her concern. "Patrick told me to take care of you," he said. "And you will not ride off, will you?"

"Nay," she said. "I willna go back to Abernie." And she only meant to lose them for an hour or so.

Alex nodded. "I have already asked Donnie to saddle three horses."

Marsali looked more closely at him. She had seen him infrequently, and they had exchanged only a few words at meals. He, as much as Elizabeth, seemed bent on appearing to be invisible. Yet he was a handsome young man, tall and slender, with a face both sensitive and eager. He looked very much like Patrick had at seventeen, though his eyes were lighter. And as he stood there in front of her, obviously proud of making a decision, of pleasing her, she knew suddenly that she could not go through with it: She could not lie to either Alex or Elizabeth.

She would not try to escape them. But what *would* she do?

She did not know. But she had several hours to think about it: It would take that long to reach the pass that led to the hut.

"I am ready," she said.

Alex led the way out of the castle, his air seemingly more confident than Marsali remembered. They met inquisitive eyes at the stables, but Alex ignored them, offering his assistance first to Marsali, then to his sister, in mounting. He settled into the saddle of his own horse, and the three of them left through the open gates.

It did not take Marsali long to determine that she never would have been able to lose Alex anyway, not on horseback. He rode as if he had been born to it, far better than most men she knew. And Elizabeth, though obviously less comfortable, also rode competently.

The sun broke through the heavy clouds, transforming drops of rain clinging to yellow broom and purple heather to glimmering jewels. 'Twas one of those Highland days that made the spirit sing in gratitude for life itself. But the persistent veil of fear would not allow Marsali to enjoy it.

She kicked her mare's sides, briefly leaving the others behind as she galloped toward the hills that sheltered the small hut. Alex, either in deference to his sister's lesser skills or her own need of freedom, did not try to catch her, though he could easily have done so.

When she reached the pass, she waited for them. A few minutes later, they drew up beside her, and Alex looked at her inquisitively.

She chewed on her lower lip for a moment, then made her decision. "Will you trust me to go on alone? I swear I will return within three hours."

Alex studied her. "Why?"

"Alex, I donna know any other way to say this. I think your brother might be in danger, and I have to warn him."

Alarm flashed in the younger Sutherland's eyes. "If Patrick is in danger, then why did you not say so before? We should have brought help."

Marsali shook her head. "No. I donna know what the danger is. I have . . ."—she waved a hand in a helpless gesture— "I have only a feeling—a *strong* feeling—that something is wrong, that something or someone will hurt him. I have to warn him."

Relief flooded through her when Alex did not question her sanity. Indeed, he seemed to accept her unsatisfactory explanation without hesitation. Still, he offered one protest.

"Why can we not go together?" he asked.

Marsali tamped down her frustration. It was a reasonable question. Yet she could not tell Alex or Elizabeth about Quick Harry. Patrick felt Harry's survival depended on absolute secrecy.

And now *she* knew exactly how he had felt when she had asked questions that he could not answer. It was a miserable experience.

Finally, she let out an exasperated sigh. "I canna explain," she said. " 'Tis for your own good, but it all has to do with Patrick's plan to end the feud between our families."

Elizabeth's eyes sparkled with curiosity, while Alex's narrowed with speculation.

"Patrick's plan," he said. "You mean like the . . . *raids* on the Gunn cattle herds?"

Marsali stared at him. He knew about the mock raids? His tone made it obvious that he did, and she supposed Patrick had told him when he had taken Alex along on the last raid. Still, she doubted that Alex knew about Quick Harry.

"I wasna aware you knew of the raids," she said. "But they are only part of it. I am not certain I know all of it. Patrick believes very strongly that the fewer who know, the fewer there are who must lie."

Alex was not mollified. "He does not trust us."

" 'Tis not that," she said, no longer able to keep the impatience out of her voice. "He doesna want to put you—or your sister—in the position of having to lie to your father. And if you continue on with me now, you will *both* be forced to lie about things other than cattle raids."

Alex scowled, and Marsali could see him struggling with the choices before him. She glanced at Elizabeth, not surprised to find the girl listening avidly.

"Are you going to Father's hunting hut?" she asked.

Of course, both Alex and Elizabeth would know their

own land. And what other destination could she possibly have in this isolated corner of the Sutherlands' domain?

"Aye," she said. Then, meeting Alex's gaze once more, she added, "Please. Trust me."

She was counting on Alex's need to protect his sister winning out over his desire to prove that he could be trusted. And, in the end, it did.

He held her gaze steadily for a long moment. Then he gave her a single nod. "We will wait here. But if you do not return by the time the sun is overhead, we will go in."

Marsali felt humbled by his trust, glad that she had told him what truth she could. "I will be back."

She started up the path that went through the pass, looking back once to wave to the brother and sister, who were dismounting. She guided her mare as quickly as sense permitted through the narrow, rocky pass. When she came out into the open pasture, she kicked the animal into a gallop and headed for the hut.

It was empty. And there was no sign that anyone was about. Dismounting, she led her mare carefully through the woods to the cave, trying to be quiet.

Apparently, she was not quiet enough. As she reached the mouth of the cave, a huge figure stepped out, pistol in hand.

"Hiram!" she exclaimed.

His brow furrowed, and he slowly lowered his weapon. "Lass?"

"I am looking for Patrick. Is he here?"

"He left some time ago," Hiram said.

"I hoped he would take you with him," she replied worriedly.

"Someone was nosing around the hut yesterday," Hiram said. "They didna find anything, but Patrick didna think it safe to leave Quick Harry alone."

"How would anyone know to look in the hut for Quick Harry?" she asked.

He shrugged. "No one has found his body. Perhaps

someone feared he might still be alive. 'Twas not far from here that he saw the raiders."

"But then they would have to know of this place."

"Aye," Hiram said.

"Did you see who it was?"

He shrugged. "I was trapping some hares and saw two men on horseback. I couldna see the faces, and they were no' wearing plaids but doublets and trousers." Frowning, he added, "How did you come to be here, lass? You shouldna be riding alone. Patrick will have some heads for this."

Ignoring his questions, she grabbed his arm. "Hiram, you have to go after him. He shouldna be alone."

Hiram's brows furrowed. "I donna ken ye, lass."

"Something is wrong. I know it."

"*How* do ye know?"

"I simply do. It is a feeling I canna explain. I only know that he is in danger. Please, Hiram"—she squeezed his arm—"please go after him."

"He will ha' my head," Hiram muttered, but Marsali recognized his worried scowl and knew he was taking her seriously.

"I can stay with Harry for several hours," she said. "Where was Patrick going?"

"An hour's ride from here," Hiram said.

"Can you catch him?"

"Mayhap. My horse is fresh."

"Go. Please go."

Hiram waited no longer. He disappeared into the cave and brought out his horse, mounting quickly.

"I will wait here for you," she said.

He started to argue, then quieted at the stubborn set of her jaw. Instead, he dug his heels into the horse's flank and galloped off through the clearing.

She turned toward the cave, hoping against hope that she had sent him chasing after nothing more than shadows.

* * *

Patrick rode hard toward the place he was to meet Rufus, wishing all the while that he was headed in the other direction: toward Brinaire and Marsali. For the first time in his life, he was responsible to a woman for his actions. His wife. He had told Marsali he would try to take someone with him, but it had turned out to be neither convenient nor wise. As a result, though he believed he had made the right decision, he felt guilty. And that, he supposed, was part of what it meant to be a married man.

Seeking to assuage his guilt, he vowed to be especially cautious. And God help him if something did happen; Marsali might never forgive him for ignoring her concern.

As he drew closer to the Sinclair border, Patrick quickened his horse's pace. It was bloody close to midday, the time he was to meet Rufus, and if he missed the appointment, it would be three days before the next scheduled meeting. Keeping a careful eye on the trail, he came upon scattered signs that someone had passed this way not long ago. He slowed his horse out of caution, and guided the animal off the trail, into the woods, pausing to listen for sounds of riders.

He heard nothing and finally reached the meeting spot, a small glade marked by an outcropping of rock shaped like a castle tower. The sun was directly overhead. Midday. He dismounted and tied his horse to a low branch, then checked the dirk and pistol tucked into the heavy belt around his waist.

A large hollow log bisected the small clearing; it was covered by vines and moss; its center had rotted long before it had fallen and now offered shelter for untold settlements of small creatures. It also provided a perfect spot to hide a message. Patrick walked to one end of the log and searched inside. There was nothing. Rufus either had not or could not come.

As he stood considering the possibilities, most of which

were cause for concern, he heard the high-pitched whistle of a titmouse. *Here, here, here, here.* Relieved, he whistled back. Suddenly, Rufus stood in front of him, a crooked grin on his face.

"Lord and master," he said impudently. "I thought Hiram would be here."

"Hiram is otherwise engaged," Patrick said, "and I wanted to see for myself that you were still in one piece."

"I am, and pleased that ye be concerned," Rufus said lightly. "Or is it my task that gives ye more concern?"

"A bit of both, if you must know," Patrick said, smiling. "Now, what do you have to tell me?"

"In a hurry, are ye?" Rufus teased. "To get back to the fair Marsali?"

"To end this bloody nonsense," Patrick replied in as stern a voice as he could manage, which, with Rufus, was not very stern. The man always made him want to laugh. In kinder days, he thought, and given a better choice, Rufus would have made a wonderful court jester. As it was, he had learned to put his charm and wit to use as a spy.

"I do have some news for ye," Rufus said. "A mon named Foster, an Englishman I think ye ha' met, has joined with Sinclair."

Patrick felt his heart miss a beat. "So it's true. He does live," he murmured.

"Aye, he lives," Rufus nodded. "Though he can barely speak. Took a blow to the throat with a sword, it seems."

Patrick held the other man's gaze for a moment. They both knew who had sliced Foster's throat.

Edward Sinclair was nothing but a spoiled, cowardly child compared to Foster. Aye, Sinclair was causing much grief, and he had to be stopped. But Foster was another matter altogether. Patrick had never met a man more evil, and Foster had sworn to kill Patrick even before nearly dying at Patrick's hands. He was cunning and dangerous . . . and a superb swordsman. Patrick had barely escaped their last encounter. The man was now a wounded wolf, bent on striking back regardless of the danger to himself.

"He did not recognize you?" Patrick asked.

"Nay. I was in helmet and armor that day ye fought him. And covered with blood as well."

"What is he doing with Sinclair?" Patrick muttered.

"No good," Rufus replied. "He and Sinclair are planning another raid on Abernie. They be a wee bit impatient with the earl, and they speculate tha' the young lord, yer boyhood friend, might be in league with ye. They believe another nudge is necessary."

Patrick stared at his friend. "You have learned all that?"

Rufus looked wounded. "Of course, my lord. Ye know I have fine ears. The best in all Scotland, I would wager."

"And they trust you?"

"As much as any mercenary. My greed seems as real as any. I asked for near a fortune, and they granted it. Not like some miser Scots I could name."

Patrick raised an eyebrow. "Thinking about changing sides?"

"Ah, Patrick, you wound me. Yer friendship more than compensates for yer lack of coin."

"I am glad to hear it," Patrick said dryly. "When do they plan this raid? And where?"

"I suspect in the next few days," Rufus said. "Sinclair was nearly livid wi' outrage when he heard tha' ye had kidnapped the Lady Marsali, and his impatience keeps pace wi' his fury. His language grows more colorful every day. He has even talked of raiding Brinaire and taking the lady. His honor, such as it is, has been impugned, he says."

"Honor?" Patrick nearly choked on the word. "He gave that up years ago, and it was all his own doing."

Rufus shrugged. "I canna say I like the mon. But he is a cunning one, and careful. He has someone at Abernie who spies fer him, and I fear the spy may be following the young lord."

Patrick nodded. He was certain Gavin was being careful, but he would warn him of the need for special caution. "What about Brinaire? Have you heard of any spies there?"

Rufus shook his head. "Nay. But that is no' to say there are none."

"I will ask Gavin to have men cover their farming settlements to the north," Patrick said. "Did you hear anything of the Lady Margaret?"

"Nay, and I asked, pretending an interest in yer father's being cuckolded. But I did learn that Sinclair owns a keep on a small island. Gordie said it would be the perfect place to hide if one is in need of sanctuary."

"Is it well guarded?" Patrick asked.

"Only by water, and secrecy. Sinclair has brought every man he can here."

Patrick thought for a moment. An island. It could be in a loch or the sea. He would look into Sinclair's holdings. "Do you know its location?"

Rufus shook his head. "Nay, but I can find out. Gordie is a gambler and braggart. A few cups of wine and a few games, which I allow him to win, and he becomes loose tongued."

"Do it," Patrick said. "And be careful."

"Och, ye do care."

"It would be such trouble finding another spy."

"Ye wound me, Patrick."

"No one wounds you, Rufus, but I do miss your impertinent presence."

"Patrick."

"Aye."

"Ye be careful. Foster is no' with Sinclair out of coincidence. He is a crazed mon, and he wants his revenge on ye. Nor will he rest till he has taken it."

Patrick gave a short nod. "I know what Foster wants. And I will be careful."

Rufus studied him for a moment, then, seeming to be

satisfied that his warning had been heeded, he grinned. "And how is the fair Marsali?" he asked, his eyes twinkling.

Patrick's mouth sloped into an answering smile. "Very fair, indeed. We were handfasted."

Rufus's mouth actually fell open, and Patrick knew a moment of true satisfaction. He had not thought anything on earth could shock Rufus.

"Was that wise?" Rufus asked after a moment.

"No," Patrick said. "But inevitable if she was to stay at Brinaire."

"Do either of yer fathers know?"

"Nay, not yet."

Rufus muttered something under his breath about being daft. "And yer friend, the young Gunn?"

"Aye," Patrick replied. "Gavin stood as a witness, along with Hiram and Quick Harry."

"Quick Harry?"

"A Gunn clansman who was wounded in the raid. He made his way to a hut about an hour's ride from here."

"He lives?" Rufus said incredulously. "Sinclair's men have combed the countryside fer his body. They believe him dead but want to make sure."

Patrick shook his head. "He was close to dead when I found him, but he is fully recovered now."

Rufus whistled.

Patrick added, "He saw Foster's face. He described him to me, though, until you confirmed it, I couldna be sure. I had hoped him in hell these past years. Quick Harry will emerge at the right time, and he will make a bloody fine ghost. I want more than that, though. I want to catch Sinclair in the act, and perhaps now—"

Patrick broke off when, out of the corner of his eye, he caught movement in the brush behind Rufus.

Lowering his voice, he said, "Behind you. We have company. Could you have been followed?"

"I didna think so," Rufus said.

"Mount and ride out as if nothing is amiss. I will take care of our visitors. Wait for me on the other side of the trees. I canna have you go back to Sinclair unless we are sure you are safe."

Rufus gave no indication he heard, but then he did not have to; they had been together a very long time. Making it appear as if their meeting had reached a natural conclusion, Rufus gave a nod, walked calmly to his horse and mounted. Patrick followed suit. They both lifted their hands in a parting gesture, then started off in opposite directions.

Keeping his mount to a reasonable pace, given the wooded terrain, Patrick rode for several minutes. When he was well out of sight of the glade, he slipped down from the saddle and quickly tied his horse. Removing his sword from its scabbard, he ran back toward the glade, keeping his steps light and nearly silent. By now, he knew Rufus would be doing the same from the opposite direction, both of them hoping to catch sight of the trespassers.

Suddenly, Patrick heard a branch snap. Then a rustle of leaves in a bush to his right. They were the only warnings he had. In the next instant, he was surrounded.

Eight men. All armed. And all wearing Gunn plaids.

Chapter 19

Bloody hell. How could he have been so foolish?

Patrick's first thought was followed quickly by another: *Marsali was right.* The next time, he would pay more attention to her warnings.

If there was a next time.

Noticing that Gavin was not among the band surrounding him, he held perfectly still. The eight men encircled him, swords drawn and fury stamped on their faces. They carried no pistols, but all had swords and dirks.

" 'Tis the bastard Sutherland," one said.

"And a fine hostage he will make to trade for our lady," said another.

"Our lord would better prefer a corpse after what he did to Quick Harry and the others," another growled, moving closer.

Patrick lifted the sword defensively. He had faced many an enemy, and he could not count the number of times his life had been at risk. Yet he could remember no time when the stakes had been as high. No time when it had mattered as much that he survive. If he was killed, any hope of ending the feud between the Gunn and Sutherland clans would die with him. His father would declare all-out war on the Gunns, damn the consequences. They would fight each other to the death.

And Marsali . . .

Quite simply, his only choice was to survive.

Eight against one. Not very good odds. Where in bloody hell was Rufus?

The Gunn clansmen surrounded him warily. He recognized

several. One, Black Fergus, was a bully and seemed to be the leader of the group. He kept looking uncertainly at Patrick's sword, and for once, Patrick was grateful for every outrageously exaggerated tale and every outright lie that had been told about his battlefield deeds and his prowess with weapons.

"Tie him," Black Fergus told one of the others.

The man he had addressed took a backward step. "He has a sword."

"Jack?" Black Fergus said.

"Not me," said another man.

Patrick had to resist the sudden urge to laugh. Truly, there was nothing amusing about the straits in which he found himself; if they attacked, he was a dead man. Yet none seemed to want to be the first to approach him.

Assuming his most arrogant battle stance—the better to maintain his intimidating reputation—Patrick gave Black Fergus a slow, wicked smile. "What about you, Black Fergus? Do you want to tie me?"

Before Black Fergus could respond, the quiet forest air was pierced by the shrill call of a titmouse. The sound came from the north, and Patrick breathed a little easier. Rufus was still there. But then another call, identical to the first, came from behind him—from the south.

Hiram? Patrick recognized his friends' distinct whistles, though he doubted anyone else would. But what was Hiram doing here? Even as he wondered, another birdcall—Rufus again—brought the band's attention snapping to the northeast.

Clearly nervous, the Gunn clansmen began looking around. Another whistle came from the west. And another from the southeast a few seconds later. The Gunns started backing away, convinced now that they were surrounded.

Patrick would have liked to let them slip away, but he knew he could not. They had seen him with Rufus. They might have seen Rufus come from the north, from Sinclair land; regardless, they surely would report his clandestine meeting with a stranger to the earl if he let them return to Abernie. That would be the end of Rufus's spy mission.

Patrick swore silently. He would have to take them all prisoner.

"Put down your weapons," he demanded. "My men have you surrounded."

The Gunns looked to their leader. It was immediately obvious that they had no appetite for a fight. Black Fergus's gaze darted from one side to the other, trying to follow the birdcalls, which kept coming with gratifying regularity. His face grew red as he realized his leadership and courage were in question.

But he appeared to be ready to drop his weapon and Patrick was about to breathe a sigh of relief—when suddenly Black Fergus lunged at him, his sword in motion.

"Whoreson," the Gunn said as the tip of his blade ripped into Patrick's shoulder.

The movement was so unexpected that Patrick had no time to block the blow. He could only turn so that the sword hit his left rather than right shoulder.

Pain rushed through him as Black Fergus pulled the blade from his body and started to lunge again, rage mottling his face. Lifting his own sword, Patrick parried the blow. Black Fergus's movements were awkward, his attack driven more by anger than skill, and Patrick knew he could kill him without much effort. But he most fervently did not want to kill. More bloodshed would surely end any chance for peace.

His broadsword was heavy and usually required two hands, but his left arm dangled uselessly at his side. With mammoth effort, he was barely able to parry and thrust, waiting for an opportunity that would damage but not kill. The Gunn clansmen had backed away. Out of the corner of his eye, Patrick saw Hiram standing to his right, pistol in one hand and sword in the other.

Patrick felt the blood seeping down his arm and chest,

dampening his shirt and plaid. He knew he was weakening. He had to finish this. He turned as Black Fergus thrust, and the blade went past him. Whirling, he brought his own sword up, hit the underside of Black Fergus's weapon, and sent it flying. An instant later, the point of his blade was at the man's throat.

"Yield," he said, "or I will slit your throat."

For a long, heavy moment, fear and bravado warred in his opponent's eyes. Finally, fear won.

"I yield," Black Fergus said, his voice a low, grudging rasp.

Patrick looked at each of the Gunn clansmen. In turn, each one nodded as they met his glare.

He lowered his sword and turned to Hiram. "Tie them."

Hiram lifted an eyebrow, gesturing toward the surrounding woods. "And your men?"

"Leave them there," Patrick said as he tore off a piece of his shirt and tied it tightly around his bleeding shoulder. "In case there are any other intruders."

He looked at Black Fergus, who was allowing Hiram to tie his hands behind him with a piece of his own plaid. "What are you men doing here?"

"Looking fer Quick Harry's body," Black Fergus said sullenly. "He is married tae my sister."

Patrick wondered then whether these were the men who had been at the hut. Perhaps it had not been Sinclair's men after all. Yet the two trespassers had been on horseback.

"Have you any horses with you?" he asked.

Black Fergus stared at him insolently.

"Do you want to taste my sword again?"

Still, the man did not answer, and Patrick's respect for him rose. He might have been a bully as a boy, but he was a braw man now.

"You wouldna want them to starve," he said, "if you tied them up."

One man stepped out, the reminder of the mount's fate

loosing a reluctant tongue. "We have one horse, an old nag I borrowed. Fer Quick Harry's body. He's over yon beyond the stream."

"Have you visited a hut on my land?"

Several of the men looked at each other. Black Fergus looked confused. "A hut?"

So it had not been Gunns. It must have been Sinclair's men. Which also meant that Rufus's ears were not the best in Scotland, else he might have heard something of it. Or mayhap he was not so trusted by the Sinclairs as he thought.

Black Fergus shifted. Patrick saw his gaze flicker to the wound he had inflicted. "Wha' do you plan to do wi' us?" he asked.

"Make you our guests for a few days," Patrick replied.

He whistled and received an immediate call in return. Seconds later, another whistle came from a different direction. The Gunn men kept looking around, expecting an army to step out from among the trees.

Hiram moved quickly, before anyone had time to wonder why no one appeared to help him. When he had tied the last man, he turned to Patrick, scowling when his gaze took in the copious amount of blood.

Patrick shook his head, warding off Hiram's concern; he had no time for it.

"I will get the horses," Hiram said, handing Patrick his gun, which he could hold much more readily than his sword. But he did not need it now, not with all the Gunns bound.

His father would be pleased, Patrick thought. He, however, was not. A few days in the Sutherland dungeons for Gunn clansmen would not help relations between the two families. Yet he had no recourse. The consequences of them reporting his meeting with Rufus were simply too grave for all parties concerned.

Sweet heaven, his arm hurt. He had survived far worse, and the thought of Marsali's healing touch gave him some consolation. But before he could surrender himself to his wife's ministrations, he and Hiram had to get their prisoners back to Brinaire. No easy task over the passes for men on foot. He swore, wondering if God really had any interest at all in peace—or if He might simply be testing him.

Hiram returned then, their horses in tow along with a third, unlikely-looking beast.

"Start them toward Brinaire," Patrick said, his voice lowered so that only Hiram could hear.

"Ye need someone to look at the wound," Hiram said sternly, and with a twinkle in his eye, he added, "and I know someone who will be waiting to do it. Marsali is at the cave."

Patrick's brow shot upward. "The devil you say."

"The devil had nothing to do with it." Hiram grinned. "My lady had a . . . *feeling* that ye were in danger. She insisted that I come after ye."

A shiver ran down Patrick's spine, and he made a silent vow never—*never*—to discount Marsali's intuition again. He would be dead, and mayhap Rufus, too, if Hiram had not appeared. Rufus alone never could have made the Gunn clansmen believe they were surrounded.

Giving Hiram a nod, he asked, "Can you handle these prisoners alone for a few moments? I need to talk to Rufus. Then I'll send him to join you, and I will go to the cave. After I see Marsali, I will catch up with you and Rufus, and Rufus can return to the Sinclairs."

"Aye. I can manage them even if they were not tied," Hiram said contemptuously, his gaze flitting over the prisoners. "With the gloaming, we should reach Brinaire by dark."

Patrick did not like Hiram handling eight men on his own. He also did not want to leave Marsali at the cave with only Quick Harry, yet he could not take her to Brinaire with the Gunn clansmen; the Gunns would wonder at her helping the Sutherlands. And Rufus needed to return to Sinclair's land before he was missed.

The problem was, Patrick realized, he needed ten hands, not two, one of which was of little use.

Mounting his horse, he rode over to the Gunn clansmen. "I want your parole," he said. "I will untie you if you give it. If not, I will have you bound one to the other, and you will walk that way to Brinaire."

The men looked at one another. Each knew the hazardous nature of the mountains. One misstep could mean death.

Black Fergus nodded.

"Swear it," Patrick demanded, waiting until every man had spoken the words.

He nodded, satisfied. No Highlander would violate such an oath. It would bring shame down upon the clan.

"Untie them," he told Hiram.

Hiram flinched, but he took out his knife and walked his horse past the line of men, cutting each man's bonds. "Get moving," he said to them.

They started walking, heading south out of the woods toward the steep path that would lead them to Brinaire. Hiram followed on horseback, the nag trailing him on a lead.

Patrick's arm throbbed, and he could feel the blood trickling down his chest and arm. He watched until Hiram and his party disappeared, then he rode in the direction from which the last titmouse had trilled its piercing whistle.

The titmouse, in the guise of Rufus, moved out from the cover of the trees. "I see we cozened them."

"Even I believed an army was out there," Patrick said, wincing. "You and Hiram move quickly."

Rufus's eyes narrowed, his gaze dropping to the bloody evidence of the afternoon's work. "Someone needs to look after ye," he said, shifting in his saddle to study the wound.

"It did not touch bone," Patrick said. "I have had worse."

"Aye, ye have," Rufus agreed. "Still, ye need to have it tended."

"Marsali is at the hut—the place where I told you I found

Quick Harry," Patrick said. " 'Tis only an hour's ride. I will stop there. But I need you to follow Hiram until I can catch up to him again."

"Aye," Rufus agreed. "And I will return to Sinclair wi' yer bloodstained plaid and say I killed another Sutherland. That should satisfy them as to the reason I was gone so long."

Patrick nodded. He took his dirk and cut off the top part of his plaid. The cloth of the shirt beneath had turned scarlet across the expanse of his chest and down to his waist, and it clung to him, dripping.

Rufus looked as if he thought they should revise their plan.

Before he could suggest it, Patrick said, "I will catch up to you in two hours."

Sighing, Rufus agreed. "Hiram and I will take care of them." Using Patrick's saturated plaid, he smeared blood on his face, then pulled his bonnet down. With his face thus disguised, he looked more demon than human, and Patrick thought the very sight of him would keep the Gunns loyal to their parole.

Rufus flashed him an irrepressible smile, and Patrick could not help but smile back. "Get on with you," he said.

"Aye," Rufus said. "I will see you soon." He spurred his horse into a trot toward the trail Hiram had taken.

Patrick watched him go, then turned his own horse onto a path that would lead him directly to the cave. And Marsali.

Elizabeth chewed her lower lip as she studied her younger brother. Alex had kept his word. They had waited until the sun was overhead. But there was still no sign of Marsali, and Elizabeth knew Alex was anxious to take action.

"I think we had better look for her," he said.

Elizabeth paled. She did not want to incur Patrick's wrath any more than her father's, and Marsali had said that Patrick did not want anyone to know who—or what—was at the hunting hut. Yet as she took in Alex's determined look, she knew there would be little she could do to stop him. He had changed. In just the few weeks that Patrick had been back at Brinaire, Alex had begun to emerge from his books.

She felt more adventuresome, too, a state she attributed to Marsali's presence. She had watched, fascinated, as Marsali managed the cook and housekeeper with honey-laced suggestions and compliments. The results were, to Elizabeth's thinking, nearly miraculous. The soiled rushes in the great hall had been replaced by fresh ones, the wall hangings had been cleaned and aired, and the food had improved appreciably. Marsali had brought brightness to the gloomy keep. She had brought hope.

Elizabeth did not want anything to happen to her.

And so she gave Alex the nod of approval she knew he was waiting for. A few weeks ago, she would not have had the nerve. Nor would she have considered following him when he started his horse through the treacherous mountain pass. They both knew where the pass led: to the hut where Margaret was rumored to have met with her lover.

When Alex spurred his horse, Elizabeth followed. The pass terrified her. The path was narrow and fell off to a sheer drop below. Her hands clenched her mount's reins, and her fingers curled around the front of her sidesaddle. If she leaned a fraction of an inch in any direction, she was certain that she and the horse would go sliding off the cliff.

She said a prayer, then another. After what seemed like hours, the trail leveled off, and the sheer cliffs opened up into a meadow. She relaxed with a trembling sigh.

Alex held his horse back until she drew up beside him. "Are you all right?" he asked.

She nodded.

"You managed that well. 'Tis not an easy ride."

An understatement if ever Elizabeth had heard one.

They urged their horses into a trot, a sense of urgency

taking hold of them. Elizabeth followed Alex's lead, until Alex pulled his horse to a halt, motioning for her to do the same.

They heard voices and moved quickly off the path, into the trees. A few moments later, eight men on foot appeared, followed by two men on horses. Elizabeth recognized Hiram; the other man on horseback—the one with blood painting his face—seemed vaguely familiar, but she could not place him.

She stayed hidden while Alex nudged his horse onto the path beside them.

" 'Tis Alex Sutherland!" Rufus exclaimed. "Hiram, call a halt!"

Hiram glanced back, giving the order to halt to the men on foot.

"Lad," Rufus said. "I didna expect you."

"Nor I you," Alex replied as Hiram approached them. "I barely recognized you under that grisly mask. What is going on here?"

"Gunn prisoners," Hiram said. "They ambushed Patrick. One wounded him."

Elizabeth's breath caught. Urging her horse out of hiding, she said, "Is he hurt badly? Where is he?"

"Nay," Hiram answered her question, a frown marring his broad, warrior's face. "He took a small cut in the shoulder. 'Tis all. But, Lady Elizabeth, what are ye doing here?"

Alex answered. "I told Lady Marsali that we would wait for her on the other side of the pass. She did not return in the time we agreed upon, and so we have come to find her. I couldna leave Elizabeth to wait alone."

Elizabeth smiled inwardly at her brother's lordly tone. She liked seeing him so confident.

Carefully studying Alex, Hiram said, "We could use your help in getting these men to Brinaire."

"I am going to find Marsali," Alex insisted. "She is my responsibility."

"The lady is not lost," Hiram replied, his tone dropping to a murmur. Casting the prisoners a quick glance, he continued, "She is safe, not far from here." When Alex looked at him askance, he sighed. "She is wi' Patrick. I swear it. And ye will be doing yer brother a larger favor by coming wi' me."

Alex's expression cleared, and Elizabeth could almost feel the burden of responsibility lift from his shoulders.

Alex spoke to Hiram. "What about Elizabeth?"

Hiram and Rufus exchanged looks. Elizabeth did not like being talked about without being consulted, but that brief irritation was replaced by cold fear at Hiram's next words.

"She can come with us."

The pass again! Elizabeth fought the urge to beg them, please, to take another route home. She had hoped there might be another way, even if it meant a full day's ride. But she could not voice her fear now, not in front of Patrick's friends and Gunn clansmen. Nor would she badger them with the many questions pounding in her head. She understood not a bit of what was happening, had only the vaguest clue that it had to do with the Gunn and Sutherland feud. In her romantic fourteen-year-old way, she liked the notion that it all had to do with Patrick and Marsali—and their love for one another.

But there was one question she had to ask. "Is Patrick truly all right? He will not . . . die, will he?"

Hiram gave her a kind smile. "Nay, Lady Elizabeth, he willna die. The sword struck only his shoulder. Marsali is a healer, and she will soon ha' him hale and hearty." His gaze went back to his captives, who, Elizabeth noted, were eyeing them with interest.

"We canna linger here," he said, and under his breath he muttered, "And when Patrick hears tha' ye ha' been traipsing about the country wi'out protection, I donna wish to be around."

Elizabeth shot a glance at Alex and saw his face redden. "I have Alex," she said loyally.

Hiram looked embarrassed. "Aye, ye do at tha'. But even Patrick needs more than one mon with him, and today he saw the truth of it."

Elizabeth was pleased to see Alex relax in the saddle, his pride assuaged.

"Lad?" Hiram prompted, motioning toward the captives.

Alex nodded. "We will go back with you."

Hiram nodded, then turned to Rufus. "You can return, then. The young Sutherland and I can handle these ruffians."

Alex beamed.

Rufus inclined his head in assent, then turned to Elizabeth. "Ye are a bonny and brave lass," he said with a quick smile that sent a flutter through her. Few men had ever said she was bonny.

Before she could reply, Rufus had turned his horse around and was trotting back the way he had come.

"Where is he going?" she asked Hiram, no longer able to entirely quench her curiosity.

Hiram shrugged. "Who knows wi' that one," he said. "We had best get moving. I want to get these blackguards to Brinaire before dark."

Elizabeth bit her lip, but Hiram nodded encouragingly. "Ye *are* a bonny and brave lass," he said.

"No, I am not," she protested. "I was frightened out of my wits coming through that awful pass."

"That is what I mean, lass," he said. " 'Tis no' brave to do something that doesna frighten you. 'Tis bravery when ye are frightened and ye do the thing that must be done, *despite* yer fear."

Elizabeth sat up straighter in her saddle. The pass would not be nearly as daunting now.

She glanced at Alex, and he gave her a warm, knowing

smile. Then they both kicked their horses to follow Hiram as he yelled to their captives to get to their feet.

Patrick stopped at the cave's entrance, his eyes straining to see into the dark cavern. "Marsali? Quick Harry?" he called.

He heard Quick Harry's "Milord! 'Tis ye?" at the same time he heard Marsali's choked cry. In the next instant, she appeared from the recesses of the cave, a smile on her face as she ran to greet him.

But she stopped short at the sight of his bloody clothing. Quick Harry came up behind her, a pistol in his hand. Patrick motioned for Quick Harry to give them a moment of privacy, and he obliged, withdrawing into the cave once more. Patrick took Marsali's hand and led her a short distance from the entrance.

"Dear God, Patrick," Marsali whispered, her shocked gaze flickering from his face to his shoulder and back again.

" 'Tis nothing," he said.

But her hands were already busy ripping his shirt to get a better look at the damage beneath. As she grasped the saturated linen, blood oozed over her hands and wrists, and when she untied the piece of cloth with which he had bound the wound, the blood began flowing in earnest.

She gasped. "Patrick, 'tis not *nothing*. 'Tis deep." Quickly, she bound the wound once more.

"I have suffered worse," he said, keeping his tone light. She had seen the scar that bisected his belly.

"Who did this to you?" Her gaze lifted to his.

"Black Fergus," he replied. "He and seven other of your clansmen ambushed me. If it hadna been for Hiram, Rufus and I might well have been killed." He was silent a moment. "Hiram told me that you sent him?"

"Aye," she said. "I shouldna have let you go this morning. Patrick, I . . . I had a feeling. I have never had such a thing, and I wouldna have known how to explain it to you. But I shouldna have let you go."

"Ah, love," he said, the fingers of his good hand brushing her cheek. "Donna fret so. You tried to tell me. I didna listen. But I swear, the next time you get such a feeling, I will give heed to it." He tried a smile. "I didna know I was acquiring a wife who had the Sight."

She looked mildly chagrined. "Nor did I. But I am grateful for whatever possessed me to send Hiram to you. And now I must tend your wound before Hiram's efforts come to naught."

She took his good hand, and they began walking toward the cave.

"The men who attacked you?" she asked, her tone anxious. "Are they . . . ?"

"They are alive," he said. "Not even a cut. Hiram is taking them back to Brinaire as prisoners. I fear they saw too much."

He caught the surprise in the sideways glance she gave him. "You let them live after they ambushed you?" she asked.

"Did you think I wouldna?" he asked gently. "Do you think me such a villain, I would kill your clansmen without a thought?"

"Most men would, under the circumstances," she murmured.

"I am not most men."

"Nay." She gave a tiny smile. "I am coming to see that you are not."

"Good. And I would like to linger and discuss my finer qualities with you at greater length, but I canna." He gave her a regretful smile. "I must ask you to hurry and do what needs be done to this shoulder so that I can catch up with Rufus and Hiram."

She came to a halt at the cave entrance. "But, Patrick, you shouldna be riding anymore with that wound. You need to rest."

He shook his head. "I do not like the idea of one man

taking eight to Brinaire, and I must be there when my father sees them." In truth, he did not know how he would make it. His head was starting to spin, and he felt cold to the bone. He recognized the feeling, knew it was from loss of blood.

At the mention of his father, worry flooded Marsali's blue gaze. "He willna harm my clansmen, will he?"

"Nothing of a fatal nature," he soothed her. "But they gave me their parole, and I would see them as comfortable as possible."

"Gave their parole?" she asked incredulously. "When there were only three men against them?"

"Well," he said slowly, "they thought there were many more. Almost an army." He could not help but grin. "I donna think they will be pleased when they learn there were so few of us."

For a moment, she seemed disgusted that her clansmen had been so easily fooled, then a flash of humor erased her distaste. But all disappeared in a frown as her gaze went back to his wound.

Though he did his best to hide it, the bloody thing was starting to worry him, as well. He did not want to alarm her, but he was not certain how much longer he could remain on his feet. Apparently, his efforts to pretend he was unaffected were being wasted, for she suddenly took charge.

"Come inside," she said.

"I canna linger," he said again, but his eyes closed for a moment, and when he opened them again, the world was spinning.

"You will have to," she said. "If you donna stop losing blood, you will be lingering permanently."

"A few moments," he conceded. "Only a few moments. Then we must go." He tried to take a step, but he staggered and ended up leaning against the rock wall a few feet inside the cave. Dear God, but he was tired.

"Patrick!" he heard her exclaim. "Quick Harry! Help!"

Patrick felt his legs giving way beneath him, felt himself start to slide down the rock. Marsali's arms came around his waist, but she was unable to support his weight. Another pair of arms encircled his chest. Together, Marsali and Quick Harry dragged him into the cave, around a bend in the rock wall to the place Harry had made camp. There, beside a small fire, they lowered him to the ground. He blessed them silently for the care they took in the process.

The sudden authority he heard in Marsali's voice as she barked orders at Quick Harry caught his attention. He opened his eyes, blinking several times to focus on her face, bent worriedly over him. He let himself sink into the lovely, soothing depths of her eyes as her fingers gently untied the binding from his wound, then inched his shirt from under his belt. He did his best to cooperate when she, with Quick Harry's help, pulled the shirt off him. But when they lifted his left arm, fire ripped through him, and he could not entirely swallow the groan the agonizing pain evoked.

"I will have to sear the wound to close it," he heard Marsali say. "He is still bleeding."

"I will be about building a fire," Quick Harry said. "And I will put my knife in it to make it ready fer ye."

"He says he needs to be on his way," she said, worrying her lip with her teeth.

"Hmph. He willna get far," Quick Harry said. It was clear to Patrick that he was outnumbered. And this time, neither Hiram nor Rufus would be coming to his rescue.

Marsali's fingers were exploring the rip in his shoulder. When she caught him watching, he smiled at her.

"Donna look so worried, lass," he said, wondering if his words sounded as slurred to her as they did to him. "I am not dead, and I donna plan to be. Naught else matters."

Her mouth pursed. "Men," she muttered.

He sighed and let his eyes drift close. He had no idea how many minutes passed before he heard Marsali's voice calling him.

"Patrick?"

His eyes flickered open, then closed. He tried again, this time able to bring her into focus.

"I have to burn the wound to stop the bleeding," she said.

"Do it," he mumbled. "Then I must . . . I must go."

Her whisper came close to his ear. "Patrick, I love you, but you are being a fool. I will hit you over the head if I must, but you willna leave here until I say you are able."

"You would . . . hit me, lass?" he asked, his lips twitching in foggy amusement. "Not proper for a . . . lady to hit . . . her lord."

"Nay, I am quite certain it is not. But I will do it if I must."

Quick Harry's voice came from the direction of the fire. "The knife is ready, my lady."

She rose, and through sheer effort of will, Patrick kept his gaze focused, watching as she selected a small piece of wood from the pile of kindling. He saw Quick Harry pull the knife from the fire and quickly wrap a cloth around its handle. He handed it to Marsali. She dropped to her knees at his side; in one hand she held the knife, and in the other, the piece of kindling meant for him to bite against the pain.

Her gaze met his, and though his brain was not working as it should, he recognized the anguish in her eyes. He knew the cause of her hesitation; it was not easy to hurt someone you loved.

"Do it, lass," he said quietly.

She looked at him for another moment, then offered him the kindling. He took it in his mouth and bit down. The blade glowed white-hot in Marsali's hand. He looked at it once, then, giving her a nod, he let his eyes close.

An instant later, a bolt of shattering pain sent him careening into oblivion.

Chapter 20

Donald Gunn, laird of the clan Gunn and earl of Abernie, insisted upon looking over the purloined cattle himself.

He surveyed one of the herds feeding in an eastern pasture from the back of his sleek gray stallion. "Scrawny beasts," he observed critically. "Hardly worth stealing. Sutherlands have no care for their animals."

Sitting astride his bay beside his father, Gavin heaved an inward sigh. The cattle had been brawny a month ago. But a month of being stolen back and forth, from Gunn to Sutherland pastures, as often as twice a week, had taken its toll. He was only grateful that the beasts were on Gunn land at the moment, for he was beginning to feel a little like they looked: haggard.

How much longer could the deception continue? How many more times could he send his clansmen out to search for Quick Harry—in all the wrong directions? How many more places could he look, and fail to find so much as a trace of Cecilia? How much longer could he and Patrick keep this preposterous scheme from falling down around their ears?

Not much longer, Gavin thought. He had already had to confide in several men, the smarter ones, who had realized it was altogether too easy to steal Sutherland cattle. He was certain Patrick had been forced to do the same. He shuddered at the thought of one particular man's reaction when he learned what his son had been doing. And Gavin had no doubt at all that his father would discover the truth. It was only a matter of time.

The earl of Abernie was regarding his recent bovine acquisitions with a possessive eye. "We will fatten them," he said.

Not bloody likely, Gavin thought, nodding in agreement.

"I am sending Duncan to Edinburgh," his father said, "with a request for the king to have Marsali returned to me and the Sutherlands outlawed for breaking the peace."

Once more, Gavin nodded. Indeed, he was delighted to hear that Duncan would soon be out of the way. The old man had been asking far too many questions about the raids, and why there were no casualties, nor prisoners.

"I have been thinking about sending Jeanie to Brinaire," he said.

His father's gaze snapped to his. "Send another Gunn to be held captive? Are you daft?"

"Nay, she would go as Marsali's maid," Gavin explained. Actually, he was more concerned that his sister have a friend than a servant at Brinaire. "Jeanie could report back to us about the castle defenses," he added for his father's benefit.

His father's eyes lit at the thought. "Do you think they would let her return?"

"She is naught but a maid," Gavin said indifferently. "They would not be keeping too sharp an eye on her."

"I willna rest until I have my daughter back," his father said. "Poor child."

Gavin's lips thinned. His father's compassion for his daughter was coming a bit late. As had his own, he acknowledged. At least, his had not come too late. And if it took his last breath, he would see his friend and his sister properly wed.

"Will she go?" his father asked.

"Jeanie? Aye, she would give her life for Marsali."

God, he hated this deception. Hated the dishonor he felt every time he lied to his father. But he was no longer sure where honor lay: in his duty to his clan or his loyalty to his father? He wished he had Patrick's certainty. Or did Patrick, too, have doubts?

Gavin had longed to be like Patrick for years, a warrior who inspired songs of cunning and bravery. But now he had seen the toll of those brave deeds on Patrick's face. War did not always mean valor. Could honor and dishonor go hand in hand?

"Gavin?"

His father was staring at him.

"Aye, Father?"

The earl reached across the short distance separating their two horses and laid a hand on his knee. "I am proud of you, lad," he said.

He almost told him. At that moment, awash with guilt, Gavin felt an overwhelming urge to tell his father everything. About the cattle raids and the handfast. About Quick Harry and the near certainty that it had been Sinclairs, not Sutherlands, who had killed and burned out their crofters. He almost told him about Patrick's belief that Sinclair was responsible for having Margaret disgraced and for her subsequent disappearance.

Ironically, it was his father's own words that renewed his sense of purpose.

"Sinclair is asking about Cecilia again."

"Fa, in truth, you wouldna give Cecilia to him, would you?" Gavin asked, feeling suddenly cold.

His father looked at him in surprise. "I would honor my word to Edward. I thought ye agreed that a match with Sinclair was advisable."

"*You* thought," Gavin corrected him. "I never actually said what *I* thought. And I am sorry for that, for waiting so long. I should have spoken before. I should have argued against it, because I knew Marsali didna want Edward. Nor did I believe him to be the right man for her."

"And why would that be?" his father asked, his eyes narrowing.

Gavin gathered his courage. "I have always had suspicions about Edward Sinclair," he said. "I allowed my own grief for Margaret to blind me to them. I donna want either of my sisters wed to him."

Gavin met his father's hot stare.

" 'Tis a bit late to be having second thoughts," the earl said.

"Aye, but not too late," Gavin replied, his eyes on every twitching muscle in his father's face.

"You would prefer that devil's spawn of a Sutherland?" his father said, his chin jutting.

I would prefer any man to one who would order the slaughter of innocents. Gavin bit his tongue. He had already said too much. But, dear God, it felt good to speak his mind, to say things he should have said months ago. Aye, he thought, it was high time he stopped living in his father's shadow. The earl of Abernie was a good man, had been a good father and a good laird. But he was not infallible. Especially when he was angry.

And there was no one but himself to stay his hand— to offer another opinion. Even he had held his tongue far too long.

"I have said what I intend to say on the subject," he said, holding his father's gaze. "I wouldna approve a match for either Marsali or Cecilia with Edward Sinclair. I donna like or trust the man, and that is the truth of it." With that, Gavin pressed his knees to his horse's sides and started toward home.

His father's voice followed him. "I want more men guarding the cattle!"

Without slowing, Gavin lifted a hand in acknowledgment. Aye, he would see that the cattle were well guarded. As well guarded as they could be by Gunn clansmen who were deaf, dumb, and blind. He wondered how many of them he could find.

Patrick awoke to hell's own blaze searing through his shoulder. But his head was resting on something warm and soft and infinitely comforting. A hand soothed his cheek, and sweet whispered words floated in his ears.

His eyelids fluttered open, and he saw Marsali smiling down at him. Sighing, he let his eyes close once more. She tucked his blanket closer around his good shoulder, then went back to stroking his brow.

He swallowed against the dryness in his throat, and when he spoke, his voice was a low rasp. "How long . . . have I been . . . ?"

"Just the night," she said. "Rufus stopped by. Your brother helped Hiram take Black Fergus and the others to Brinaire."

Patrick frowned. "Alex?"

"Aye," she replied. "He and Elizabeth rode with me yesterday, from Brinaire. I left them on the other side of the pass, but when I did not return at the agreed-upon time, they came looking for me."

It took a moment for the full import of her words to sink in. When it did, his eyes flew open. "Elizabeth? She rode through the pass?"

Her hand held him down when he tried to sit up. That she succeeded with so little effort shocked him.

"Elizabeth is fine," Marsali assured him. "Rufus told me she was very proud of herself. So, I think, is Alex."

Patrick relaxed, basking in the luxury of being cosseted by his wife. A lovely experience, indeed. But his mind was clearing rapidly, and a myriad of thoughts intruded to disturb him.

Again his eyes flew open. "Quick Harry?" he asked. "Is he still here? Is he all right?"

"He is perfectly all right," Marsali replied. "He is gathering wood." Then, as if she had read his thoughts, she added, "I donna believe anyone else will come here. Whoever came before found the hut empty. They wouldna think there was reason to return."

She was right, of course. Still, Patrick did not like her being here, with only two wounded men for protection. She should be back at Brinaire where he could keep her safe. And the prisoners—he had to make certain his father did not mistreat them.

He needed to be home.

But first, he needed to stand.

Patrick planted his right hand on the ground and tried to shove himself into a sitting position. When Marsali tried to stop him, he said, "Nay. I must," in a tone that brooked no argument. She relented.

Waves of pain radiating from his shoulder assaulted him with every movement, but he gritted his teeth and kept trying until he sat upright. His head swam a bit, and his shoulder hurt like bloody hell, but otherwise he seemed to be all right.

Glancing at Marsali, he said, "Help me up, lass."

She hesitated, then stood and offered him a hand. He shoved the blanket off of himself, and found he was naked underneath. Using Marsali's slight form for balance, he got to his knees, then his feet. He leaned against the wall of the cave for a moment, then tried a step. And another. Fighting to breathe through the pain, he looked down at his shoulder. It was swathed in bandages that were damp with a yellow, bloody stain. The bandages themselves were a fine linen, and he realized they must have come from Marsali's shift.

He looked up to find Marsali's gaze on him. Without a word, she picked up what was left of his plaid, which he saw had been washed of blood, and brought it to him. He did not need to ask about his shirt; even if she had been able to wash out the blood, he would not have been able to put his arm through the sleeve. She helped him wrap the plaid around his waist and belt it. He leaned on her throughout the process.

Still she did not speak. She neither protested nor tried to stop him, yet she had to know that he meant to leave.

"You are a rare lass," he said, trying to smile through the pain. "You have more courage than any man I know."

"Nay," she whispered. "I died a hundred times in the past day alone."

"I am sorry, lass."

"You should be," she scolded, but he saw tears shimmering in her eyes.

He bent his head to kiss the tears that hung in her thick eyelashes. He felt the strength in her, the resoluteness, and yet she was trembling. He knew she was afraid for him, yet, when he looked at her, she smiled.

Love flowed through him like a warm breeze on a sunny Highland day, overcoming the pain in a gentle rush. His good arm went around her, holding her tight against him, in part because he needed her support, but mostly because he simply needed her. It had nothing to do with lust and everything to do with belonging and tenderness and a quiet splendor. He wanted to stay here with her forever.

"Ye be alive, then?"

The sound of Quick Harry's voice brought Patrick back to reality.

Marsali backed away a little, and he turned. Quick Harry stood watching them with a smile on his face. Patrick's prize witness looked well; he had gained weight, and his color was back. But Patrick did not remember his red beard being laced with quite so many white hairs before.

Patrick nodded. "Aye, Quick Harry, I live," he said. "Thanks to my lady."

"Aye, she be a fine healer." Quick Harry hesitated. "Do ye know when I can go home? I ache to see my wife and son."

Patrick had to smile. He understood exactly what Harry meant, although a month ago, he might not have.

"My men say that Sinclair will probably act soon,"

Patrick said. "Be patient, Quick Harry. I think it willna be long before we capture the raiders who burned your homes. Then we can produce the dead man who can prove it."

Quick Harry nodded reluctantly. "I heard it was Black Fergus who stabbed you."

"Aye," Patrick said. "He has been taken to Brinaire, but I swear to you he will be well treated."

Quick Harry grimaced. "I donna care fer 'im myself, but my wife ha' a soft spot for 'im, 'im being 'er brother."

"He is a brave man," Patrick said.

Quick Harry nodded. "Ye be wantin' to leave, do ye not?"

"Aye, I must get back to Brinaire."

Again, Quick Harry nodded. "I will saddle yer horses."

"You will be safe here alone?"

"Aye. Whoever came didna see anything to bring them back. Yer Hiram brough' enough supplies to keep me fed fer weeks. Ye ha' my word I willna leave until ye tell me. I owe ye my life."

"Marsali saved it, not I," Patrick said, embarrassed by the emotion in Quick Harry's voice.

"I am in debt to ye," Quick Harry insisted, then turned to fetch the horses.

When he returned, Patrick allowed Quick Harry to help Marsali mount her horse, but he refused any help for himself. He gained his saddle, but not without considerable pain. It was going to be a hellish ride.

He nodded to Quick Harry. "I will send Hiram back to see how you fare soon," he said.

"I will be fine, milord," Harry replied. "Just see to it that this bloody mess gets over wi', so we can all get on wi' our lives."

Quick Harry's words echoed in Patrick's mind as he and Marsali rode for Brinaire. Aye, it was high time they were all able to get on with their lives.

* * *

How could a father and his son be so completely different?

Marsali stood at Patrick's side in front of Gregor Sutherland at the entrance to Brinaire. Where Patrick gave warmth and caring to those he met, his father was the coldest human being she had ever known. It was a mystery which she doubted she would ever unravel.

They had been warned about the marquis's mood. Hiram had met them with ten other Sutherland clansmen a few miles south of the pass. Having heard that his son had been wounded, Patrick's father had exploded in rage. It had not improved matters when he learned that Alex and Elizabeth had left Brinaire with the Lady Marsali. The very angels themselves, Hiram insisted, must have heard him bellowing. He had dispatched Hiram to find his son and his Gunn hostage. He had confined Elizabeth and Alex to their rooms. And the prisoners, being the nearest and most vulnerable targets, had been thrown into the dungeons.

Marsali had seen the fury come over Patrick at the news. He had promised the prisoners that they would not be mistreated. And his brother and sister were being punished for trying to help him. Nothing would do, then, but to increase their pace, despite the wound she knew must be causing him agony.

The marquis had been waiting for them on the castle steps, forewarned of their arrival. He stared at Patrick for several minutes without a word, and Marsali thought she saw a flash of concern in his eyes. Then he turned to glare at her.

"Your doing, I ken," he said, waving a gnarled hand toward Patrick's shoulder.

"Nay," Patrick interceded. "She saved my life."

"Now, how is that so?"

Patrick hesitated. He could not say that she had had a premonition. Nor could he explain how she had found him.

"She is a healer," he finally said.

His father snorted. "Get to your room, gel. I will talk with my son."

Patrick started to object, but she shook her head. Her presence would only serve as a further irritant to his unreasonable father.

Patrick held her gaze for a moment, then nodded. "Thank you, Marsali," he said, making it clear that she left because she chose to.

She heard the anger in his voice, though he had spoken softly. Some men thundered when they were angry. She had learned that Patrick grew more and more quiet. His silence, Marsali thought, was far more formidable than his father's shouting.

She climbed the stairs to her bedchamber slowly. Would it ever be possible for her to be part of Patrick's family? She feared that, as long as his father was alive, none of them would have any peace.

In her bedchamber, Marsali went directly to her ferrets' basket. Isolde and Tristan eyed her indignantly when she lifted the cover; neither hopped out to greet her.

"Angry that I deserted you, no doubt," she said to them.

Picking them up, she carried them to her bed, sat cross-legged upon it, and deposited them on her lap. Even then, they cast accusatory looks at her, reluctant to forgive.

Finally, Isolde curled up on her lap and Tristan wrapped himself around his mate. But they made none of their happy little chittering noises. Marsali stroked them with her fingers, muttering small apologies.

Her fingers continued to stroke their soft, thick fur as she waited for—and worried about—Patrick.

Only a few minutes had passed when a soft knock came at the door. She spilled the ferrets onto the bed and hurried to open it, then had to hide her surprise to find Colly, the cook, standing in her doorway with a tray of food.

"The young lord's man—that Hiram—he said ye might be needing a wee bit to eat," Colly said awkwardly.

Marsali looked at the tray. There was much more than a wee bit on it. It was full of pastries, and meat pie, and fish of some kind.

"I used eggs in the pastries," Colly said with a hint of defensiveness. "And some of that salt Lady Elizabeth bought."

"It looks very good, Colly," Marsali replied. "Thank you."

"Hiram said you saved Lord Patrick?"

Marsali shook her head, wondering what tale Hiram was spinning. Just then, one of the ferrets jumped down and darted toward Colly's feet. She screamed and the tray went flying—up, then down, with a resounding crash of pewter plates hitting the floor. When the plates settled, food lay everywhere. The startled ferrets ran under the bed, then peeked out and, seeing food, cautiously inched forward, noses twitching. Isolde dipped her face into the meat pie and emerged covered with pastry, which she started to lick happily.

Colly stared at them with horror, backing toward the door. "What are them doing in here?"

Marsali bit her lip to keep from laughing. She leaned down and picked up Isolde and Tristan, scolding them. "They are ferrets, Colly. They are usually better mannered than this. I can see that Lady Elizabeth has brought them food and water since yesterday morning, but they are accustomed to me doting on them. They become testy and sullen when I leave them, and I think they are getting their revenge."

Isolde started chittering, trying to get back to the meat pie. Tristan licked his mate's face. Colly, apparently satisfied they were not wild beasts, looked at them with fascination. A smile crept onto her face.

"I thought they were big rats."

"Nay, they are usually gentle little creatures," Marsali replied with chagrin. "Except they donna care for Patrick."

The cook's eyes sharpened, and Marsali scolded herself.

She should not have said his name in such a fond and intimate way. She was a prisoner. He should be *Lord* Patrick.

"I am sorry about your food," Marsali added hurriedly. "It was so kind of you to bring it."

Colly was still staring at her thoughtfully, and Marsali was afraid she would soon be the subject of kitchen gossip.

"I will clean the spilled food," she offered.

"Nay," the cook said. "I will send the lad to do it, and he can bring ye some more food." She looked at the ferrets. "Can I be touching them?" she asked.

Marsali handed her Tristan, the less temperamental of the two, and Colly took him with two large, work-roughened hands. She leaned down and took a piece of fish from the floor and offered it to the ferret, letting him nibble from her fingers. Isolde started squirming with jealousy, and Marsali found her a piece of fish.

"I ha' a boy," Colly said nervously. "He lives wi' my sister. He loves animals. Might I bring him to see them?"

Marsali nodded. "Isolde will be having kits soon. Mayhap he would like one."

Colly beamed. Then, as if she felt she might have overstepped her bounds, she handed Tristan back to his mistress and began to back out of the doorway. "I will send the lad," she said, then stopped. "We all like Lord Patrick. And ye bring light into this old place." With that, she was gone.

Stunned, Marsali stared at the closed door. Finally, with a pensive frown, she put both ferrets on the floor and watched as they nibbled at the fish, then the meat pie.

"We all like Lord Patrick." The words echoed in Marsali's mind, as did Patrick's words to his father. *"She saved my life."*

Sitting beside her now-sated ferrets, she stroked their fur, saying, "My pets, I fear I love a very devious man." He was even using his injury to create goodwill for her.

While she had to admire Patrick's cleverness, and she had no doubt that his intentions were honorable, she could not help but worry what would happen when all of their lies became known. Nor could she help but wonder whether she and Patrick, in the midst of all this deception, were building a life together on a foundation that must one day collapse.

She wanted a home filled with his children. And she wanted their children to be free from hate. And from deceit. Could they build such a home and raise such children when, at this very moment, she knew he was telling his own father fewer truths than lies?

Could she expect to raise children who were honest when she was sitting comfortably on the bed in which she had lain with her husband, while her father believed she was being held against her will?

Marsali could only hope that the price they were paying to live together and raise their family in peace was not so high that it destroyed them.

Chapter 21

Patrick steeled himself for the worst. It was imperative that he not show even the slightest sign of weakness. The only thing his father understood was strength.

He had not expected to come home to a power struggle. He certainly had not wanted it. He wanted peace and contentment. He wanted a wife and children. And somehow he had almost forgotten how indifferent to his feelings his father was. How ruthless. He had thought merely of home, the mountains and rich blue sky and foaming sea. He had thought of Marsali.

As he looked now at his father's worn and bitter countenance, he felt a stab of pity. The man had lost three wives, had ruined his relationships with his children, and was at war with the only man he had ever considered a friend. What did he have to show for his life?

Nothing but his honor. Honor that he now had to depend upon his son to uphold, for he was too old and gout-ridden and dispirited to do it himself. For a proud man, it had to be the worst form of torture.

Aye, Patrick could feel pity for his father, despite believing that the man had brought most of his troubles on himself. But, he could not allow his father's wounded pride to ruin the lives of everyone around him. It had been the old man himself who had taught him that his duty to his clan was more important than anything else. Now the honor his father told him was so precious demanded that he do whatever was necessary to prevent his father from destroying that which he had spent his life protecting.

Even if it meant lying.

Even if it meant standing on his feet and fighting when he knew he could be knocked over with a feather.

"I want the Gunns released from the dungeon," Patrick said. "I gave them my word they would be treated honorably in return for their parole."

"I made no such promise, and you had no right," his father retorted. "Brinaire still belongs to me. I havena died yet."

Patrick heard the frustration in his father's voice.

"Several of these men have fought at your side," he reasoned. "They have been our allies. You canna treat them like vermin. Those dungeons have not been used in years. They are infested with rats and damp enough to kill the heartiest man."

"The bastards almost killed you!" his father roared. "Do you think I will let that pass unnoticed?"

There was an odd note in Gregor's voice, and for an instant, it almost sounded as if the old man actually cared. But his gaze flickered away, and Patrick thought he must have been mistaken.

"They were looking for one of theirs, a man they thought I had killed," Patrick said. "I canna blame them for that."

"Then you are weak," his father replied, glaring at him. But there was no fire in his voice; it was almost as if he were repeating words spoken too many times already.

Patrick stared him down, waiting until his father's gaze dropped. Then he said softly, "I want them released. And I donna want Elizabeth and Alex punished for doing what I told them to do."

His father's gaze snapped to his face. "*You* told them to take the Gunn wench outside these walls?"

"She has given her parole, as have the other Gunns. She is entitled to some freedom, and I told Alex and Elizabeth to take her riding if it pleased her."

"Pleased her?" his father exploded. "*Pleased* her?"

"Aye," Patrick said. "I came home to a pigsty. In the little time Marsali has been here, she has managed to see to it that the keep is clean and that the food is edible. She is teaching Elizabeth how to manage a household, a process which should have begun years ago. Whether you choose to admit it or not, she is making this place a home again, and I intend to do everything possible to encourage her efforts."

His father's swollen hands clenched into fists and his face turned red, but he said nothing.

Patrick persisted. "The Gunns?"

Gregor stared at him in silence. Then, with an unmistakable note of defeat coloring his bitter tone, he said, "Do as you will. And if there is more Sutherland blood shed, let it be on your head."

Patrick's eyes narrowed, yet he sensed no deception. Rather, it seemed as if his father simply did not have the will to argue further. This assessment gave Patrick no personal satisfaction at all.

"And Alex and Elizabeth?" he asked.

A muscle worked in the stern jaw. "What have you done to them? They used to be obedient."

"I have done nothing but treat them with respect . . . and love. Something they should have received from you," he retorted. "They are scared to death of you."

" 'Tis as it should be."

"No," Patrick said softly. " 'Tis not as it should be. A child needs . . . deserves love. I received precious little from you, but it is not too late for them. At least, I hope to God it is not."

He had to leave before he said more than he should. More than was wise.

And before he fell down.

Patrick mounted the first step to Brinaire's massive front doors, thinking that collapsing at his father's feet would not enhance whatever power he had won that day. If only his bed were not so far away . . .

Placing each foot with great deliberation, he climbed one

step, then another, determined not to falter. A night's rest. A good meal. Then he would be ready to do battle again with an unreasonable old man. But now he felt dizzy and sick, and he was not sure he could continue to speak, much less do battle.

He heaved a sigh as he reached the top step. Hiram was waiting, leaning against the door, his gaze fixed on his friend. Patrick started toward him, intent on making the door under his own steam. But with a muttered oath and a look of disgust, Hiram strode quickly to his side and put an arm under his right elbow.

It was enough. With Hiram's help, Patrick made it inside, across the hall, and up the stairs. He wanted Marsali, but he could not take the steps toward her. Hiram helped him onto the bed, then pulled his boots off.

"Release the Gunns," Patrick said.

"Your father?"

"He agreed, but he willna give the order," Patrick said, closing his eyes. "They can sleep with the other men in the great hall."

Patrick felt a big, callused hand cover his forehead.

"First I will fetch the lass," Hiram said. "Ye are much too hot."

" 'Tis only from arguing," Patrick replied sleepily. He was bloody relieved to be lying down. "You can release the Gunns as long as they continue to pledge their parole."

"To hell with them," Hiram said. "I am going to fetch the lass."

"Hiram, I will be fine," Patrick insisted, turning onto his right side in blessed anticipation of sleep. "I only need rest. I want you to release the Gunns before my father changes his mind. And you must wait for Rufus at the glade. I must know when Sinclair has planned the next raid. We canna afford to be blamed again."

Hiram hesitated.

"Go, Hiram," Patrick ordered, the force of his words lost in a sigh.

"Aye, my lord," Hiram said.

With his eyes still closed, Patrick smiled. Hiram never used his title unless he was truly disgruntled.

"I wish I had a dozen of you," Patrick said. "But I have only you. And Rufus."

"You have your brother," Hiram said.

Surprised, Patrick opened his eyes again.

"He is ready, Patrick. Ye should ha' seen him on the ride with the prisoners. He was proud to be of service to ye, and he did a fine job of it."

Patrick considered it. Alex seemed so young. He could not bear it if something were to happen to him.

"Ye have to start trusting someone."

"I do," Patrick protested.

"Rufus, myself . . . who else? Yer lady and her brother, mayhap." Hiram cocked an eyebrow down at him. "Alex is *yer* brother, and he is ready."

"He is too young."

"He is older than ye when ye went off to battle, Patrick. And 'tis not necessary that he be ready fer war to wait on a message. Let him go to meet Rufus. He has courage, if ye will but till it."

Patrick stared at Hiram. He was right—about Alex and about him. Somewhere in the past twelve years, he had lost whatever ability he might have had to trust. That lack had come close to costing him Marsali. Out of sheer desperation to keep her, he had been forced to begin the uncomfortable, difficult process of learning to trust someone. And, in truth, he was reaping unexpected rewards for his efforts. Mayhap it was time he learned to trust others, as well. What better place to start than his own brother?

"Very well." Wincing, Patrick levered himself up on one elbow. "Send him to me."

"Aye," Hiram said happily. "And I will send yer lass to tend that wound."

Patrick watched him walk to the door. "Hiram?"

He turned with his hand on the latch. "Aye?"

"I am grateful for the day you dropped upon me."

Hiram grinned. " 'Twas not a poor day fer me either," he said, disappearing through the door.

Adjusting the pillows, Patrick hauled himself into a semi-upright position. Sleep would have to wait.

But he was in fact dozing when a knock came at his door. He opened his eyes to see Alex enter, a tentative, even wary expression on his face.

Fighting off sleep and waves of dizziness, Patrick smiled and gestured for Alex to come stand beside him. His brother stopped a few feet short of the bedside. Patrick met and held his gaze.

"I believe you saved my life," he said. "If Marsali hadna reached Hiram yesterday, you would be heir to Brinaire today."

Patrick watched Alex's expression change, saw pride slowly replace his uncertainty. A smile twitched at the corners of his brother's lips, and, gradually, the smile became a grin.

"Having to name me heir would give Father apoplexy," Alex said. "And I have no wish to *be* heir. If it comes to taking the brunt of Father's anger, better you than me, brother. I have not your courage."

No, but you have your own, Patrick thought, *and it is quite as fine as any other man's.* He knew Alex would not believe it, though. Not yet.

"I would ask you to do something for me," he said.

"Anything," Alex replied, his eyes sparkling.

"Hiram thinks a great deal of you. He believes you are ready to help us."

The young brow puckered.

"He also believes you can be trusted to keep silent. So do I."

Alex's frown deepened, but he nodded.

"Sit," Patrick commanded, gesturing with his good hand toward the straight chair by the window.

Alex went to fetch the chair, and Patrick used the moment to gather the remnants of his strength. He had nothing left in him to ward off either pain or exhaustion, and knew they must be stamped on his face with every breath he took. Alex confirmed his thought when he returned with the chair.

"Patrick, I should go. You need to rest. We can talk later, can we not?"

Patrick rolled his head back and forth on the pillow in denial. "Nay, time is of the essence. We must talk now."

Alex shot him a skeptical glance but did not argue. Perching on the edge of the chair, he said, "I am listening."

Dear God, what a pleasure it was to discover he genuinely liked his brother, who, after all, had been not much more than a babe when he had left to go to war. Feeling deeply grateful, Patrick began, "The raid on the Gunn crofters—it was made by Edward Sinclair's men. They plan another in the near future."

Alex leaned forward.

"Rufus is working for Sinclair," Patrick continued. "A spy for us. He . . . will let us know . . . when a raid is planned. I must know . . . immediately." A wave of dizziness struck, forcing him to stop.

"Patrick, let me fetch someone. You should be—"

"Nay. 'Tis only dizziness from loss of blood. It will pass." Taking a deep, slow breath, he went on. "I need someone to meet Rufus, and I am asking you to do it."

Alex nodded quickly. Too quickly.

"It could be dangerous," Patrick warned. "I donna want you to take chances."

"I will be as careful as you would be," Alex said.

Patrick gave a weak laugh. "Brother, take a good look at my body, and you will see how far from careful I have been."

Alex's eyes slid from the scar on his brother's face to the bandaged shoulder. "Then I should have said that I will be as careful as I always am. For while you have been planting your body in the way of enemy swords"—he raised an eyebrow—"*I* have been perfecting the art of avoiding our father's wrath. And I think it altogether possible that I am more cautious than it ever would occur to you to be."

Patrick drew back, astonished by Alex's perception. For an instant, a vivid picture of his brother as a baby flooded his memory: a solemn little face, a pensive frown, a wary manner that held him back from activities into which a more reckless, carefree child would have blundered with a happy, innocent grin. How odd, he thought, to meet that child full grown and see the same qualities manifested to advantage.

Patrick was still coming to terms with the reality that his baby brother truly was on the precipice of becoming a man.

"So I am to meet Rufus and get news of Sinclair's plans," Alex said, his eyes clear and bright.

Without further hesitation, Patrick answered. "Aye. Hiram will tell you the place. 'Tis on our northern border, an hour's ride from the pass."

Alex nodded.

"You may have to wait several days," Patrick warned.

Alex's tone was dry as he replied, "I willna be missed."

"By me, you will be," Patrick said.

Alex stared at him for a second, then let his gaze fall to the floor. A muscle worked in his cheek, and a hint of pink crept up his neck.

Patrick wished he could make up to Alex—and to Elizabeth—for all the years of coldness and loneliness they had been forced to endure, but he could not.

All he could do, when Alex finally looked at him once more, was smile and say, "Take care."

"Aye," Alex said. "I will. You have my word."

He rose to leave, and Patrick saw the strength of purpose in the set of his jaw and the straightness of his back. Aye, Alex might be only seventeen, but he was a man.

When Alex left, Patrick hung on to that thought as he finally gave way to sleep.

Rufus leaned against the wall as he listened to Sinclair, Gordie, and the Englishman, Foster.

"I want more men this time," Sinclair said. "I want a raid that Gunn canna ignore."

"We donna have enough Sutherland plaids," Gordie pointed out.

"In three days' time, you will. The women are preparing them."

Gordie scowled, and Rufus could see the question poised on the tip of his tongue. He willed the man to ask it, for he could not. He was a newcomer, a mercenary who should have interest in naught but killing.

"I have seen no women at weaving or dyeing," Gordie said finally.

Foster and Sinclair exchanged glances. Foster's heavy frown showed he was clearly against giving Gordie the information. After a moment, though, Sinclair shrugged.

"They are at Creighton," he said.

"Creighton?" Rufus said, moving cautiously into the opening Gordie had made. "I ha' not heard of it. Is it far?"

Sinclair frowned. " 'Tis none of your affair."

Rufus shrugged. "But 'tis my affair to be here when ye need me, is it not?"

"Have you other plans?" Sinclair asked, his mouth tightening. "I pay you to stay here."

"Aye, but I like to keep my aim true by hunting," Rufus said. "Yer kitchen has benefited from my efforts." He knew

Sinclair could not argue. He had brought in two stags last week, each killed with one arrow.

"Be here three days from now at dawn," Sinclair said.

"Aye," Rufus agreed, annoyed at not getting more out of the man. "And the spoils from the raid?"

"You can keep what you take."

"And the women?"

Sinclair shrugged, giving his approval to rape and pillage.

Rufus moved slightly, keeping his anger in check. God knows, he had seen enough brutality. He had even participated in it before joining Patrick, who would skewer any man—even his own—he saw attacking a woman. But over the years, Patrick's ethics had become his own.

"Who can we trust?" Sinclair asked Gordie.

Gordie shrugged. "I have ten men. Mayhap twenty of yours. And, of course, Foster."

Rufus noted he was excluded, but Gordie, who was Sinclair's second-in-command, had been jealous of him ever since he had entered Sinclair's gates. That he had been included in this meeting had not pleased Gordie at all. Nor did it please Rufus that Sinclair apparently had taken a liking to him; it was like bile in his throat. But it was necessary.

Sinclair nodded. "You will attack at dawn three days from now. There is a cluster of Gunns fifteen miles northeast of the village of Kilcraig. Take it. Leave one or two witnesses."

Rufus nodded with the others and started to leave.

Until Sinclair gestured for him to stay. Gordie frowned. Foster's expression was inscrutable. But both left without a word. Sinclair had a reputation for a towering temper.

Sinclair poured two cups of wine, offered him one, then sprawled in a chair, eyeing him with interest. "Gordie does not like you."

"I ha' noticed," Rufus said with a shrug.

"He questions your absences."

"Do ye?"

Sinclair looked thoughtful. "A soldier should be obedient."

"Then ye can find one that is," Rufus said. "I am a rest-less mon. I see nothing good aboot indolence and over-feeding a big belly." That shot was aimed at Gordie, whose large size included a protruding stomach.

Rufus drained the contents of his cup and again moved toward the door.

Sinclair stood, eyeing Rufus with speculation. "Nay. Do not leave yet. The other men like you, even Gordie. You have something he does not." His eyes narrowed. "Will you consider staying?"

"I told ye. I am a restless mon. I will do a job for ye, and do it well for good pay, but then I leave." Rufus knew he was treading a dangerously thin line. Sinclair had questions about him, questions nagging at his brain. He could see them in the man's eyes.

"I will go hunting with you," Sinclair said.

"I prefer hunting alone," Rufus said with a touch of inso-lence. He watched Sinclair's face redden, and he wondered just how far he could go before sparking the man's famous temper.

"*I* do not," Sinclair said through clenched teeth.

Rufus realized he had no choice. He would have to take Sinclair with him today; then mayhap the man would be sat-isfied and leave him alone on the morrow so he could meet Hiram.

Rufus shrugged. "If ye wish."

"I wish," Sinclair said. "I will have the horses saddled."

Mayhap Sinclair's demand was a fine thing after all. May-hap he could discover something about Creighton. What-ever and wherever it was, it was a good place to keep women whose task it was to make plaids they had no business mak-ing. Mayhap it was also a good place to keep other people, whether they were willing—or not.

*   *   *

Marsali washed the sweat and grime from Patrick's face. That he did not waken, or even stir, told her how truly exhausted he was. The tightness of his jaw gave evidence of the pain he felt even as he slept.

Concerned about the redness she saw surrounding his wound when she removed the bandage, she had sent Hiram to the woman who had provided the healing herbs for Quick Harry. She wished Hiram would hurry.

The sight of Patrick's seared flesh made her stomach knot. Nothing in her life had been harder than holding the hot knife to his wound. She had stitched the flesh and set the bones of other men, and she had ached with sympathy for them. But that did not compare to the deep agony she had felt yesterday. Only the knowledge that he would bleed to death if she did not do it had given her the strength.

As she gently washed the area around the wound, Marsali's gaze traveled over her husband's body. He had so many scars. So many signs of pain endured. A battle ravaged body with a peacemaker's heart.

A soft knock sounded at the door. She jumped up to open it, gasping when she saw Jeanie standing next to Hiram. Hiram wore a sheepish look and held out a sack to her.

"I met the lass coming into the gates," he offered.

With tears stinging her eyes, Marsali took the herbs and threw herself into Jeanie's waiting arms. Unable to speak for several moments, she took in the comfort and warmth of the familiar embrace.

"There, lovey," Jeanie crooned. " 'Tis glad I am to see ye, too, and looking so well as ye are, at that."

"But what are you doing here?" Marsali took a step back to meet Jeanie's gaze. "Why are you—I mean, how—"

"Gavin thought you might need me," Jeanie said.

Dear, sweet Gavin. She pulled the door of Patrick's room closed behind them. "And Father—does he know you are here?"

Jeanie nodded. "He agreed, though at first he didna like

it." She cast a slightly wary look up at Hiram's broad face, then lowered her voice to a whisper. "Gavin convinced him I could be used to spy."

Marsali's eyes widened. Gavin was becoming as devious as Patrick.

Taking note of Hiram's rather silly grin, Marsali saw that he, too, was pleased to see her maid. But she worried that there might be others at Brinaire who would not be so pleased.

"What did the marquis say about you being here?" she asked.

"I donna think he knows," Jeanie said with a smile. "He apparently is abed and ordered that no one disturb him."

Marsali bit her lip. "Jeanie, Patrick has been wounded. I need to get back to him, but I would be ever so glad for your help."

Jeanie shot Hiram an accusing glance. "Ye didna tell me."

"I had no time, lass," he said. "But donna fret, either of ye. Patrick has been dealt worse and has survived. He has the nine lives of a cat."

His attitude made Marsali want to stamp her foot or scream or do something—anything—to vent her frustration at men and their casual acceptance of wounds and war and violence.

Knowing Jeanie would understand, she said, "I fear it might be festering."

"Then we best get to work," Jeanie replied, shooing Marsali into the room ahead of her. Hiram started after them but was quickly stopped by Jeanie, who pushed him resolutely out the door.

When Marsali looked at her with raised eyebrows, Jeanie merely shrugged. Then, with a hand on her arm, the older woman said, "I ha' been sick with worry since ye disappeared. Ye are all right, lovey? Truly?"

"Aye, truly, I am fine," she replied. After a moment's

hesitation, she added, "Jeanie, we were handfasted. Patrick and I. Gavin witnessed it."

Jeanie stared at her, eyes wide. Slowly, her breath left her body in a soft "Och!"

" 'Tis true," Marsali said, smiling.

"And Gavin . . . ?"

"Aye," she nodded. "He and Patrick have been working together to end the feud."

Jeanie's wide-eyed surprise turned to open-mouthed shock. "But how . . . ? Gavin . . . ? Then mayhap he meant it—he did send me as a spy. Or a messenger, at least." And reaching into her dress, she brought out a piece of parchment. "He sent this for ye, love. I had almost forgot."

Marsali took it and opened the seal. She saw immediately that it was really meant for Patrick and that it was not good news. At least, to her it was not. Marsali stuffed the note inside a fold of her overskirt. Time enough to deal with it when Patrick was awake.

"Come," she said to Jeanie. "Help me ready the herbs." Marsali laid the back of her hand on Patrick's forehead. "His skin is much too warm."

"Who did the burning?" Jeanie asked, her brow furrowed as she studied the sleeping man's wound.

"I did," Marsali replied.

"And died a little doing so, I ken."

"Aye."

Jeanie held her gaze for a moment, then, giving a short nod of approval, she turned to the business of emptying the bag Hiram had brought onto the table.

Examining the items, Marsali was pleased to see that, once again, the healer had provided exactly the things she would have chosen herself, as well as one or two she might not have thought of. Mayhap she could meet this woman and learn from her. Mayhap when the feud was over, she could meet many of Patrick's clansmen in harmony.

Sighing, Marsali began mixing the herbs. "I canna hardly

believe you are here. It seems so long, though I know it has only been a few weeks."

Folding the empty bag, Jeanie smiled. "Abernie has been a quiet place. I admit to ye, it gave me pause, thinking aboot coming here. But I couldna say no. I missed ye." With a grin, she added, "And the wee beasties, too."

"They will be glad to see you," Marsali said, adding the final ingredient to the mixture. "They donna like Patrick, though. I donna understand why."

"They are jealous, lovey," Jeanie said. "They sense he means more to ye than most."

Marsali frowned. "But I love you, and they like you."

"But I was wi' ye before they came," Jeanie said. "They had to accept me."

Marsali soaked a piece of cloth in the bowl of water, wrung it out, and covered it with the powder she had mixed. Sitting on the edge of the bed, she spread the cloth on Patrick's wound. His body jerked slightly, but he did not awaken.

"He has so many scars," Marsali said.

"Aye, he is a warrior."

"But a gentle one." Marsali felt her heart constrict, watching him.

"Ye love him."

Jeanie's softly spoken words were not a question, but Marsali nodded.

"And does he love ye?"

Marsali hesitated. He had never actually said the words. Yet he called her his love, and she believed in her heart that it was so.

"I think so," she whispered. "Though I am not sure he knows it."

Jeanie gave a soft snort. "Men. They are always the last to know what they feel. If ye wait for them to tell ye, ye will die waiting. 'Tis by their actions ye must know their hearts."

Marsali smiled, looking at her husband's handsome,

scarred face. "Aye, he loves me, then," she said. "I canna doubt it."

When they had done all they could for Patrick, Marsali led Jeanie up to her own room. She wanted to stay with Patrick, but she feared that he would be disturbed by their voices.

The moment she opened the door to her room, the ferrets started chittering in their basket. Marsali went to them, picking up both and fondling them. They allowed her a moment's affection, then jumped out of her hands and ran to Jeanie, tumbling over each other in excitement.

"Traitors," Marsali mumbled. She watched them affectionately for a moment. Then, knowing it had to be faced, she said, "Tell me about Father. How is he?"

"He worries about ye and yer sister," Jeanie said, "but he is proud of Gavin."

And how long would his pride last, Marsali wondered, when he found out that his son had been deceiving him?

"Does he talk with Sinclair?" she asked.

"Hmph," Jeanie snorted, carrying the ferrets with her as she came to stand by the bed. "Sinclair sent an emissary asking about ye and Cecilia, demanding that yer father fulfill the contract."

"Cecilia's still safe, then," Marsali whispered. She had feared that someone might indeed find her sister, despite Patrick's assurances.

"I think Sinclair's insistence is straining yer father's patience," Jeanie said. "He ha' stopped talking about a match, but is sending out demands to Parliament and the king that ye be returned to him and that the Sutherlands be outlawed."

Marsali took one of the ferrets, stroking its fur.

"He is lonely," Jeanie said. "He frets over ye."

Marsali sighed. "I miss Abernie. All of you." Then she grimaced. "The servants and the cook here badly need instruction. And Elizabeth—"

"The Sutherland's daughter?"

"Aye, I must go and see her. I think her father was very displeased with her." She took Jeanie's hands. "Come with me. You will like her. Then we will see about some broth for Patrick, for when he wakens."

Jeanie looked at her compassionately. "And ye want to go back to your Patrick, not stay with an old woman."

"You are not old," Marsali said, adding with a grin, "And Hiram certainly doesna think so."

Jeanie looked pleased for a moment. "He is a braw man."

"Aye, he is," Marsali said. "Loyal and sweet and—"

"*Sweet?*"

"Handsome," Marsali continued merrily.

"Ye *are* daft. What ha' the young Sutherland done to ye?"

Marsali smiled. "He has made me happy. Happier than I ever dreamed was possible. And I want the whole world to be as happy as I am. Especially people I love, like you."

Jeanie rolled her eyes, but Marsali could tell she was pleased.

"I should go back and sit with him," Marsali said.

Jeanie gave her a fond look of approval. "You do that."

"Stay in my room for the night. I will find you a room of your own in the morning."

Jeanie looked uncomfortable, and Marsali cocked her head, questioning.

"Hiram has spoken to a woman called Colly about lodgings for me," she said. "She seems to ha' an eye for him."

Marsali wrinkled her nose. "Colly?"

"Aye," Jeanie replied, her tone hinting of jealousy.

Hiram? A heartbreaker? The very idea tickled Marsali, making her want to laugh outright.

"Colly asked Lady Elizabeth," Jeanie said, "and she said tha' I might have the room next door, so I can look after ye. So ye donna need to be concerning yerself wi' me. I will see to some straightening here, then find the kitchen and see about the broth. Now go on. Go back to yer mon, where ye belong."

Marsali did not hesitate. Jumping off the bed, she gave Jeanie a quick hug, then ran lightly toward the stairs. She wanted to be there when Patrick awakened, though she tried to convince herself that it was not out of any real concern for his life. He would be all right. As Hiram said, he had the nine lives of a cat. Still, she intended to make very certain that he had not come to the end of the last one.

Chapter 22

Marsali watched as he finally woke. His cheeks were stubbled, his eyes red-rimmed as they fluttered open. He moved slightly, then expelled a sigh.

Sun was flooding through the window, and he blinked once or twice against the light before his gaze found her, and, as she had hoped, he gave her that slow smile she loved.

He started to sit up, but her hand urged him to stay where he was.

"Rest," she commanded.

" 'Twas but a scratch, lass," he said, but he obeyed all the same, which worried her. Still, his tousled, sleepy gaze made him look so appealing.

"You are a lovely lass," he said, smiling at her with such tenderness her heart jerked.

"A worried one, no matter what you say," she replied, her voice stern at his lack of concern for himself. "You were fevered last night."

"I was but tired," he said. "I just needed some rest. And your touch."

"I will get you some food," she said. "And Gavin sent this for you." She handed him the piece of parchment.

"Gavin?"

"He sent Jeanie to be with me. At least, that was the excuse," she said.

Patrick sat up, slowly at first, then more surely. The cover fell from him, but he seemed unconcerned. His nakedness quickly aroused feelings now so familiar to her: the ache in the center of her being, the rapid beating of her heart that should have contradicted the heated slowing of her blood. Yet it did not.

He did not seem to be having the same problems. Instead, he stared at the writing on the parchment for several moments, then tried to stand, wincing as he did so.

"It is too soon for you to go riding again," she said, already knowing the contents of the letter. Gavin wanted to meet with him. Today.

"I must," he said. "He doesna know Hiram."

"I can go," she offered.

"And how would you leave Brinaire? My father insists that you stay inside the walls."

"Alex?"

"He has already left," Patrick said, taking several tentative steps.

"You shouldna be doing that."

"I have stayed abed long enough," he replied. "There is too much to do."

"You have not been abed nearly long enough," she chided. "Hiram says you have nine lives, but looking at your body, I think you have used up at least eight."

"Does it offend you?" he asked, his eyes suddenly shuttering, and she wondered how he could ask that after the past few days.

"Nay," she said. "Only the pain I know you have suffered. That does offend me." She bit her lip. "And knowing that I . . . the burn . . ."

"You did what had to be done," he said gently, "and I am grateful for it. I never wanted a timid wife who swooned at the sight of blood." His hand took hers. "I never thought to be so . . . blessed by a wife with courage, and skill and heart."

It was the loveliest speech he had ever made to her, that anyone had ever made to her. Women had little value other than bringing about a good marriage and producing children. Her father had taught her that. So had Gavin.

But now he *wanted* to go, to be the manly protector, despite the cost to himself. He was doing it partly for her, partly for their clans.

Would she ever be able to keep a man like him safe? Would he always be fighting for something? She did not feel brave at all then—only frightened, so very frightened for him. She wanted to run away with him, away from feuds and sword fights and hatred. But she knew he would not go, not until he had finished what he had started.

He pulled her to him then, as though he knew exactly what she was thinking. "I will take Hiram with me," he said. "But I must go. Gavin will be expecting me."

"I wish I hadna given you his message," she said.

"Nay, love. You knew I would go." His arm squeezed her closer to him. His lips touched her forehead, then he stepped back. "Help me dress," he said, forcing her to become an accomplice to something she fervently wished he would not do.

Marsali swallowed hard.

"Lass?"

She finally went to the huge armoire and took out a clean linen shirt and a plaid. She already knew the difficulties of fitting the plaid with two good arms. With only one, it was near impossible. She wondered what he would do if she refused to help. Unfortunately, he would probably find someone who would.

She helped him pull the shirt over his head, then fit the plaid over his head and wrapped it around his waist, clenching it with the heavy belt. And amazingly, he seemed to gain strength with every movement, rather than losing it.

"How are the dragons?" he asked. Did he mean to distract her from the fear probably too evident on her face?

"The dragons?"

"Isolde and Tristan," he said, his mouth turning up at one corner. "A foully named pair."

"They were pleased to see Jeanie," she taunted in return. But he could not completely tease the worry from her.

"Is there anyone they donna like but me?"

"Nay," she said as she fastened his clan badge to his plaid. She stood back and looked at him. His dark hair was tousled, and stubble darkened his cheeks, but she thought she had never seen so handsome a man. His green eyes seemed more vivid, mayhap because a trace of fever remained in them, or mayhap because they were regarding her so warmly.

And she *felt* warm inside. She always seemed to melt in his presence, her legs becoming weak, her heart beating erratically, her mouth spouting nonsense.

His touch warmed her even more, sending streaks of heat through her, pulsing at her very core.

"Donna look at me like that, lass," he said, "or I will never go."

She tried to look even more seductive, but she had little experience with such wiles. She had never wanted anyone but him, and he had been gone so many years. Even now that they were handfasted, their time together was so short.

"Donna look so sad," Patrick said.

"I am not looking sad," she protested indignantly. "I am looking seductive."

Patrick chuckled. "I will try to remember the difference," he teased, his finger tracing her mouth, pushing up the edge that was trying to frown. "And you are always seductive, love."

"Will you at least eat some broth and bread before you go?"

"Aye," he said. "The message from Gavin said he would be at the waterfall at noon." He looked out the window at the sun overhead. "I have an hour before I need to leave."

"I will fetch the food and order Hiram to keep you safe." She heard the fierceness in her voice even as she saw amusement twinkle in his eyes.

"You will terrify him, lass." He sat on the ledge below the window, looking relaxed, his legs stretched before him. Legs, Marsali noted, that were really terribly attractive beneath the plaid. She had never noticed a man's legs before. But then, she noticed everything about Patrick Sutherland. And everything was quite perfect.

Her gaze wandered up to his eyes, and she flushed as she realized he had been watching her. She felt the heat in her face, and with a shy smile at the man who made her act so foolishly, she fled.

Marsali had been right. He had needed the hot broth, bread, and cheese she brought him. His arm pained him, but it would have pained him if he had stayed in bed, as well.

Hiram rode silently at his side. He, too, had protested this meeting. His mouth was uncharacteristically grim and he was muttering unintelligible phrases to himself. Patrick did not believe them complimentary.

"Speak up," he finally commanded after nearly an hour.

"Ye should be resting."

"I have seen you riding with worse wounds."

Hiram grumped another indecipherable insult.

Patrick smiled despite the burning pain in his shoulder. Bloody hell, but the riding *did* jolt what was tolerable into thrusts of pure agony.

He sought a way to distract himself.

" 'Tis not just my wound that worries you," he charged Hiram.

"Ye willna listen to anyone," Hiram countered.

"Ah, Hiram, how could you make such a charge? I have always listened to you and Rufus."

Hiram raised one bushy red eyebrow, eloquently expressing his opinion of such a claim. "Then go back, and let me meet wi' this mon," he said.

"You are a stranger to him," Patrick said. "And I fear that it might take my persuasion to keep him on course."

"Ye risk too much," Hiram said.

"I am wagering the future, Hiram," Patrick said softly.

"Ye should take the lass and leave. No one wants peace except ye."

"You are wrong. Quick Harry. Gavin. My clansmen. Theirs. None of them want war. Sinclair started this, and by God, I will end it."

Hiram's frown deepened. "Ye canna save the world, no matter how hard ye try."

"My aims are much smaller, Hiram." Then, because they had always respected each other's privacy, he hesitated before commenting as innocently as possible, "Marsali said Jeanie is here."

"Aye," Hiram said, throwing him an odd expression.

"You mentioned her before," he ventured.

"I may ha'," Hiram admitted.

"Is she as bonny as I remember?"

"Aye," Hiram said after a moment's pause. Then his mouth clamped shut.

Patrick smiled to himself. He liked the idea of a besotted Hiram. Hiram had been as close in many ways as any brother. He had always been a shy giant of a man who had avoided women. Now that Patrick had savored the wonders of making love to a woman who owned his heart, he wanted his friends to know the same joy.

They were silent the rest of the way. Patrick led Hiram to the waterfall, as he had never been to this particular spot. Patrick went first for fear they might scare off Gavin, who expected only him. He thought about leaving Hiram a short distance away, but it seemed like high time they met.

Both Patrick and Hiram dismounted, and Patrick took a seat on a low, flat rock. He felt dizzy and sick again. The world slid around him in odd ways. Then he heard a whistle. It was the same whistle he and Gavin had used as children, the one he had taught Rufus and Hiram.

Hiram looked at him in surprise. Patrick shrugged as he

returned the whistle and saw a movement above. In minutes, Gavin stood in front of him, looking suspiciously at Hiram.

"Your sister wouldna allow me to come without him," Patrick said.

Hiram interceded rudely. "One of your clansmen ripped his shoulder open. He still bleeds from the wound."

Gavin's gaze went immediately to the bulge under the plaid and the stiff way Patrick held his left arm to his side.

"Who?"

"Black Fergus."

Gavin groaned. "Where is he now?"

"Eating and drinking in our hall. He and seven others are paroled prisoners. One way to defeat us would be to send us more prisoners. They will eat us into surrender."

But his jest did not produce a smile.

"None are hurt?"

"Nay," Patrick said.

Gavin looked closely at Patrick. "How badly were you hurt?"

Patrick shrugged the question aside. He was tired of all the bother about little more than a prick. "You wanted to meet?"

"Aye," he said. "Father is sending an emissary to Parliament, asking that you be outlawed. I suggest you send someone to plead your case."

Patrick nodded.

"I want to know what is going on," Gavin continued. "I donna like lying to my father."

"Neither do I," Patrick said curtly, the pain in his shoulder sharpening again. "I donna think we will have to wait much longer. I have a man with Sinclair. He says Sinclair is becoming impatient. There will be another raid soon." He hesitated. "How many men can you send to guard the border farms?"

"A hundred," Gavin replied. "Mayhap more."

"Bring the women and children into Abernie," Patrick said. "Concentrate ten men at each farm but keep them out of sight. Station others on horseback throughout the woods so they can carry messages and call your people to wherever the attack takes place. If I can, I will send a warning as to exactly where the raid will be. I will also send men to join you. They will wear black bands around their arms and any kind of clothing other than Sutherland plaids. I donna want them attacked by Gunns."

Gavin's brows furrowed as he listened to the rapid-fire orders.

"That would leave Abernie and the cattle herds virtually unprotected," he finally said.

"Aye," Patrick agreed steadily. Now he would find out exactly how far Gavin trusted him. He was asking his friend to leave his keep—his family—unprotected. If Patrick was lying, the Sutherlands could walk into Abernie.

"Father would never agree."

"He would if he thought the Sutherlands might raid the crofters," Patrick countered.

Gavin sighed, looking away. Patrick wondered what he was thinking. But he knew he could not push his friend.

Patrick leaned to the side to relieve the damnable pressure in his shoulder, and Hiram instantly started toward him. But Patrick shook his head, and Hiram paused, looking from Patrick to Gavin and back again. Then he retreated. This was not the time—Patrick would have to manage on his own.

A minute went by, then another.

Finally, Gavin turned back to Patrick, his gaze searching his friend's face. Then he nodded.

"I will try to do as you ask," he said. "I will have to say that the warning came from Marsali through Jeanie. That is the only thing my father will believe."

Patrick did not like the idea, but he had little choice. If anything went wrong, he would make sure the blame was diverted elsewhere, anywhere other than onto Jeanie or Marsali.

He held out his hand and the two men clasped each other's wrists in friendship. Patrick saw Gavin's gaze go to his shoulder again.

"Take care," Gavin said. "Give my love to my sister."

"Aye," Patrick said.

Gavin looked over at Hiram, but the big man only glowered at him. Hiram apparently blamed all Gunns for Patrick's recent wound. "Take care of him," Gavin said, and Hiram's frown faded slightly.

"I will get the horses," he said, leaving Gavin and Patrick alone for a moment.

Patrick smiled. "How are the cattle?"

"Weary," Gavin said. "My father believes Sutherlands are uncaring villains for allowing their cattle to get so thin."

"The poor beasts will be as glad as any of us to have this finished," Patrick said.

"But who ends up with the mangy beasts?" Gavin asked, a combative gleam in his eyes. "Possession, you know . . ."

Patrick tried to laugh, but his shoulder hurt too bloody badly.

"My man in the Sinclair stronghold says there is talk of a secret place . . . perhaps an island. Do you know anything of it?"

Gavin's brows knitted together. "There is Creighton, but it was abandoned years ago when the sea washed away the foundations and made it an island."

"Aye," Patrick frowned. "I thought it had crashed into the sea."

Gavin stared at him. "What are you thinking?"

Patrick moved away from the supportive rock as he saw Hiram approaching with the horses. "Mayhap naught," he said, using his right hand to help him mount. Once he had gained the saddle, he looked down at Gavin. "Hiram will bring you any message. He has been at Abernie before and would not be suspect."

Gavin nodded.

"I will have men on the border by tomorrow night," Patrick said. "But there must be Gunns if we are to catch Sinclair. Your father wouldna believe a Sutherland."

"They will be there," Gavin said.

Patrick looked down on his boyhood friend, remembering all the fine days they had spent together, the games, the adventures, the shared secrets.

Now they shared something much larger: the fate of their clans.

"God go with you, Gavin," he said.

Gavin grinned. "More like the devil."

Alex perched in the leafy branches of a tree, composing a poem in his head. Marsali was the inspiration. He greatly admired her, and envied Patrick the looks he received from her.

Occasionally, he looked out over the forest for movement, but he had been here a day and a half now and had seen little but the scurrying of squirrels and an occasional rabbit. He had spent the night shivering inside his plaid, reluctant to start a fire which might give him away. At dawn, he had climbed into his tree again, eager to be of help to his formidable brother.

Now he was beginning to despair that anyone would come. His attention was wandering, and his mind occupied itself with the poem he planned to put to his harp.

He heard a low whistle, like the song of a bird, but he had not heard a bird sing in these trees the whole time he had waited. His skin prickled. His heart beat faster when he heard the soft neigh of a horse. He peered out from between the branches and saw a lone horseman. The poem fled from his mind as he studied the approaching rider.

As he drew closer, Alex recognized the lanky form of Rufus, and, eager again, he slipped down from his perch.

Rufus had a pistol out, and Alex knew a moment's fear before Rufus lowered the weapon. "God help ye, lad, has no one warned ye not to drop in on someone like that?" He frowned down at Alex.

Alex stood speechless for a moment as his watery legs tried to keep him upright. Then to his embarrassment, he stuttered as he started to explain. "Pa—Patrick sent me."

Rufus grinned suddenly and dismounted. "I thought to find Hiram. He has a habit of dropping from trees, too."

"Hiram?" Alex said with surprise. "Is he not too large?"

"Ye would be surprised, lad. He can get in trees I canna."

Alex grinned back, feeling suddenly at ease with this warrior. He was, after all, a friend of Patrick's. From what Alex had seen, Rufus was the fastest man with a sword who had come this way in quite some time. He had defeated five Sutherlands in a row before throwing his sword down, saying there was no challenge there.

Rufus threw an arm around Alex's shoulder and walked with him to the fallen tree trunk. "Patrick must greatly trust ye to send ye here. No one knows about me being at Sinclair's, other than Hiram and your brother."

Alex tried to keep from grinning with pleasure; he wanted a face like stone, just like Patrick's. "I was afraid you were not coming."

"I was much delayed by Sinclair and his sudden desire to go hunting. Thank God, ye waited." Rufus grinned again and sprawled on the log. "I tired him out and made sure he wouldna wish to come again. Still, I canna stay long. I promised Sinclair a wild boar or stag. Even a rabbit will do. Tell your brother Sinclair plans to attack at dawn tomorrow. The Gunn farms fifteen miles northeast of Kilcraig. 'Tis close to the northern border between Gunn and Sutherland land."

Alex tried to assimilate the outpouring of information, the jumble of disconnected facts. "The northern border," he said. "I know it."

"Good lad," Rufus said. "Dawn. Also tell him that Sinclair has women at a keep named Creighton. 'Tis there they are making Sutherland plaids. I wouldna be surprised if they were keeping something else there also."

"What?" Alex asked, bewildered.

"The keep is said to be abandoned," Rufus said, "and yet they send guards and have women there. Now, why do you suppose that is?"

"I donna know," Alex said.

"A captive, mayhap?"

Alex knew he should understand. Rufus looked so expectantly at him, as if he need say no more.

"Your stepmother," he explained finally. "Patrick knew yer father could have naught to do with murder, though I wonder why he is so sure. The marquis seems perfectly capable of anything to me. And the Lady Marsali is equally positive that her aunt would ne'er ha' killed herself."

Thoughts tumbled through Alex's mind. He, too, doubted his father would murder a defenseless woman. Even in a rage. Honor meant too much to him. Alex often thought it was the only thing that did mean anything to him.

And if Margaret was indeed alive, being held prisoner, then . . .

"But why would Sinclair keep her alive?" Alex asked.

Rufus shrugged. "I wouldna be knowing that. 'Tis only a possibility, lad. Probably a slim one. But 'tis something I thought Patrick should know. Now ye best be getting back with the news."

Alex nodded. "I tied my horse deeper in the woods."

Rufus nodded with approval. "Smart lad."

Alex grimaced at the "lad." He was feeling very much like a man now. Patrick, after all, had gone to war at sixteen. Still, pride glowed inside him that this friend of Patrick's thought him capable. He decided to return to his horse before he made a fool of himself.

With only one backward look, he saw Rufus mounting his horse. Alex quickened his steps. Patrick would be waiting.

Patrick would be pleased.

Chapter 23

Marsali had learned long ago that being a woman had many disadvantages. A woman was not considered intelligent enough to learn to read or to have opinions. She could make few of her own decisions. She could not choose her own husband. Yet the past week had nearly convinced her that the advantages of being a woman overshadowed, if not outweighed, the disadvantages.

For one thing, when she and Patrick lay together, she felt as if she were a treasure of untold worth that meant more to him than life itself; he made her feel deeply grateful that she was a woman, and nothing could have convinced her otherwise.

But how did a woman go through life waiting to see if her love would return home in one piece—or if he would return at all? How did she wait in ladylike grace when what she wanted to do was grab the first steed and ride to her love's side? How did she spend hours planning a meal or sewing a platitude, all the while knowing that momentous events were occurring that would change her life forever?

Marsali did not believe she would ever learn the trick of it. She thought she would always feel as she did that day: frightened, anxious, her stomach in knots and her throat aching from the effort of holding back the sudden urge to cry. It was dreadful, and in her turmoil, she leveled the blame at Patrick. One minute she felt like strangling him. The next she wanted only to throw herself into his arms and kiss him.

To distract herself, Marsali surrounded herself with Elizabeth and Jeanie. And they pulled her into the kitchen, where Jeanie started talking to Colly as if the woman were an old friend.

Colly's frown quickly disappeared, and she chatted happily about her son. As Marsali listened, she wondered whether the woman's previous bad temper had come simply from insecurity. She was not altogether surprised when Colly admitted that she had lied about her experience to obtain the cook's position. She was only a widow with a young child, and desperate.

Leaving Jeanie but with Elizabeth in tow, Marsali returned to her room determined to ask Patrick if he could find an empty room for Colly's child in the keep. If the poor woman had less to fret about, her cooking might improve.

The ferrets were fussing in their basket, and brushing past her, Elizabeth ran to release them. She plopped immediately onto Marsali's bed to play with them. But to the neglected creatures' dismay, Elizabeth's attention was caught by the sight of the illustrated book Marsali had left lying open on the bed.

Elizabeth looked at Marsali in amazement. "Do you read?"

"Aye," she replied, picking up Isolde as she sat beside Elizabeth. She stroked her pet as she explained, "I took lessons with Gavin, after Patrick left. I made a terrible nuisance of myself until Gavin asked the tutor to include me. I think, with Patrick gone, he disliked having the tutor's full attention."

Marsali watched Elizabeth, whose gaze was fixed on the book. Elizabeth's green eyes came up to meet hers, and her voice was filled with both reverence and longing as she asked, "Will you teach me to read? The vicar taught Alex, but refused to teach a girl."

Marsali smiled. "Aye, I taught my sister, and I would be glad to teach you." Indeed, she would welcome having a valuable way to pass time.

Without looking up, Elizabeth spoke shyly. "I am so glad you are here."

"So am I," Marsali said, reaching to take the girl's hand. "Though you are not to say that to anyone. I am supposed to be a prisoner, you know."

Elizabeth rolled her eyes. Then she spoke with sudden and uncharacteristic boldness. "I hope Patrick marries you."

Marsali had to bite her tongue. Of course, she wasn't completely lying by not responding—they were really only handfasted. If they did not deny their handfast in a year's time, then the union would become official.

"When do you think he will return?"

Elizabeth's question brought a frown to Marsali's forehead. "By dusk," she replied. *If he returns at all.*

"I am sorry," Elizabeth said softly. "I didna intend to make you worry any more than I know you already are."

A little surprised at the girl's perception, Marsali gave her a rueful smile. "You know, you remind me of Cecilia," she said. "She always knows what I am thinking." And, with a sigh, she added, "I miss her."

"I like Cecilia," Elizabeth said. "I have missed her, too, since . . . since our families no longer visit."

Marsali's lips thinned, recalling all the times the Gunns and Sutherlands had spent together. Visits with her aunt, feasts at winter solstice. Being betrothed, she had stayed with the women, but she knew her sister had become friends with Patrick's sister during those happy occasions. Those times were gone, though, and as she looked at the shy, lonely girl sitting beside her, she counted yet another casualty of the senseless feud that had divided their families.

"Cecilia likes you, too," she told Elizabeth honestly. "I know she was looking forward to having you as a real sister, once Patrick and I were married."

"Truly?"

"Truly." Marsali smiled, picturing her sister as she had seen her last—dressed in lad's clothing, sitting behind Rufus atop his big bay, her eyes sparkling with excitement. "And now she has gone off on an adventure of her own," she murmured without thinking.

"Tell me about it."

Her gaze snapped to Elizabeth, realizing she never should have said anything so obviously destined to pique the girl's curiosity. But Marsali hesitated over the decision only a moment. She knew Elizabeth was trustworthy. And so she told her the story, about her and Cecilia being kidnapped on her wedding day by Hiram and Rufus, and about Cecilia going with Rufus to his home in the Lowlands.

Elizabeth's eyes grew wider and wider as the story progressed, and by the end, her mouth was actually hanging open. When Marsali finished, she sighed. "I would never have been so brave," she breathed.

Marsali did not try to dissuade her, though she disagreed. Elizabeth would have to find her own worth. No one else could convince her of it.

Picking up the book, Marsali asked, "Would you like to have your first reading lesson now?"

Elizabeth's face lit up, and Marsali thought again how pretty she was when she smiled. She would have to make sure Patrick found the right husband for his sister. And mayhap he would have to look no further than—Gavin. Her brother needed a wife, and although he seemed in no hurry to find one, she could not think of a sweeter mate than Elizabeth.

Catching Elizabeth's curious glance, she tamed the smile tugging at her lips, moved Isolde off her lap, and rose to find some parchment and a quill.

Patrick saw the walls of Brinaire, and his heartbeat quickened. He loved the mountains and rolling hills that surrounded the keep, but he had never truly considered Brinaire his home—until now. At that very moment, when he saw the majestic towers looming against the backdrop of the mountains, and he knew Marsali was there, waiting for him, Brinaire *became* home. Just the sound of her name, whispered in his mind, eased the tension in his gut.

It was dusk, and a translucent moon hung waiting in the sky even before the sun had painted its final brushstroke across the horizon. Brinaire's gates were open, and he rode through them with Hiram at his side. Impatient now, he dismounted and threw the reins to a stable lad, then strode across the courtyard and into the great hall, his gaze searching for his blue-eyed lass. When he did not see her, he did not bother to ask any of the clansmen present if they knew her whereabouts but, instead, took the stone stairs directly to her room. Reaching her door, he knocked once, threw it open, and entered without waiting for an invitation.

He stopped at the sight of Marsali and his sister sitting on the bed, their heads bent together over a book, a ferret in each of their laps. The picture they made warmed his heart and filled him with a love so strong he could not have imagined an adequate way to express it.

Marsali and Elizabeth raised their heads and saw him at the same moment, their faces both lighting with pleasure. With a small cry, Marsali leaped from the bed and ran to him. He caught her in his good arm, feeling her own arms encircle his waist. He buried his face in her hair, hugging her tightly against him, and for a long moment, neither of them spoke or moved.

When she finally lifted her face to meet his gaze, the relief and love he saw in her eyes made his heart lurch. He could no more have resisted the pull of her soft, parted lips than he could have resisted breathing. Without a thought in his head but how much he adored her, he brought his lips to hers and kissed her. He felt her tremble, felt her body press closer to his, felt her melt against him as the kiss deepened into something fierce and full of need.

Only the awareness of movement in the room reminded him that they were not alone. Opening one eye, he caught sight of Elizabeth, who was tucking the ferrets into their basket. Closing the lid, she tiptoed across the floor, attempting to slide past them and make a quiet exit.

Reluctantly, Patrick raised his head. "Elizabeth, wait." His voice sounded hoarse as he fought to control his breathing as well as the outrageous conduct of his body—which should have been too weak to react as precipitously as it was.

"I . . . I . . . was just leaving," his sister stuttered.

Keeping Marsali tucked at his side, he half turned to see Elizabeth making an effort not to stare at them—and failing.

He glanced at Marsali, who met his gaze only long enough for him to see her embarrassment.

Patrick's jaw clenched. This had to end. Now. He would not have Elizabeth believe her brother to be a blackguard who would seduce a hostage. Nor would he have Marsali feeling guilty for expressing her love. Bloody hell, this house had known little enough of love, and he was determined to do whatever he could to encourage its growth—including kissing his wife whenever he chose to do so.

Giving Marsali a quick, reassuring smile, he spoke to his sister. "Marsali and I handfasted a week ago."

He heard Marsali's tiny gasp and felt her body grow tense in the circle of his arm.

His sister's eyes were as round as saucers. "Truly?" she asked.

"Aye," he said.

A smile spread slowly across her face as she looked from him to Marsali, then back again. "Then Marsali is truly my sister. But, Patrick—" The smile disappeared abruptly, and she whispered, "Does Father know?"

He shook his head. "Nay, he doesna—else you would have heard the roars clear to the sea."

"And Alex?"

"Not yet." Hesitating only a moment, he said, "We had

three witnesses, though. Gavin, Hiram, and a man you donna know."

Elizabeth sighed, her hands clasped together in front of her. "Oh, I am so glad." Then, with a blush creeping into her cheeks, she added, "But I must go now. Thank you for telling me. I promise, I willna tell anyone else." And before he could stop her, she fled the room, leaving the door sitting open.

"Alone at last," Patrick growled, striding across the room to kick the door closed with his foot. When he turned, he found Marsali watching him, her expression nearly as astonished as Elizabeth's had been. He smiled, walking slowly toward her.

"I didna think you would tell her," she said as he approached. "I am glad you did. I know we can trust her."

Stopping in front of her, he tugged her into his full embrace, ignoring the pain in his shoulder to put his left arm, as well as his right, around her. "I want to tell everyone," he murmured, his lips brushing hers. "I want to tell the world that you are mine."

Then his mouth covered hers, and any need for speech ceased to exist. They sought each other frantically—mouths locked, bodies clinging, desperate to get closer. He warned himself to be cautious, but the warning went unheeded. And soon he was lost. Completely, ecstatically lost.

Marsali snuggled in the crook of Patrick's right arm, reveling in the feel of her bare skin against his. She ran her hand over his chest and downward, over his hard stomach.

"I should let you rest," she said.

"I am resting," he murmured.

She sighed again. He was resting but only after very strenuous activity. She had tried to make it easy for him, allowing him to guide her on top of him. She had felt a bit shy at first, and she had been uncertain what to do. But when he had begun moving, her body had responded instinctively.

The recent memory of the way it had been, with her riding him, sent tiny spasms of pleasure through her. Such a glorious ride.

He had slept for a time afterward, and she had watched, content to have him beside her. She would have let him sleep all night, but some scattered noise drifting through the window from the courtyard below had awakened him a few minutes ago. Marsali was wondering whether she could persuade him to go back to sleep when a soft knock at the door decided the question.

"Oh!" She sat bolt upright, suddenly realizing that it would not do—nay, it would not do at all—to have someone find Patrick naked in her bed. "Quickly!" she whispered, hopping up to search frantically for something to put on.

Snatching her nightdress from the end of the bed, she yanked it into some semblance of order around her nude form. A glance at Patrick increased her panic, for he seemed completely unconcerned as he casually got out of bed and went about looking for his clothing.

The knock came again, insistent, and Marsali hurried toward the door, afraid whoever it was would grow tired of waiting and just walk in, for the door had no lock. With her hands on the latch, she cast a glance over her shoulder at Patrick, which made her groan. He had pulled his shirt over his head, but he could only manage to get his right arm through the sleeve; he might as well not have bothered.

Hoping he would stay out of sight, Marsali opened the door a crack and peeked out. Relief flooded her when she saw Jeanie standing in the corridor, with Hiram lurking behind her.

"The marquis is looking fer his son," Jeanie said quietly.

Marsali felt Patrick close to her, and she turned to see him standing at her shoulder. His barefooted approach had been utterly silent.

He wrapped his fingers around the edge of the door and

opened it wider. She watched Jeanie's gaze take in his tousled hair and the plaid he had draped haphazardly over his shoulder. It hung nearly to his knees, covering the essentials, but its condition made it obvious what they had been doing.

Jeanie did not seem in the least bothered. "Yer father wants ye in the great hall fer supper tonight," she said to Patrick, her eyes twinkling.

"You can tell the marquis," he said, "that the earl and his lady would be pleased to join him for supper. No, wait. I will tell him myself."

Marsali saw Hiram's eyebrow lift and heard Jeanie's quick intake of breath.

Her own heart was in her throat as she looked at him. "Are you sure?" she asked.

"Aye," Patrick said. "Half the castle must know where I am. 'Tis time to tell my father and everyone else where I stand. I have no heart for sneaking and skulking." He held her stunned gaze. "Are you ready?"

She was not. The marquis frightened her. She was not so frightened of what he might do to her, as of what he might do to Patrick. She did not want to be the cause of Patrick's being disowned.

"Are you *really* certain you wish to do this?" she whispered.

"Aye," he smiled. "I am really certain."

"But—"

He silenced her with a swift kiss, then said, "I want you protected if anything happens to me. I believe Father will protect my wife, even if she is a Gunn. He wouldna do the same for my mistress, no matter who she was."

He sounded so confident that she had to wonder what he knew that she did not.

He gave her no time to consider. "I will return in an hour's time for you," he said. "Jeanie can help you dress." He leaned down and kissed her nose, tickling her as he did so and extracting a smile.

"Are you going to walk to your room like that?" she asked, smiling as her gaze raked over him.

"Nay," he grumbled. "Help me with the shirt, then wrap this bloody plaid."

She did as requested, while Jeanie bustled into the room and began straightening things. Hiram stood in the doorway, looking disgruntled as he watched her dress his friend. Doubtless, he thought he should be helping Patrick, but Marsali did not agree. It was a wife's right and privilege to help her husband. And she felt like a wife. A true wife. And soon everyone would know.

Including her father. If the handfasting was made public at Brinaire, 'twould not be long before word reached Abernie. A shudder ran through her at the thought.

Hiding her distress, she finished buckling the wide belt around Patrick's waist, then gave him a tremulous smile.

"I will be all right, love," he said.

She should have known she could not hide her feelings from him.

"I love you," she whispered.

"Aye, I know," he replied softly. "I am counting on it."

And then he was gone.

Patrick walked down the hall toward the stairs. Hiram followed, muttering to himself.

"Now what are you complaining about?" Patrick tossed the question over his shoulder.

"Women," Hiram grunted. "Best to stay away from them. I would ha' fixed the plaid fer ye."

Patrick chuckled. "Forgive me for preferring a gentler touch."

Hiram mumbled something else, but Patrick heard enough to understand the gist of it.

Stopping at the top of the stairs, he waited until Hiram caught up. "Jeanie?" he said.

"Stubborn woman," Hiram muttered, plodding down

the stairs with such force that Patrick was thankful they were made of solid stone.

"How is she stubborn?" he asked.

"Says she is no' interested in a husband." Hiram looked at him plaintively. "Wha' kind of woman is no' interested in a husband?"

"Have you someone particular in mind?" Patrick queried.

Hiram mumbled again.

"I didna hear you," Patrick said.

"Nay," Hiram said finally. Reaching the last step, he started down the corridor, waving a hand as he spoke. "I just think a bonny woman like her . . . Well, she shouldna be alone."

Patrick fell into step beside him. "Did you ask to court her?" he asked.

Hiram drew himself up to his full height and looked at him indignantly. "Nay."

"I am afraid to ask how the subject of marriage arose."

"I simply said she needed a mon, a fine braw mon like me." He threw his arms wide. " 'Twas a simple observation."

Patrick groaned. "And what did she say?"

"She chased me from the kitchen with a broom," Hiram replied despondently.

Stopping before his father's chamber door, Patrick asked, "Then how did you come to be at Marsali's door together?"

"I couldna find ye, and didna think I should come to the lady's room alone."

"So you asked Jeanie to help you?"

"Aye," Hiram said, a smile spreading over the battered face.

Patrick's lips curved in a slow, sly smile. Mayhap his big, awkward friend was not as inept in the ways of courtship as he had feared.

"I might try some flowers, were I you," he suggested.

"*Flowers?*" Hiram sounded horrified.

"Flowers."

Patrick's good humor faded as he turned to his father's door.

"Do ye wish me to wait?" Hiram asked.

"Nay." Patrick gave a soft snort. "I donna think he will shoot me. Yet."

Hiram looked dubious, but he turned and walked back down the hall. Mayhap on his way to find some flowers. The thought made Patrick smile again as he raised his hand and knocked.

"Whoever the hell ye be, go away," his father roared.

Ignoring the order, Patrick straightened his back, opened the door, and entered the chamber. His father was sitting in a chair by the cold hearth, a goblet in his hands. A pitcher sat on a table next to him. Wine. Evidence of it showed in his father's red-rimmed eyes.

"Hiram said you wanted me."

"At supper, lad. At supper. 'Tis time you sat with me at the high table. You are always gone," he complained in a voice that, to Patrick's surprise, seemed to tremble.

Patrick nodded. "I will be leaving in the morning. A raid."

"On the Gunns?" the marquis asked with drunken satisfaction.

"On the border," Patrick replied. His father could believe what he wished—for now.

"I wish I could go with you," Gregor said.

Patrick blinked. Was that a tear in his father's eye?

Abruptly, Gregor tried to stand, his hand waving Patrick away. But he could not do it. With a cry of pain, he fell back, and Patrick stepped forward to catch him with his good arm and lower him into the chair. His father's gnarled hands battered at him to leave him alone. Suddenly Patrick realized that his father was embarrassed—water *did* glimmer in his eyes, and he did not want anyone, not even his son, to know.

Stunned, Patrick stared at his father, remembering the fierce, proud man he had respected in his youth. Bloody hell, he had *loved* him, no matter how little love his father had shown him. Ironically, looking at the shadow of a man whose own pride had destroyed him, he realized that he had never loved his father more than he did at that moment.

He had to steel himself to speak, to say the words that would hurt his father even more. He had to ensure Marsali's safety and the safety of their child, if there was one. He could not discount the possibility that Foster might yet find a way to make good on his threat.

His father was looking at him strangely. Waiting.

He took a deep breath and spoke. "I wanted to tell you that Marsali will be with me for supper."

His father shrugged. "I care not what the wench does."

"Good. Then you willna mind when I seat her beside me."

His father drew back, his green eyes sparking. "A Gunn? A *hostage*? She will sit at the end of the table."

"Nay, Father," he said, forcing calm into his tone. "She will occupy the seat at my right. As my wife."

With a wiry strength fueled by anger, his father shoved himself out of his chair to stand, his right foot wrapped in cloth. "Never!"

Patrick counted to three, then said, "It is done. We were handfasted a week ago."

His father's jaw dropped.

Before he could speak, Patrick brought out his greatest weapon. "With luck, there is an heir already on his way," he said.

The ploy worked. Just. His father's mouth clamped shut, and he stood trembling from his graying head to his gout-ridden toes. For a full minute, he simply stared. Then, with a sly smile, he said, "A handfast must be made public."

Patrick nodded. "There were witnesses."

"Who? That fellow of yours? I willna have it."

"You *will* have it—or you will never see me again."

His father fell back into his chair, his face disbelieving. "You are my son. You will do as I say."

Quietly, Patrick replied, "You arranged my marriage twelve years ago. I agreed, then, because it was your wish. I honored that contract for twelve years, and in doing so, I honored you. I wouldna dishonor you now by putting it aside so easily."

"A pretty speech," Gregor Sutherland said. "I see you have learned guile as well as warfare. But you know my feelings about the Gunns. I willna have one in this family."

"Then my wife and I will leave by week's end. You will never see your heir."

"I will make Alex my heir."

"As you wish." Patrick nodded and started for the door.

"Wait."

Patrick turned to face his father.

The old man took a long time before, finally, he said, "You know we canna fight the Gunns and Sinclairs without you."

Patrick remained silent.

His father lifted a hand in a helpless gesture. "Alex would die trying," he said.

"You realize that, do you?"

His father glowered. "I was trying to make a man of him."

Patrick shook his head. "You have caused much misery, Father. Too bloody much." He headed again for the door.

"Patrick."

But he did not turn.

"Patrick. Donna . . . donna leave."

He stopped a foot from the door. His father was standing again, and as he watched, the old man took a step toward him. But his body swayed, his hand flailing. In a moment, he tumbled back into the chair.

"Bloody gout," his father grumbled.

Patrick knew his father was ashamed of his illness, which he considered a weakness. He prayed he would never grow so foolish in his old age. He stood by the chair, waiting for another tirade. But it never came. For a long time, his father stared at the cold hearth, his hands gripping the chair arms.

Finally, he began, "She reminds me of . . ." He trailed off.

"Margaret?" Patrick said.

"Aye. Be careful, lad. Women are treacherous." The anger was gone from his voice, leaving it hollow. Lonely.

Patrick had never seen his father the least bit vulnerable, and wondered if he would ever see him so again. Choosing his words carefully, he said, "Sir, I do not believe that Margaret betrayed you. I think someone wanted you to believe that she did."

Weary eyes looked up at him. "She has been gone two years. If she didna betray me, where is she? I didna kill her."

"Aye, I know," Patrick said.

"Nor did she kill herself. Oh, I know"—he waved a hand at Patrick's surprised look—"I said she threw herself into the sea, but I knew it wasna true. You are my son, and I trust you to know that, in her heart, Margaret never gave up her Catholic beliefs. She wouldna have killed herself." He paused, staring again at the hearth. "She was my wife. I would never have revealed her faith to anyone. I would never have betrayed her. I thought she . . ."

"You thought . . . ?" Patrick prompted.

But his father only shook his head. "It doesna matter."

"Mayhap 'twill matter a great deal," Patrick said, "if I can prove Margaret was not unfaithful to you."

His father's head snapped up. "What do you know, lad? And sit. My neck grows stiff looking up at you."

Patrick seated himself on the edge of the chair opposite his father's. Leaning forward, he said, "I believe Edward Sinclair hatched a plan to destroy the Sutherlands, and the first step was to make you think Margaret had been unfaithful."

His father looked at him as if he had gone daft, but he did not interrupt. "He knew Margaret was the key to creating hatred between you and Donald Gunn. I believe he meant for you to declare war against the Gunns, and force the earl to look to him for help—which is exactly what happened. I am sure he was gracious when he accepted the earl's offer of his daughter's hand in exchange for help against our clan. The alliance would have given him the strength to fulfill his ancestral pledge to destroy our clan." Raising an eyebrow, he added, "You and I both know we would never win against the Gunns and Sinclairs together."

Gregor nodded but still did not speak.

"More than that, though," Patrick continued, "in marrying Marsali, Sinclair knew he would be hurting me. And that, I think, was at least as important to him as destroying our clan."

Gregor's eyes narrowed. "Why?"

"The man hates me," Patrick said. "I saw him cower and run from battle, leaving other men to die. He hoped I was one of them. He claims to have performed valiantly, and I am one of the few men alive who can say otherwise."

His father scowled. "Why have you not?"

"I am responsible for myself, my own acts, my own honor. No one else's. I would never have spoken of it, had he not attacked my family."

His father studied him, and Patrick thought the old man's gaze was every bit as sharp as it ever had been.

"So you have foiled Sinclair's plan," his father said. "You came home too soon."

His body might be weak but there was nothing weak about his father's mind, Patrick realized. "Aye," he said. "To be exact, I came home one day too soon. Had I been a day later, Marsali would be married to him."

Surprise flickered in the old man's gaze. "You *did* have something to do with her crying off the wedding, then?"

"Aye," Patrick admitted. "She was only going through with it because, if she hadna, her father would have put Cecilia in her place. She wouldna allow it. So I secreted Cecilia in a place where the earl willna find her. Marsali endured a month in her room on bread and water for refusing to go through with the marriage, but she didna yield. She has courage and honor, Father, as great as any man's."

His father was silent, and Patrick dared to hope that the fire he saw in the faded green eyes was admiration. Aye, the marquis of Brinaire would admire someone, man or woman, who had true honor.

Finally, his father spoke in a tone that came close to wrenching Patrick's heart—a brusque but futile attempt to cover pain. "How certain are you, then, about Margaret?" he asked.

Patrick replied, "I am certain that Sinclair's men, dressed in Sutherland plaids, attacked the Gunns. I am certain they will do it again. Of these things, I have proof. I think Sinclair convinced Abernie to petition the king to have us outlawed."

At the mention of Donald Gunn, his father's look became shuttered, and Patrick was afraid he had lost him. "Donald Gunn is as much a victim as we are," he said. "He truly believes you attacked his crofters only for revenge."

His father leaned back in his chair, a thoughtful gaze on his face. Patrick saw a glimmer of the man his father had been. A man respected for making hard decisions, for his valor and his cunning—if not for his loving nature.

"You have plans," Gregor finally said.

It was a statement, not a question, and Patrick knew he had to be careful. This was not the time to tell his father about the scrawny cattle or his renewed friendship with Gavin, much less that he was taking Sutherland clansmen to the Gunns' northern border to fight against the Sinclairs.

"Aye," Patrick said. "I have plans. And they include finding out what happened to Margaret."

"Tell me," his father ordered, though not in the same autocratic tone he might have used an hour earlier.

"I hope to let Abernie catch Sinclair in the act," Patrick said, praying he was not asked to elaborate. After all that had been said in honesty, he did not want to have to lie again.

He exhaled slowly when his father growled, "Aye, you make certain Abernie is there to see it. Then he can come crawling to me with apologies."

Patrick sighed. "He believes you mistreated his sister. At the very least."

"She . . ." Gregor Sutherland stopped. He turned his head away, and Patrick saw his throat move as he swallowed hard.

Finally, his father spoke in the quietest tone Patrick had ever heard him use.

"Bring the Gunn wench to supper," he said.

"You will be courteous to her."

"You ask too much."

"She will be the mother of my children."

"Then God help you." Some of the spirit was back, but it lacked the force that Patrick remembered.

"You *will* be kind to Marsali, Father. And you will look after her if anything happens to me."

His father's gaze came back to meet his, and Patrick was surprised to see the aging green eyes cloud again with something that, in another man, he would have thought was concern or mayhap fear. It was too much to believe. It contradicted too many years of expecting and receiving nothing; he simply could not believe his father had come to care about his welfare in the course of one conversation.

Yet when his father spoke, the harsh voice was merely gruff and held no hint of resentment.

"I will look after her," he said.

Patrick left his father's chamber feeling as if he had already won a war.

Chapter 24

The marquis kept his promise. Almost. Patrick had known cordiality was too much to hope for. Civility would have been nice. Instead, his father grumped his way through supper, acknowledging Marsali's presence with a single nod. Still, it was far more than Patrick had expected, and the grins of the Sutherland clansmen at hearing of the handfasting more than compensated for his father's lack of enthusiasm.

It was clear the clansmen liked Marsali. Patrick already knew that the Sutherlands associated a marked improvement in their food with Marsali's arrival. How she had accomplished it, they did not know. They only knew that—within a matter of weeks—Brinaire seemed a brighter, happier place. Fresh rushes covered the floor, dishes were clean, and a smile graced young Elizabeth's face.

He accepted the sincere congratulations of his clansmen, who, he noted, pointedly ignored his father's glowering countenance. Then they drank to his and Marsali's happiness. And drank some more, until the hall was filled with ribald comments and good cheer.

Marsali's face, Patrick was gratified to see, glowed at their obvious goodwill. Still, he caught an occasional mist in her eyes and a worried frown on her brow. She knew he was leaving again after supper tonight.

He wished he could wait for Alex's return, but he dared not; Sinclair could strike at any time, and he had promised Gavin that he would have men in the hills to support him. He had chosen twenty of his most trusted clansmen. Each man had been told not to wear his Sutherland plaids and, once away from the keep, to put a black ribbon around his arm. Cautious lest there be a spy of whom he was unaware, Patrick had issued orders for the clansmen to begin leaving, two or three at a time, after supper.

He himself would leave a bit later, when he had said goodbye to Marsali. Privately.

Patrick looked at his father, who had steadfastly refused to join in the toasts and was staring down at the contents of his goblet. He was not drinking as much as usual, and his gaze seemed more alert as it moved from Patrick to his daughter, then to Marsali.

A sudden movement at the opposite end of the long table caught Patrick's attention, and he looked to see Hiram push back his chair and stand. When the red-haired giant cleared his throat, and it became clear he intended to speak, Patrick was stunned. He had never, ever, seen Hiram seek the center of attention.

His face red with embarrassment, Hiram looked toward the marquis and lifted his cup. "To the bonniest lass in Scotland, and the truest mon," he said. "Two braw hearts."

Cups raised, and fists pounded the table. "Two braw hearts," echoed the thirty men and five women seated at the tables, as well as the ten servants standing against the walls.

Patrick's gaze remained fixed on his father, who sat as unmoving as a stone. Gregor Sutherland looked around the room, then at his oldest son. His heir. Their gazes met, held, and the hall quieted. Then the marquis of Brinaire slowly raised his cup, his gaze never leaving Patrick's.

"Two braw hearts," he said. Then he took a sip, very carefully pushed back his chair and stood, and limped from a room now wrapped in stunned silence.

Patrick looked at Hiram and arched an eyebrow.

Hiram plopped down on his chair with a noise that brought laughter from the hall. Nervous laughter at first, but then it deepened, and the hall seemed to ring with it.

* * *

Marsali tried to smile as she bade Patrick farewell, but it was futile; she was terrified, and surely he knew it.

He was dressed in a dark brown doublet, overlaid by a jack, and dark breeches that hugged his legs. He looked fierce, menacing—and irresistible.

She looked at the face that was so incredibly dear to her and could not imagine living without seeing it again. Mayhap it was her imagination, but she thought some of the deep furrows around his eyes had smoothed out. The scar still bit deeply into his cheek, but it was part of him, a symbol of what was fine and decent and honorable.

She burrowed into his embrace, her hands wrapping around his neck.

"It will not be long, sweeting," he said. "A day or two. No more than three, I think."

His voice was calm and reasonable, and, oddly, his apparent lack of fear sent even stronger shivers racing down her spine. One day or three: It might as well have been a lifetime.

His hand touched her hair, then his lips came down on hers, possessing them. Marsali clung to him, feeling as if she were drowning in love—and terror. She wanted to be brave, but the bulge of cloth on his shoulder, under his clothing, was evidence that he was not invulnerable.

A cry of pure anguish ripped from her as his lips left hers. "Oh, Patrick, donna go," she said. "You are not well enough."

"I must," he said softly. "I started this, and I must be there to see it through to the end." He gave her a crooked smile. "Hiram willna allow anything to happen to me. He wouldna dare, knowing he will have to answer to you."

She was neither humored nor comforted: Hiram had been with him the last time he was wounded.

"Father said he would look after you," Patrick added.

Her eyes widened in surprise. "He agreed to that?"

"He wants to see his grandson," Patrick said with a smile.

A blush crept into her cheeks. "Even one that is half Gunn?"

"Aye," he replied. "Even one that is half Gunn."

She sighed. "I wish you didna have to go. I donna understand why you canna send Hiram to meet Gavin."

His look was mildly chiding. "I gave Gavin my word, lass. I canna leave him and his out there alone. The Gunn clansmen have not the weapons nor the experience." A frown furrowed his brow. "I had hoped Alex would return by now, but Rufus may have had a problem meeting him. I canna wait." He took her chin in his fingers, tilting her face upward. "When Alex returns, send him to the hut. I will put a man there who can find me—and I will make sure Quick Harry knows he is coming, lest he decide 'tis best to shoot a trespasser first and ask questions later."

Marsali nodded, her insides churning. He was leaving. And nothing she said or did would stop him.

Yet he did not move. She saw the glitter of anticipation in his eyes, and she felt the impatience to be gone in the tension in his body. And still he stood there, his fingers stroking her cheek, his gaze moving slowly over her face.

Then, suddenly, his arms went around her, clasping her tightly, and he kissed her, hard and fierce. When he pulled back, his hands framed her face, and his gaze locked with hers.

"I love you, lass," he said. "Donna ever forget it."

Then, without looking back, he strode quickly from the room.

For a moment, Marsali stared at the empty doorway, her breath caught in her throat. Then, filled with both glory and anguish, she burst into tears.

Patrick rode with grim determination through the moonlit Highland night. The vision of Marsali's face, tears hovering in her eyes and lower lip trembling, was like a lead weight on his heart. How he had wanted to stay. Yet it was for her that he had to leave. For them.

And he was about to break his oath, the oath that he would never fight another Scotsman. God help him, he hoped this would be the end of the violence.

And the end of Foster. The man was evil as well as mad, and he had sworn to kill Patrick even as Patrick's sword stroke had apparently altered his voice. He would not give up. As long as Foster lived, Patrick knew that he and everyone he loved would be at risk.

"My lord?"

Patrick glanced at Hiram, riding beside him. "Do I want to know why you are using that 'my lord' nonsense again?"

"Ye ha' that fierce 'my lord' look."

"You donna look too happy yourself."

Hiram sighed. "Aye, I must be getting old. I ha' started to think I might like a small piece of land. Terrifies the bloody sap from me."

"I am thinking you might want something else to go wi' it."

Hiram grinned. "She told me to be looking after m'self— *after* she told me she would beat me with a broom were I to allow a single additional bruise to my lord. Ye wouldna be responsible for my untimely death, would ye?"

"I will do my best to preserve your bonny hide," Patrick said.

"Speaking of bonny hides, how is the shoulder?"

" 'Twill do. I will be able to hold a sword." And that, Patrick knew, was what Hiram wanted to know. Pain—and there was enough of it—meant nothing. The ability to fight was all.

Just then, several dark-clad Sutherlands who had left Brinaire before them rode up to swing their mounts in line beside theirs. They rode in silence for an hour, when another ten clansmen joined them. Together, they pounded on, across the hills, toward the Gunn border.

* * *

Alex rode into Brinaire, well past midnight, on a winded horse. He had spotted riders, none of whom wore Sutherland plaids, so he had been forced to take a longer route. He could not risk being taken by either Sinclairs or Gunns.

He woke a stable boy, who took his horse and gave him the news that Patrick had left hours ago, as had Hiram and at least a dozen other clansmen. Burdened by a sense of failure, Alex headed for Marsali's room.

He knocked, waiting quite a while before she opened the door. Her eyes were red and puffy, and she still wore a shift and overdress, from which he gathered that she had been crying and unable to sleep.

When she saw him, her eyes grew wide, and she opened the door to allow him entrance. Her gaze flickered briefly over his unkempt state, then rose to meet his. "You have news for Patrick?" she asked.

"Aye," Alex nodded. "But the stable lad said he is gone."

"He has taken clansmen to aid the Gunns if the Sinclairs attack. He couldna wait for you."

"Bloody hell," Alex muttered, then remembering himself, quickly offered an apology.

Marsali dismissed his belated efforts at politeness with an impatient wave of her hand. "Patrick said to tell you to take your news to the hut. He will have a man there to meet you." She hesitated, her gaze sweeping over him. "You look tired."

Alex shook his head in denial. "I will get a fresh horse."

"Please." Her hand gripped his forearm. "Tell me what you learned."

"Sinclair plans a raid," he replied. "Tomorrow at dawn. The Gunn farms northeast of Kilcraig, near our northern border." He hesitated, then continued. "Rufus—Patrick's man—believes Margaret might be on an island Sinclair owns."

Marsali gasped. "Creighton?"

"Aye," Alex said, his heart racing. Everyone who knew the Sinclair clan knew of Creighton. The old keep sat on a strip of land which had once jutted into the sea. But its impregnable defense had also brought about its demise, as the inexorable, crashing waves had washed away its attachment to land and undermined its foundations. As far as anyone knew, Creighton had not been inhabited in a hundred years.

"But 'tis abandoned," Marsali said. "Edward told my father that the keep has all but washed away."

"Mayhap so," Alex agreed. "But he is using it, nonetheless. Rufus claims he has women there making plaids. And guards."

"But Margaret—" She shook her head quickly. "Why would he have kept her there—*alive?*"

"I donna know," Alex said. "I wonder the same. But why else would Sinclair be guarding abandoned ruins?"

Marsali's forehead creased in a frown. "It seems impossible," she said slowly, "but if Margaret *is* alive, what will Sinclair do if his plan fails? What will he do *tomorrow* if he and his men are caught raiding—and his scheme is exposed to my father?"

Alex knew immediately what she was thinking, and it made his blood run cold and face pale.

Marsali's tone suddenly held a note of panic. "Alex, if Edward knows his scheme has been exposed and knows he will be outlawed, he willna risk having Margaret found. Alex, he will kill her!"

Alex's hands knotted into fists. He would give everything he had to bring Margaret back, not only for her own sake and because he had cared for her but because her loss had sent his father and Brinaire tumbling into despair. If she were indeed alive . . .

But the if was such an enormous one.

Marsali, however, did not seem to think so. Her eyes brightened as she gripped his arm with both hands. "Alex, can you bring me some of your clothes?" she asked.

"Why would you want—" He stopped abruptly. "No. Marsali, Patrick would never forgive me. You canna—"

"I must," she insisted. Then, in a much softer tone—a tone he suspected was meant to persuade him to something he knew was wrong—she said, "Alex, I am not suggesting something foolish. I only mean to take your news to the hut. I will give it to the man whom Patrick has left there."

"Mmm, I donna know . . ."

"I will be safe," she added. "And I know the way."

Alex looked at her dubiously. She sounded far more confident than he thought was wise. Nonetheless, he could not think of a valid argument against the plan. She did know the way, and she was a fine rider; with a bright moon, she would have no trouble getting through the pass.

Warily, he asked, "And what are you proposing that *I* do?"

"Go to Creighton," she said instantly. "Watch for Sinclair. Take some men and—" She broke off abruptly, her face falling. "But Patrick has taken all the men he said he trusted."

"I know some," Alex offered.

She frowned. "Who?"

He gave her several names. He did not give her ages. "I know them well," he said, "and I trust them. Patrick doesna know them, but they are good men, I swear it." If one considered a sixteen-year-old a man.

Marsali did not appear completely satisfied, but she nodded. In truth, they both knew they had no other choice. Someone had to take the news of the dawn raid to the messenger, and someone had to watch for any move Sinclair might make on Creighton; the stakes were too high to forgo either task, and there were only two of them to perform both.

"You will be careful," she said. "You willna do anything precipitately."

"Precipitately?" He raised an eyebrow as he had seen Patrick do, although he knew very well what she meant.

"You will not do anything *dangerous*," she clarified. "I

will make certain Patrick's messenger tells Patrick where you have gone and to meet you there. But until Patrick arrives, you will only keep watch." She was worrying her lip as if she were having second thoughts.

He certainly was. It was plain that if, while he was "watching," anything happened—like Sinclair arriving to kill Margaret—he would be forced to do something other than watch.

Alex held Marsali's gaze for a moment, and he felt an understanding pass between them.

"I will get you some clothes," he said. "While you dress, I will have the horses saddled."

"Alex, wait."

He stopped.

Her gaze fell from his for a moment, and he could have sworn she was blushing. But her voice was clear and strong as she spoke.

"Alex, I know Patrick wouldna want you to hear it this way, but I canna let you go off, possibly to meet danger, without knowing. Patrick and I handfasted a week ago. He told your father, and he announced it at the evening meal."

Alex stared at her. A wide grin spread of its own accord across his face, but at the same time, he felt a twist of jealousy. He quickly dismissed the latter, stepping forward and grabbing her hand. He lifted it to kiss the backs of her fingers. "Welcome, sister," he said. "Welcome to the family."

When he looked at her, he saw tears welling in her eyes. "Thank you," Marsali said. "I am proud to call you brother. But now, I think we best go."

Still grinning, Alex nodded and left her chamber. In less than five minutes, he was back with a doublet and jack, a pair of trews, and a helmet that would cover her long hair.

She took the clothes, agreeing to meet him in the courtyard, and he headed for the stables. Watchful, he took the stairs two at a time. But the corridors were empty, many of the men gone with Patrick, the others abed.

With the help of the sleepy stable lad, he saw to the saddling of four horses, picking the mounts with special care: the most surefooted for Marsali, the swiftest for himself and the two friends he intended to take with him. He led the saddled horses into the courtyard, explaining to the guard at the postern gate that he and a friend would be riding out to meet Patrick. The clansman merely nodded, and Alex was grateful for the strange comings and goings of late that made his own departure seem normal.

He collected a pistol, a sword, and several torches, then mounted his horse. As he did so, he saw Marsali crossing the courtyard toward him. He barely recognized her, dressed in men's clothing. She moved swiftly to the horse he indicated, mounting the heavy saddle astride without hesitation. Keeping her head down, she followed him as he led the two riderless horses toward the postern gate. The guard simply nodded as they passed, then closed the gate behind them.

With Marsali keeping pace at his side, they rode until Alex knew they were out of sight of the walls, then he pulled his mount to a halt. Marsali stopped next to him.

They would be going in different directions now. Marsali would head for the mountains. He would gather his friends and ride toward the sea.

He handed her the torches, then hesitated. Were they doing the right thing? Or should he simply follow Patrick's orders and forget about Creighton? It was such a long shot anyway—Margaret could not possibly be alive.

But the thought that she could be would not leave him alone.

Alex sighed, wondering how many times over the past twelve years Patrick had faced the kind of choice he now faced. More times than his brother could have remembered, he supposed. Mayhap he did not want to be like Patrick after all.

"Take care," Marsali said to him.

"Aye, and you," he replied. Then, giving her what he hoped was a rakish grin, he turned and galloped off toward the sea.

Chapter 25

Patrick watched the first silvery fingers of a chilly dawn creep over the mountains. He shivered, not so much from cold as from growing uneasiness.

He stood with Hiram and fifteen other men, waiting to hear where Sinclair planned to strike. Others were scattered over the surrounding area, watching the approaches to Gunn crofts; they had been instructed to watch from trees, having learned—reluctantly—the art of perching from Hiram during their training. Patrick did not like having his forces divided, but until he knew Sinclair's plan, he must be ready for any possibility.

Where was his messenger? Had Alex made it back to Brinaire? Had Rufus indeed reached Alex? He paced back and forth across the clearing.

He felt Hiram's gaze on him and knew his friend was worried. In truth, this was not like him. Before a battle, he was usually calm; he had learned to hold his energy inside, to focus it, for he believed it wasteful—and deadly—to spend it until there was a need. But tonight . . . tonight was different. He found it difficult to maintain any pretense of calm, and indifference would have been impossible.

Bless the saints, his life and the lives of everyone he loved were at stake. Yet here he was, helpless, waiting to be told where to go. He hated—truly despised—having so little control over the course of events.

The sound of a low whistle, coming from the leafy bower to the south of the clearing, brought Patrick's attention into immediate focus. He whirled to look in the direction from which the signal had come, squinting in the semidarkness in an effort to see through the trees.

Horses thrashed through the underbrush. Then, suddenly, a large bay, ridden by a man clad in jack and breeches, broke from the trees and galloped into the clearing. The rider, a slight figure, yanked the horse to a rearing halt and jumped from the saddle before the animal's front hooves had touched ground. In the dim light, Patrick recognized neither the horse nor the rider and was about to motion Hiram to the alert when the rider tore off his helmet.

Long, dark hair tumbled down around a face he most surely did recognize.

"Marsali!"

She threw herself into his arms at the same time another horse broke into the clearing, Quick Harry clinging awkwardly to its back for all he was worth.

With his hands clutching metal buckles where he was accustomed to feeling soft flesh, Patrick scowled at his wife. "What in the devil are you—"

"Rufus met Alex," she broke in, speaking in short gasps for breath. "The attack will be at dawn. Northeast of Kilcraig. The farms near the border."

"The ones around Sandy Gunn's croft," he recalled, glancing at the pink glow hovering over the mountaintops.

"Aye." She nodded, her chest heaving as if she had been running, not the horse.

"But why did you come? Did something happen to Alex?"

She shook her head. "He has gone to Creighton. Rufus said he thinks Sinclair"—a quick breath—"could be holding Margaret there. If she truly lives"—another gasp—"we feared Sinclair might kill her, or order her killed . . . if his men are recognized."

"And Alex has gone to stop him? *Alone?*"

"Nay, he took others. I said to watch and wait for you . . . or somebody you send."

"Bloody young fool," Patrick muttered. "But that still doesna tell me why you came. Where is Fergus—the man I left—"

She waved her hands impatiently. "His horse stumbled and fell on the pass. I found him on my way to the hut. His leg is broken and . . . and the horse ran away."

"Sweet *Jesu*."

"Fergus couldna ride. And I feared sending Quick Harry alone. He doesna ride well. But he wouldna have me come alone, so—"

"So you came together."

Completely winded, she nodded.

Patrick noted that Hiram and the other men had sensed action, and were already mounting their horses. "Dawn is breaking," he said. We must ride hard." He sprinted across the clearing to collect his horse, issuing orders as he ran. "John, go collect our men. Tell them to converge at Sandy Gunn's croft. 'Tis the central one in the cluster nearest the border."

"Aye, Patrick."

"Tommy?"

"Aye?"

"Take Hector and ride to Creighton. Ride *hard*. Find Alex. Stay with him. I will join you when I can."

"Aye, Patrick."

The two men turned their mounts to gallop toward the coast.

Giving Marsali a leg up into her saddle, he told her, "I would send you and Quick Harry home, but these woods are crawling with armed men. You will be safer with us. But you are both to stay back. *Far* back." Swinging into his own saddle, he shot Hiram a quick look. "Take care of her."

"Aye," Hiram said without question.

He would have preferred to have Hiram at his side, but Marsali's well-being came before his own. With a quick glance at the remaining clansmen, he chose Cadman, another whose skills he respected.

Giving the man a piercing look, he said, "You, too, will protect my lady."

"Aye, milord."

"On your life?"

"On my life."

Patrick spurred his horse eastward, his men behind him. They were nearly five miles away from where Sinclair would attack, and dawn was upon them.

As they rode, other men joined them. Some wore plain clothes with black armbands, others wore Gunn plaids. Gavin had done his part. He looked over his shoulder—once was all he would allow himself—to see Marsali's small figure flanked by three larger ones dwindling in the distance.

They were at least thirty strong when they reached the first croft. No one was there. No women. No men. The only sign of life was a pig staring at them from behind the fence of his pen. And the only reason the place would be empty was if an attack had begun on a neighboring croft. Spurring his horse forward, he motioned his men to follow.

The first sign of conflict ahead came in the clanking of swords and the cries of battle shattering the still morning air. As he and his band drew near, Patrick saw that the battle was fully engaged. He and his band came thundering into their midst, and some men wearing Sutherland plaids broke off from their fighting and began backing away.

Catching sight of Gavin fighting hand-to-hand with a man wearing a black helmet, Patrick barked out orders to two men. "Get their horses! I donna want one man to escape. I want them *all* sent to Abernie as a present!" As the two galloped to do his bidding, he turned to the others. "The rest of you, attack the men wearing our plaids!"

Turning his mount in a tight circle, he searched for Rufus and found him clashing swords with a man wearing a Sutherland plaid. As Patrick's feet hit the ground, he saw

Rufus run his opponent through. Rufus held up a hand in salute to Patrick before turning to meet another attack.

Drawing his sword, Patrick ran to aid Gavin. His friend's attention was fixed on his duel with the man in the helmet, and he did not see the enemy moving in behind him. Patrick intercepted the second attacker, his sword deflecting a blow meant for Gavin's back.

The man turned on him, his sword arm raised. But he hesitated, distracted for an instant by the influx of new-comers, and Patrick seized the moment. Knocking the sword from the man's hand, he leveled the point of his sword at the man's heart.

Two of his men ran to take the prisoner as Patrick stayed to guard Gavin's back. Gavin's opponent was good, bloody good. But so was Gavin. Knowing his interference would not be appreciated, he stood watch as both men drew blood.

All over the croft, more raiders were surrendering, real-izing they were trapped, surrounded by superior numbers. One after another was taken prisoner and tightly bound.

Yet the man fighting Gavin seemed not to care that the odds against him were overwhelming. Instead, his attack grew more ferocious. Gavin was no mean swordsman, and he parried and thrust with competence. But his opponent was better. Gavin fell back a step, then another. In that in-stant, Patrick saw the enemy's face—his eyes—and his heart leapt to his throat.

God's blood! Foster!

It took every ounce of discipline Patrick possessed not to run immediately to Gavin's aid. Only the certain knowledge that Gavin would be humiliated in front of his own clans-men held him back. Yet as it became clearer and clearer that Gavin could not win, Patrick prepared to finish it.

Gavin fell back another step, then stumbled on a rock be-hind him, falling to one knee. Patrick moved forward, sword raised. But he was too late. Foster lunged, grabbing Gavin and placing the blade of his sword next to Gavin's neck.

"Do not move," he told Patrick, "unless you want him to die."

Several drops of blood dripped from Gavin's neck. Patrick stood perfectly still, dropping his sword to his side. One movement from Foster's hand, and Gavin would die.

"Go ahead," Gavin said. "Kill the bastard."

The sword pinched his neck tighter and the drops became a steady stream.

"What do you want, Foster?" Patrick could barely contain the rage in his voice.

"You," Foster snarled. "But for the moment, I will take a horse. A good one." He looked around. "That black over there looks just fine."

Patrick returned his stare, hatred radiating from him. God's blood, but he did not want to let the man go. As much as he had wished for peace, had wanted to put killing behind him, he could barely control his rage. This one man had caused so much pain, so much destruction.

But he would not—could not—sacrifice Gavin for vengeance. He nodded to one of his men. "Bring him." Then he looked back to Foster. "You are only delaying things, Foster. I *will* find you. 'Tis only a matter of time."

Foster shrugged. "Mayhap that is exactly what I have in mind. But not against such odds."

"Release Gavin and fight me. I swear that if you win, these men will let you go."

"Ah, but I am not as trusting as you, my lord."

"Coward!"

"Oh, our time will come. Now I have another bone to pick with you. You brought these men?"

"Aye," Patrick said. "I brought them. To put an end to your game—yours and Sinclair's."

Foster sneered. "Still playing the hero, Sutherland? Well, one day, I promise you, I will see you dead. But now I go to join a friend."

The horse was brought within a few feet of Foster, until

the villain barked, "Far enough. Now all of you move backward. And you," he added, pointing at the men holding the
horses, "let them go."

Gunns and Sutherlands looked from Gavin to Patrick.
Gavin managed a strangled "Nay."

But Patrick nodded, his gaze still on Gavin.

"Scatter them," Foster said. "The prisoners, too." He
turned to Patrick. "That should keep you busy for a while."

But Patrick shook his head. "The prisoners stay where
they are." He was bargaining dangerously now, betting that
Foster cared less about his unfortunate colleagues than his
own skin. He must know that if he killed Gavin, he was a
dead man.

And Patrick needed those prisoners. He needed them to
convince Abernie of Sinclair's treachery. Otherwise, all
would be for naught.

Foster hesitated a moment, then nodded. "Scatter the
horses. The prisoners are yours."

His mercenaries began to shout as they realized his betrayal. But Foster spared not a backward glance for them.
Instead, he kept his eyes on Patrick.

"Back off," he ordered.

Patrick retreated several steps. Foster pushed Gavin to
the ground, then swung into the saddle of the black, digging
his heels in and galloping toward the woods.

Patrick ran to Gavin as several of his men started after
the loosed horses. Blood was dripping from the neck wound,
but it was not a fatal cut. He tore a piece of cloth from his
bloodied shirt and tied it around the wound.

"You stay here," he said. "I am going after the bastard."

"I am going with you," Gavin said, getting to his feet.

"Bloody hell you will."

"We do not have time to argue."

They did not, and Patrick knew it. He had a good idea
where Foster was going, and they could not waste time.

Foster would destroy any loose ends. That meant Margaret, if she still lived. And Alex had gone to protect her.

But first, he had to make sure Abernie learned the truth.

His gaze moved to the men in Sutherland plaid. Those not lying on the ground had been tied and seated together, awaiting his pleasure. A few of his men stood guard over them.

One of the captives was already loudly blaming the attack on Sinclair, saying they were provided the Sutherland plaids by their laird.

Patrick moved to stand in front of him. "Where is Sinclair?"

The captive shrugged.

With calculated deliberation, Patrick walked over to where he had dropped his sword, picked it up, and walked back to the man. He brought the tip of the blade up to rip the edge of the plaid the man was wearing, drawing a fine line of blood.

"That you are wearing my plaid offends me," he said coldly. "That you have dishonored my name offends me even more. I am not known for patience, nor for temperance. Now, where is Sinclair?"

The sword tip lingered at the man's throat, and when he swallowed, the movement caused the tip to bite into his flesh. The flow of blood down his neck increased, and his eyes stretched wide with terror.

"In the woods," he gasped. "Awaiting word."

"Too cowardly to come himself," Patrick said. "And what do you know of Creighton?"

The man blinked several times, swallowed hard again. "He will kill me."

"Not if you are already dead."

The man shuddered, but Patrick felt no compassion. The man and his fellow raiders had attacked the croft with the intention of killing and raping, and they had used the Sutherland plaid and name to do it. At that moment, Patrick thought he understood his father better than he ever had:

His clan *was* everything, and it was his duty to protect it, along with its name and its honor, above all else.

Suddenly fearing what he might do, Patrick took a step backward. Still, his sword remained poised to strike.

"I want to know about Creighton," he said again.

"I donna know," the man said desperately. "I know only that men are sent there occasionally."

"Why?"

" 'Tis said a woman is kept there," another captive said. "But none of the guards the laird sends to the keep ha' ever seen her. At least, tha' is what they claim."

Patrick studied the talkative captive. "Are you a Sinclair?"

"Nay," the man said. "A Macnab."

"A mercenary?"

"Aye," the man said hopefully. "Are you in need of one?"

"Not one that would kill women and children," Patrick snapped. "But you will live if your information is correct and you are willing to give it to Parliament."

The man nodded. So did another.

At that moment, one Gunn clansman who had been listening to the confessions fell to his knees and started babbling a prayer. Patrick looked around for the cause of the man's odd behavior. When Patrick saw a man climbing clumsily to the ground from the back of a horse, he had the answer. But while his mouth curved into a crooked grin, the men around him gasped.

"A ghost," one man uttered in reverence.

"Quick Harry," said another in awe.

"He is dead," said a third.

Patrick could see that Quick Harry enjoyed the attention.

"Be he or be he not?" a Gunn asked plaintively.

Quick Harry chuckled. "I be," he stated with assurance.

"But . . . but . . ." one man stuttered.

Quick Harry did a little jig, smiling broadly. Patrick could guess how glad he was that he could finally go home.

But Quick Harry's smile faded as he looked at Patrick and Gavin. Marsali, who had ridden with Quick Harry, had run to Gavin's side and was fretting over his bloodied neck. Patrick smiled briefly, afraid to even look at her when he knew he must leave here quickly.

Instead, he ordered Rufus and Hiram to take the prisoners to Abernie, curtly cutting off any dissent. He trusted only his two friends to make sure Abernie heard the truth.

Satisfied, he grabbed the reins of what looked to be the fastest of the retrieved horses and swung up into the saddle. Gavin jerked loose from Marsali and took the reins of another.

Patrick rode over to him. "Stay here."

" 'Tis only a scratch," Gavin said, "and I have unfinished business."

Patrick swore but dug his heels in his mount, galloping off in the direction Foster had taken—toward Creighton. He had no more time for further argument. He had already wasted precious minutes.

Foster and Sinclair could not guess that he knew about their hideaway. And Alex was there. Patrick rode harder, barely aware of Gavin at his side, of the sound of other horses behind him.

Chapter 26

Alex reached the coast with his two friends at daybreak. He had roused both Jock and Rory from their beds, telling their families their laird had need of them. He had met with no objections, either from the families, who were proud that their sons were chosen, or from his friends, who craved adventure. Before they came in sight of the derelict keep, they dismounted and tied their horses to a stunted, sea-swept oak. Keeping low, they snaked their way through the tall grass.

The keep loomed ahead, dark and foreboding, stark against the sea that had swallowed chunks of its foundation.

Alex gestured for Jock and Rory to stay down, and the young men flattened themselves on their bellies as they inched their way to the very edge of the grass, where the beach began. As one, they peered through the tall stalks. Alex had never seen Creighton. He had only heard of it, and at any other time, he might have enjoyed studying the place. It was, after all, one of the oldest keeps in the Highlands. But this was no time for a history lesson.

With a less appreciative eye, he forced himself to note the fortifications. Only a small strip of sea separated it from the beach, but the sea was rough and the currents strong. They would need a boat if they were to cross.

But the shore was bare.

"They *must* have a boat," Alex said.

"Perhaps it comes from the keep," Jock guessed.

Rory asked, "How would they know when to come?"

"A signal of some kind," Alex offered.

Jock looked puzzled. "What do we do now?"

Alex was at a loss, and for a moment he wished Patrick were there. But Patrick was *not* there, and Alex needed to stop wishing and start thinking. In answer to Jock's question, he said, "We keep out of sight until we see someone approach. Then mayhap we can learn the signal."

"Hide where?" Jock said dubiously.

The three of them looked around. Trees were sparse on the windswept coast, as were rocks large enough for their purpose. They had probably all been taken to build Creighton.

"We will dig holes," he said. "Shallow ones."

The other two looked at him askance.

Alex said, "And cover ourselves with grass."

Jock and Rory considered for a moment, then nodded.

Still crawling on their bellies, they searched for a place soft enough to dig. They found one several yards away from a path carved through the grass by horses' hooves. Using their dirks, they shoveled out three shallow holes in the ground, and Rory and Jock stretched out in two of them. Alex crawled to the path and checked for riders in both directions. He saw only the long grass waving in the cold Scottish wind. Returning to the others, he stretched out in the third hole, worrying about what was happening on Gunn land, fretting over whether Marsali had reached Patrick safely, and wondering how long he and his friends would have to wait.

And what on earth would they do if a troop of men approached?

He had the two pistols from the armory, and his friends both carried dirks. Jock and Rory had started training and knew how to use both dirk and pistol, but none of them was really proficient with any weapon. More than ever, Alex realized they would have to rely upon stealth and wits if they were to succeed.

He kept his eyes on the path. He did not want to think of Margaret in the dank, desolate keep. Mayhap she was not there at all. Mayhap he was endangering himself and his friends needlessly. But then, he wondered for the hundredth time since his meeting with Rufus, why would Sinclair guard an empty, crumbling heap of rock?

Aye, Sinclair was hiding something. And if it was not Margaret, it was something else of value.

Alex felt a chill and knew it was not from the cold ground beneath them. The cold came from inside, from the fingers of dread creeping up his spine. The excitement he had felt when Patrick had asked for his help had long since faded. He was more frightened now than he had ever been in his life.

Yet he was committed to seeing this through. He would not turn back. He finally understood what Patrick had meant the night of the cattle raid when he had said, "Bravery has nothing to do with the use of arms. . . . Real courage is being true to yourself and what you believe is right."

Did real courage mean risking your life even though you were shaking through and through?

He did not know the answer. He only knew the fear.

Edward Sinclair's horse grew restive beneath him, and he cursed, too impatient himself to calm the animal. He had been sitting on the bloody beast all morning, waiting in a wood at the edge of his land where it bordered the Gunns'. Waiting for news from Foster.

At midmorning, when Foster had not arrived, he had dispatched one of the two men with him to the crofts that were targeted for attack. It was now past midday, and no one had returned.

Something had gone wrong. Edward was certain of it. But how could anything have gone wrong when everything was planned to the last detail? He had sent his best men— his *very best*—with Foster. Men he knew he could trust. Men without consciences. The combination was not easy to find. When he had inherited the keep fourteen years ago from his cousin, he had discovered, to his disgust, that the fealty of the men-at-arms was attached, blood and bone, to the Sinclair name, not to himself. His coin had bought mercenaries, but not his clansmen. And it had been those well-paid mercenaries whom Foster had taken on the raid.

What in bloody hell had gone wrong?

Foster *never* made mistakes. In truth, though he disliked the man personally, Edward admired Foster a great deal. To him, the madman had been a godsend—and indeed, he was mad. But he was brilliant. While Edward had tried for years to devise a way to relieve the Gunns and Sutherlands of their rich grazing lands, Foster had come along and, in no time at all, nearly solved the problem. He had even suggested a way to include the fair Marsali as part of the victory when Edward thought there was no hope of having her. After all, she had been betrothed for years to Patrick Sutherland.

It had all seemed quite simple, really: Divide the clans, then reap the rewards. Make them hate each other, watch them kill each other off, leaving their lands for the taking. By offering to "help" the Gunns, he could have Marsali, who by that time surely would no longer be betrothed to a Sutherland. In the end, he would have the land and the woman. Foster would have the revenge he wanted on Patrick Sutherland—which was to his own liking, as well.

Edward admitted only to himself that, when Foster had suggested how they could cause strife between the earl and the marquis, he had paled. He did not mind making the marquis believe that his wife had cuckolded him, but kidnapping her had seemed a very risky thing to do. Frightening, the thought of getting caught. And charged. And hung.

But Foster had assured him it would work. And it had. Exactly the way Foster had said it would. Hatred born of anger and grief flared between the two old men like fire in a dry forest. Marsali's betrothal to Patrick Sutherland had been cried off. And Sinclair had stepped in with gifts and offers of assistance to the Gunn in his feud against the Sutherland clan—in exchange for Marsali's hand in marriage, of course.

The earl had agreed. Everything was set. Then Patrick Sutherland had come home and ruined everything.

He was the reason Marsali had abandoned him at the altar. *He* was the reason Cecilia had disappeared. And *he* was certainly the reason Marsali was a hostage at Brinaire. And somehow the accursed Patrick Sutherland had brought the feud Foster and he had brewed to a grinding halt. Cattle raids. Och! Where was the *blood*?

Still, all had not been lost. The clans were still at war, a war helped in no small measure by the burning out of the Gunn crofters. And while he might not have Marsali, he would, if it came to it, have another Gunn to marry.

Because he still had Margaret. Poor Margaret, who believed it was her husband who kept her prisoner.

Foster had wanted to kill her immediately. But Foster was a rash man, and he was not. It had been a risk to keep her alive, but Edward was willing to take it. For what if Marsali were killed in the feud? Or what if he had not been able to convince the earl to give him either of his daughters in marriage? Then he could have waited, and when the earl of Abernie and the marquis of Brinaire had killed each other off, he could have "rescued" Margaret and married her. Such a union would have strengthened his petition to the king for the Gunn and Sutherland lands.

Edward did not find the thought of marrying Margaret Gunn Sutherland pleasant. She had been neither young nor beautiful when they had kidnapped her, and he imagined two years of imprisonment had taken its toll. But it could be done. If necessary.

For two years, he had stood firm against Foster and kept Margaret alive. But as Edward sat on his horse and looked at the sun sinking toward the western horizon, he began to think the time had come to let Foster have his way.

At three hours past midday, Edward heard a rider approaching. He strained to see movement through the thick forest but was not relieved when he saw Foster. Especially when he reined up and Sinclair saw his mottled, enraged face.

"A trap," Foster said between pants. "The young Gunn . . . and Sutherland were waiting. They captured our men. I barely escaped."

Edward felt the color draining from his face. "They know . . . the raiders came from me?"

"Aye. And now they have proof."

"Creighton?" Edward could barely manage the word.

"I do not know whether they know of it or not, but I suspect they will soon. One loose word . . ."

"Margaret," Edward said. "If she is found on one of my properties . . ."

The thought terrified him. He might be able to cry innocence of the raid, claiming that Foster had ordered it without his knowledge. But kidnapping a highborn lady? His neck would undoubtedly stretch.

Foster nodded. "We have to get rid of her. I told you that, but you . . . you were too cowardly. And now both of us might well be put to the horn. We have time, though, to remedy the situation. I expect Sutherland believes I will make for your keep. He wants you as much as me." He said the last with obvious satisfaction.

A shiver racing up his spine, Edward damned the man silently. But he still needed him. Foster must kill Margaret, for he had not the stomach for it himself.

At least, he thought, only a few of the men who had guarded Creighton knew about Margaret. And they would not easily reveal the secret, since it would convict them as well.

Margaret had to die. Now. Her body had to be thrown into the sea or buried where no one would ever find it.

Edward saw his beautiful scheme unraveling before his eyes. All the intricate, careful planning. Wasted. And he laid the blame squarely on Patrick Sutherland.

He glanced at Foster, who had drawn down his helmet

again. His face was invisible, yet Edward felt his tense fury. Nodding to the man, Edward dug his spurs into the side of his mount, and they started toward Creighton.

And murder.

Rory kicked Alex and pointed toward the east. Two horsemen were riding rapidly along the beach.

They were coming from the south, from Sutherland land. Alex looked up at the sun. They had been there three, mayhap four, hours.

His gaze returned to the two men, and as they drew closer, Alex recognized them as Sutherlands, even though they did not wear their clan plaids. They were Patrick's men, two of those who had been training for weeks in the courtyard.

Alex scrambled to his feet, keeping his body bent nearly double, and ran toward the riders. Catching sight of movement, one drew his sword.

Alex cried out softly, "A Sutherland."

He breathed in relief when the men recognized him and the weapon was lowered. They pulled their horses to a stop and waited until he reached them.

"Patrick sent us," Tommy Sutherland told Alex. Hector, the second man, nodded.

"Continue as though you were riding down the coast," Alex ordered. "Circle around and hide your horses. Then come back—but keep low." The orders issued from his mouth, surprising him with how confident they sounded.

Tommy and Hector did as they were told, continuing north and turning their heads toward each other as if in conversation. An hour later, they came wriggling through the grass to stretch their bodies beside Alex and his friends.

Hector spoke in a harsh whisper. "Wha' the bloody hell is going on?"

Alex tried to put authority in his reply. "Lady Margaret may be in the keep. We thought that if Patrick's plan to catch the Sinclair raiders was successful this morning, Sinclair might try to kill her."

"Lady Margaret?" Tommy Sutherland asked in surprise.

"Aye," Alex said. "Tell me about the raid. How did it go?"

Hector shrugged helplessly. "Patrick sent us ahead to join you. We know nothing."

Anxiety ate at Alex. Still, he had his own job to do. "My friends and I have been trying since we got here to think of a way to get over to Creighton. But there doesna seem to be one."

"Patrick would want ye to wait for him," Tommy said.

"Aye, and I will unless someone comes to cross," Alex said, glancing at Tommy and Hector. He noted that their bodies came close to the top of the grass. "Scoop out two more holes," he said.

"A Sutherland doesna hide," Hector said indignantly.

"He does if he doesna want to be the cause of Lady Margaret's death," Alex countered.

The two men glared at him for a moment, then, with a glance at each other and a shrug, they complied.

After another hour, they were all growing impatient, and he began to worry that his authority over them, tenuous as it was, would not go the distance. Just as he was trying to think of a way to pacify them, he heard voices. His hand shot out to still the murmurings of his companions.

He watched as three horses came into sight. They all wore Sutherland plaids, he noticed, but something about them warned him to remain still. As they came closer, he peered at the faces. He recognized none. Then he noticed the flash between the island keep and the newcomers. A mirror? A piece of metal?

A couple of seconds later, Alex saw the glint of something bright coming from the island. After a moment, the flashes disappeared, and the three men dismounted.

They must be replacement guards. Wearing Sutherland

plaids, damn their souls. What would Patrick do? Quiet the anger and use his head, Alex answered himself.

Tommy started to move, and Alex gripped the back of his jerkin to stop him. "We have to take them without any sound," he whispered. "No one from the keep must know. And," he added, "Patrick will want them alive."

Tommy nodded, and he and Hector began snaking their way forward through the grass. Alex, with Rory and Jock behind him, followed.

The newcomers tied their horses to a gorse bush, then started through the tall grass toward the beach. When Alex judged that his little band was close enough, he threw a stone to land behind them. All three turned to look.

As they did, Tommy grabbed one of them around the throat and quickly lowered him to the ground. Hector used the butt of his pistol on the second man's head, and Alex, Rory, and Jock tackled the third man, wrestling him to the ground and thrusting a piece of cloth in his mouth before he could cry out. The men were down, and out of sight, within seconds.

Hector made quick work of gagging the two conscious men. One struggled frantically until Tommy put his dirk to his throat and promised a lingering death. The man quieted instantly and both obeyed instantly when told to disrobe. Rory disrobed the still-unconscious guard.

Once all three were stripped naked, the two conscious men shivering both from fear and cold, Hector, Jock, and Tommy bound them with cloth from their own shirts.

Alex told the two older men to don the discarded clothes of the two larger men. He donned the plaid of the third himself. They changed quickly, knowing the boat might not approach if the men rowing it did not recognize the plaids. As Alex finished belting the plaid, still shielded by the grass, the horses, and the gorse bush, the boat was already halfway to shore.

Alex looked at Rory's and Jock's expectant faces and nodded. Five were better than two.

"We will go together," he told Tommy, not waiting to hear any objections he might have about the inclusion of the youths. Alex could hardly believe they were following his commands. He only hoped they couldn't tell how close he was to getting sick.

The five of them started toward the beach with Tommy, Hector, and Alex wearing the guards' plaids and walking in front. The boat was just landing, and one of the two rowers jumped out to pull it up onto the rocky shore. Apparently, they were so busy fighting the tide they did not look closely at the men approaching them. It was enough that they had seen the signals.

Tommy jumped into the boat and with one great swing knocked out the man inside. Jock, at the same moment, hit the second man with his pistol.

Alex prayed like blazes, as they dragged both men into the grass, that no one was watching from the keep's windows. Rory and Jock took the rowers' plaids, donning them over their own shirts and discarding their trousers.

Once in the boat, Hector and Jock rowed. Halfway across, Tommy muttered, "We should ha' waited for Patrick."

His words were an echo of Alex's thoughts. But, in truth, he knew they could not have waited. What if the men had been told of the ambush and ordered to kill Margaret?

As they approached the back side of the castle, Alex saw a small dock and a man waiting for their arrival—or rather the arrival of the men whose plaids they had stolen. Alex breathed a quiet prayer that the man was truly alone. The place would not need an army, after all. And it did *look* deserted.

Tommy kept his face averted as the boat swung in, and Jock threw the rope to the man, who caught it deftly. Alex jumped onto the dock and pressed his pistol into the man's stomach.

"Tie it," he ordered.

The man stared at the pistol for two long seconds. Then, quickly, he tied the rope to a piling, and stood as the other four men climbed up onto the wet planking.

"How many guards are there?" Tommy demanded.

The man hesitated until Alex thrust his gun more firmly into his stomach. With the hard metal against his ribs, he gulped several times before muttering, "Eight."

"Including those in the boat?" Alex asked.

Another thrust from the gun prompted a reluctant nod.

"How many others are here—*besides* the guards?"

The man hesitated. Alex leaned toward Tommy and inquired in what he hoped was a dangerously soft voice, "Do you recognize this kinsman of ours?"

The prisoner stiffened, realizing at last who his captors were.

"*I* donna know him," Tommy said.

"Neither do I," Jock said.

"Ye wouldna be thinking some blackguard would pretend to be a Sutherland?" Hector said. "Why, Patrick Sutherland would tear him limb from limb. *Before* hanging him. They say he's killed a hundred men wi'out mercy."

" 'Tis true," Alex said. "My brother told me himself."

The prisoner's eyes grew wild, flicking from one man to another.

"Aye," Tommy said. " 'Tis Patrick's own brother, Alex. He takes after his brother, he does, despite his young-looking face. Just killed one of those dogs comin' to relieve you. Stuck 'im in the gut wi'out wincing."

"I am just following orders," the man cried. "I would be killed myself if I didna."

"Sinclair is dead," Alex said, following Tommy's lead. "So now you will follow my orders. Who else is in the keep?"

Convinced now that he was in the hands of madmen, the

captive started babbling. "A lady. Three women who tend her. Five other guards."

"Where are the guards?"

"Three are asleep," he said. "Two others would be in the guardroom."

"Who saw the signal?"

"I did. One of us is always up in the tower window."

"Is anyone there now?"

"Nay, I was to return as soon as the relief arrived."

"They willna be arriving now," Tommy said.

"Are they . . . really dead?"

"Ye donna see them, do ye?" Hector replied roughly. "Now take off that plaid ye ha' dishonored."

The man rushed to comply, his hands fumbling with the belt that held the plaid in place. With Tommy's none-too-gentle help, he soon stood there in only a dirty, thin shirt.

Jock tore part of the shirt off to tie the man's hands behind him, then ordered him to show them where the guards slept.

In less than an hour, they had all of the guards bound and locked in a damp cell on the lower level of the decrepit keep. The "lady," they said, was in a tower room, up four flights of stairs. One woman was always with her. Two others alternated in caring for her.

Alex took the steps two at a time. When he reached the top step, he startled a woman coming out the door. A key hung from a piece of leather around her neck.

"No need to lock that," he said, pushing her aside. She tried to stop him, but Hector was right behind Alex and he grabbed her.

Alex entered the chamber, his heart pounding so hard his chest hurt. The room had no windows. Only one candle provided any light. He saw a woman lying on a narrow bed, and in a few steps he was kneeling on the floor next to her, his hand reaching for her thin, pale arm.

The face was familiar, but it was gaunt and very wan. Dazed blue eyes looked at him listlessly.

"Margaret," he said softly.

She blinked, her eyes focusing suddenly. "Alex?" she breathed. "Mother of mercy! Alex, is it really you?" She struggled to sit, and he stood to help her.

She was dreadfully weak, and her eyes kept seeming to lose their focus. "I canna . . . I drank the wine, and now I willna be able to stand."

"They have drugged you?" he asked.

"A little. A little each day. And night." She looked up at him. "Your father . . . is he . . ."

"He is at Brinaire," Alex said. "Do you know where you are?"

She shook her head. "The sea. Somewhere on the sea."

"You are at Creighton. Edward Sinclair put you here."

"Sinclair?" She shook her head again. "Oh, aye, Edward Sinclair. I remember. But it was Gregor who put me here." Her gaze was beseeching. "Please . . . help me home."

"Nay, it was not Father," Alex said gently. "Father didna put you here, Margaret. He thinks you are dead and that you . . . that you may have killed yourself. Your brother believes my father killed you. They have been . . . at war."

She stared at him blankly. "It wasna Gregor?"

"Nay," he said gently. "It wasna. I swear it."

"How long have I . . . ?"

"Two years."

"I donna remember . . . the wine . . . I feel so . . . so weak when I drink it, yet it makes it more . . ." She swallowed hard. "More bearable."

Alex felt his heart break. Her clothes hung on her as if they belonged to a woman twice her size. He wanted to kill Sinclair.

Rising, he took her hand. "Come, Margaret. I will take you home." He lifted her in his arms. She was so thin and light that it frightened him.

When he reached the door, Hector held out his arms to take her. Alex started to protest, then stopped. Hector was stronger than he, and they had four flights of stairs to descend. Alex handed Margaret to Hector as if she were a piece of fragile glass. "Be careful with her."

"Aye," Hector replied. "On my life, I will be."

They hurried down the stairs and out of the keep, to the small boat bobbing on the sea.

"What about the guards?" Jock asked.

"We will lock them in the tower room. Tommy, you and Jock stay with them. It should not be long before we can send others for them," Alex said. "And I suspect my brother would like to take care of them himself."

Tommy grinned at him, and Alex grinned back. He felt ten years older. And wiser.

Chapter 27

Standing on the steps of Abernie, the earl watched the men stagger through the gates of his keep. His clansmen were on horses he had never seen before, and they led nearly twenty bound men, all on foot.

He looked for his son, sick at heart when he did not see him. He noted three horses carrying wrapped bodies. Please, God. Not Gavin. And then the last man rode unsteadily through the gates, a short, wiry man more accustomed to running. The sight took his breath away.

Quick Harry? A spirit? The earl could not believe his eyes. What the devil was going on? Gavin had told him they were going on another raid. But where was he? Dear God above, had his insistence on revenge cost him his only son?

The earl stood as if paralyzed while Quick Harry rode up to him and nearly fell off his horse dismounting. Two men he did not recognize dismounted and stood next to Quick Harry.

"I donna know how you came to be alive," the earl said to him, "but your explanation can wait. Tell me, where is my son?"

Quick Harry hesitated a moment, then said, "Gone t' take the carrion who has been devilin' us."

"The Sutherlands?" the lord of Abernie asked. "But I knew that."

"Nay," Quick Harry said, climbing the steps toward him. "Not the Sutherlands. Sinclair." He spit on the ground. "If it had not been for Patrick Sutherland, yer son would be dead."

"Where is he?" the earl roared. "Where is my son?"

"He went wi' Patrick Sutherland after Sinclair. They believe he ha' to do with yer sister's disappearance."

"You are daft, man. It was Sutherland."

"If ye will listen, my lord, I will explain," Quick Harry interrupted.

Abernie's gaze went to the prisoners, who had come to stand in a crooked line in the middle of the courtyard. They were nearly naked, wearing only dirty, sweat-stained saffron shirts.

Frowning, the earl brought his gaze back to Quick Harry.

The clan's messenger waved a hand toward the prisoners. "These craven cowards attacked our crofts in the nor'east, jest as they attacked mine. They were wearing Sutherland plaids, but they are mercenaries paid by Edward Sinclair."

"Sinclair!"

"Aye. He ha' been raidin' our land and makin' ye think it were the Sutherlands. But Patrick Sutherland found him out and made a plan to stop him."

None of it made any sense. "And Gavin?"

"Aye, the young Sutherland and Lord Gavin ha' been workin' together to catch Sinclair in the act."

Donald Gunn scowled. "Nay, Gavin has been raiding the Sutherlands. He has no' said a word to me about Sinclair or working with that spawn of the devil, Sutherland."

The look Quick Harry gave him was about as accusatory as any a crofter could give his lord and get away with it. "Lord Gavin couldna tell ye his suspicions," Quick Harry said. "Nor could he tell ye that he and Patrick Sutherland were together in a scheme. Ye wouldna ha' listened."

That, the earl acknowledged, was certainly true. "And so when Gavin told me last night that he was taking clansmen to raid the Sutherlands, it wasna true?"

"Nay, it wasna," Quick Harry confirmed. "He and the Gunn clansmen joined with Patrick Sutherland's band to foil Sinclair's attack on the crofts north of Kilcraig. They were hoping to catch Sinclair in the act, and they caught him proper. I tell ye, sir, it wa' a sight to see." He sighed. Then, frowning, added, "But a mon named Foster—the Sinclair's leader—he would ha' killed Lord Gavin, but Patrick Sutherland stepped in and saved his life, jest as he saved mine."

The earl was trying hard to understand Harry, who spoke as rapidly as he ran. "Yours?"

"Aye, sir. That devil Foster carved me up the night of the raid on my croft. He left me for dead, but I wa' able to get to that old huntin' hut on Sutherland land. Lord Patrick found me, and he brought Lady Marsali to tend me. The young Sutherland is a good mon, sir, I tell ye straight."

When Quick Harry finished his recital, Abernie stood stunned. A Sutherland had saved his son? Helped save Gunn crofters?

Unable to accept that everything he had believed the last two years was a lie, the earl said, "Are you certain Sinclair was behind the raids?"

"Aye." Quick Harry nodded. "And he had his men wear the Sutherland plaids. 'Tis why they be half naked. The Sutherlands didna favor their plaids bein' used so foully."

"These men admitted this?"

"Aye." Quick Harry gestured to one of the Gunn clansmen guarding the prisoners. "Bring the ugly one to me."

"They all be ugly, Quick Harry."

"The one that talked to Lord Patrick."

One of the prisoners was pushed out of line and dragged to the bottom of the steps.

"Tell the earl," Quick Harry ordered.

" 'Tis the truth, sir," the man admitted. "Edward Sinclair paid me and the others ye see here to raid yer crofts. We had orders to kill all. Women and children, too. Patrick Sutherland said he would spare my life if I told ye the truth, and I ha'."

Abernie had to look away. Rubbing a hand across his

face, he turned, staring over the walls of the keep at the hills beyond. He could barely breathe, could think of nothing but the fact that he had nearly married his daughter to a murderer.

The earl's jaw worked as he fought for control. Finally, he said quietly, "And my daughters?"

"I know the whereabouts of only one," Quick Harry said, "and I believe 'tis by her choice that she stays at Brinaire."

Abernie suddenly felt very old. His son had lied to him. The son of the man he considered his greatest enemy had saved his own son's life. His daughter preferred to stay at Brinaire. A man he had chosen as son-in-law had tried to kill the people he was pledged to protect.

"Take the prisoners to the cells below," he said wearily. "We will give them over to the king's justice." He hesitated, looking at Quick Harry. "You are sure my son lives?"

"I could not swear by it, my lord," Quick Harry replied. "But he wa' only slightly wounded when he rode with Patrick to find Sinclair and the man named Foster."

Donald looked toward the two men standing next to Quick Harry. "And who are these two?"

"Friends of the Sutherland, ordered to accompany us and make sure we arrived safely," Quick Harry said. "One was at Sinclair's keep on Patrick Sutherland's orders. He can tell ye more."

But Donald did not need to hear more. The evidence was before his eyes.

"I will go after Gavin," the earl said. "I will not risk his life now. Fetch fresh horses. We will leave as soon as I talk to Duncan."

Abruptly, Abernie turned and went into the castle. He sent a messenger for Duncan, then went directly to his study, where he flopped into the chair behind his desk and buried his head in his hands. His head was filled with ugly thoughts, thoughts of remorse and fear. Most of all fear— for his son's life.

Gavin. His pride. His joy. Defying his father to join with Patrick Sutherland to defeat a common enemy. The earl tried and failed to be angry. He was too proud of his son.

If Gavin died trying to prove his father wrong, the earl hoped God would take him, too, for he would not want to live.

He had driven away the three people he loved most in the world. They had run from him. They had felt compelled to lie to him. A single tear fell from the corner of his eye to trickle down his cheek. A tear for his son, for his daughters, and for himself.

With Foster at his side, Sinclair reined in his horse as they neared the coast. He looked back. No one in pursuit. Mayhap luck was with him. He took a piece of metal from his sporran and flashed it toward a window in the keep.

There was no response. He flashed it again. He had no time for this. The cursed guards were lazy.

He glanced at Foster. His companion's back was stiff, the man's gaze moving cautiously over the sea grass and mounds of sand. When he spurred his horse forward, Sinclair followed.

Ahead, Foster leaped down from his mount, taking his dirk from its sheath. Sinclair guided his horse to the same spot and looked down incredulously at three nearly naked men bound with cloth strips.

Mumbling an oath, he slid off his horse and stood at Foster's side as the man knelt to cut their bonds. One man was conscious; the other two made no movement.

"What in the devil's name?" Sinclair muttered.

"I believe someone has discovered your secret," Foster said. He glared at the one conscious man now trying to rise, even as he averted his eyes from his lord.

"Coinneach Sinclair," Sinclair said. "What happened?"

"I donna know, laird," the man said, his eyes filled with fear. He knew well the price of failure. "We came to relieve the guards, gave the signal as always, and 'twas answered. Then a horde of men were upon us. I know naught else."

"A horde?"

"Aye, ten or fifteen at least," the man said.

"Come now," Foster broke in. "Was it really ten or fifteen?"

Coinneach Sinclair lowered his eyes. "They came from behind."

"Then you donna know?"

Coinneach bent his head but persisted stubbornly. "There were many."

Sinclair looked out over the water and for the first time saw the small boat coming around from the back of the keep.

Foster's eyes followed his gaze. "It seems someone is coming, and it is time for me to leave Scotland." He stood.

Fear suffocated Sinclair. Foster was a mercenary. He could go anywhere. But all Sinclair had was his land, and he saw it slipping through his fingers.

"We donna know who is out there," he said. "There are three of us . . . mayhap four," he added. The second guard was coming to. "We can take them by surprise."

"Ten or fifteen?" Foster said, raising a brow.

"I see only three in the boat. We have pistols. And they will not suspect anything."

Foster considered the odds, then Coinneach, who'd insisted there were more attackers. He looked at the footsteps leading down to the boat. Five, mayhap six different sets.

"Jewels," Sinclair said desperately. "I will give you the rest of Margaret's jewels."

They had battled once about that. Foster had meant to take them all, but unfortunately Sinclair had more men than he. They had divided them.

Foster nodded once. He gave his dirk to Coinneach, keeping his sword and pistol for himself. Sinclair kicked the second man as he awoke, thrusting his dirk into the man's shaking hands. "You have a chance to get your clothes back," he said. "Otherwise you can walk back naked."

The boat was approaching the beach. Sinclair hoped they could not see the horses, and he quickly signaled one of the newly freed clansmen to take them farther inland. Dropping close to the ground, the others moved away from the one unconscious man still lying in the sand.

Sinclair was afraid the beating of his heart would give him away. But the rowers had not killed his guards, which meant he had the advantage. Foster would never have let them live.

Peering through the sea oats, he saw one man carrying a woman. Margaret! So they had found her. Two slender young men followed. Boys? Could boys have bested his men?

As the three approached, he saw Foster stand and level his pistol. " 'Tis far enough," Foster snarled.

The three stopped mid-stride.

Swallowing hard, Sinclair stood, too. As did Coinneach.

Foster approached them slowly. "Ah," he said, his eyes studying the dark-haired boy, who moved just a step ahead of his companions. "Could this be the Sutherland's brother?" He didn't wait for an answer. "And Margaret? How impolite to leave our hospitality."

None of them said anything. But dismay flickered over the dark-haired boy's face, and Margaret cowered against the man who held her. Sinclair was heartened by their fear.

"Who else is with you?" Foster asked.

No one answered.

Foster nodded to Coinneach. "Mayhap you can persuade someone to answer me. Try the woman first."

Coinneach did not move. Foster looked at him impatiently, then handed him the pistol. "You can shoot, can you not?"

Coinneach looked at his laird, then at the pistol, and shook his head.

Foster gave a snort of disgust and took a step forward.

The younger Sutherland did, too, placing his body in front of Margaret's.

"You will not touch her, not as long as I live."

Sinclair's finger was poised on the trigger of his flintlock pistol. One shot. Only one shot before he must reload. A Sutherland. Mayhap not the Sutherland he wanted, but a Sutherland nevertheless. He hesitated only a moment before he pulled the trigger, the sound of the shot piercing the late afternoon quiet. But his shaking hand had sent the bullet wide.

"You bloody fool," Foster roared. Then he turned to Alex, his sword raised. "I have no more time to waste. One of you will tell me who else is with you or this boy dies."

Patrick and Gavin were nearing Creighton when they heard the shot.

Patrick's heart stilled a moment, then he dug his heels into his mount, racing toward the keep . . . and the sound of the pistol shot.

Gavin was by his side, and he was aware of another rider behind him. He turned, his breath catching in his throat as he saw Marsali racing to keep even.

He swore and slowed his mount as they approached the beach. It would do no one any good if they rushed in without knowing what awaited them, and he would not further endanger Marsali. Why in blazes had she not stayed behind?

He tried to breathe evenly as he waited for Gavin and Marsali to reach him. He wanted to rail at her. But as she pulled her horse to a stop, she looked at him with eyes full of anxiety . . . not for herself, but for him. And her brother.

"I couldna stay," she whispered. "I have waited too many times alone."

He could do nothing now, anyway, other than gain her promise to stay out of sight. "If you wish to help us," he said, "stay here, and hold the horses."

She started to protest, but Gavin held up his hand. "If you wish to aid Margaret, do as he says."

Marsali looked from one to the other, then nodded reluctantly.

Patrick nodded to Gavin, and they both dismounted, each going in a different direction—one to the east and one to the west. 'Twas the same as when they were boys; they knew instinctively what to do.

Patrick worked his way in the direction from which the shot came, stopping when he heard voices. Gavin would be coming from the opposite direction.

One shot. He had heard one shot, which meant at least one of them had a pistol. He struggled to remember. Did both Foster and Sinclair have guns? There might be others with them now, as well. And where was Alex?

He crept closer.

An oath sounded, then another.

"Who else knows about Creighton?" Foster's voice. Patrick heard a grunt of pain.

Another step, then another, and he saw them. Foster held a sword close to Alex's face. Blood was already streaming down the boy's cheek. Hector held a pale but very much living Margaret, whose face was contorted with confusion and fear. Sinclair was standing, the pistol in a hand pointed at the ground. Another man clothed only in a linen shirt held another pistol at the ready.

Patrick unsheathed his sword and stepped quietly out of the tall grass. Gavin emerged opposite him, shouting a curse that drew the attention of all, leaving Patrick unnoticed. Foster and the man holding the gun whirled on his friend, and Patrick's sword struck the latter's arm just as the gun went off.

Blood exploded from Gavin's arm. Still, his friend rushed Sinclair, at the same time Patrick went for Foster with his sword raised. Out of the corner of his eye, he saw Hector lower Margaret and attack the man who had held the other pistol.

Patrick's thrust at the gun had given Foster time to register what was happening, and now he stood in front of Patrick, his eyes gleaming with malice.

"I've been expecting you, Sutherland." His sword sliced through the air to clash with Patrick's.

Patrick parried the blow, knowing full well he was at a disadvantage. His left shoulder and arm were weak, and the pain and stiffness in them would affect his agility. As he had observed watching Gavin fight Foster, the man was still a superb swordsman. That had not changed. Neither had his cold, dark eyes.

Those eyes, Patrick noted as the two circled, each taking the other's measure, lingered on the scar on his face. Foster had carved that scar ten years earlier, although not on the battlefield. He and Rufus had come upon Foster and two other men raping two girls, neither of whom had been a day over thirteen. Enraged, Patrick had killed the first man while Rufus dispatched the second. Then Foster had engaged him, and they had fought while Rufus helped the girls escape. Foster's blade had ripped open his face, and he had slashed Foster's throat, thinking that if anyone had ever deserved death, it was this man.

And he had left Foster for dead, only to learn years later that the man had lived and sworn an oath of revenge. It had been a mistake not to make certain that Foster no longer drew breath. A mistake he was about to rectify.

Gathering his strength, Patrick tried a riposte. The Englishman stepped back, recovering quickly, then lunged. Patrick sidestepped, and Foster's sword went past him, but again Foster swung around, striking faster than Patrick thought possible.

He managed to get his blade up to block the blow, but the impact sent a river of pain shooting up his arm to his shoulder. Again and again, their swords clashed and disengaged. Minutes went by, grueling minutes of no respite and no quarter. Not from either side.

Vaguely, Patrick was aware of sweat coating his face and blood trickling down his arm. He realized he had been cut again, but he felt nothing save the agony in his shoulder. Nor did he care. He cared only about killing Foster.

He began to have difficulty drawing a breath. And it was becoming harder and harder to keep his feet moving fast enough to sidestep blows that kept coming and coming. He was running out of time. He needed an opening, needed it soon, but Foster allowed none. The man's strength, fueled by madness and a passion for revenge, was greater. As was his taste for blood. Truly, Patrick had lost such a taste long ago, if indeed he had ever had one. . . .

Patrick yanked himself back from that thought. If he did not destroy Foster now, Foster would kill him. And he was not ready to die. He had too much to live for.

Just then, he saw her. Her face was drained of color, but he tried to dismiss the sight of it from his mind, tried to gather his wits as well as his remaining strength. He let his feet stumble a little in the sand. Foster, sensing victory, raised his sword, preparing to strike a death blow. But in doing so he bared his own heart, and Patrick plunged his blade into Foster's chest, driving it in up to the hilt.

He stood only inches from Foster, his gaze fixed on the man's face. With his arms still raised to strike, Foster lost his grip on his sword, and it fell to the ground. Patrick felt it graze his leg in passing. But he held on to his sword, pulling it free only as Foster's body collapsed, crumbling backward to hit the ground as if boneless.

Patrick felt himself sway but managed to stay on his feet. Nearly blinded by either sweat or blood, he did not know which, he looked down at his body and saw blood. Was it his? He felt no pain. Somewhere in the past few minutes, his body had gone numb, and the only sensation he could identify was weariness.

He looked at Foster lying at his feet and knew he should feel satisfaction. Yet as he stared at the open eyes and saw the puzzlement trapped there at the moment of his death, he felt no satisfaction at all. Instead, he felt sick.

An instant later, he was saved from his own thoughts when Marsali hurled herself into his arms.

Flinging her hands around his neck, she sobbed against his chest. "Oh, Patrick! Oh, dear God, I thought he would kill you."

From somewhere inside him, a weak laugh rose. "Such wee faith," he murmured, burying his face in her hair. Dropping his sword, he put his arms around her and crushed her to him. He would have liked to lie down right there, in the dirt, with his head in her lap, and sleep for the next week.

But all at once, he remembered the others. He lifted his head. Alex, his face bloodied, held a dirk with steady hand to the neck of Sinclair, who knelt on the ground. Hector had his sword point aimed at the heart of the man who had shot Gavin. Gavin sat, alive, holding his hand against his arm.

He looked down at Marsali. "I thought I asked you to wait."

"Aye," she said, her hand reaching up to touch his face, as if to convince herself he was truly alive. "But I couldna live without you, and I couldna stay and imagine what might be happening."

"Will you never obey?" he asked gently. Glad she had not. Glad she was in his arms.

"In all things but your carelessness with your life, my lord," she said with mock deference, but then her slight smile disappeared as she turned toward her brother.

"Gavin . . ."

Together they walked to where Gavin sat, and Marsali knelt next to him.

"Took you long enough to down that Sassenach," Gavin

growled, and Patrick was relieved to hear that although his friend's face was pale, his voice was as strong as ever.

For a moment, Patrick could not speak around the lump filling his throat. Gavin had risked his own life by diverting their enemies' attention for the split second Patrick had needed. And he had done so without regard for his own life.

He held out his good hand to Gavin's good one, and the two men clasped them together, bound together now by more than friendship. Patrick allowed himself a slight grin at Gavin's jibe, although they both knew quite well that if the fight had continued, it would have ended another way.

Patrick watched as Marsali tore a piece of cloth from her shirt and began tying it around Gavin's arm. The bullet would have to be removed, but it did not look dangerous.

He turned to Alex, who was still guarding Sinclair. The bleeding wound in the young man's cheek looked painful, but neither deep nor dangerous with good tending.

And Margaret—dear Margaret—was lying on the ground nearby, half conscious, her eyes closed.

"Margaret?"

"They drugged her," his brother said. "I am not sure she even knows what is happening."

Patrick stooped beside her. "Margaret," he said gently, holding back his rage at her condition. "You are safe now. I will take you home to Brinaire. Or would you rather go to Abernie?"

Margaret didn't answer but moved slightly as Patrick lifted her. He could wrap one of his hands entirely around her upper arms with his fingers overlapping. She was dressed only in a shift, but a Sutherland plaid had been wrapped about her; beneath the clothing, she was nothing but skin and bone.

"Margaret." Her eyelids flickered and Patrick was even more disturbed by the glazed, unfocused look he saw in her eyes. Drugs, he thought. Not enough to render her senseless but enough to make it difficult for her to control her movements or focus her thoughts.

"Margaret," he said again, seeking a response, any response.

"Patrick?" She turned her head, trying to see his face. "But they told me . . . they said Patrick was dead. They said . . ." She gave her head a little shake, murmuring something about wine and wishing she had not taken it. With an impatient sound, she took a deep breath, and when she looked at him again, her eyes seemed to focus.

"Patrick! Oh, merciful heaven, 'tis really you! You are no' dead as that wretched Foster told me."

"Nay, I am not dead," Patrick replied. "But some are not so lucky."

Her eyes followed his to the man lying on the ground. "Foster?"

"Aye," Patrick said. "He willna be hurting you again."

Her gaze fell from his. "He didna hurt me. At least, not in body. But the things he said . . ." She shuddered. "Terrible things." She raised her gaze to his once more. "Alex said . . . he said that Gregor . . . that he didna put me here. That he . . . that Gregor believes I . . . Oh, dear God . . . that I killed myself." She burst into tears.

Patrick hesitated, glancing down at the blood covering him. Then, swearing silently, he hugged her to him. She needed comfort. "Ah, Margaret," he murmured. "Father knows you wouldna kill yourself. He told me that himself. He was told that you left him for a lover, but I donna think he believes that any more than the other. I think he doesna *know* what he believes. But 'tis plain to everyone that he has missed you sorely."

"I thought he put me here," she sobbed. "I thought he loathed the sight of me and couldna stand me near him. Foster said it, and I believed him. Oh, Patrick, I want to go home. Please . . . please take me home."

"Aye, you shall go home," he said, patting her back gently. "Alex and I will take you to Brinaire, and you will—"

"Nay." Her hand moved against his chest in negation. "Not Brinaire. I canna face Gregor. Not like this. Please. I want to go home, to Abernie where I . . . where I will feel safe."

Patrick closed his eyes, feeling his heart break for her. "No one will force you to do anything, I swear to you." Holding her away from him, he leaned down to kiss her cheek. "You will go to Abernie with Hector." Then he added, whispering under his breath, "To hell with the consequences."

"Take good care of milady," he said, handing her gently to Hector. He turned to Sinclair, who was still kneeling with Alex's dirk at his throat.

Patrick placed his arm on Alex's shoulder. "You did well, Alex. Marsali will tend that wound once she finishes with Gavin."

" 'Tis nothing," Alex said with a nonchalance that made Patrick's smile wider. He wished his father were there.

But his smile faded as he looked at Sinclair, who had risen from his kneeling position once the knife was removed from his throat.

"You wanted a fight," Patrick said, taking Foster's sword and offering it to Sinclair. "I will give you one."

He heard Marsali's cry, Gavin's muttered objection. He was tired, it was true. But somehow he knew it wouldn't matter.

Patrick watched as, instead of taking the sword, Sinclair took a step backward. His retreat pulled Patrick forward, Foster's sword in one hand, his own in the other. He wanted to kill.

"Take it," he ordered Sinclair, who stumbled and fell partly to the ground, his eyes wide with terror.

I will never kill another Scotsman. Still, his hand itched to plunge the blade into Sinclair's chest. Longed to with all his being.

"Patrick." Marsali's soft voice. Steady and pleading.

Sinclair held his arm in front of him as if to ward off a blow. Patrick's sword hung in the air, then slowly, very slowly, he dropped it to his side and closed his eyes. The hate drained from him. Her voice took it away.

He felt Marsali at his side, her arm around him. He opened his eyes. Alex was already binding Sinclair's arms.

Sinclair *would* pay. But he would pay through His Majesty's justice. And Patrick would make sure he paid dearly.

Marsali clutched his hand. "Let us go home," she said. Home. A good word. A fine word.

He nodded and leaned down, touching his lips to hers. And feeling whole for the first time in his life.

Chapter 28

Patrick decided to fetch Tommy and Jock from Creighton and risk leaving the remaining Sinclair prisoners locked in the same room where they had held Margaret until others could return to take them.

Patrick would accompany Margaret to Abernie, along with Hector. He could not rightly send the man alone; neither did he fancy leaving Margaret's care in the hands of Alex's two youthful friends, regardless of their bravery.

He sent the others back to Brinaire. Gavin needed attention, and Brinaire was far closer than Abernie. Marsali wanted to stay with her brother until he was out of danger, but that was just as well, for Patrick was not yet willing to chance losing her again.

He took Alex to one side. "Tell me everything that happened."

Alex shrugged, but his eyes were bright, proud. "Everyone did their part. But, Patrick, all the guards were dressed as Sutherlands. Margaret really believed Father was holding her."

Patrick could think of no punishment that would pay for all the grief and misery that Edward Sinclair had caused. He was, in that moment, glad he hadn't killed him. Death was too good for him. Too easy.

"Those two friends of yours . . ."

"Rory and Jock," Alex said eagerly.

Patrick nodded. "The three of you did the Gunns and the Sutherlands a great service this day," he said. "I am proud of you. And our family owes a great debt to Jock and Rory. Tell them that. They have only to ask a boon, and it will be done." Meeting Alex's gaze, he said, "Since you found Margaret, I think you should ride ahead to Brinaire and tell Father. And that we are bringing Gavin in—as our guest."

Alex's grin broadened. "Aye," he said as he mounted and spurred his horse, racing toward Brinaire with a brief wave over his shoulder.

Patrick turned to Gavin. His friend looked pale, but his back was straight, and he tried a smile. "Do you think your fa will throw me in the dungeon?"

"I am not so sure your own father won't do exactly that to me," Patrick said, trying to make his smile reassuring. "At least, they can exchange us this way." Careful of Gavin's arm, he embraced the other man, muttering, "Take care of my wife."

"Aye," Gavin said. "The Gunns will owe you a great deal."

"Nay," Patrick said. "My father with his bloody pride was every bit at fault."

He looked at Marsali—his lovely Marsali. "Take good care of him."

"I will," she said, her eyes filled with worry. "I will be waiting for you."

He leaned over and kissed her. It lasted longer than he intended. He cared not if others watched. He savored the sweetness, the gentleness of her mouth on his. He never wanted to let her go, not even for the next few hours.

"Take care," she whispered.

"Aye, and I *will* hurry," he replied.

He helped her into the saddle and watched as she and the others started toward Brinaire. He watched until they disappeared from sight, then turned to Sinclair.

"Make him comfortable," he told Hector.

"Aye," Hector said as he tossed Sinclair over the saddle like a sack of grain and tied his feet to his hands under the horse's belly. "Verra comfortable."

* * *

The following day, Patrick rode beside the earl of Abernie toward the gates of Brinaire. He had met Abernie and his men halfway the evening before. Despite Abernie's concern for his son, he had returned to his own keep, accepting Patrick's assurances that Gavin was in no danger. And Margaret desperately needed her brother now.

Patrick had stayed the night, making sure that Margaret was well and comfortable. And he *had* slept, despite his need to see Marsali. He had been tired to the bone. . . .

Behind them rode Hiram and Rufus, flanking a bound and ragged-looking Edward Sinclair. Margaret had remained at Abernie in the care of several teary-eyed clanswomen, who had not yet stopped expressing their gratitude and joy over her seemingly miraculous return from the dead.

The earl cleared his throat, and Patrick looked at him.

"I donna know how to say this," the earl began. "I have had little practice with such things. But say it I must." He drew himself up in his saddle until his back was washboard-straight. "I have wronged you, Patrick, and 'tis sorry I am. I remember the day you left Abernie, and how you looked— so tall and proud to be going off to do your duty for your clan. I was proud of you that day, lad. Proud to have had a hand in preparing you to be a mon. And I look at you now, and I look at what you have done these past weeks to help our clans, and I am proud of you all over again. I think I must have taken leave of my senses these past two years. I willna e'er know how I could have thought you anything but honorable and decent. I am sorry, Patrick. I hope you can find it in your heart to forgive me."

For a first effort at eating humble pie, Patrick thought the earl could not have done a finer job. " 'Tis done," he said simply, leaning across the saddle and extending his hand.

The earl looked at it, meeting his gaze, then leaned forward to clasp his arm in friendship.

Straightening once more, the earl sighed. "I wonder if my daughters will be so forgiving."

Patrick smiled. "I donna think you need fret. They love you very much. And I think Marsali worries that you will never forgive *her*."

Abernie waved a hand. "There be nothing to forgive. I donna hold anything against her or Gavin in this terrible thing we have all lived through. And Cecilia! Och! How could I blame a little lass like her for anything?" He shot Patrick a concerned look. "You are certain she is safe?"

"Aye," Patrick replied. "Rufus and Hiram will go to the Lowlands to fetch her before week's end."

"Good. Mayhap Jeanie can go with them as chaperon."

Patrick hid a grin, thinking that, with Hiram along, mayhap someone should be sent to chaperon Jeanie, as well.

A few minutes later, they passed through the gates of Brinaire.

As they approached the castle steps, the earl said, "Do you think your father has been told of our coming?"

"I sent a messenger this morning," Patrick replied.

The earl let out a heavy sigh. "Ah, Patrick, I donna look forward to facing your father. But it must be done."

His own thoughts exactly. He was not sure what to expect: to be forgiven for his deceit or to be disowned and disinherited. Gratitude was too much even to imagine, much less hope for.

Dismounting, Patrick handed his reins to the stable lad who came to collect them, then turned to yank Sinclair out of his saddle. With his hand gripping one of Sinclair's arms and the earl's hand gripping the other, they dragged the defeated, though unrepentant, laird of the clan Sinclair up the steps of Brinaire and into the great hall.

Patrick's father was waiting for them, standing in the center of the huge room with the help of a stick. Alex stood next to him. But Patrick's gaze went past them both to the bottom of the stairs, where Marsali stood looking radiant

despite a certain tension in her body. He knew she was trying to be discreet, maintaining a respectful distance, nor was
this the time or the place for their own personal greetings.
Still, he wanted her beside him.

They deposited Sinclair on his knees, and while Abernie
approached his father alone, Patrick moved quietly to her,
taking her hand in his and bringing her with him to stand
next to Alex. A worried frown flickered across her brow as
she looked from him to her father and back again. He shot
her a reassuring wink, and although her eyes widened in
surprise, her hand tightened around his.

"I love you," he whispered.

"I love you, too," she whispered back, her fingers inter-
twining with his even more tightly.

"Gavin?"

"Will be fine."

Patrick nodded, and they both turned to watch the scene
unfolding before them.

The two patriarchs were regarding each other warily.

"Gregor," Abernie said, speaking formally.

"Donald," the marquis growled.

Abernie shifted on his feet, sent a few surreptitious
glances his daughter's way, then focused once more on the
man before him. "You heard about Margaret."

"Aye," the marquis said. "My lad, Alex, told me."

Patrick smiled at the warmth and possessiveness with
which the announcement was made, and he returned the
hard squeeze Marsali gave his hand. Alex and his father, it
seemed, had made their peace.

Abernie shifted his gaze to Alex. "My thanks, lad,"
he said.

Alex nodded. " 'Twas an honor, sir. But there were others
who helped me."

"Aye," the earl agreed, "but if you had not acted when you
did, Sinclair would ha' killed her. I am indebted to you, as I
am to your brother." Bringing his gaze back to the marquis,

he said, "I accused you falsely," then added with a trace of defiance, "though I had reason."

Patrick's gaze snapped to his father's face. The old man neither replied nor moved. For a long time, he stood still as a stone, his jaw working and his throat expanding and contracting as he swallowed . . . several times . . . hard. Patrick was aware that everyone in the room, save Sinclair, mayhap, was holding their breath. As the seconds ticked by, he began to fear the outcome of the meeting. Had it all been for naught?

Finally, when the tension in the room had grown to unbearable proportions and Marsali's fingers were gripping his so hard it actually hurt, his father cleared his throat.

"How is . . . Margaret?" he asked.

Sounds of expelled breaths echoed around the room, and Patrick felt relief wash through him like a cleansing wave—in small part, at least, because Marsali had loosened her death grip on his fingers.

"She is weak," Abernie replied. "And she is verra thin. She has been given drugs. Not much, she says, but enough to confuse her and keep her quiet. Valerian, she thinks, and hops. But she will recover—at least, in body. I canna be as certain about her spirit. She has spent two years believing you had her imprisoned because you thought she had betrayed you and you couldna stand the sight of her. That is what she was told."

His father straightened to his full height, incensed. "She would believe that of me?"

"You believed worse of her," Abernie said angrily. "And *she* was innocent. Here. I brought this blackguard to tell you what he has done."

Hiram and Rufus hauled Sinclair forward until he was within striking distance of the marquis and forced him to his knees.

"Tell him," Abernie said to Sinclair. "Tell the marquis of

Brinaire everything you told me or, by God, I will see you drawn and quartered."

Sinclair shot the earl a look, and Patrick tasted bile, seeing the cowardice in the man's eyes. He was a disgrace to his clan, to the Highlands, to all of Scotland.

"You swore—" Sinclair began.

"Based on your truthful words," Abernie interrupted him.

Sinclair directed his gaze at the wall, speaking in flat tones. "The Lady Margaret met a man named Foster whilst she was out riding. He lured her to your hunting shelter by saying he had news of Patrick Sutherland but that they couldna talk where they might be seen. She went with him, and he told her that your son had been taken prisoner and that she could help him."

Sinclair stopped suddenly, mayhap, Patrick thought, because he saw the understanding—and the fury—transform his father's already formidable countenance.

"Go on," Abernie prodded.

Sinclair glanced at him, then continued grudgingly. "Your son cut Foster's throat in a fight and left him for dead. Foster swore an oath of vengeance against him, but when he couldna find him, he came here to seek vengeance against Patrick Sutherland's family. He came to me. He devised a plan that . . . that I offered aid to carry out. He would get revenge, and I would get your lands when you and the Gunns had destroyed each other. Your lady wife was the means by which we sought to start a feud between you." Drawing a shaky breath, he continued. "Your lady didna know I was involved in the plan. Foster dealt with her. He told her that your son was being ransomed, and that if the marquis learned of it, he would attack rather than pay, and your son would die. She believed it. She brought her jewels to your hunting hut to pay the ransom. Those were the meetings described to you."

The old Sutherland was actually trembling as he listened, and not, Patrick knew, from weakness or old age.

Abernie broke in. "Gregor, do you see? She believed this treacherous lie. She feared Patrick would be killed if she spoke, even to defend herself against your accusations of adultery. Remember, we had no' heard from Patrick in such a long time, and all of us were sore worried that he might be dead. When this bastard Foster came to her, saying he knew where Patrick was, she knew you would go after him with arms. She feared for your son's life—and for yours. So she tried to protect you both by buying his freedom with her jewels. It was foolish of her, mayhap, but you . . . Gregor, you are no' a temperate man."

"And you are?" the marquis exclaimed, his eyes sparking fire.

But Patrick thought the angry retort sounded practiced, like a habit formed over many years of responding to a life-long opponent. Or friend.

"Aye," Abernie said self-righteously. "More than some I could name."

His father looked at Sinclair. "And the witnesses who came to me? The ones who said they had seen my lady go to the hut?"

"Well-paid acquaintances of Foster's," the captive said.

"When she left Brinaire," the earl said, "the morning she disappeared, she was going to meet Foster to give him her jewels. But she was attacked by men in masks. She ne'er knew they had taken her to Creighton. She knew only that they said they were hired by her husband."

The marquis looked from Abernie to Sinclair, then let his gaze fall to the floor. His words were little more than a broken whisper. "And when I could not find her jewels," he said, "I thought she had run away with . . ." His hand came up to cover his face.

Patrick heard the anguish in his father's voice and realized he *had* loved Margaret—but not enough to trust her. Looking at Marsali, seeing the tears hovering in her eyes, he vowed never to make the same mistake.

Raising his head, his father glared at Sinclair, and Patrick watched warily as his father drew a dagger from his belt and limped toward the cowering prisoner. Stepping forward quickly, Patrick placed his body in front of Sinclair.

"He isna worth killing," he said.

Father and son faced each other, the older man's face mottled with rage.

"Father, donna do this," Patrick said softly. "The earl of Abernie has given his word to Sinclair that he wouldna be killed if he told the truth."

His father's glittering gaze snapped to Abernie's. "I made no such promises."

"Och, he will get the king's justice," Abernie said. "I made no promise about his raids on my land, or the murders of three of my clansmen."

Behind him, Patrick heard Sinclair start to sputter. Gesturing to Hiram and Rufus, he growled, "Get him out of here. Put him in the dungeon until we take him to London."

Everyone in the great hall watched as Rufus and Hiram grabbed the suddenly animated Sinclair by the arms and dragged him away.

When they were gone, his father looked at the earl. "Donald, what have we done?" he asked wearily.

"Been bloody fools," Abernie said. "Both of us. I donna know how we ever lived this long, being so blind and foolish. To allow carrion like that to move us around like pieces on a chessboard! 'Tis a wonder our clans have not disavowed us."

"Margaret," the marquis said. "May I . . . see her?"

"Aye," Abernie replied. "I think she would like that. It broke her heart to believe you would imprison her."

"I wronged her."

"We all wronged each other, all but our sons—and our daughters." For the first time, the earl turned his full gaze on Marsali, and his next words were colored with self-remorse.

"Lass, I came near to marrying you to that craven schemer. I willna forgive myself for that. Still, I hope"—he drew a shaky breath—"I hope you can find it in your heart to forgive me."

"Oh, Fa . . ." Marsali's voice broke as she stepped toward her father to take his hands. "I would forgive you anything. All of us—Gavin and Cecilia and I—have missed you these past two years."

"Aye, lass," the earl said, " 'tis true, I fear. You have been living with a mon twisted by the thought of revenge."

"Speaking of living with . . ." the marquis began in an ominous tone.

Patrick half turned to find his father frowning.

Looking from his son to his old friend Abernie, the marquis continued, "I have been informed that your daughter and my son are no longer strangers—in *any* sense of the word. They handfasted, and before you go bellowing, you had best know it was witnessed."

Patrick heard Marsali take a quick breath. They exchanged a look, waiting for the explosion.

It never came. The earl and the marquis scowled at each other. Then, slowly, Abernie began to smile. His smile turned into a low, rumbling chuckle.

"Gregor, we have been outwitted by our offspring."

"Aye, Donald, we have."

"And I donna believe you know the whole of it," the earl added. Patrick grew wary when Abernie arched an eyebrow at him knowingly. Speaking again to the marquis, the earl said, "I noticed some verra thin cattle on your land as we came through your upper pasture. They looked verra familiar, too, but for being a wee bit thinner than the last time I saw them. Which was last week, in my *lower* pasture."

At his father's deepening glower, Patrick held his breath for the worst.

"I donna ken what you are implying," the marquis said.

The earl seemed delighted to explain. "I am saying that

our sons have been reiving the same poor beasts, from our pastures to yours and back again, then telling *us* of their successful raids. I have wondered why there were no wounds."

His father's mouth actually dropped open, but when that intimidating glare was turned on him, Patrick stood firm.

"You did this?" his father asked.

"Aye."

"You defied my direct orders?"

"You ordered me to recover your cattle," he said. "I did. I simply made it . . . possible for Gavin to retake them. 'Twas to buy the time I needed to expose Sinclair and to find Margaret."

The mention of his stepmother's name—which was no accident on his part—made the creases in his father's face slowly smooth. Gradually, the old man's expression cleared until, to Patrick's amazement, he looked almost pleased. Amazement turned to shock when his father spoke.

"Patrick, I am proud of you," the marquis said with a chuckle. "And I will thank you for reminding me of it from time to time, should I e'er seem to be forgetting."

Swallowing against the sudden tightness in his throat, Patrick nodded. "Aye, sir. I will do that."

His father gave him an answering nod. Then, sighing, the marquis looked at Abernie.

"Donald, what say you we go sit in my chamber and have a drink? I have stood here as long as this bloody foot will allow."

"Aye," the earl agreed, turning to walk beside his old friend. "And I would like to see my son, if you donna mind."

"Of course. I am told that he is resting comfortably. Elizabeth has been with him all morning, I believe."

"Ah, a good lass. And what is she now? Fourteen?"

"Fifteen."

As the two of them slowly made their way toward the stairs, Patrick heard his father say, "You realize, do you not, that we have spawned a passel of rebels?"

"Aye," came the earl's sad-sounding reply. "I donna ken how it happened. But I tell you straight, I willna countenance any daughter of mine being handfasted. We must plan a wedding. And the sooner, the better."

"I couldna agree with you more. Donald, you canna believe how bad the food was before your Marsali came. I tell you, there were nights when I didna think to live. . . ."

Their voices faded as they climbed the stairs. Patrick followed their progress with astonishment until they turned at the second-floor landing and disappeared.

Then he took Marsali's hand and led her up to the parapet, one much like that at Abernie. It was twilight, but the first stars were appearing. She looked at him, her eyes sparkling as bright as the stars above. They stared at each other for a second or two. Then they both grinned. With a loud whoop of joy, he caught her in his arms and spun her. She clung to him, laughing, her long hair flying behind her, and when he got dizzy, he set her down and kissed her, a fierce, hard kiss filled with all the passion and happiness bursting in his heart.

Then, he said, "They are planning our wedding."

" 'Tis a miracle," she replied breathlessly. "But I expected no less from my starcatcher."

He gave her a smile that spoke of the tenderness and love he felt, thinking of the little girl he had found, standing, sad and forlorn, on the parapets of Abernie, so long ago. "If I am your starcatcher," he said, "then you are my star. That night, when I reached out to the heavens, what I found was something wondrous. I found you. Marsali, I canna imagine the world without your brightness in it. You are my heart, and I will love you until the end of my days."

"Oh, Patrick," she sighed.

And as he brought his lips down to touch hers once more, the glow from every star in the sky seemed to expand and intensify, surrounding them for all time in a lasting enchantment.

Epilogue

It was a splendid day for a wedding. Everyone said so. The sun shone brightly, its rays dappling the countryside, turning the rich green fields into emeralds and the mist on the mountains into diamonds.

Marsali stood trembling with anticipation as Elizabeth and Aunt Margaret helped her with her gown and Jeanie brushed her dark hair, entwining it with flowers. She wished Cecilia could be with her as well, but someone had to be in the great hall to welcome guests. Sounds of revelry drifted through the window from the courtyard below: laughter blending with pipes and singing.

Feeling a moment of queasiness, Marsali placed a hand on her stomach. The moment passed, though, and she breathed with relief: 'Twas only nerves, not the babe growing inside her. *That* news was to be her wedding gift to Patrick.

Margaret and Jeanie had already guessed, both having seen her run for a bowl several mornings in a row. She glanced up to find her aunt giving her a concerned look, the blue gaze, very like her own, falling to her stomach, then rising to meet hers once more. She gave her head a quick shake and smiled.

Her aunt would be going home with her tomorrow, to Brinaire. Patrick's father had been courting his wife for the past month, trying in his own rough way, Marsali thought, to compensate for what he had said and done. The truest measure of his regret was perhaps demonstrated by his not having demanded that Margaret return; rather, he had allowed her to take all the time she wished to reach her own decision. Marsali herself had wondered if the marquis's uncommonly amiable behavior was being guided by Patrick's fine hand.

In any case, it was clear to her that Aunt Margaret loved Gregor Sutherland, crippled with gout and belligerent as he was. Marsali really did not understand it, yet occasionally, she admitted, she saw flashes of humor in Gregor Sutherland and a certain charisma that had earned him his clansmen's fealty. Although he suffered from a heritage that had taught him love was a weakness and compassion a fault, he seemed to slowly be learning otherwise. Because of Margaret. And because of his son.

Indeed, she thought, love was blossoming all over the Highlands. Only last night, Jeanie had told her that she planned to say yes the next time Hiram asked her to marry him—which had become a frequent occurrence. She even giggled a little in the telling, looking years younger, the blue of her eyes sparkling like a loch under a bright sun.

As for Cecilia, her eyes followed Rufus wherever he went, and Patrick had assured her that his friend was thoroughly smitten with her sister, much to his own and Hiram's amusement. Cecilia no longer buried herself in books but, instead, was busily learning womanly skills. Though Rufus had no title, he was the eldest son of a prominent Lowland family, and her father said he had learned his lesson: He would allow his youngest child to marry whomever she wished—as long as she waited until she was sixteen. He wanted no more runaways.

And then there was Gavin. He was being gravely courteous to young Elizabeth, who had spent more time than was entirely necessary tending him while he lay recovering from his wound at Brinaire. Mayhap someday . . .

Even the ferrets had mellowed and now accepted Patrick's touch. Mayhap because Isolde, too, was expecting.

"Ye look beautiful, lovey," Jeanie said, clasping her hands together.

"Aye," Margaret agreed.

"She glows," Elizabeth added breathlessly.

"I *feel* beautiful," Marsali said. She had waited for this moment for so many years, and it was turning out to be more wonderful than she ever could have imagined.

A knock on her door told her that it was time.

With Margaret at her side and Elizabeth holding her skirts, she descended the stairs to the great hall, where her father met her. A tear seemed to glisten in his eye as he took her arm and, together, they walked to the chapel.

Standing in the open doorway of the chapel, she looked down the aisle and saw Patrick standing, strong and tall and sure, at the foot of the altar steps. His father stood next to him, his grim face seeming to soften for a moment as she met his gaze. The chapel was full of plaids, those of Sutherland and Gunn and many other Highland clans. But as she began moving down the aisle, Marsali barely noticed the people filling the rows, their faces wreathed in smiles as they watched her. She had eyes only for Patrick.

When she reached him, he stepped forward and took her hand, and the warmth of his touch spread throughout her body. Suddenly, with their gazes locked, the world seemed to shrink until it included only the two of them. She barely heard the vicar's words or her own responses. She knew only that Patrick's voice was rich and clear and certain.

And then it was over. His head bent toward hers and their lips met, not nearly long enough but as long as the present company would allow. When the chapel burst into laughter and shouts of approval, he raised his head, and their gazes met again. She smiled at him, thinking of the news she would give him that night, and as the thought passed through her mind, it seemed, somehow, to pass into his. For she saw that, suddenly, he knew. The awareness flashed in his eyes in an instant of surprise—and hope.

He arched an eyebrow for confirmation, and she nodded. His face split into a grin, his eyes sparkling with delight.

Indeed, it was a glorious day for a wedding, and the night . . .

Well, the night was waiting.

About the Author

PATRICIA POTTER has become one of the most highly praised writers of historical romance since her impressive debut in 1988, when she won the Maggie Award and a Reviewer's Choice Award from *Romantic Times* for her first novel. She has received the Romantic Times Career Achievement Award for Storyteller of the Year for 1992 and its Career Achievement Award for Western Historical Romance in 1995. She was recently nominated for a Reviewer's Choice Award for best British Isles Romance in 1996. She has been a RITA finalist three times and has received a total of three Maggie Awards. Prior to writing fulltime, she worked as a newspaper reporter in Atlanta. She has served as president of Georgia Romance Writers and currently is a member of the board of the River City Romance Writers in Memphis, Tennessee.

Patricia Potter

The award-winning national bestseller.

You've been awed by the passion of her heroes,
inspired by the strength of her heroines,
touched by the tenderness of their love,
and spellbound by the battles they must fight to be together . . .

Now, let her next enthralling
historical romance sweep you away.

Coming from Bantam Books in Fall 1998

Turn the page for an exciting sneak peak at this wonderful
tale of a man captured by fate—and a love freely given . . .

She heard something. A knock at the door.

Had Robert already heard of their tragedy? She could not imagine how, yet little escaped his notice.

She forced herself to stand up and go to the door, opening it slowly.

The Scotsman stood there. His clothes were wrinkled and filthy, although he'd made some effort to wash. His face and hands were still wet.

"You came back," she said stupidly. Anger roiled inside her. It had been his abrupt departure last night that preceded John's death. Part of her wanted to blame him. But she knew that John had been sick a long time.

"John's dead," she said shortly, holding onto the door.

He frowned, his eyebrows knitting together.

"He died in his sleep last night," she continued, hearing how calm her voice sounded. But inside she was reeling.

The Scotsman's face didn't change at the news. Was he thinking that this was his chance to escape?

She hated him then. She hated the hope he had given her husband, and then taken away. She hated him for being alive when her husband was dead. She hated him for disappearing last night when they needed him.

But after a moment, after glaring into dark green eyes suddenly filled with an emotion she couldn't identify, the hate drained away, leaving her empty. He was a stranger, here by no choice of his own.

She bit her lip to keep her tears in check, then turned away and leaned against a wall.

At least he didn't say he was sorry. She didn't think she could bear that.

"What do you want me to do?"

His voice was harsh, empty.

Yet he stood there, waiting.

What did she want him to do?

She had no idea. She knew her chin was trembling. She wanted to be strong. But she had two small children to care for, a sister who had disappeared as soon as she learned of John's death, a husband who had died suddenly, and a farm she couldn't possibly manage alone.

"Where were you?" she asked, instead of giving in to tears. Her voice was colder than she'd ever heard it. But somehow she wanted to move closer, toward the strength she instinctively felt in him.

"Downstream," he said without apology. "I don't know exactly where." Then, after a pause, he asked, "What happened?"

"He died last night. I didn't . . . even know until . . ." She took a step away from him, but she felt herself swaying. Then she felt his hand on her arm, steadying her.

Warmth from his touch was like fire to the coolness of her skin, the chill of her spirit. She jerked away, backing up against the wall as if he were an enemy.

"You'd not be thinking I would hurt you?" the Scotsman said in a curiously soft voice.

But she was thinking just that. She remembered others who had said they would help—after her father's death. Instead, they had stolen the furs her father had trapped and sought to sell her and her sister into slavery . . . or something worse.

So how could she trust this cold-eyed man who made no secret of his hostility?

She knew she could not show weakness. She ignored his question. "I want you to go with me to John's brother. I have to tell him John is dead."

His first instinct was to say no. She could see it in the

way he hesitated, in the way his eyes moved in the direction of the barn. Now that her husband was dead, there would be no one to stop him from leaving, from breaking his bond. No one to ride after him when he took one of the horses and disappeared. . . .

"John's friend in Chestertown has your papers," she said, forcing the words from her reluctant throat. "My brother-in-law would see that you're brought back." It was an empty threat. She would do no such thing. She would never give Robert such power over this man, or any other. But maybe if she could make the Scotsman stay a few more weeks, even a few more days, he would understand she meant him no harm, that they could reach an arrangement advantageous to both of them.

And she needed him so badly. The farm needed him. Dear God, her children needed him. She could never let them fall under Robert's influence.

His eyes swept her. If there had been a hint of sympathy in them, there was none now. Instead, his presence was almost threatening as he stood in the door of the farmhouse. Despite the gauntness, despite the lines in his face from the harsh treatment he had endured, he was overpowering.

All at once he bowed mockingly. "Your servant, mistress. I'll hitch the buggy."

"I have to wait until Fortune returns to look after the children."

"Where is she?"

"She went to the woods to grieve alone. She does that."

He leaned against the door frame, and for the first time she suspected the depth of the physical weakness he was trying to hide. And there was something else, a hesitancy she hadn't seen before, perhaps even a hint of regret.

She tore her gaze from him. John lay in the next room. She needed help from this man, not pity. He was a bond-servant. Her husband's bondservant; now *her* bondservant. And she had not the slightest idea how to handle him. She didn't even want to *handle* him. What she wanted, needed, was a friend.

But he was not willing to be that, not as long as he felt burdened by the injustice of his fate. She'd already realized he was not a man to accept injustice readily.

"Can you find her?" he asked.

"Yes, but I can't leave the children."

A long, low sigh came from his mouth. "I'll look after them," he said then.

She hesitated.

"*If* you trust me." It was a question.

She searched his face.

"Should I?"

He shrugged. "Probably not. Didn't your husband ever tell you not to trust the slaves?"

Her stomach clenched. *Her husband.* Her husband who was gone now. Forever. She wondered whether the pain would ever lessen. She forced herself to confront his question. "You're not a slave," she said fiercely.

"A matter of semantics, mistress," he said. "A moment ago you mentioned my papers, the papers that say you own me."

"We own your services, not you."

He gave her a dark look. "I canna leave your property without permission. I canna own anything without your permission. I canna even write a letter without your permission." His jaw worked even after he stopped talking, as if he were straining to keep from saying something else. After a moment's silence, he seemed to force himself to relax.

"I give you my word I will stay until your husband is buried. I will look after your children, and they will be safe wi' me. I promise no more."

It wasn't much, and yet she believed him. Perhaps because he'd made no promises earlier.

She swallowed hard. She had to get to Robert. If she didn't inform him of John's death before burying him, he would seek vengeance. He hadn't cared for his brother, had tried, in fact, to cheat him out of his land and small inheritance, but he did care about what he called "propriety." He would say it was his *right* to know.

Fancy nodded. "I'll go find my sister, then."

He looked down at her, and it seemed a long way. When he was so close, the disparity between their heights seemed much greater. She felt small and inconsequential. And uncertain again. Was she foolish to trust him?

Even more foolish to leave him with her children, the most precious part of her life.

They will be safe wi' me.

How surely he had said those words.

"I ha' a sister," he said suddenly. "About the age of your lad. I would never see harm come to a bairn."

His burr had deepened during their brief exchange, and she knew he had read her mind, had sensed her reluctance.

"I know," she said softly. And she did.

They said little to each other during the ten-mile trip to Robert's home. She wore a dark dress, her hair tucked under a plain bonnet.

Ian drove the horses carefully, keeping his eyes averted from the woman next to him and riveted on the road that was little more than a wide trail. He didn't want to look at her, at the sad, wistful face with the huge brown eyes that seemed just about to fill with tears.

He also wanted to pay attention to every landmark, every trail or path that ran off the rough excuse for a road. Soon enough he would need that information. Water was everywhere. Streams and rivers appeared to run through the countryside like wrinkles on an old man's face.

He had felt almost guilty hitching up these horses. They were far too fine for such work, but he was fast understanding that John Marsh had spent what money he had on developing a fine strain of racing horses, not on working animals.

Excepting himself, of course.

The reminder dimmed the brightness of the day. As did the reason for the trip. And he couldn't ignore the question that nagged at him: if he had not disappeared last night, might John Marsh be alive today?

He hadn't admitted it to the woman, but he felt the answer deep in his bones. God knew he didn't want to be responsible for another death. Nor did he want to see any more sadness in the eyes of the children. As he had while he watched them, until Mrs. Marsh returned with her sister. She had given him a grateful glance, then they had left for her brother-in-law's property. Alone.

He wondered why she had been so determined not to take the children with them, and why she seemed so tense. But it was none of his business. And, he reminded himself, he wanted no confidences that would bind him more tightly to these people. The brother-in-law would take care of them, and then he could escape, and return to Scotland.

Her quiet voice broke his thoughts.

"Thank you," she said.

"For what?" he replied curtly. "I'm just following your orders like a good servant."

"I don't think you will ever be a *good* servant," she replied tartly.

His hands tightened around the reins. The horses were high spirited and required control. But his hands were tough, heavily callused from riding and weapons training.

With similar restraint, he held back his retort. He didn't want to engage in conversation. He didn't want to know her better. He didn't want to like her.

Yet he was very aware of her presence. A soft scent of flowers clung to her, and she continued to surprise him with her flashes of spirit despite her obvious grief. She had cried; red-rimmed eyes gave proof of it. But she had not cried in front of him.

And he'd wanted to comfort her. All his instincts wanted

that. They'd wanted it this morning, and again this afternoon when he had helped her up into the wagon.

But now he knew a trap when he saw it. And he would never be trapped again.

"A good servant?" he replied after several moments passed. "No, you're right. I won't be one of those."

She looked at his heavily callused hands, judiciously changing the subject. "Did you farm in Scotland?"

"My clan raised sheep and cattle," he said shortly. She wanted to talk, obviously needed to talk, but he couldn't allow himself that familiarity.

She didn't try again, but occasionally his arm would brush hers, and the sweet flowery scent of her drifted over him, making his senses lurch. He disliked that in himself. She was newly widowed, and even if he hadn't been in the loathsome position of bondsman, he had no right to think of her that way when she was suffering.

It had been so long, though. So long since he'd felt a woman's softness. Her light scent was different from the often heavily perfumed women he had known—and a hundred times more enticing.

She had been widowed today. And by law she owned him.

But he could do nothing about his awareness of her, nor the way his body reacted to it.

At her direction, he turned up a road and was startled several minutes later to see a large brick home sitting amidst well tended fields. Behind the house lay more fields, dotted by numerous figures, some kneeling, some bending over.

Her brother-in-law's farm?

Ian had assumed that the man would be a small farmer, much like John Marsh. Why had Marsh been so desperate for labor with a brother who apparently had so many hands?

He glanced at Fancy Marsh. Her face was set and her body tense. Her hands were clasped together in a hard, tight knot. He asked her none of his questions. He must keep as much distance between him and her family as possible.

But he was plagued with curiosity. He always had been. His whole life he'd wanted to know about people and places and things. He had to tamp that insatiable curiosity now—although there was no doubt Fancy Marsh interested him, as did her sister, the mysterious Fortune who looked nothing at all like her sister and never spoke.

A lad of about twelve ran up as they approached the front of the house and took the reins from him. He stepped down, then helped Mrs. Marsh down. The door opened almost immediately, and a tall black man, dressed immaculately in uniform, stood waiting in the doorway.

Ian noticed that Fancy set her shoulders stiffly, then asked, "Is Mr. Marsh at home?"

The man's gaze flickered over Ian, rested a moment on his shabby servant's clothes, then dismissed him before returning to Mrs. Marsh.

"Masta Marsh is in the fields," he said. But at that moment, Ian saw a man galloping toward the house, and Fancy turned, watching him approach.

Ian moved to the side, instinctively knowing this man was her brother-in-law and that, for some reason, Fancy Marsh did not like him. Might, in fact, even fear him.

The rider reached the porch and dismounted, moving swiftly toward them. His gaze was intent on the woman before turning to him, raking him with the same contempt the butler had moments earlier.

"I saw your wagon from the field," the man said, turning back to Fancy and taking off his riding gloves as he switched a wicked looking quirt from one hand to the other. "This is an unexpected pleasure."

Ian noticed that though the words were courteous enough, and certainly proper, the man's eyes were not, nor was the way he'd put a hand on Fancy's arm and ran his fingers down its length in a distinctly unbrotherly manner.

Fancy jerked away. "John's dead," she said. "He died this morning. I thought you should know."

The man's hand paused in mid-air, then dropped to his side. "John? How?"

"His heart."

For a moment, no emotion crossed the man's face, then a look of concern quickly slid over it. "Ah, poor John. You must let me look after everything for you," he said.

Something about the way he said it caused a warning to ring in Ian's brain. It may have been the note of satisfaction that underlined the offer.

Taking a step backward, Ian took a long look at Robert Marsh. He was of an age with John Marsh, though he looked far healthier. He did not have John Marsh's height, but he was more substantial in body, well muscled and with an arrogant carriage that had been lacking in his brother. His hair was thinning, and his face was hawk-like, his eyes set close together: blue eyes, but a pale blue that held no warmth.

"I don't need your help, Robert," Fancy said. "I just wanted you to know. We'll be burying him under the oak tree this afternoon and we'll hold services when the circuit rider comes next week."

Ian was surprised at the strength in her voice, particularly as he recalled her earlier fear.

"You and your sister can stay with me," Robert Marsh said.

"No," Fancy replied. "I have my own home."

"Now you know you can't manage that farm alone," Robert said.

"Not when you scare everyone away from working for us," she said bitterly. "You as much as killed John. But you won't get that farm."

"You misjudge me, Fancy," Robert said. "All I've ever cared about was John's health. He never should have tried to farm that land. It belongs to Marsh Point." A hardness had crept into his voice, despite his obvious attempts to be solicitous.

Ian felt distaste boil up inside him.

"It belongs to me, now," Fancy said defiantly.

He shrugged. "You will be coming to me soon enough." He turned and stared hard at Ian. "Who is he?"

Ian tensed, waiting for her to tell him he was her bondsman.

"Ian Sutherland," she said. "He is . . . working for us."

Robert Marsh looked him over, just as the buyers had days ago when his indenture was sold, like livestock.

"He's not from around here."

"No," Fancy said, ignoring the implied question.

"Doesn't look like much."

Ian wanted to strike the man. He wanted it so badly his arm ached. He was being discussed as if he weren't even present, as if he were not human.

Instead, he forced himself to do nothing. But he couldn't force his gaze to drop. He wouldn't give Robert Marsh that satisfaction.

"He is stronger than he looks," Fancy replied.

Robert's lips turned up at the edges but by even the most generous soul the movement could not be considered a smile. He turned to Ian. "I pay far better than anyone in this county."

It was a shameless offer, made on the day of his brother's death.

Ian's fist knotted. He understood now why Fancy had been so tense as they'd approached her brother-in-law's property.

"I'll be remembering that," he said slowly, weighing the fact that Fancy had not revealed his true status. "But it looks as if ye ha' plenty of help."

Robert shrugged. "Slaves. Convicts. I can always use a good freeman to help my overseer." His gaze went swiftly to Ian's hand, looking for the telltale brand. But he saw only the clenched fingers of Ian's fist.

Robert studied him for a moment, then turned back to Fancy.

"I think we should bury John in the family cemetery."

"No," she said. "He loved that oak tree. He told me . . ." Her voice trailed off.

He ignored her words. "I'll send some of my people to get him."

"No," she said again, in a stronger voice.

"Now Fancy," Robert Marsh said, as if she were a child, "the community would expect it. Just as it would expect me to take you all in. You can't live out there by yourself—a widow and a young girl—with no one but this . . ." He searched for a word that would convey his disapproval. "Stranger," he said finally.

Ian forced himself to stand still, to say nothing. Except for Katy, he had thought his protective instincts destroyed, his heart hardened. But as he watched the slim woman stand up to this obviously cruel man on the day of her husband's death, he wanted to protect her. God in heaven, but he wanted to smash his fist in Robert Marsh's face.

For despite the man's solicitous words, the underlying threat was clear, as was the desire in his eyes. Every time Robert looked at Fancy Marsh, Ian could see the lust—so strong that the man couldn't keep his hands off his newly bereaved sister-in-law. Even now, Robert's fingers were touching her arm again, but his eyes were on her breasts.

Fancy took several steps away, toward Ian.

Ian instinctively moved in front of her, and Robert dropped his hand.

"I am going to bury him under the oak tree," she said again, "but there is something you can do."

Ian heard the reluctance in her voice. She must hate asking him for anything.

"A . . . coffin."

Robert shifted his feet. "If you bury him here . . . where he belongs."

"No," she said. "We will manage."

And she started toward the buggy. Silently, Ian followed her, helped her up, then he went around to the other side and climbed into the driver's seat. He flicked the reins, and the horses drew the buggy toward the drive.

Ian looked at the woman next to him. Her face was like marble, her back even straighter and stiffer than when they first arrived.

Then he turned. Robert Marsh was watching them, a slight smile on his face as he flicked his quirt against his leg.